Splatoon

VOL. 1

STORY AND ART BY

Sankichi Hinodeya

P9-DWT-048

CONTENTS

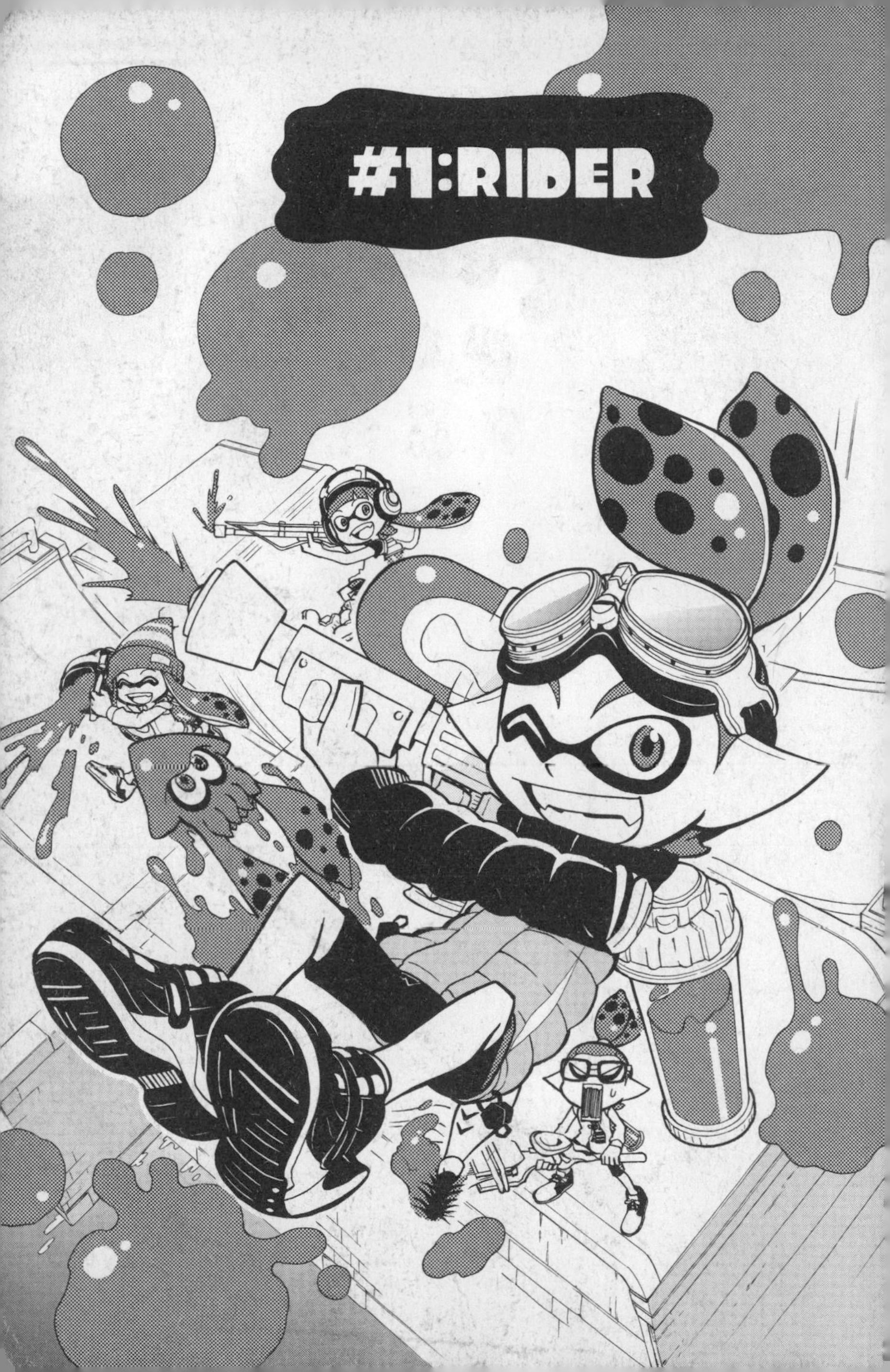
#1:RIDER

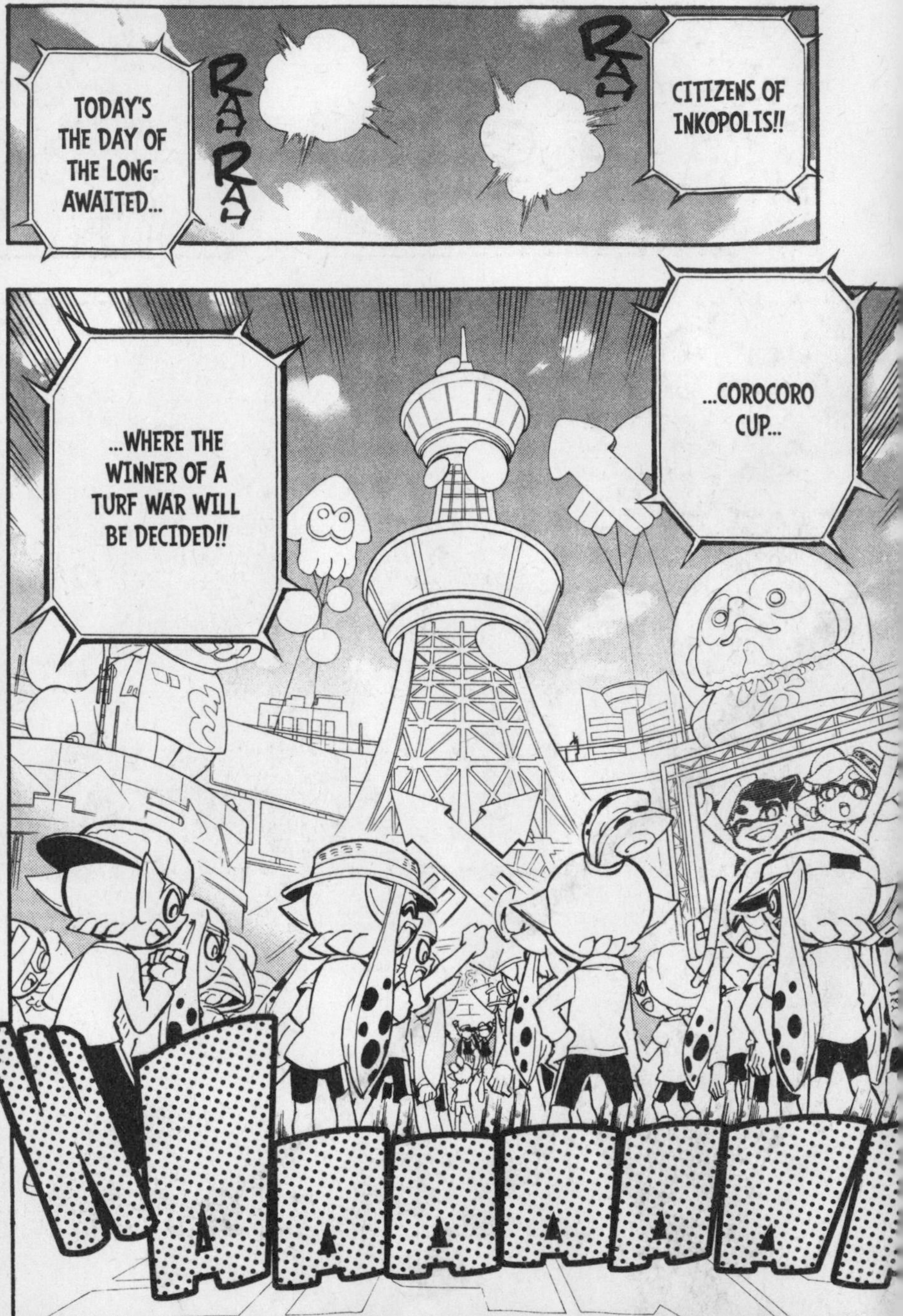
CITIZENS OF INKOPOLIS!!
TODAY'S THE DAY OF THE LONG-AWAITED...
...COROCORO CUP...
...WHERE THE WINNER OF A TURF WAR WILL BE DECIDED!!

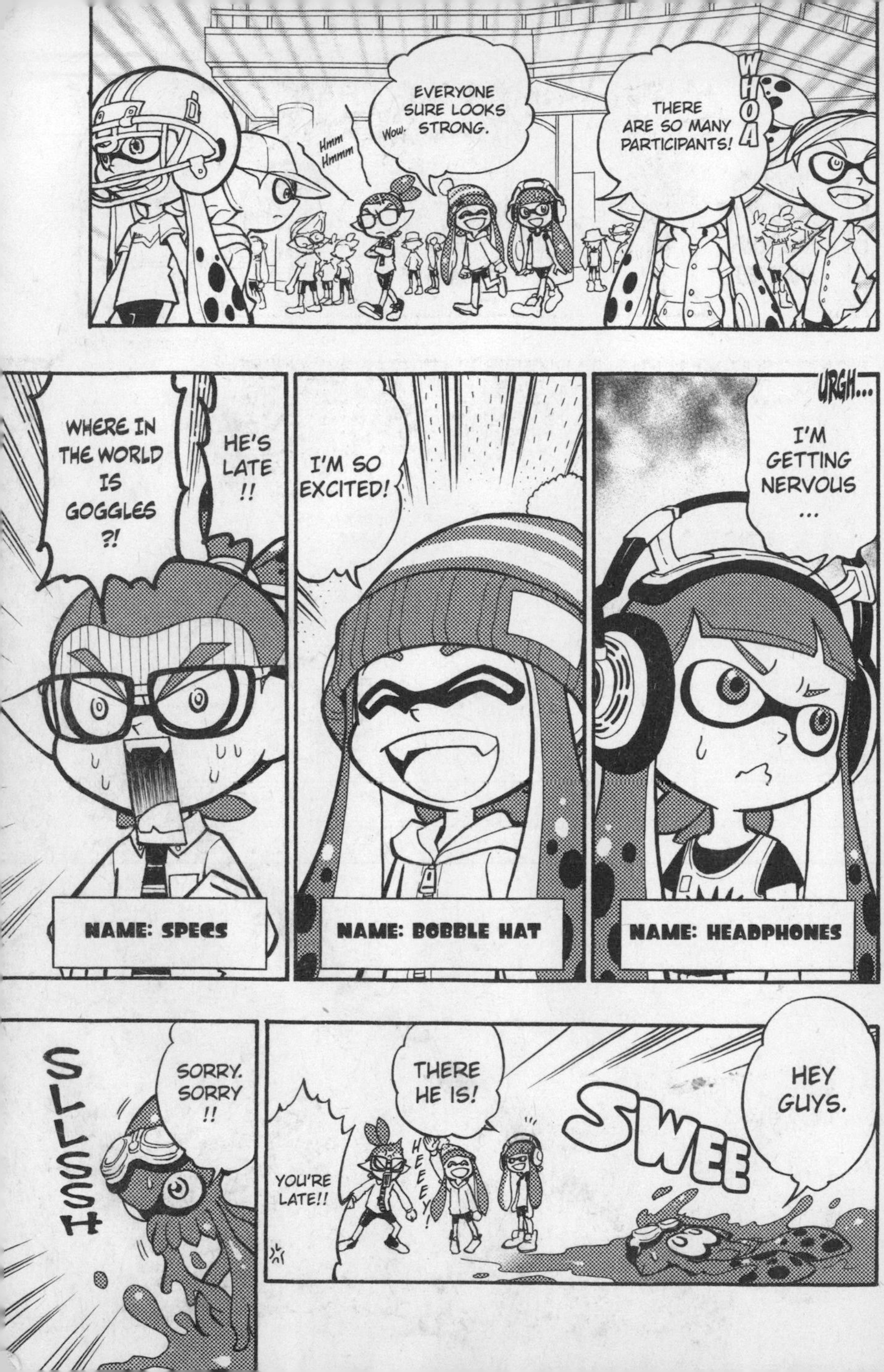
WHOA
THERE ARE SO MANY PARTICIPANTS!
EVERYONE SURE LOOKS STRONG.
Wow.
Hmm Hmmm
URGH...
I'M GETTING NERVOUS ...
NAME: HEADPHONES
I'M SO EXCITED!
NAME: BOBBLE HAT
HE'S LATE !!
WHERE IN THE WORLD IS GOGGLES ?!
NAME: SPECS
HEY GUYS.
SWEE
THERE HE IS!
HEEEY!
YOU'RE LATE!!
SORRY. SORRY !!
SLLSSH

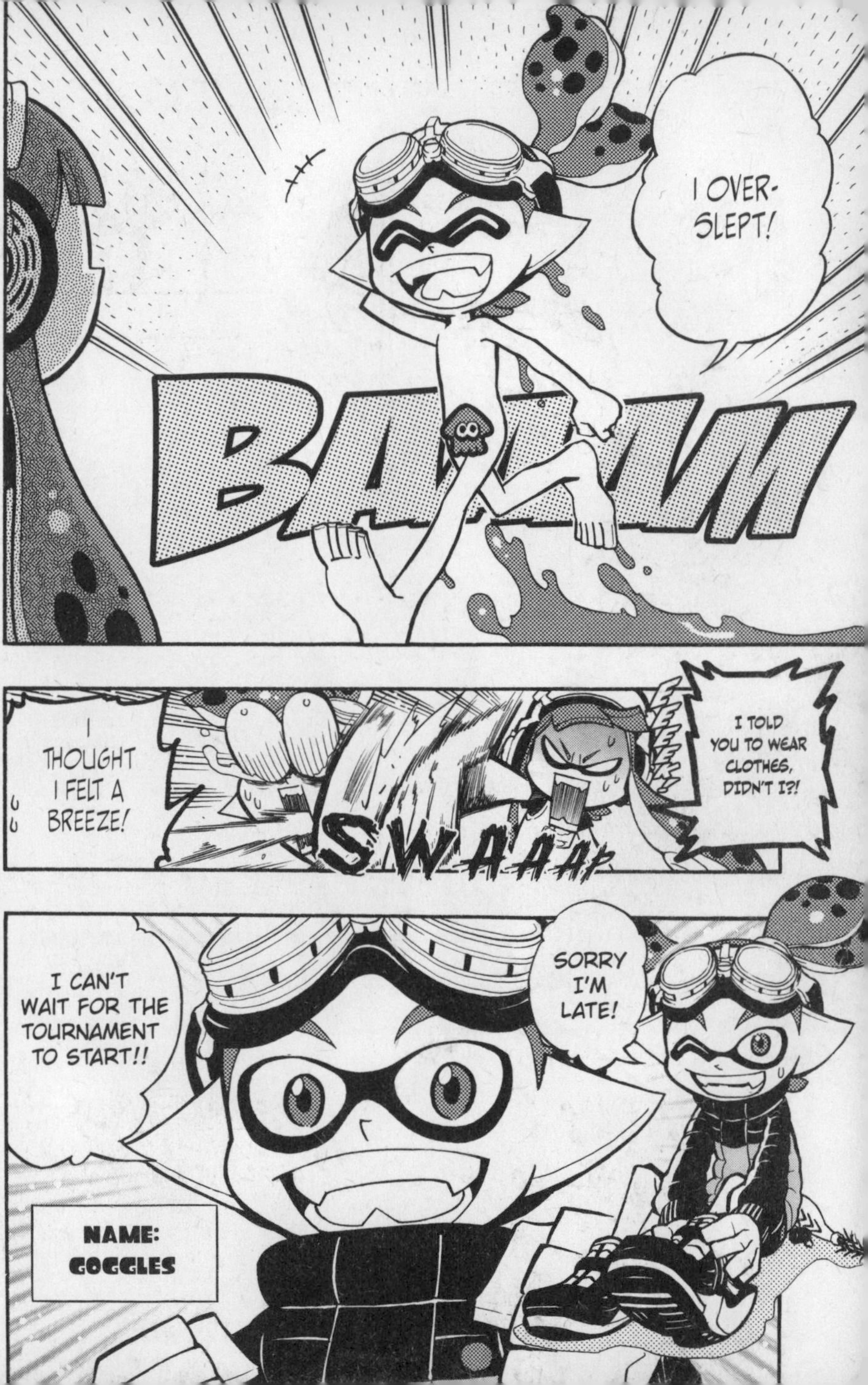
I OVER-SLEPT!
I TOLD YOU TO WEAR CLOTHES, DIDN'T I?!
I THOUGHT I FELT A BREEZE!
SWAAAP
SORRY I'M LATE!
I CAN'T WAIT FOR THE TOURNAMENT TO START!!
NAME: GOGGLES

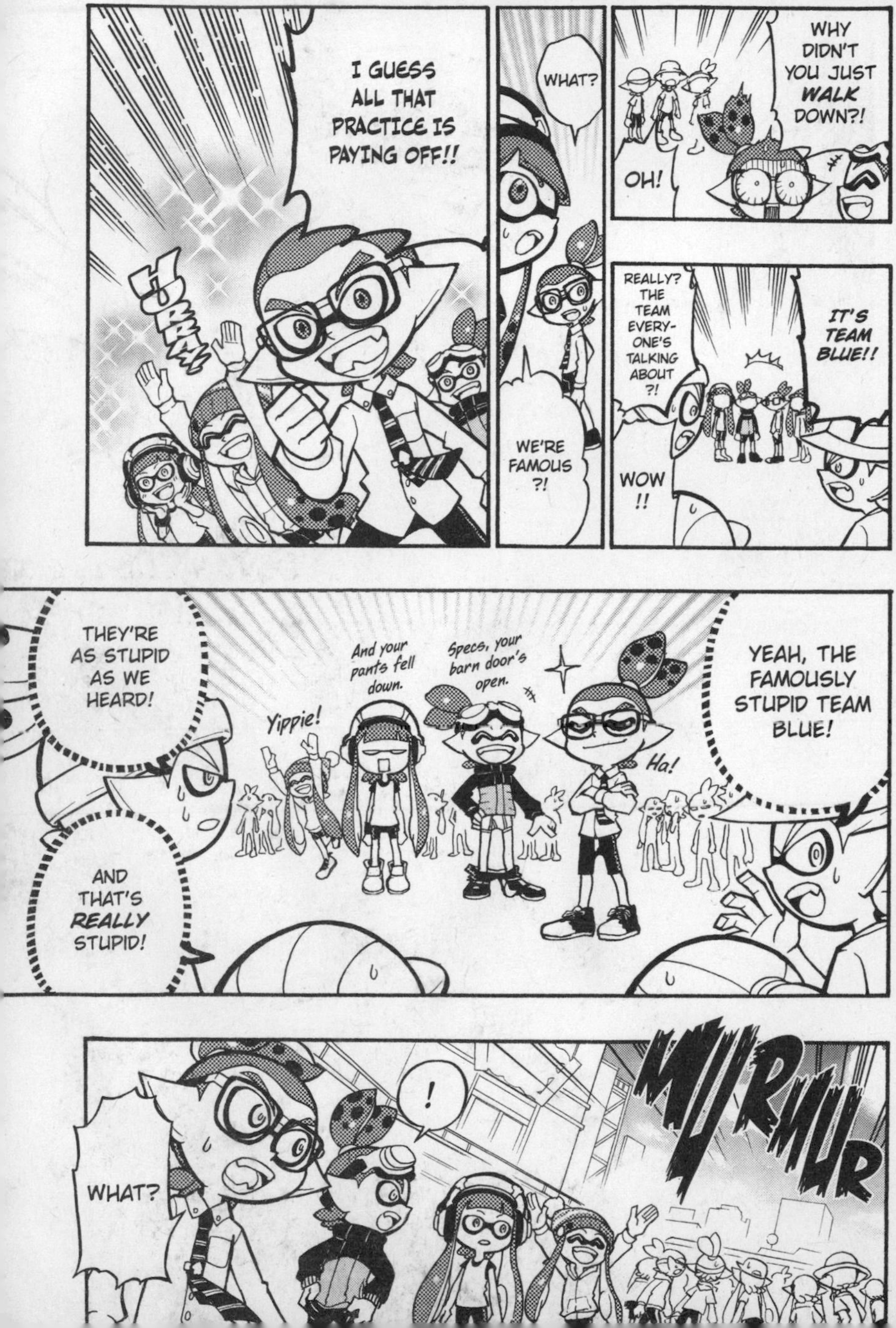
WHY DIDN'T YOU JUST *WALK* DOWN?!
OH!
IT'S TEAM BLUE!!
REALLY? THE TEAM EVERY-ONE'S TALKING ABOUT?!
WOW!!
WHAT?
WE'RE FAMOUS?!
I GUESS ALL THAT PRACTICE IS PAYING OFF!!
HURRAY!
YEAH, THE FAMOUSLY STUPID TEAM BLUE!
Ha!
Specs, your barn door's open.
And your pants fell down.
Yippie!
THEY'RE AS STUPID AS WE HEARD!
AND THAT'S *REALLY* STUPID!
MURMUR
!
WHAT?

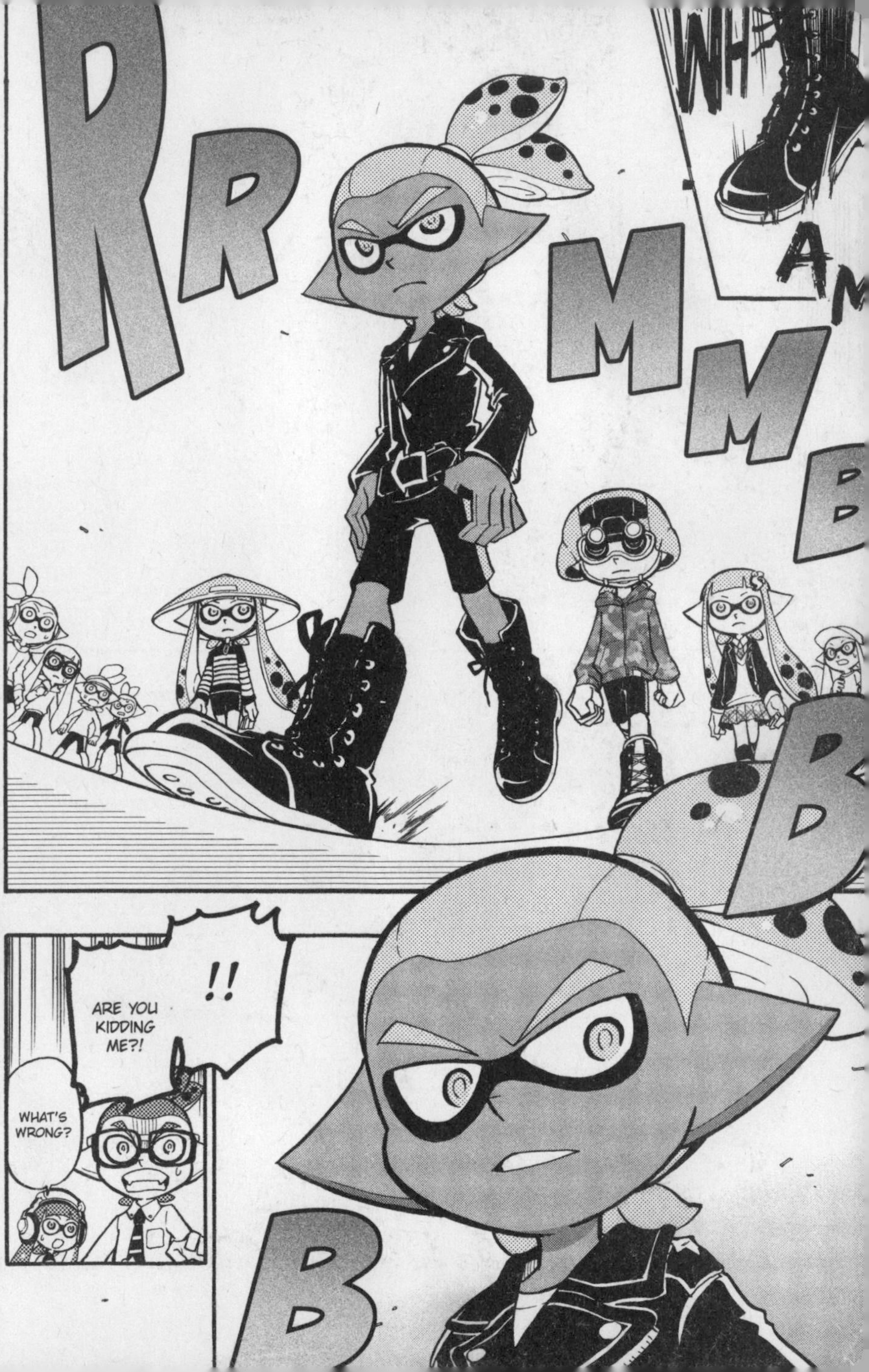
WH
AM
RRMMBBBB
!!
ARE YOU KIDDING ME?!
WHAT'S WRONG?

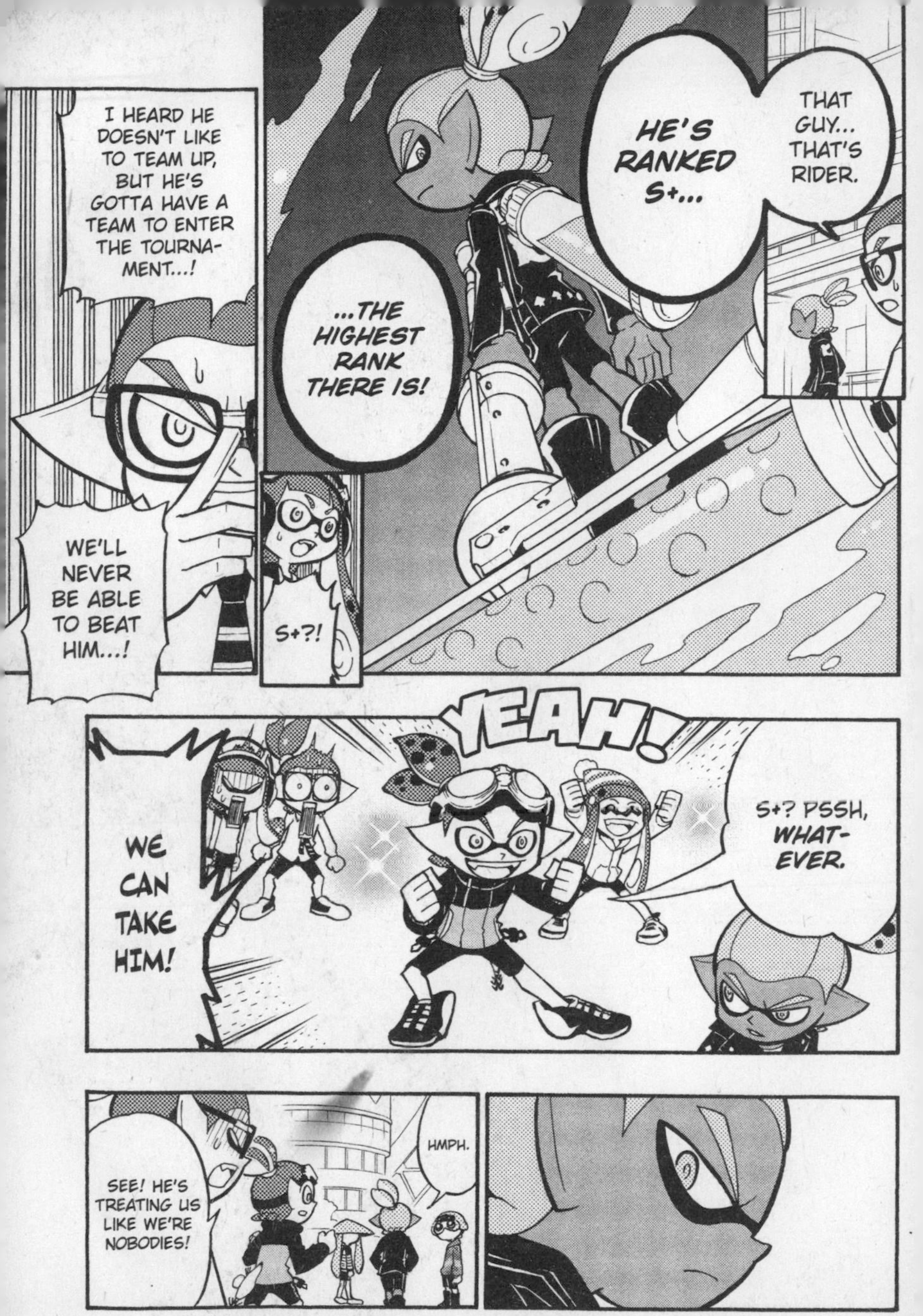
THAT GUY... THAT'S RIDER.
HE'S RANKED S+...
...THE HIGHEST RANK THERE IS!
S+?!
I HEARD HE DOESN'T LIKE TO TEAM UP, BUT HE'S GOTTA HAVE A TEAM TO ENTER THE TOURNA-MENT...!
WE'LL NEVER BE ABLE TO BEAT HIM...!
S+? PSSH, WHAT-EVER.
YEAH!
WE CAN TAKE HIM!
HMPH.
SEE! HE'S TREATING US LIKE WE'RE NOBODIES!

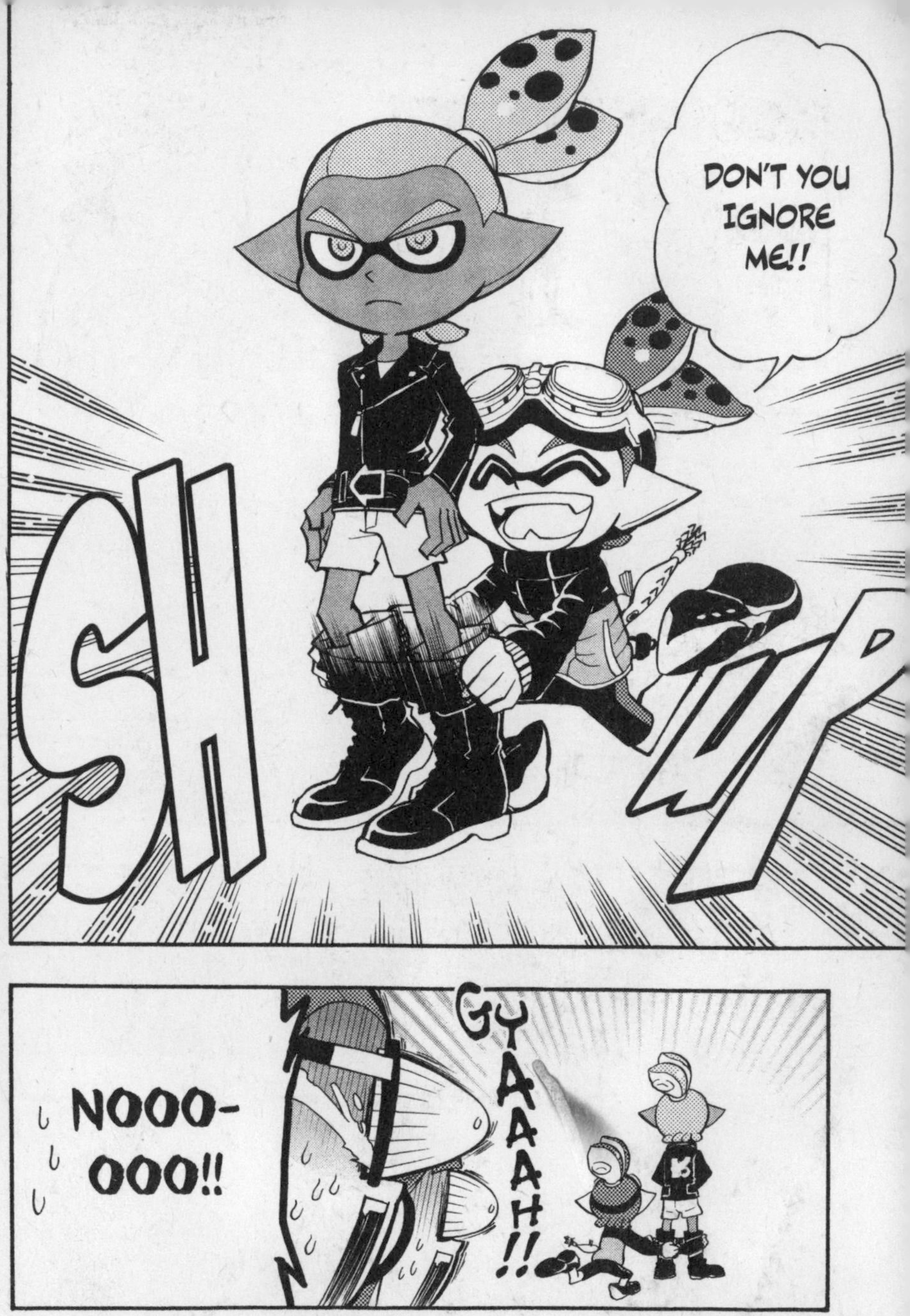
DON'T YOU IGNORE ME!!
GYAAAH!!
NOOO-OOO!!

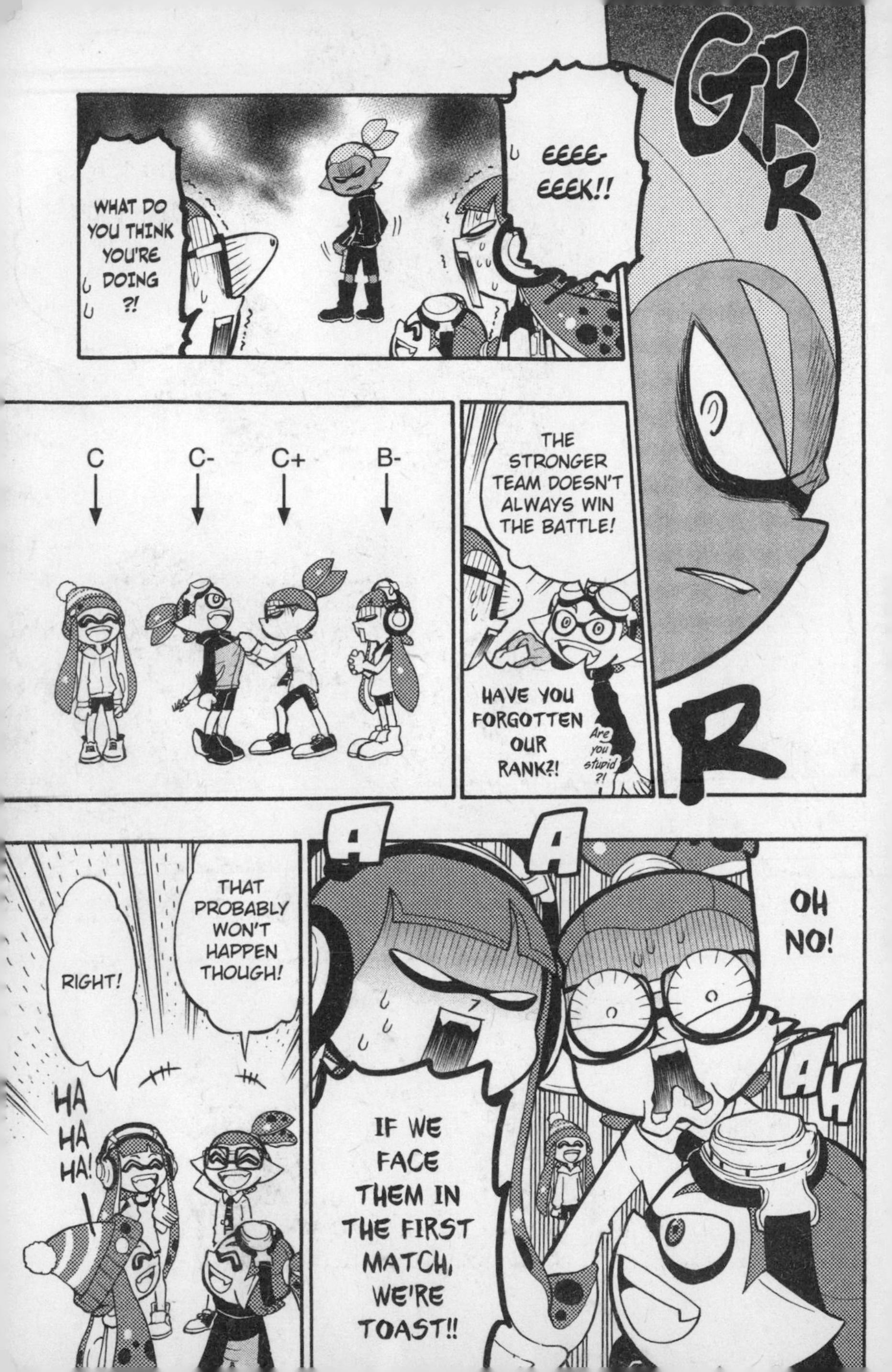
GRRR
EEEE-EEEK!!
WHAT DO YOU THINK YOU'RE DOING ?!
THE STRONGER TEAM DOESN'T ALWAYS WIN THE BATTLE!
HAVE YOU FORGOTTEN OUR RANK?!
Are you stupid ?!
C
C-
C+
B-
AA
OH NO!
AH
IF WE FACE THEM IN THE FIRST MATCH, WE'RE TOAST!!
THAT PROBABLY WON'T HAPPEN THOUGH!
RIGHT!
HA HA HA!

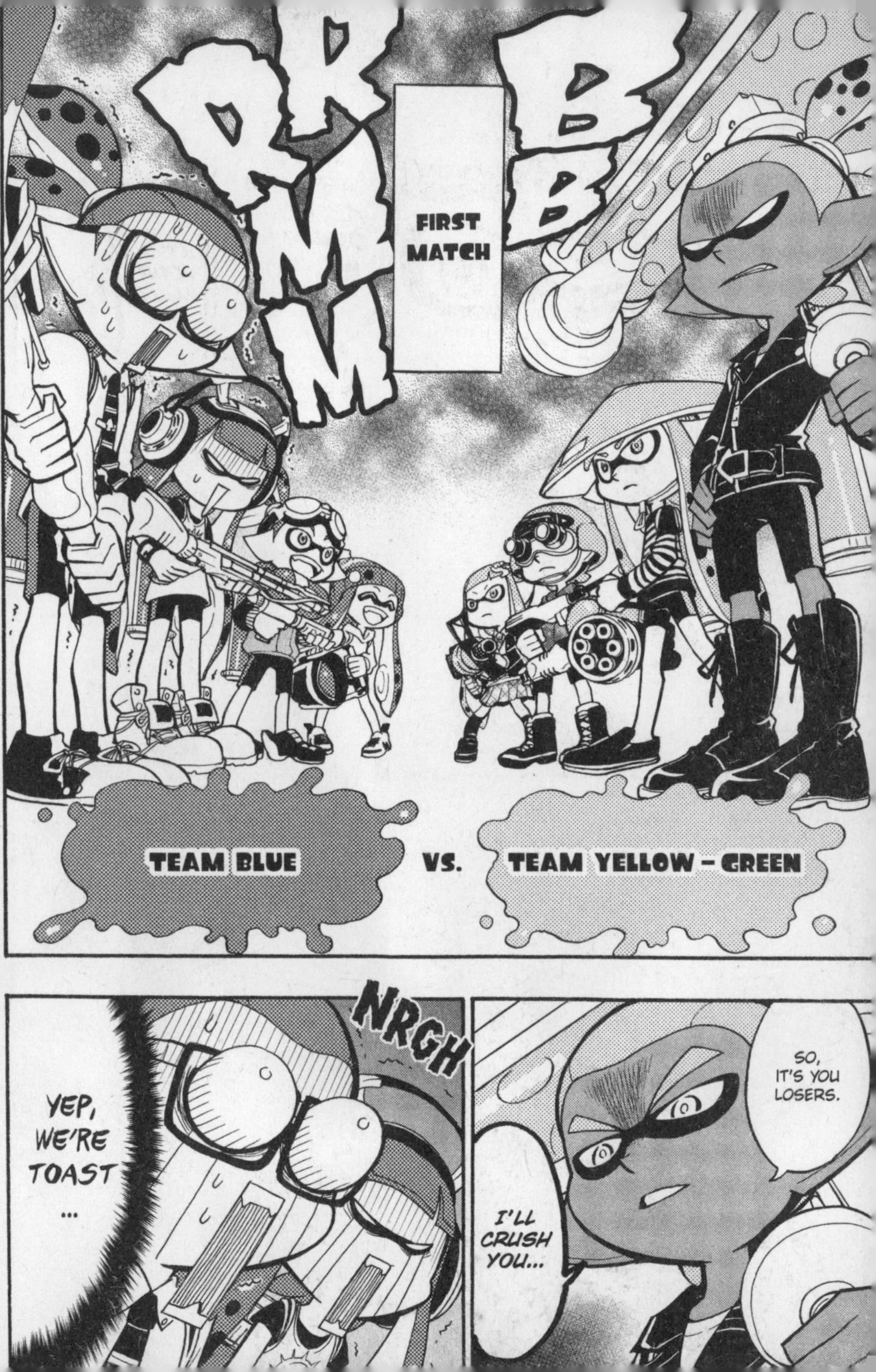

FIRST MATCH
TEAM BLUE
VS.
TEAM YELLOW - GREEN
SO, IT'S YOU LOSERS.
I'LL CRUSH YOU...
NRGH
YEP, WE'RE TOAST ...

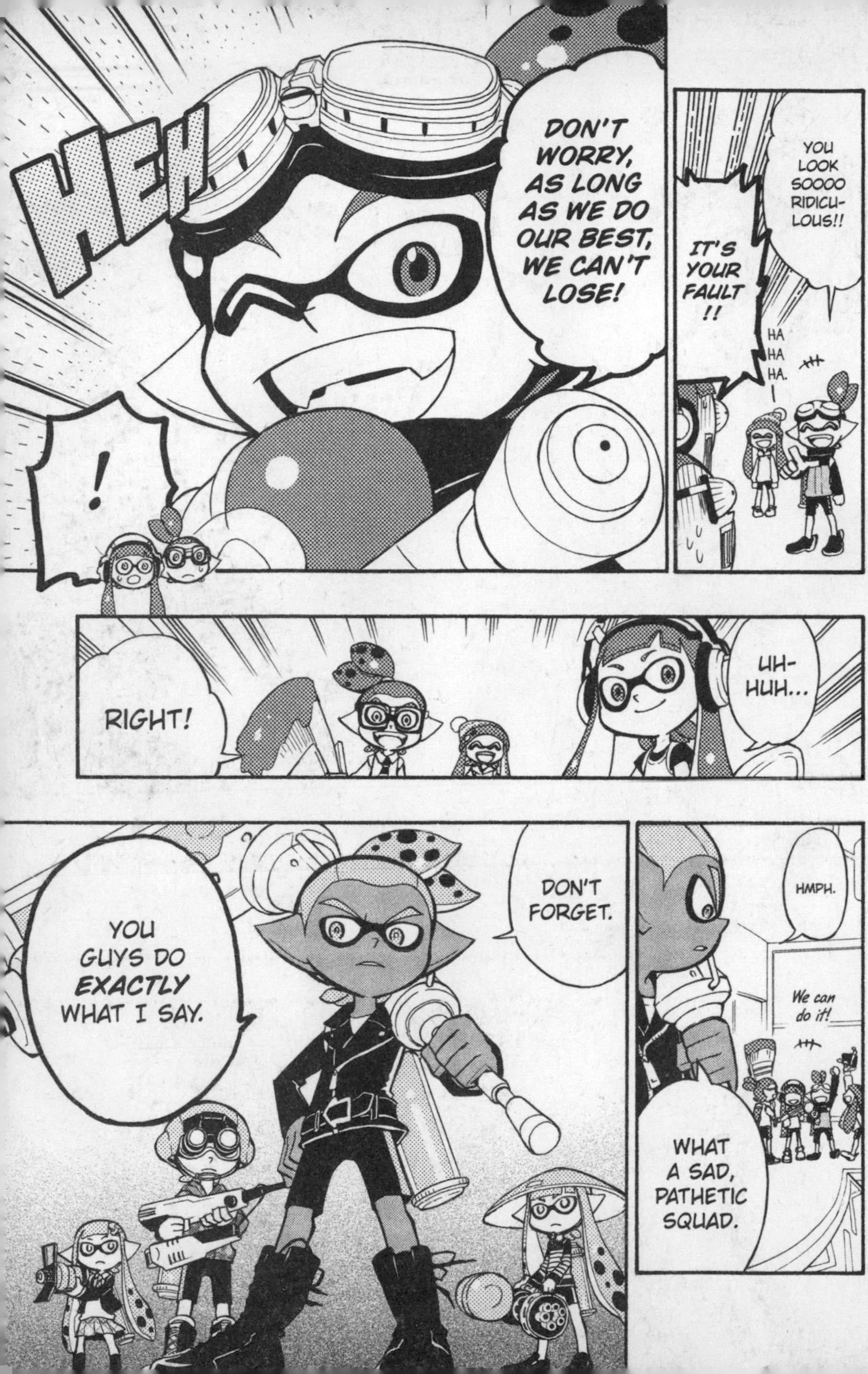
HEH
DON'T WORRY, AS LONG AS WE DO OUR BEST, WE CAN'T LOSE!
!
YOU LOOK SOOOO RIDICULOUS!!
IT'S YOUR FAULT!!
HA HA HA.
UH-HUH...
RIGHT!
HMPH.
We can do it!
WHAT A SAD, PATHETIC SQUAD.
DON'T FORGET.
YOU GUYS DO *EXACTLY* WHAT I SAY.

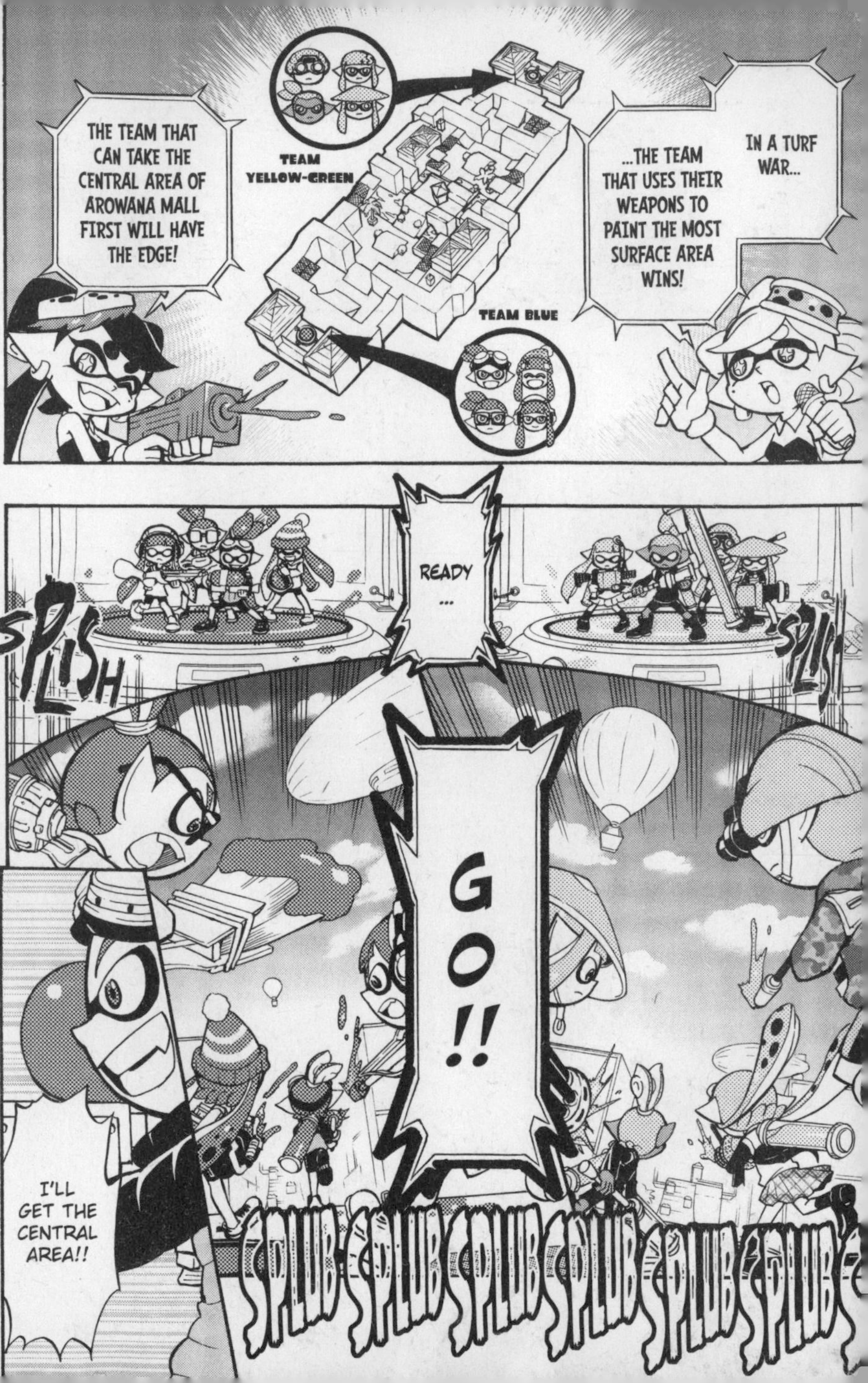
IN A TURF WAR...
...THE TEAM THAT USES THEIR WEAPONS TO PAINT THE MOST SURFACE AREA WINS!
TEAM BLUE
TEAM YELLOW-GREEN
THE TEAM THAT CAN TAKE THE CENTRAL AREA OF AROWANA MALL FIRST WILL HAVE THE EDGE!
SPLISH
READY ...
SPLISH
GO!!
SPLUB SPLUB SPLUB SPLUB SPLUB SPLUB
I'LL GET THE CENTRAL AREA!!

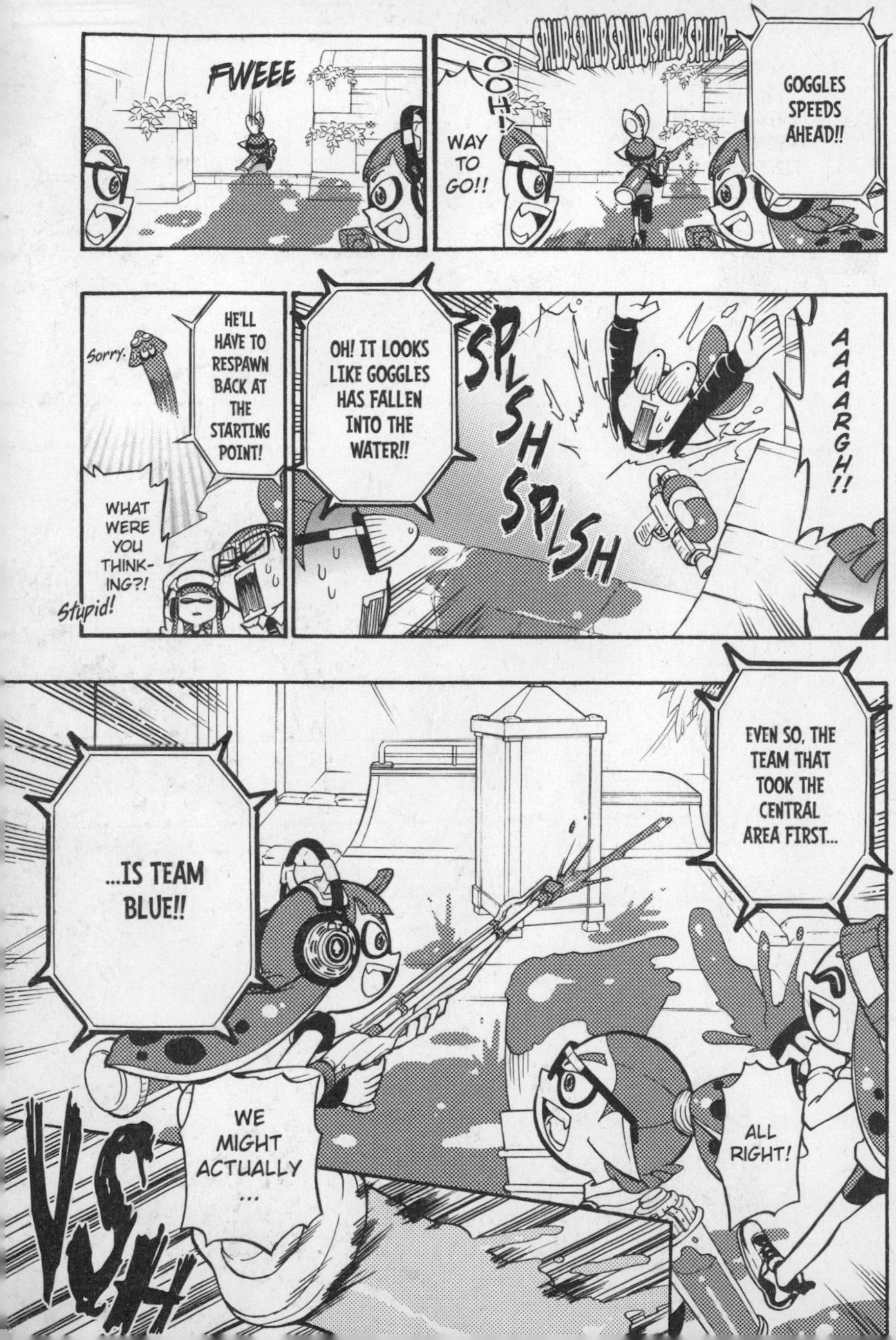
SPLUB SPLUB SPLUB SPLUB SPLUB
GOGGLES SPEEDS AHEAD!!
OOH!
WAY TO GO!!
FWEEE
AAAAARGH!!
SPLSH SPLSH
OH! IT LOOKS LIKE GOGGLES HAS FALLEN INTO THE WATER!!
HE'LL HAVE TO RESPAWN BACK AT THE STARTING POINT!
Sorry.
WHAT WERE YOU THINKING?!
Stupid!
EVEN SO, THE TEAM THAT TOOK THE CENTRAL AREA FIRST...
...IS TEAM BLUE!!
ALL RIGHT!
WE MIGHT ACTUALLY ...
VSH

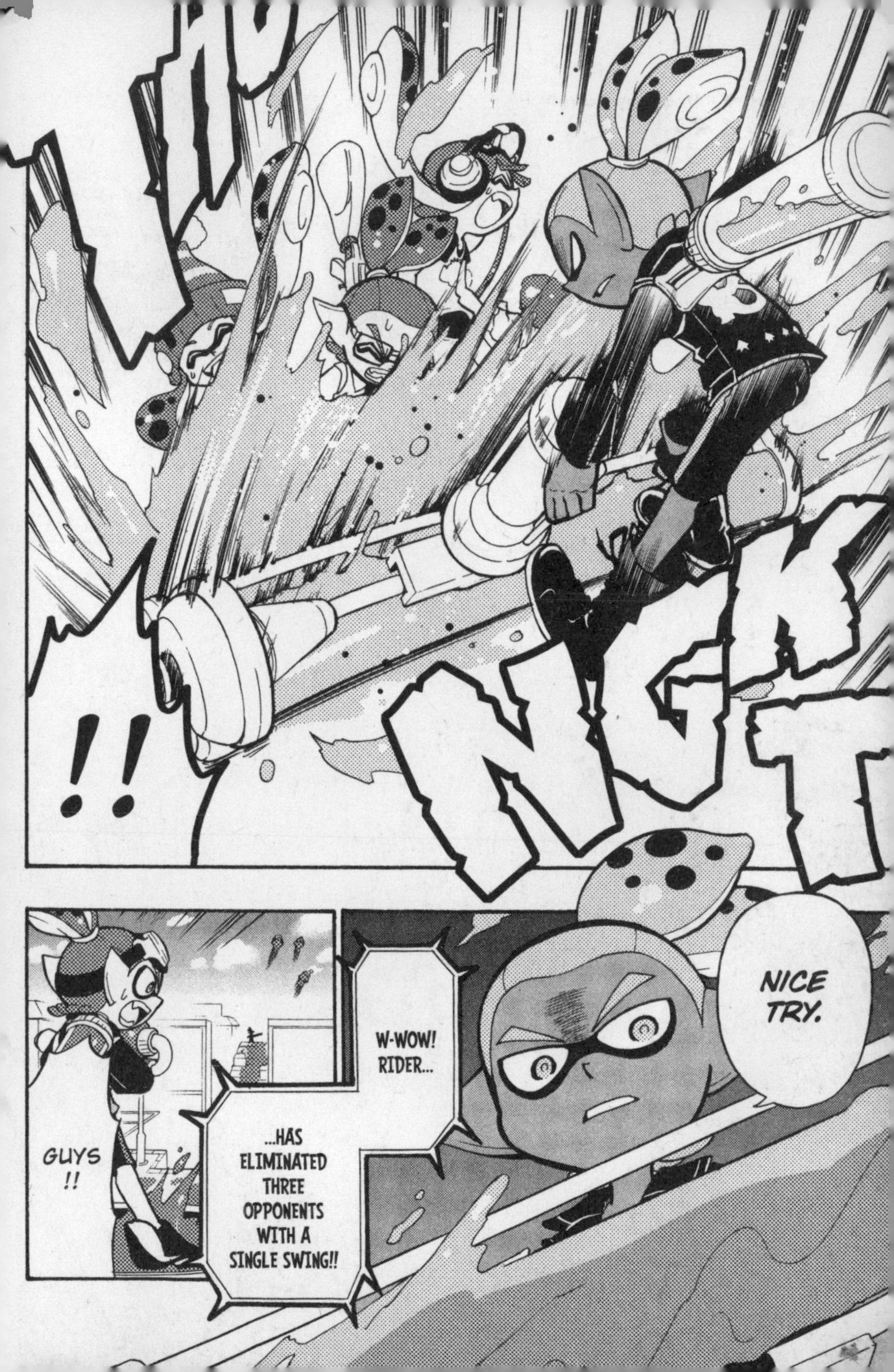
!!
NICE TRY.
W-WOW! RIDER...
...HAS ELIMINATED THREE OPPONENTS WITH A SINGLE SWING!!
GUYS !!

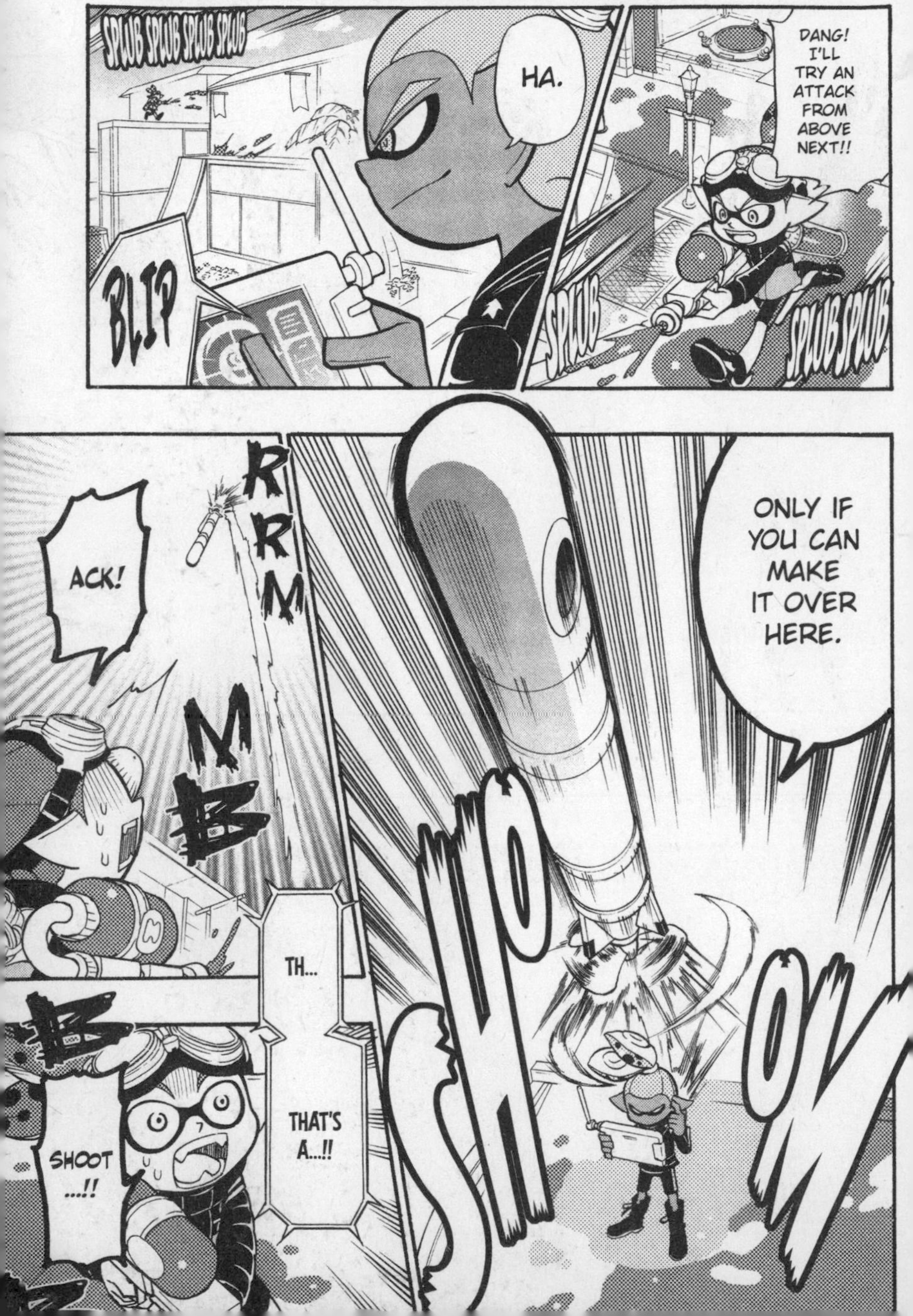
DANG! I'LL TRY AN ATTACK FROM ABOVE NEXT!!
SPLUB SPLUB
SPLUB
HA.
SPLUB SPLUB SPLUB SPLUB
BLIP
ONLY IF YOU CAN MAKE IT OVER HERE.
ACK!
TH...
THAT'S A...!!
SHOOT ...!!

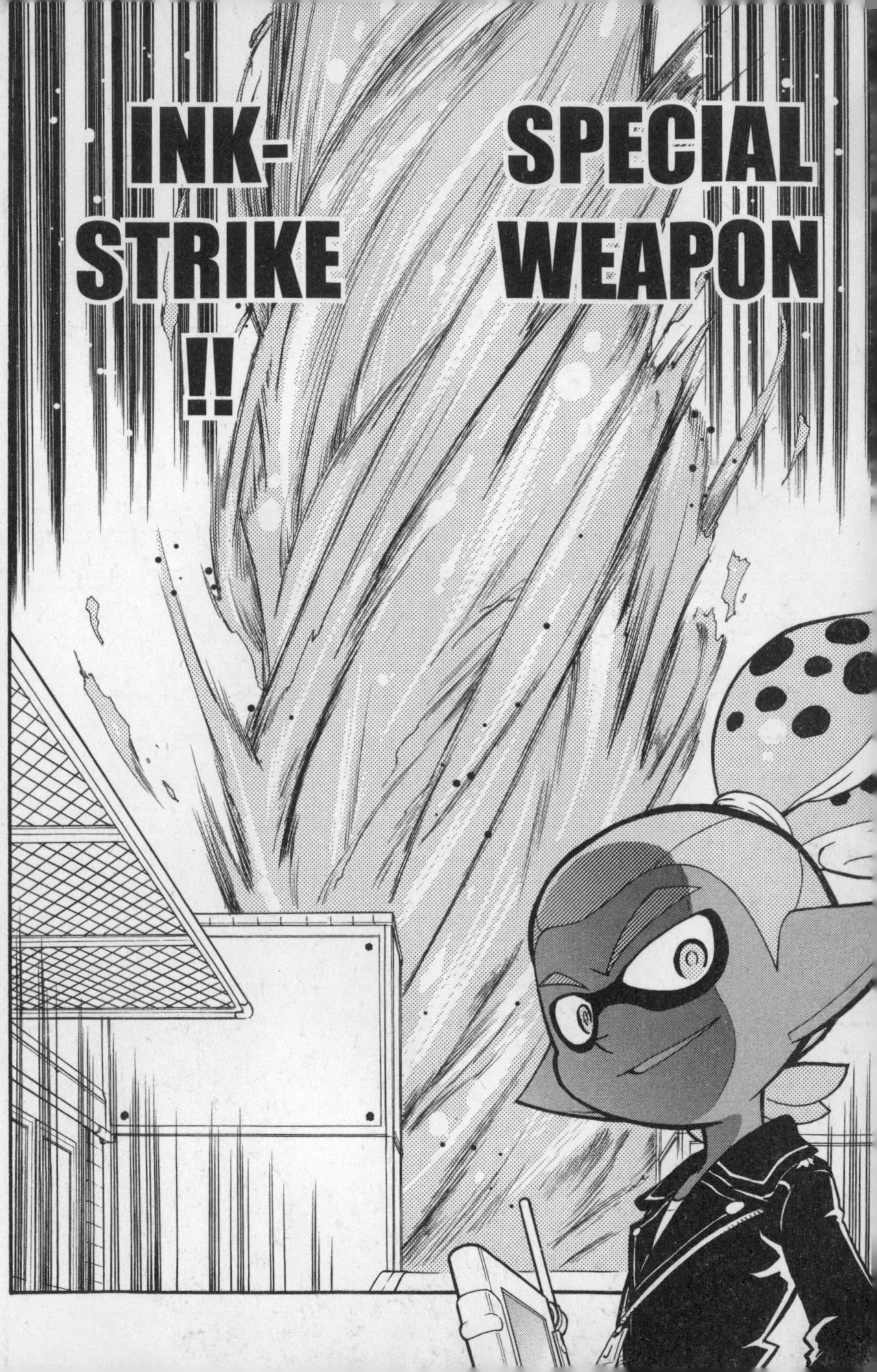
SPECIAL WEAPON
INK-STRIKE !!

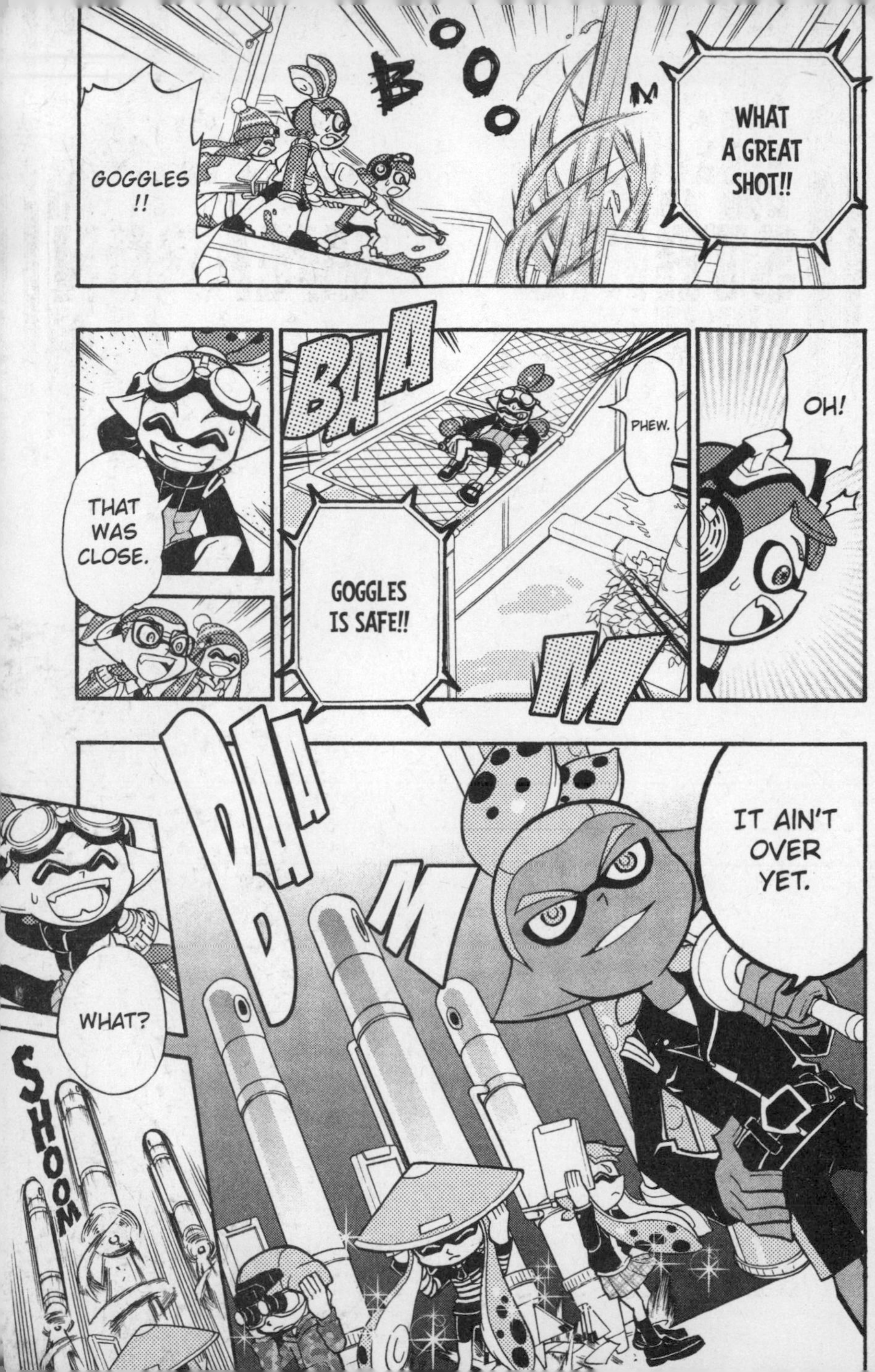

WHAT A GREAT SHOT!!
BOOOOM
GOGGLES !!
OH!
PHEW.
GOGGLES IS SAFE!!
THAT WAS CLOSE.
IT AIN'T OVER YET.
WHAT?
SHOOM

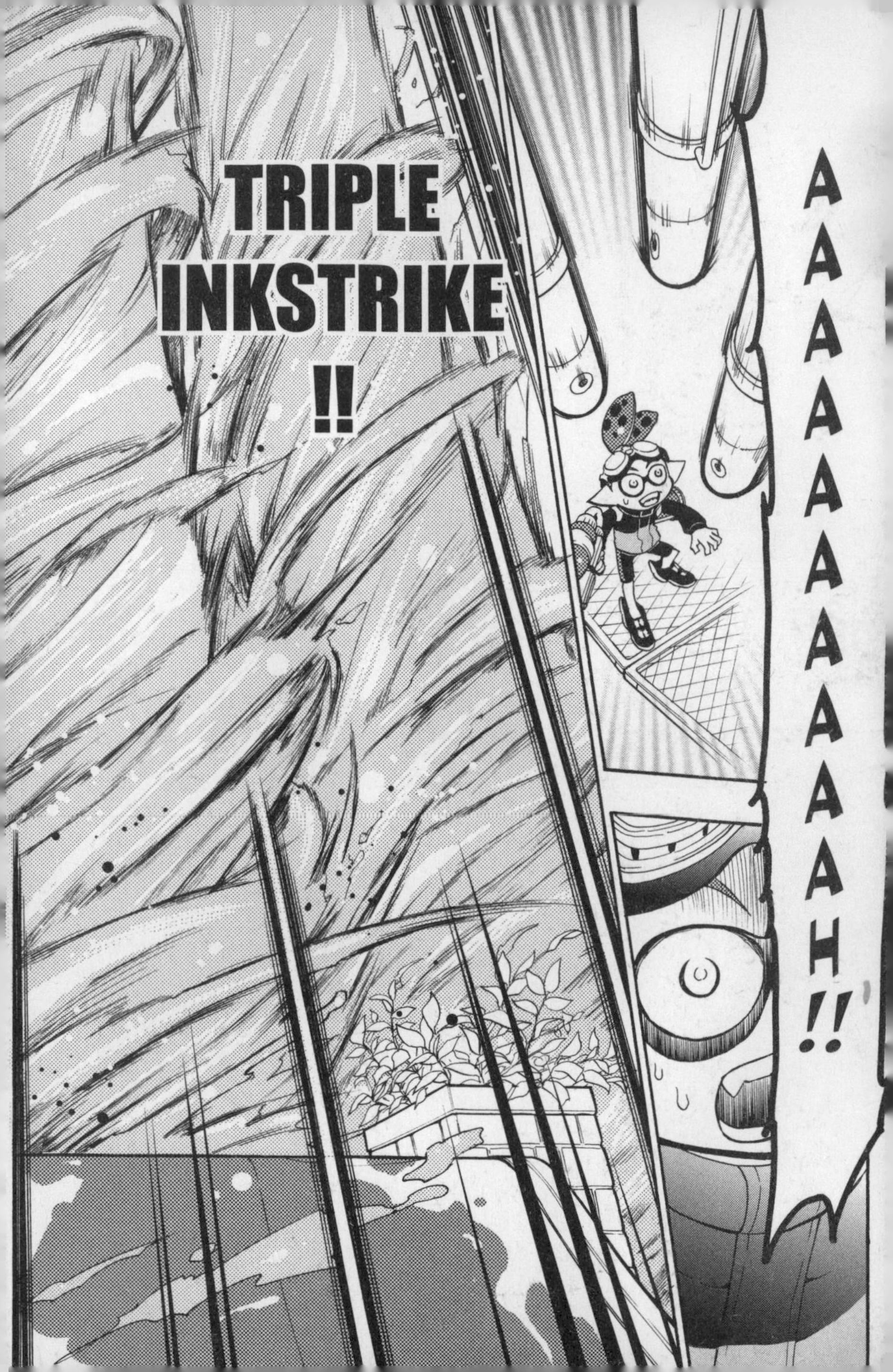
AAAAAAAAAAH!!
TRIPLE INKSTRIKE!!

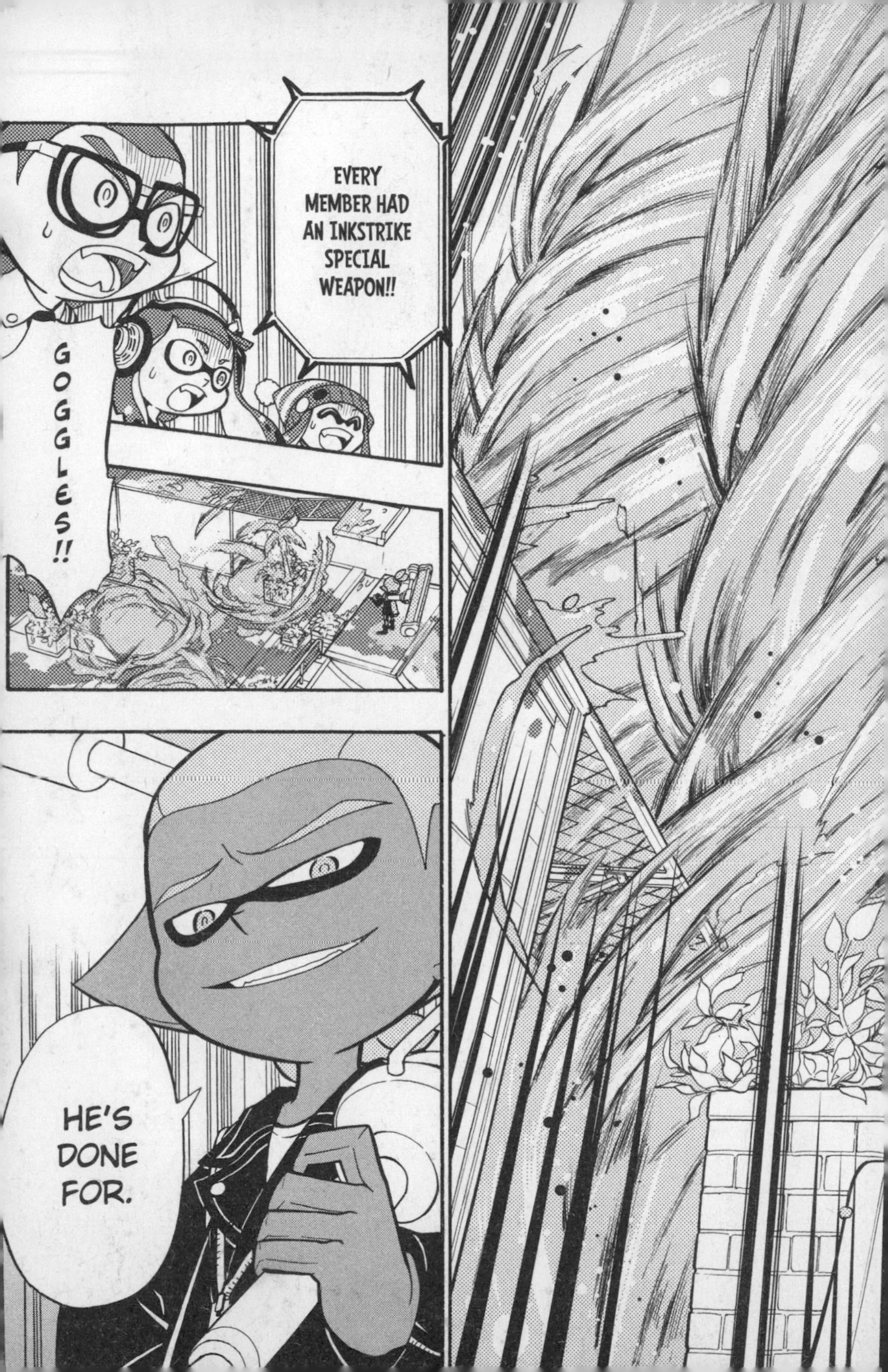
EVERY MEMBER HAD AN INKSTRIKE SPECIAL WEAPON!!
GOGGLES!!
HE'S DONE FOR.

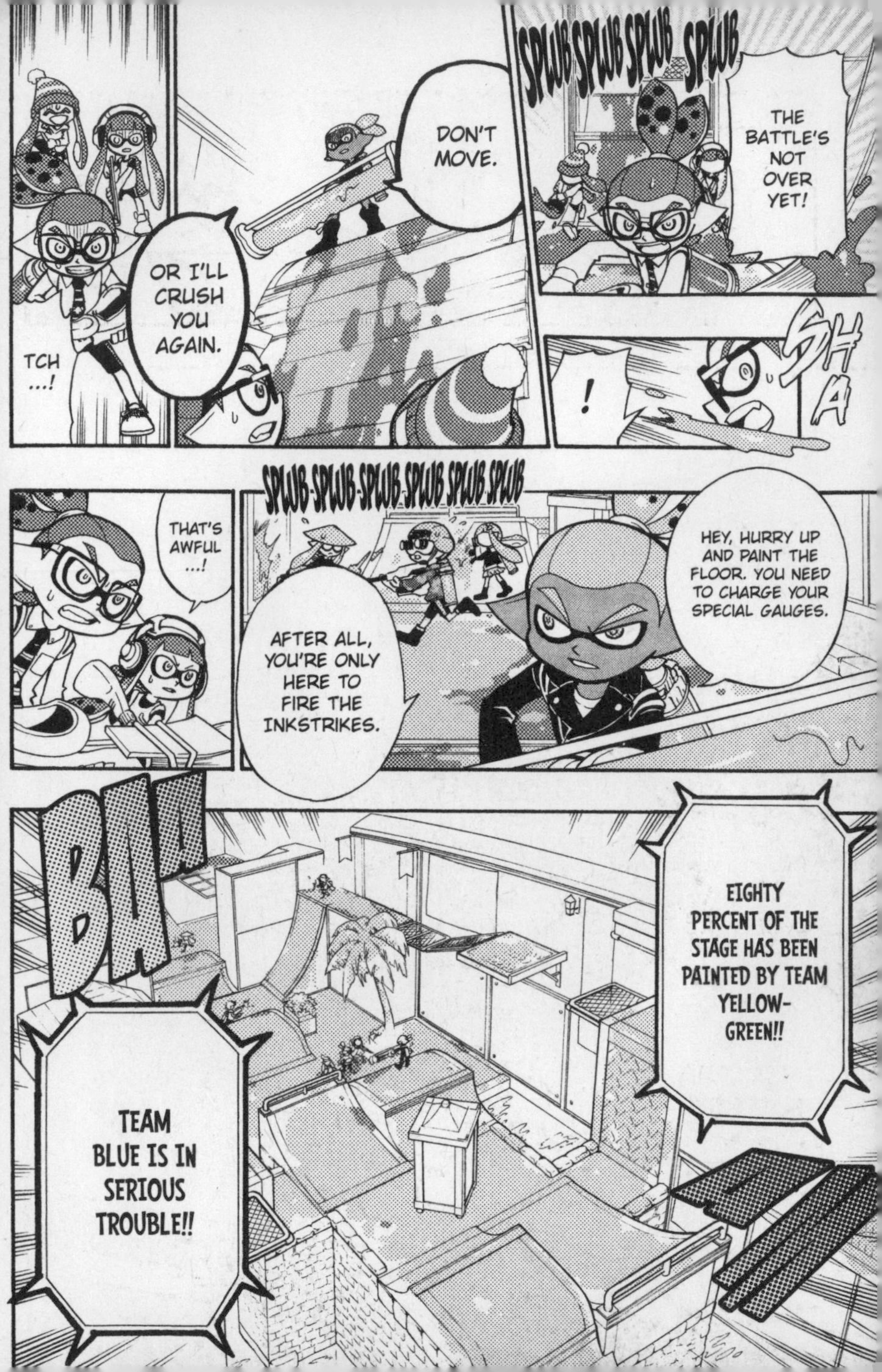
SPLUB SPLUB SPLUB SPLUB
THE BATTLE'S NOT OVER YET!
SHA
!
DON'T MOVE.
OR I'LL CRUSH YOU AGAIN.
TCH ...!
SPLUB SPLUB SPLUB SPLUB SPLUB SPLUB
HEY, HURRY UP AND PAINT THE FLOOR. YOU NEED TO CHARGE YOUR SPECIAL GAUGES.
AFTER ALL, YOU'RE ONLY HERE TO FIRE THE INKSTRIKES.
THAT'S AWFUL ...!
EIGHTY PERCENT OF THE STAGE HAS BEEN PAINTED BY TEAM YELLOW-GREEN!!
BHA
TEAM BLUE IS IN SERIOUS TROUBLE!!

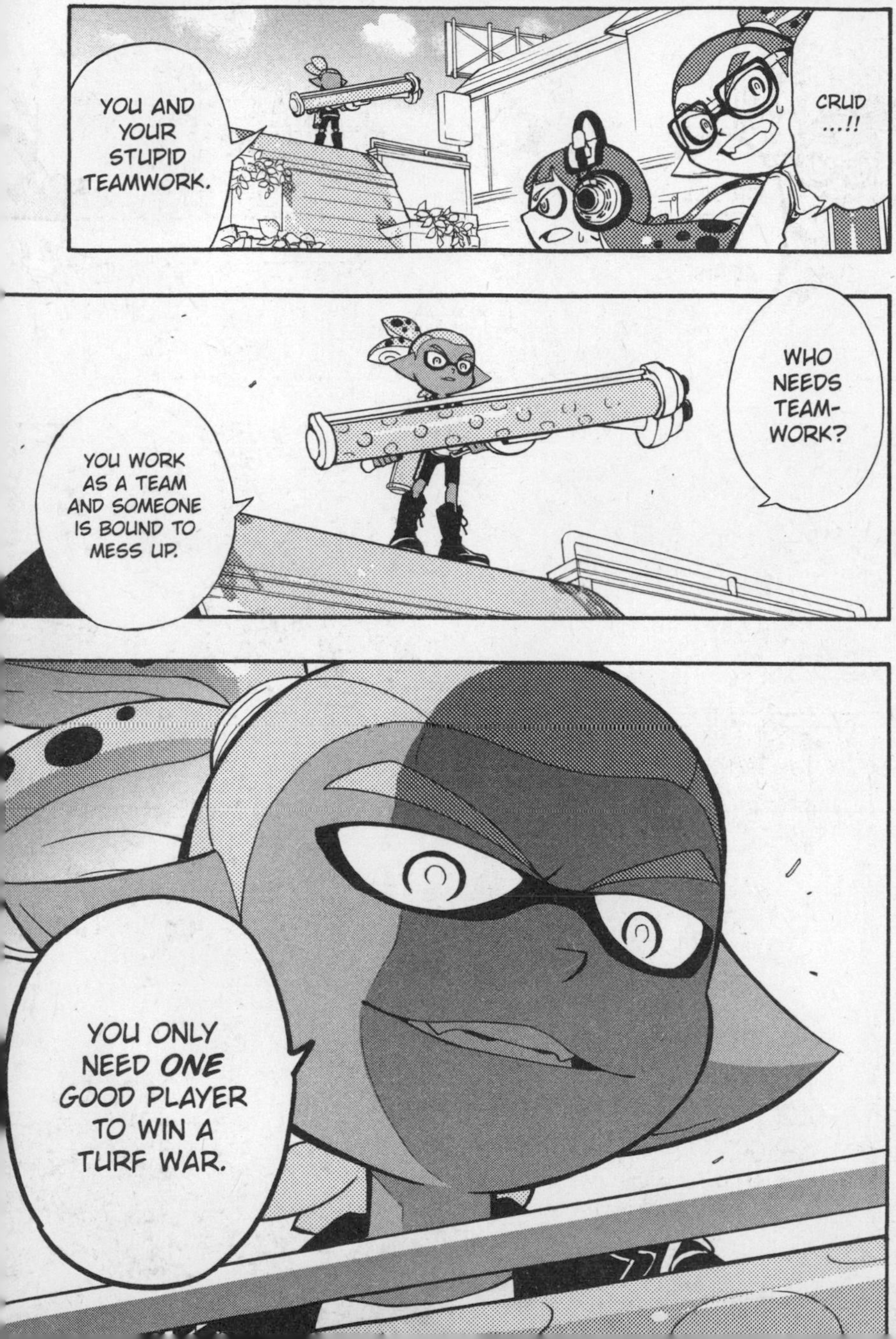
CRUD ...!!
YOU AND YOUR STUPID TEAMWORK.
WHO NEEDS TEAM-WORK?
YOU WORK AS A TEAM AND SOMEONE IS BOUND TO MESS UP.
YOU ONLY NEED *ONE* GOOD PLAYER TO WIN A TURF WAR.

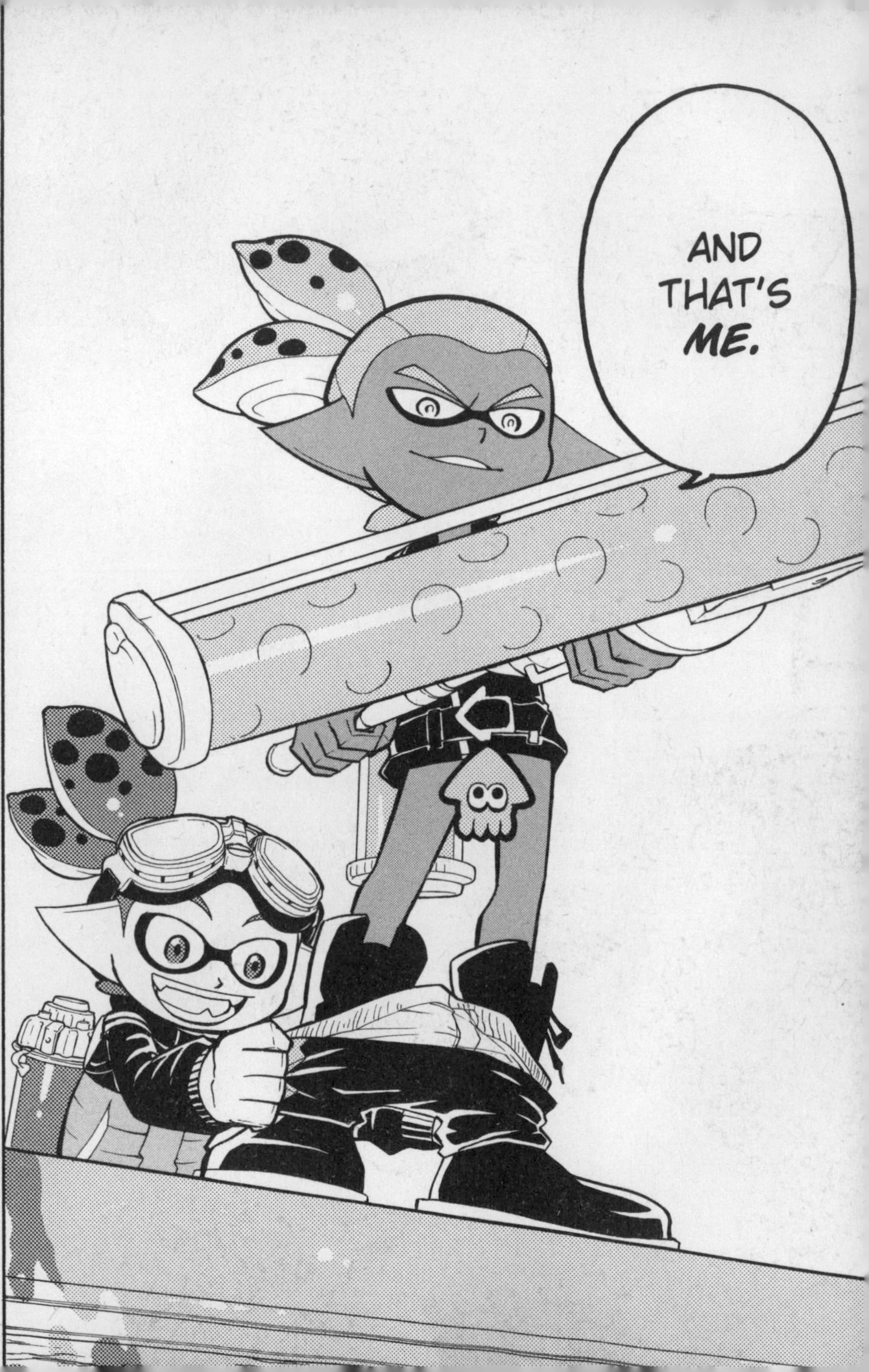
AND THAT'S ME.

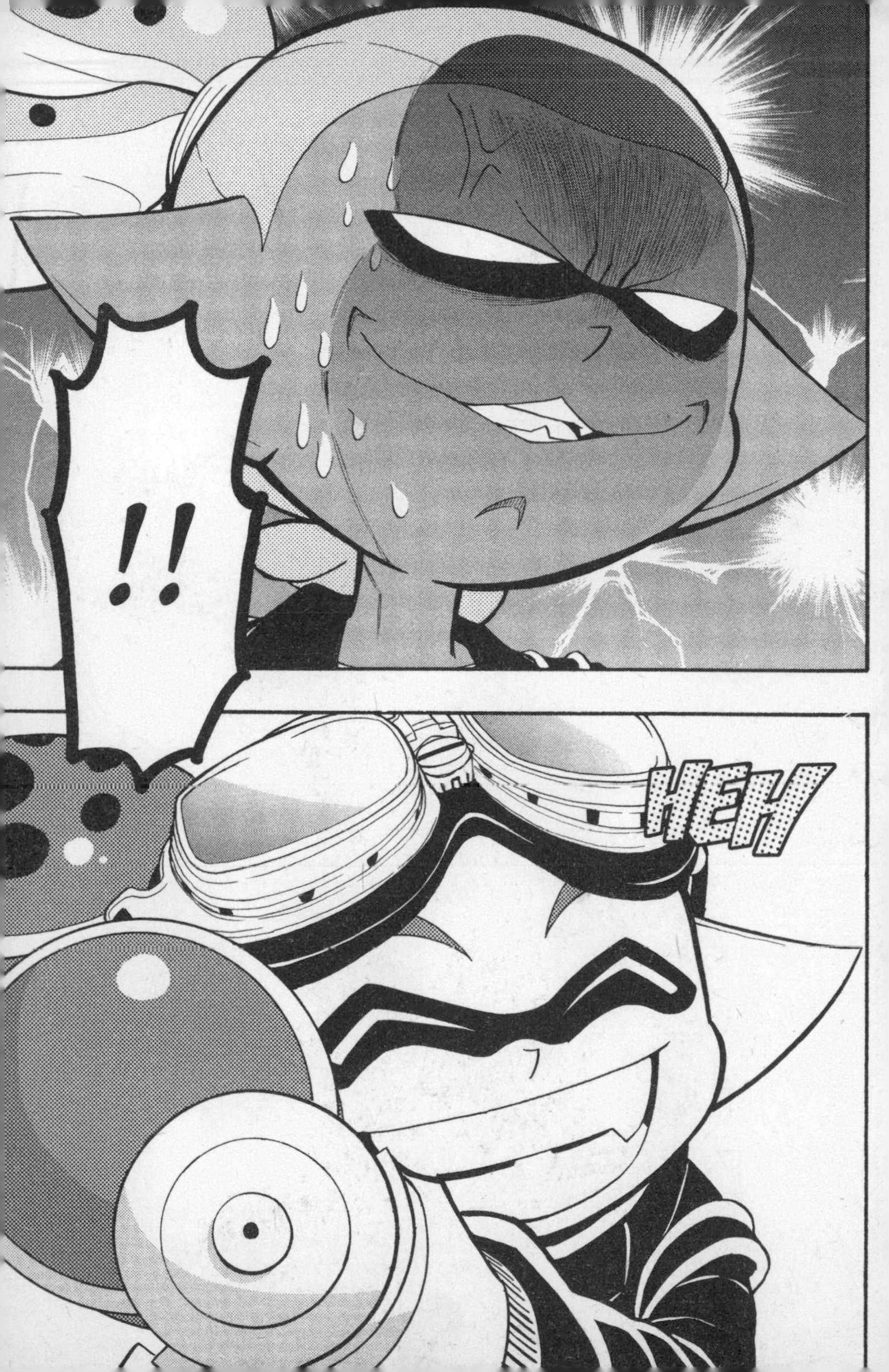
!!
HEH

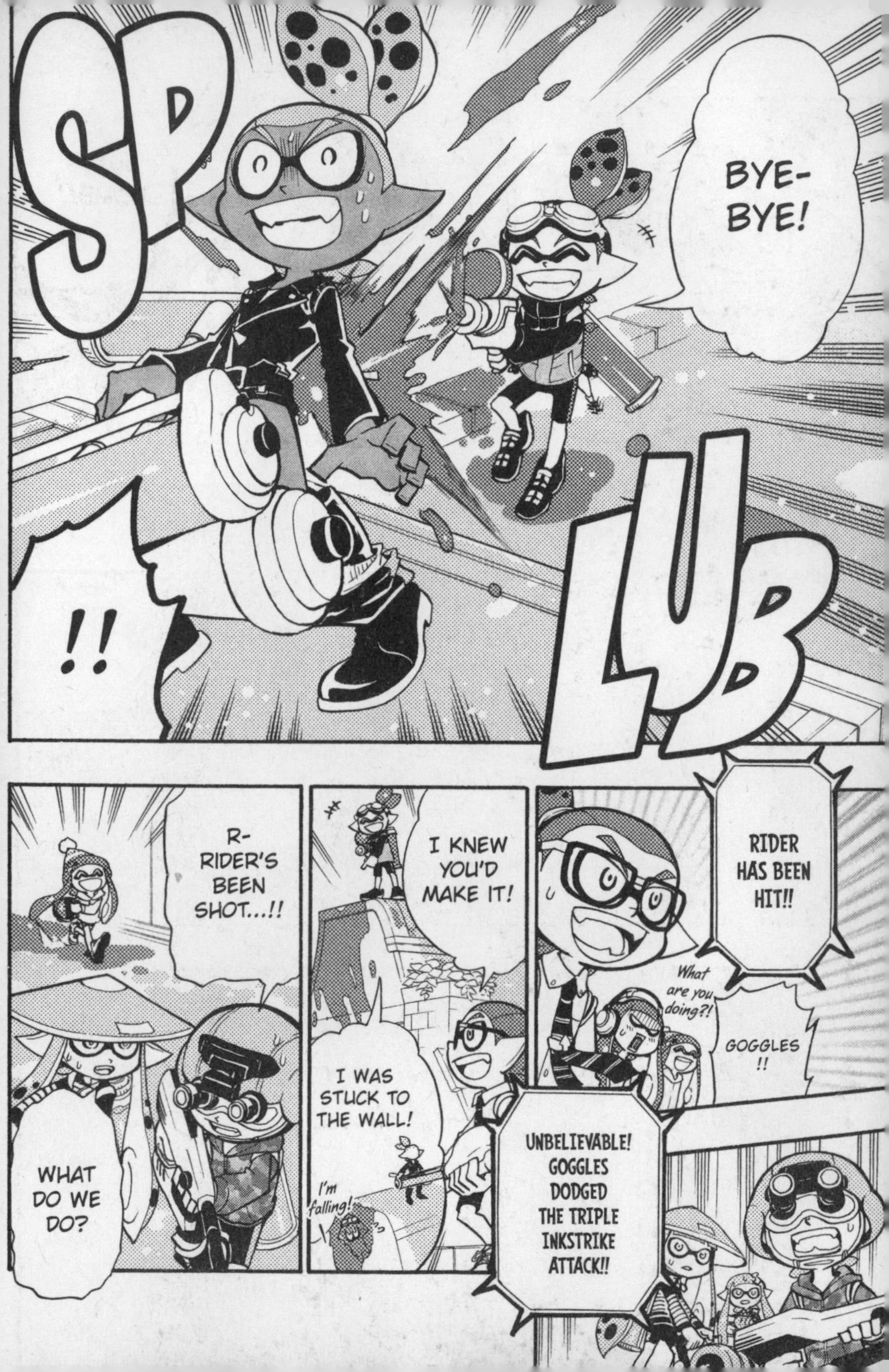
BYE-BYE!
SPLUB
!!
RIDER HAS BEEN HIT!!
What are you doing?!
GOGGLES!!
UNBELIEVABLE! GOGGLES DODGED THE TRIPLE INKSTRIKE ATTACK!!
I KNEW YOU'D MAKE IT!
I WAS STUCK TO THE WALL!
I'm falling!
R-RIDER'S BEEN SHOT...!!
WHAT DO WE DO?

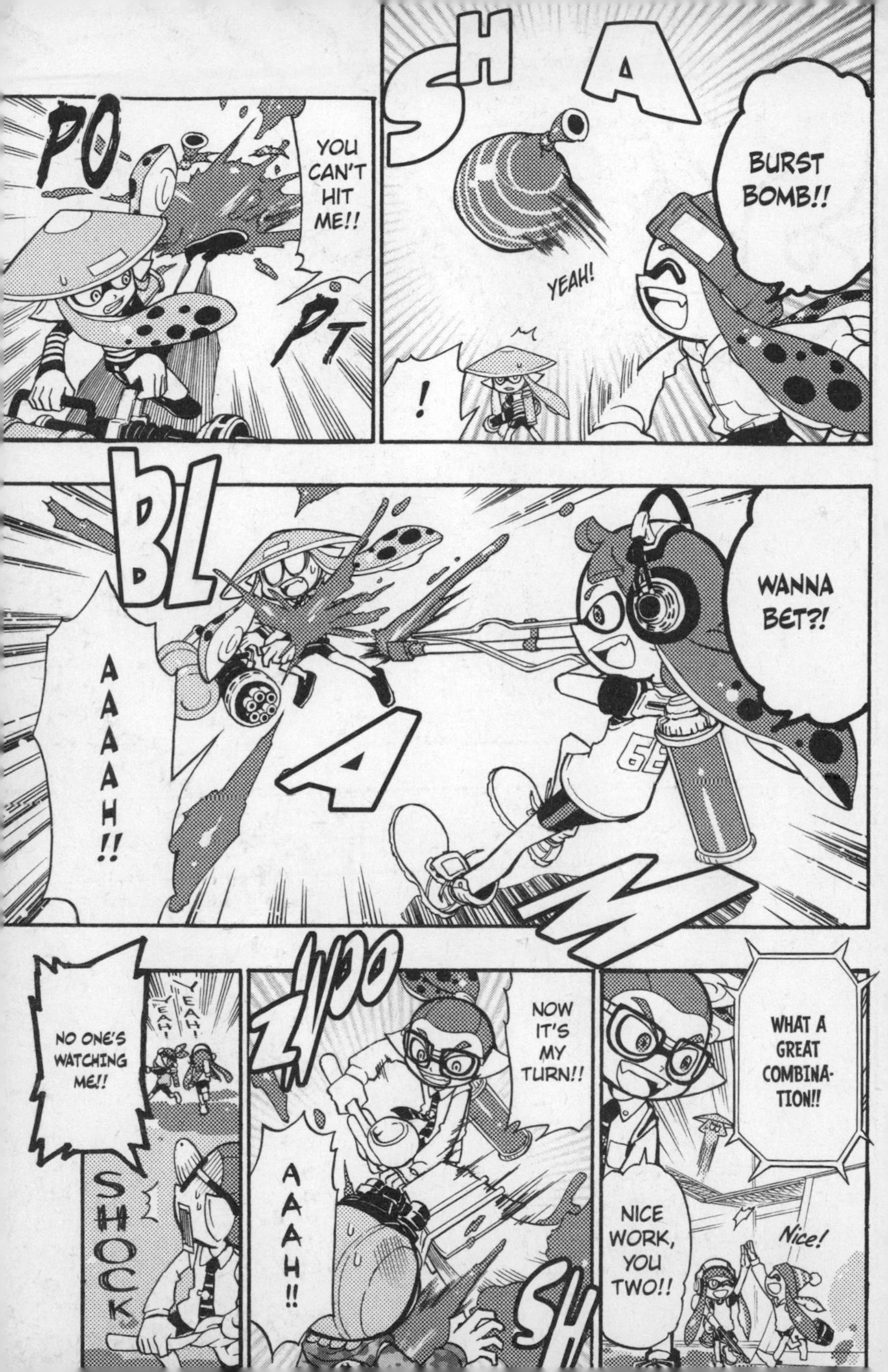
SH
A
BURST BOMB!!
YEAH!
!
PO
YOU CAN'T HIT ME!!
PT
WANNA BET?!
BL
A
M
AAAAAH!!
WHAT A GREAT COMBINA-TION!!
NICE WORK, YOU TWO!!
Nice!
NOW IT'S MY TURN!!
AAAH!!
SH
NO ONE'S WATCHING ME!!
YEAH!
YEAH!
SHOCK

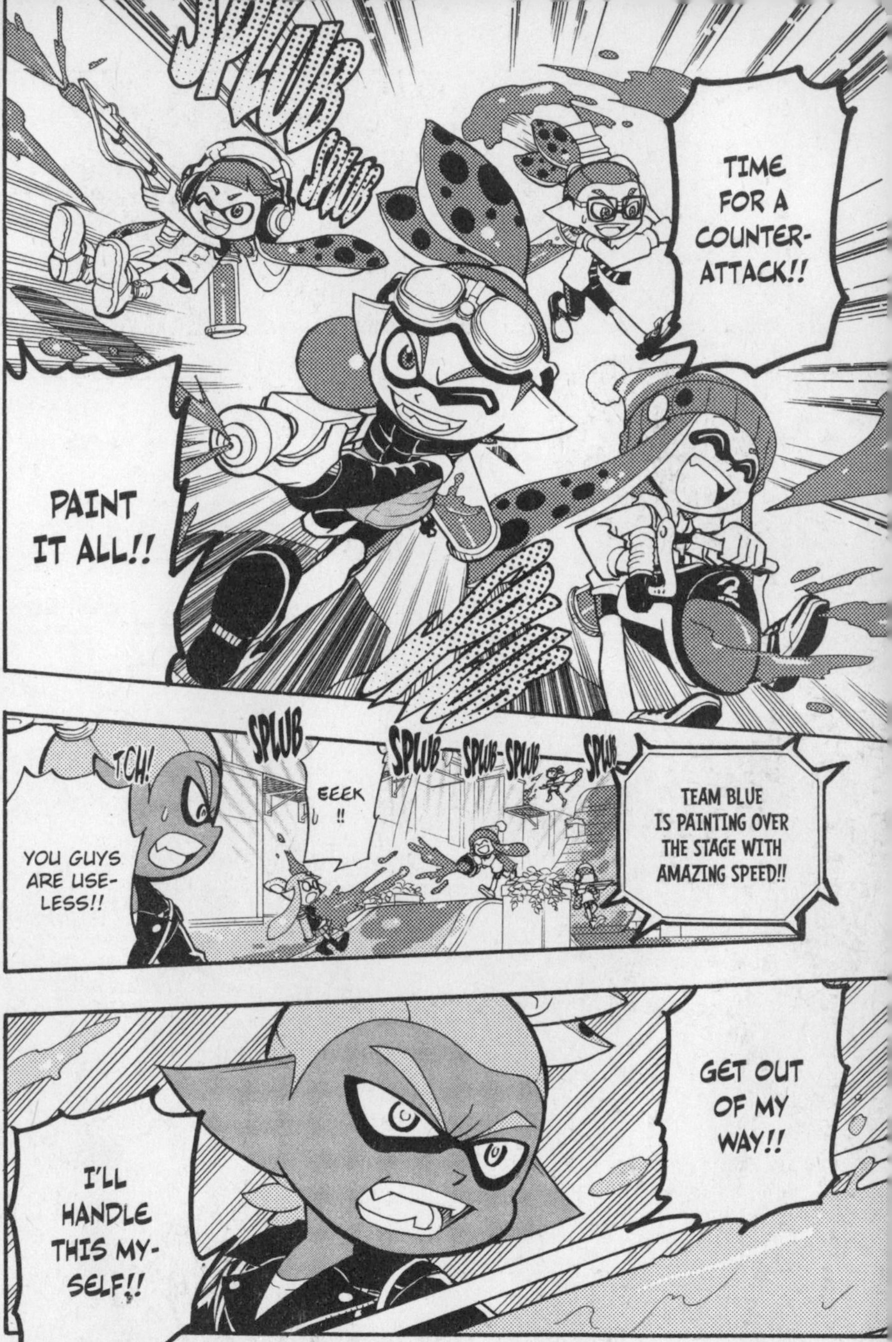
SPLUB
SPLUB
TIME FOR A COUNTER-ATTACK!!
PAINT IT ALL!!
TEAM BLUE IS PAINTING OVER THE STAGE WITH AMAZING SPEED!!
SPLUB
SPLUB-SPLUB-SPLUB
SPLUB
EEEK!!
TCH!
YOU GUYS ARE USE-LESS!!
GET OUT OF MY WAY!!
I'LL HANDLE THIS MY-SELF!!

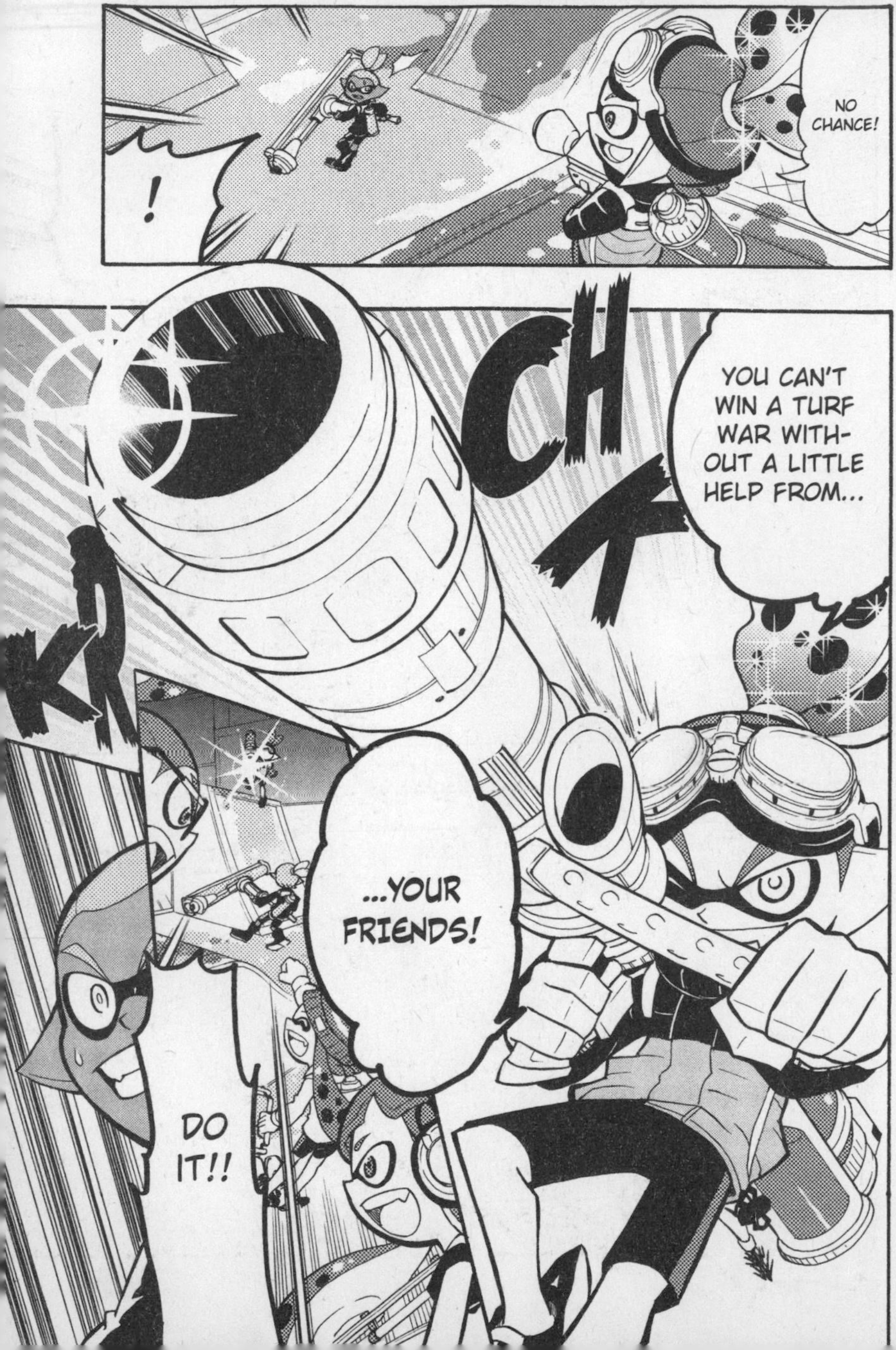
NO CHANCE!
!
YOU CAN'T WIN A TURF WAR WITHOUT A LITTLE HELP FROM...
KRCHK
...YOUR FRIENDS!
DO IT!!

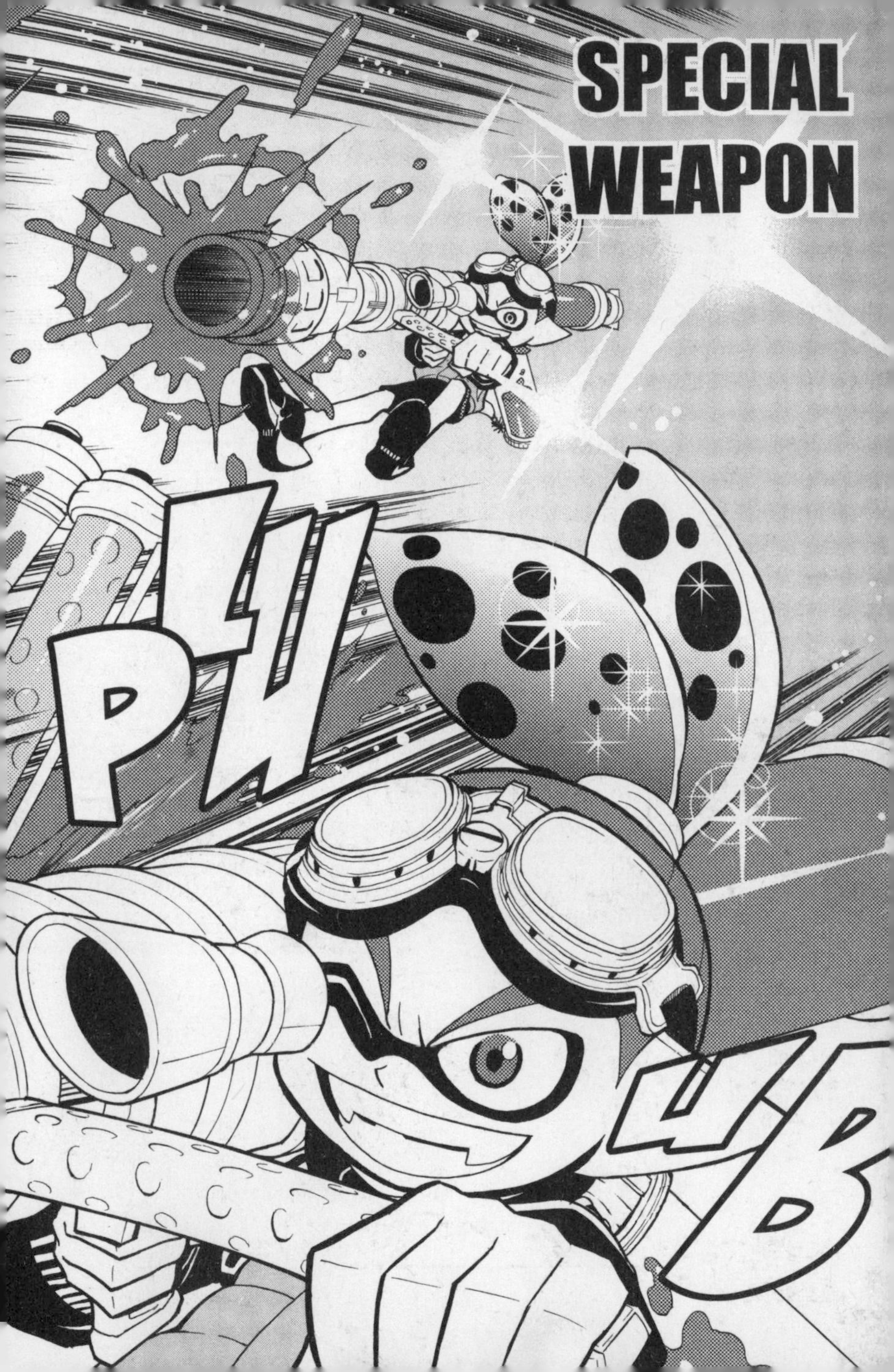
SPECIAL WEAPON
PW
UB

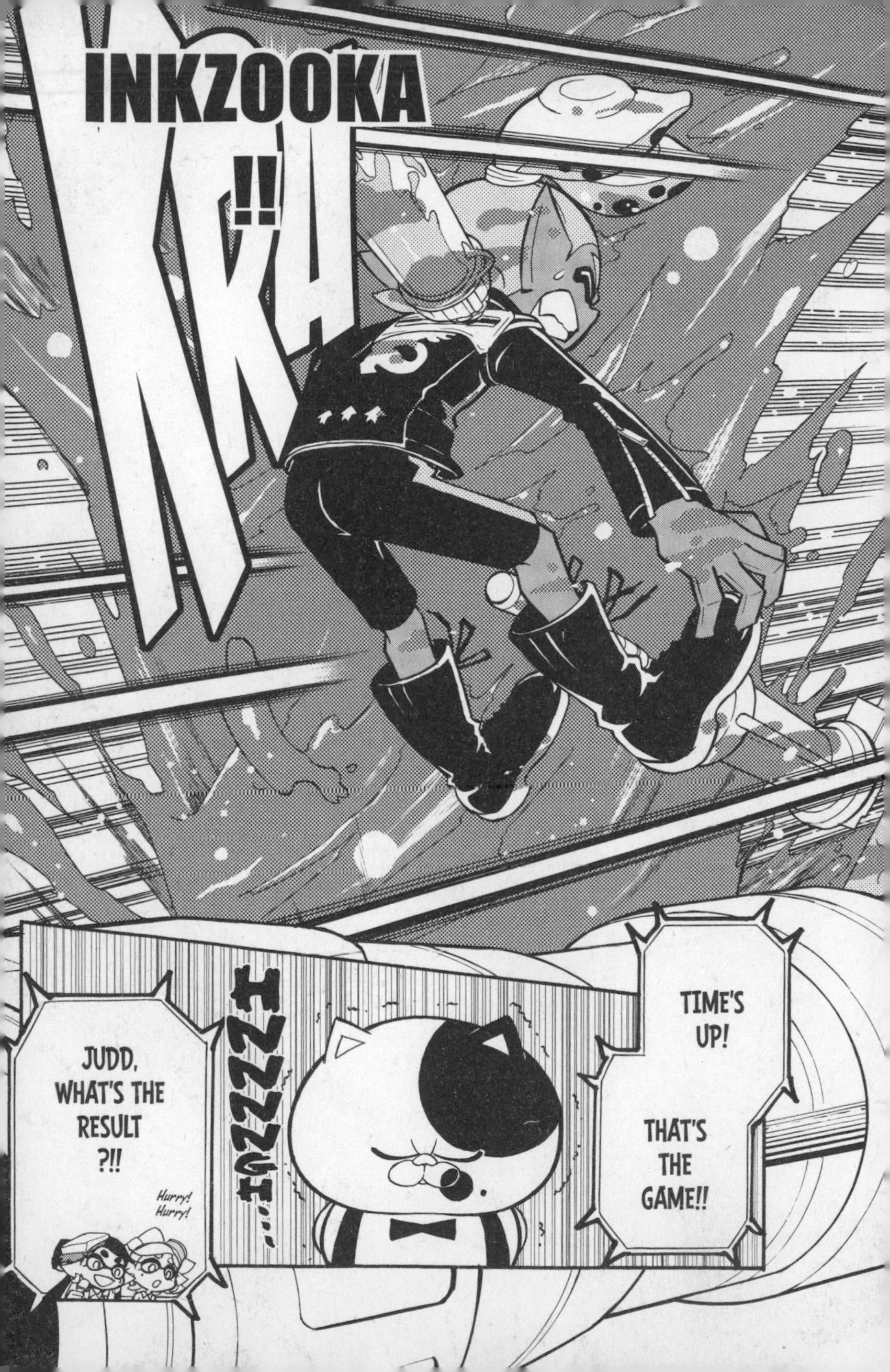
INKZOOKA
!!
TIME'S UP!
THAT'S THE GAME!!
HNNNNGH!..
JUDD, WHAT'S THE RESULT ?!!
Hurry! Hurry!

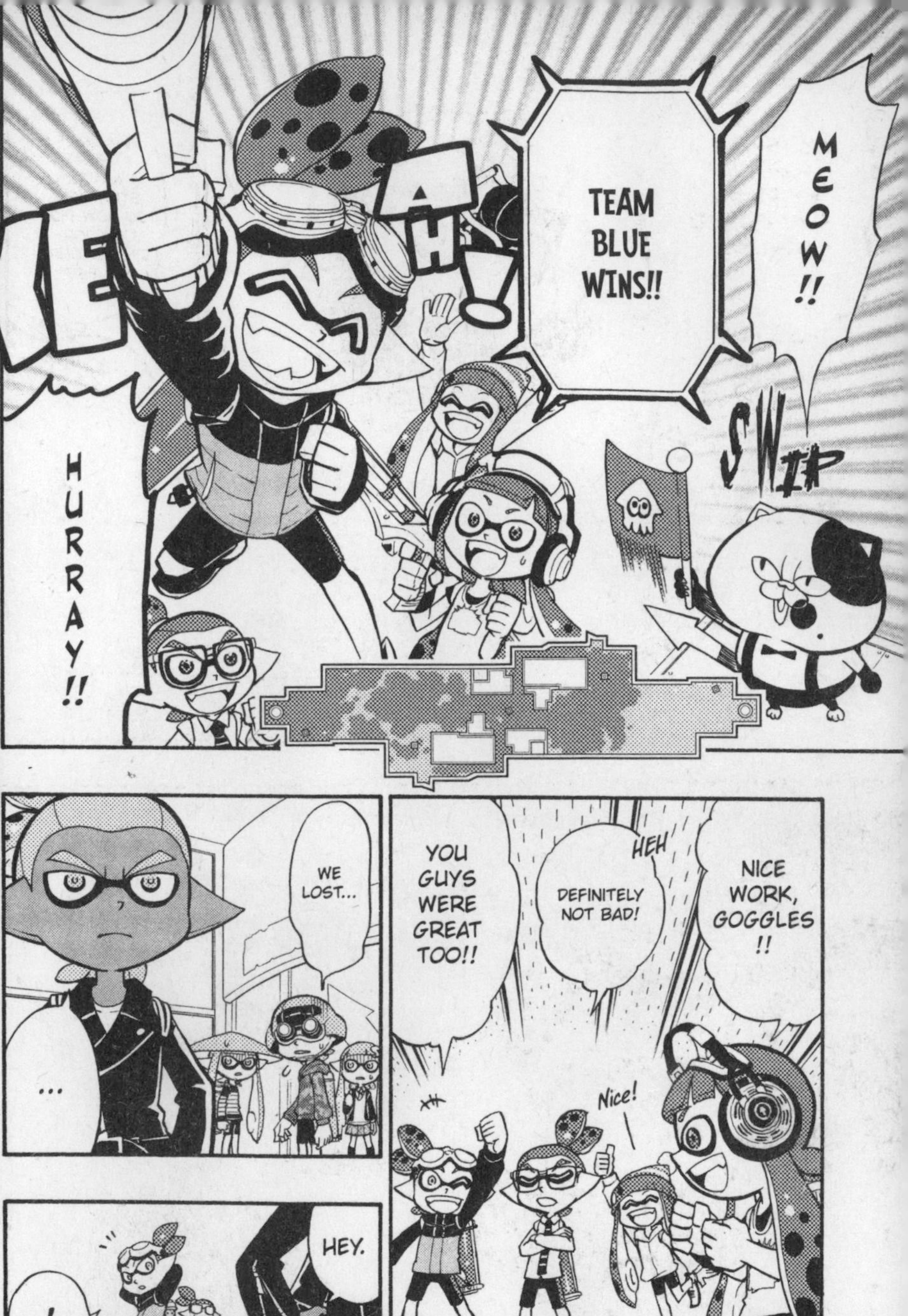

MEOW!!
TEAM BLUE WINS!!
SWIP
EAH!
HURRAY!!
NICE WORK, GOGGLES!!
HEH
DEFINITELY NOT BAD!
YOU GUYS WERE GREAT TOO!!
Nice!
WE LOST...
...
HEY.
!

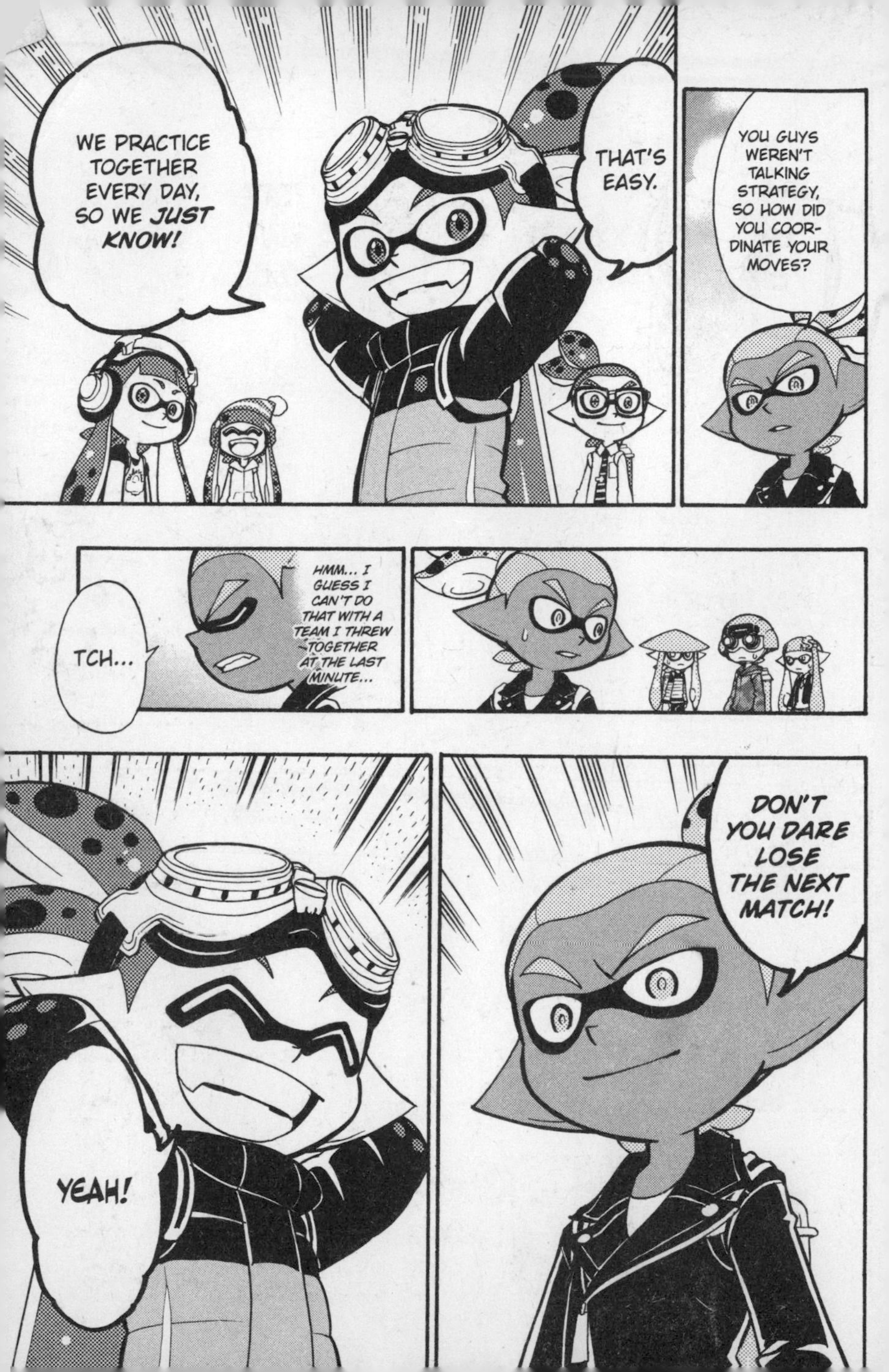
YOU GUYS WEREN'T TALKING STRATEGY, SO HOW DID YOU COOR-DINATE YOUR MOVES?
THAT'S EASY.
WE PRACTICE TOGETHER EVERY DAY, SO WE *JUST KNOW!*
HMM... I GUESS I CAN'T DO THAT WITH A TEAM I THREW TOGETHER AT THE LAST MINUTE...
TCH...
DON'T YOU DARE LOSE THE NEXT MATCH!
YEAH!

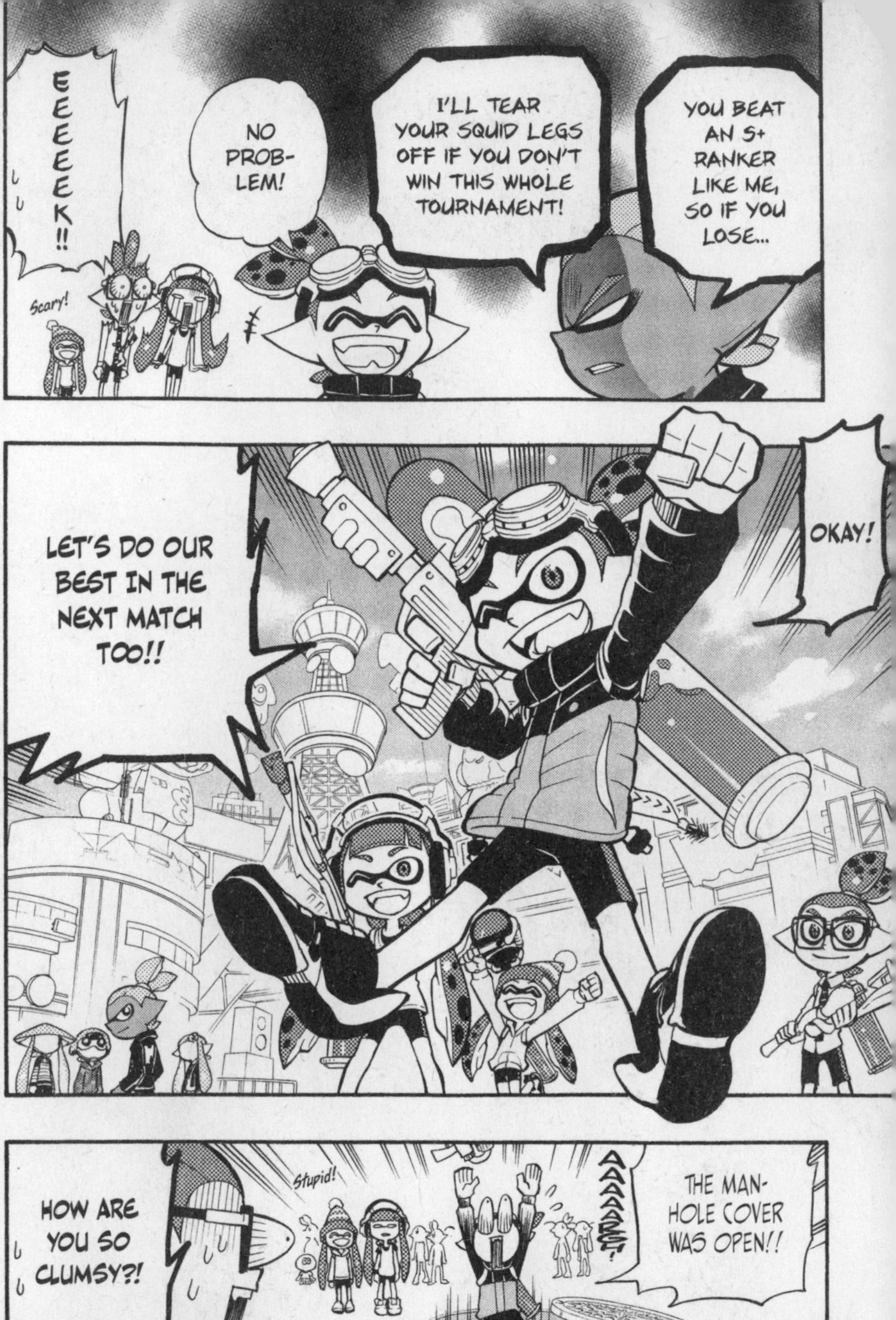
YOU BEAT AN S+ RANKER LIKE ME, SO IF YOU LOSE...
I'LL TEAR YOUR SQUID LEGS OFF IF YOU DON'T WIN THIS WHOLE TOURNAMENT!
NO PROB-LEM!
EEEEEEK!!
Scary!
OKAY!
LET'S DO OUR BEST IN THE NEXT MATCH TOO!!
THE MAN-HOLE COVER WAS OPEN!!
AAAAARGH!
Stupid!
HOW ARE YOU SO CLUMSY?!

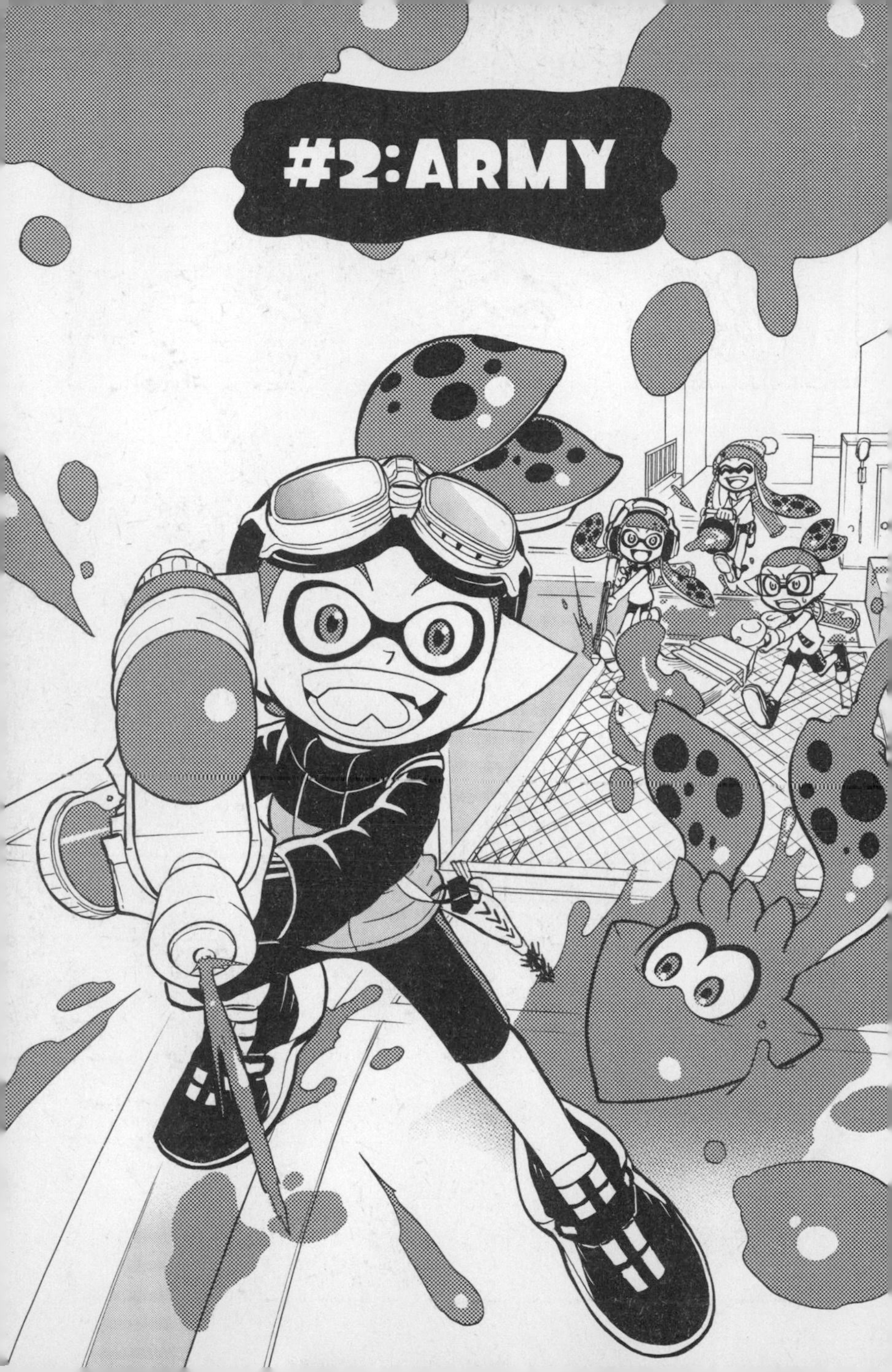
#2: ARMY

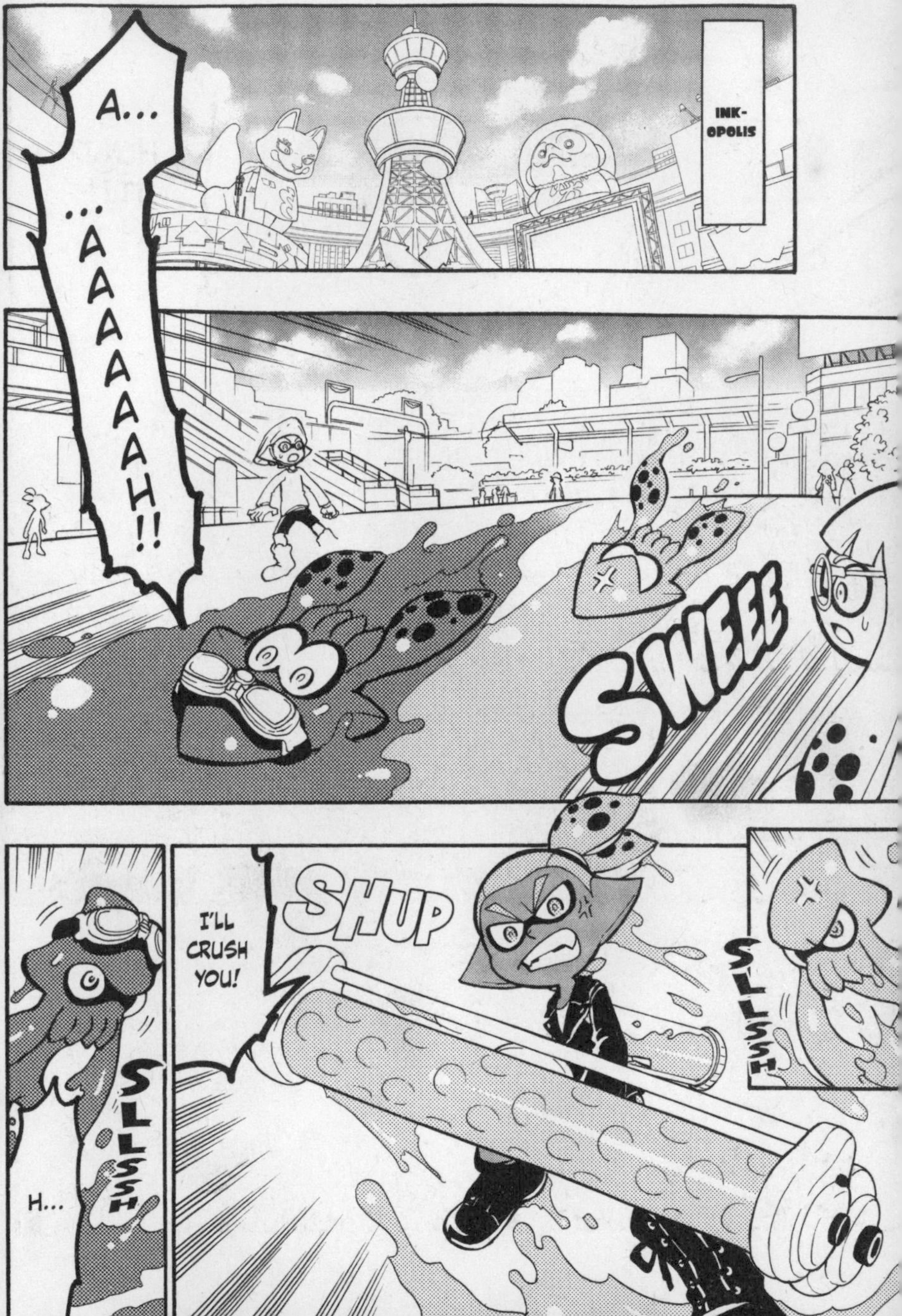
INK-OPOLIS
A...
...AAAAAAAH!!
SWEEE
SLLSSH
SHUP
I'LL CRUSH YOU!
SLLSSH
H...

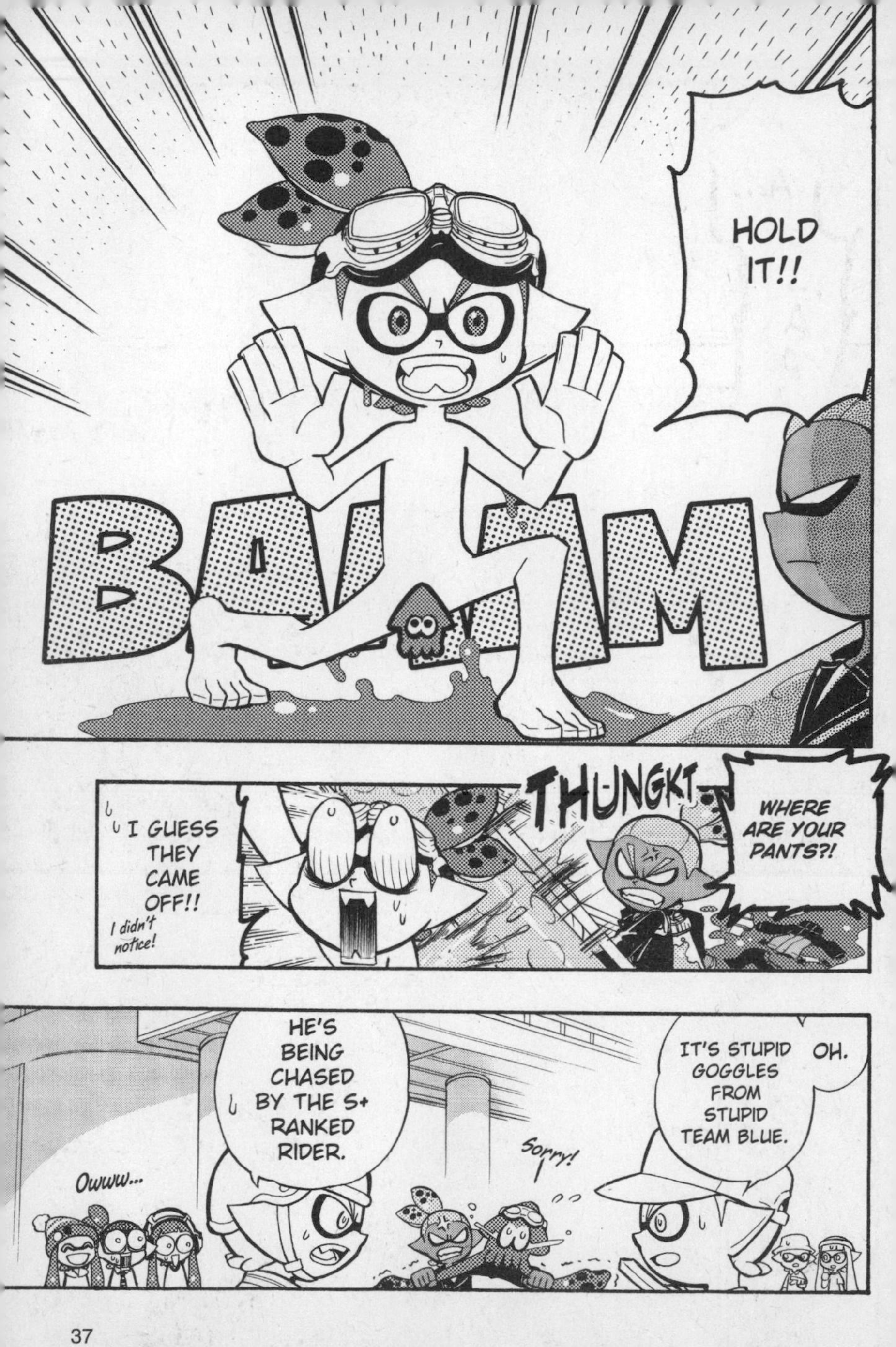
HOLD IT!!
WHERE ARE YOUR PANTS?!
THUNGKT
I GUESS THEY CAME OFF!!
I didn't notice!
OH.
IT'S STUPID GOGGLES FROM STUPID TEAM BLUE.
Sorry!
HE'S BEING CHASED BY THE S+ RANKED RIDER.
Owww...

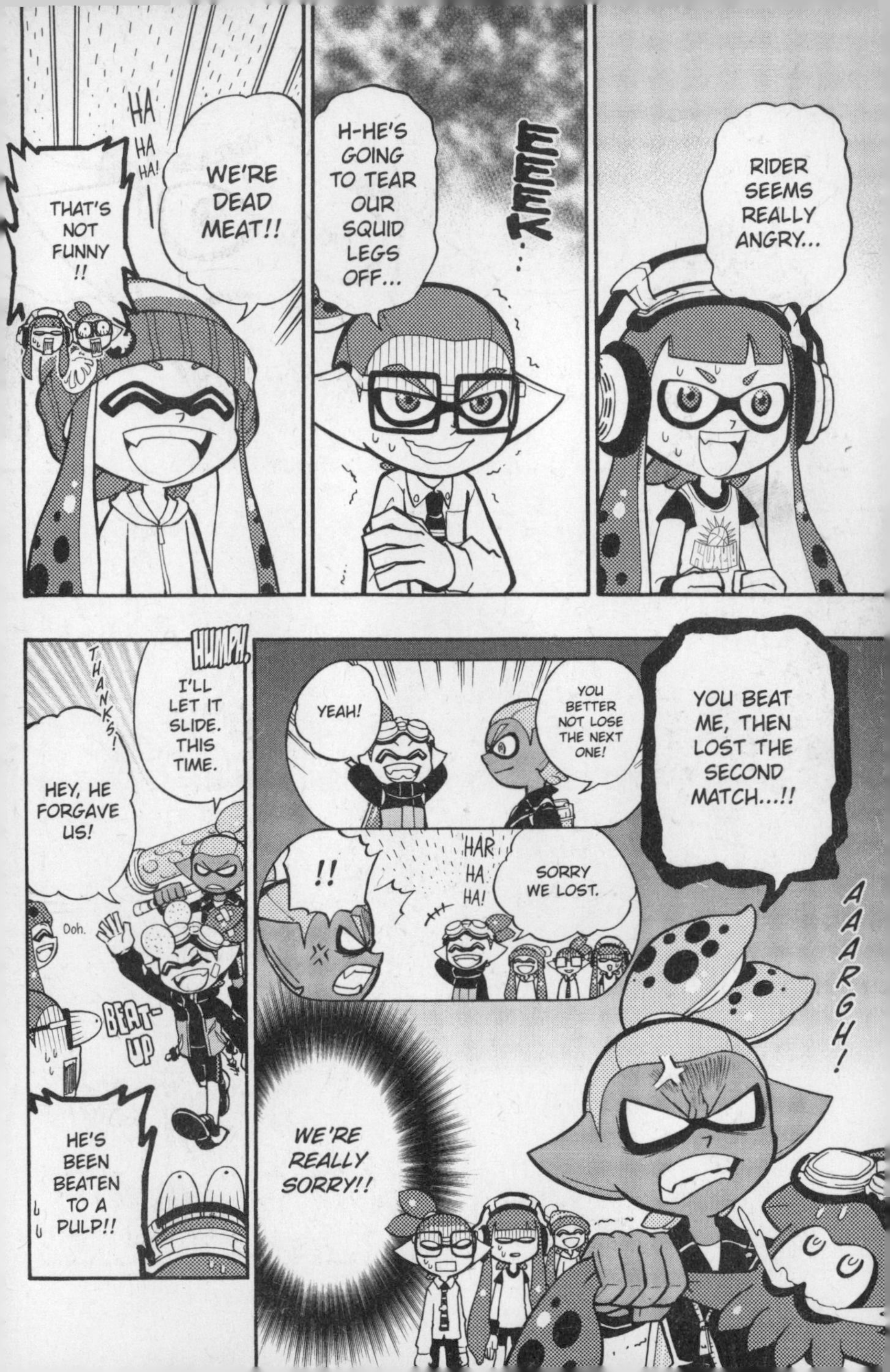
RIDER SEEMS REALLY ANGRY...
H-HE'S GOING TO TEAR OUR SQUID LEGS OFF...
EEEK...
WE'RE DEAD MEAT!!
HA HA HA!
THAT'S NOT FUNNY!!
YOU BEAT ME, THEN LOST THE SECOND MATCH...!!
AAAARGH!
YOU BETTER NOT LOSE THE NEXT ONE!
YEAH!
SORRY WE LOST.
HAR HA HA!
!!
WE'RE REALLY SORRY!!
HUMPH.
I'LL LET IT SLIDE. THIS TIME.
THANKS!
HEY, HE FORGAVE US!
Ooh.
BEAT-UP
HE'S BEEN BEATEN TO A PULP!!

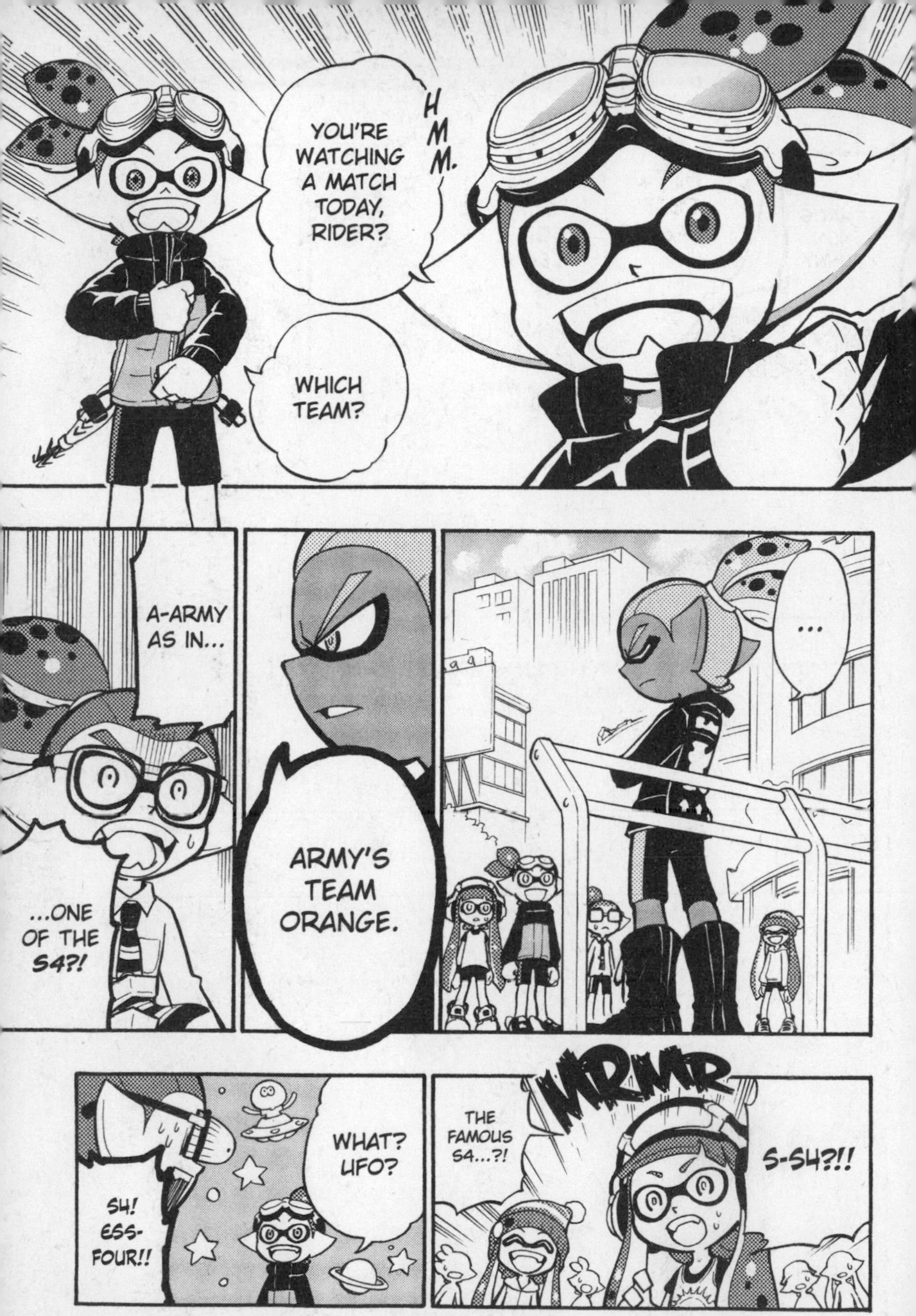
HMM.
YOU'RE WATCHING A MATCH TODAY, RIDER?
WHICH TEAM?
...
ARMY'S TEAM ORANGE.
A-ARMY AS IN...
...ONE OF THE S4?!
MRMR
S-S4?!!
THE FAMOUS S4...?!
WHAT? UFO?
S4! ESS-FOUR!!

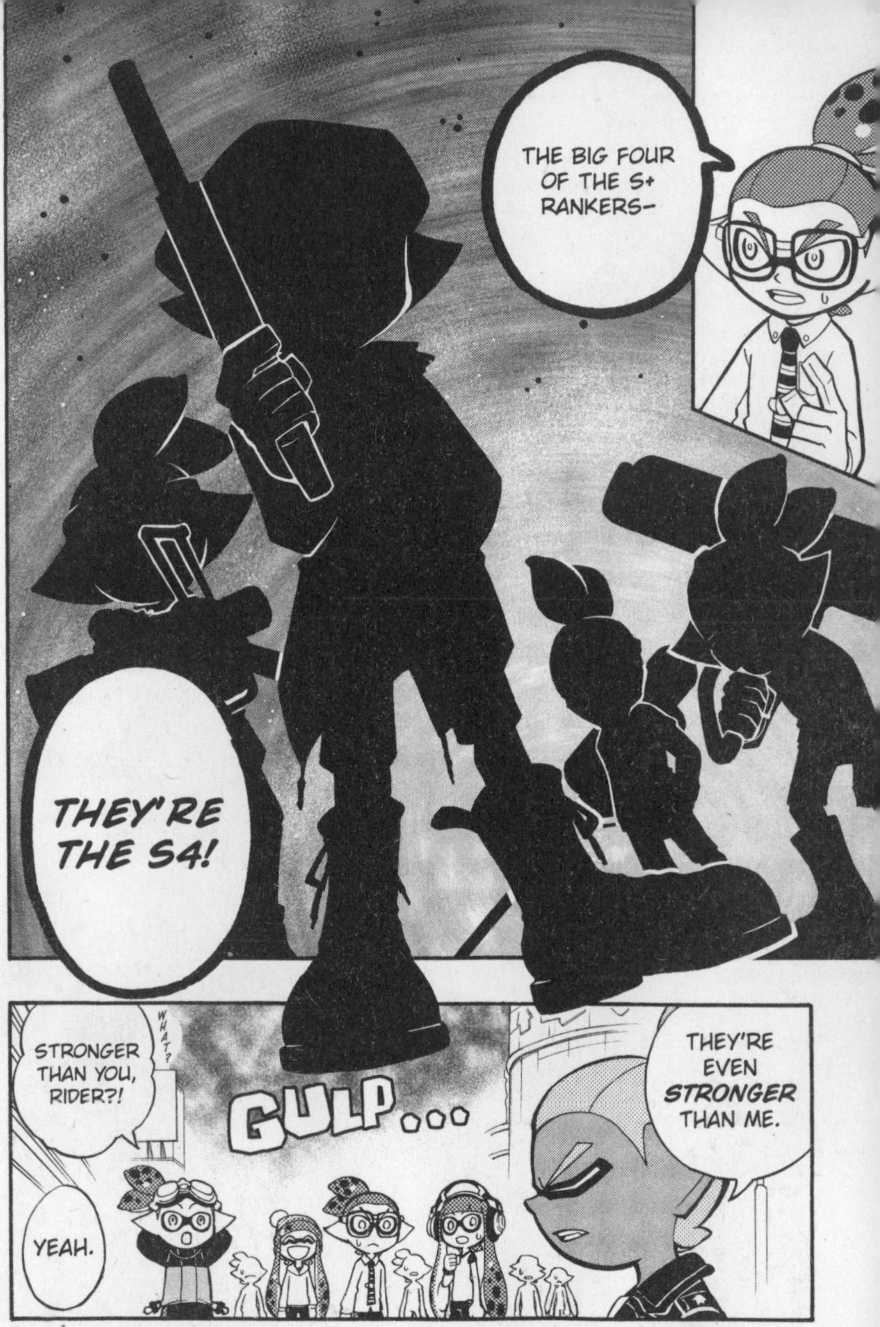
THE BIG FOUR OF THE S+ RANKERS–
THEY'RE THE S4!
THEY'RE EVEN STRONGER THAN ME.
GULP...
WHAT?
STRONGER THAN YOU, RIDER?!
YEAH.

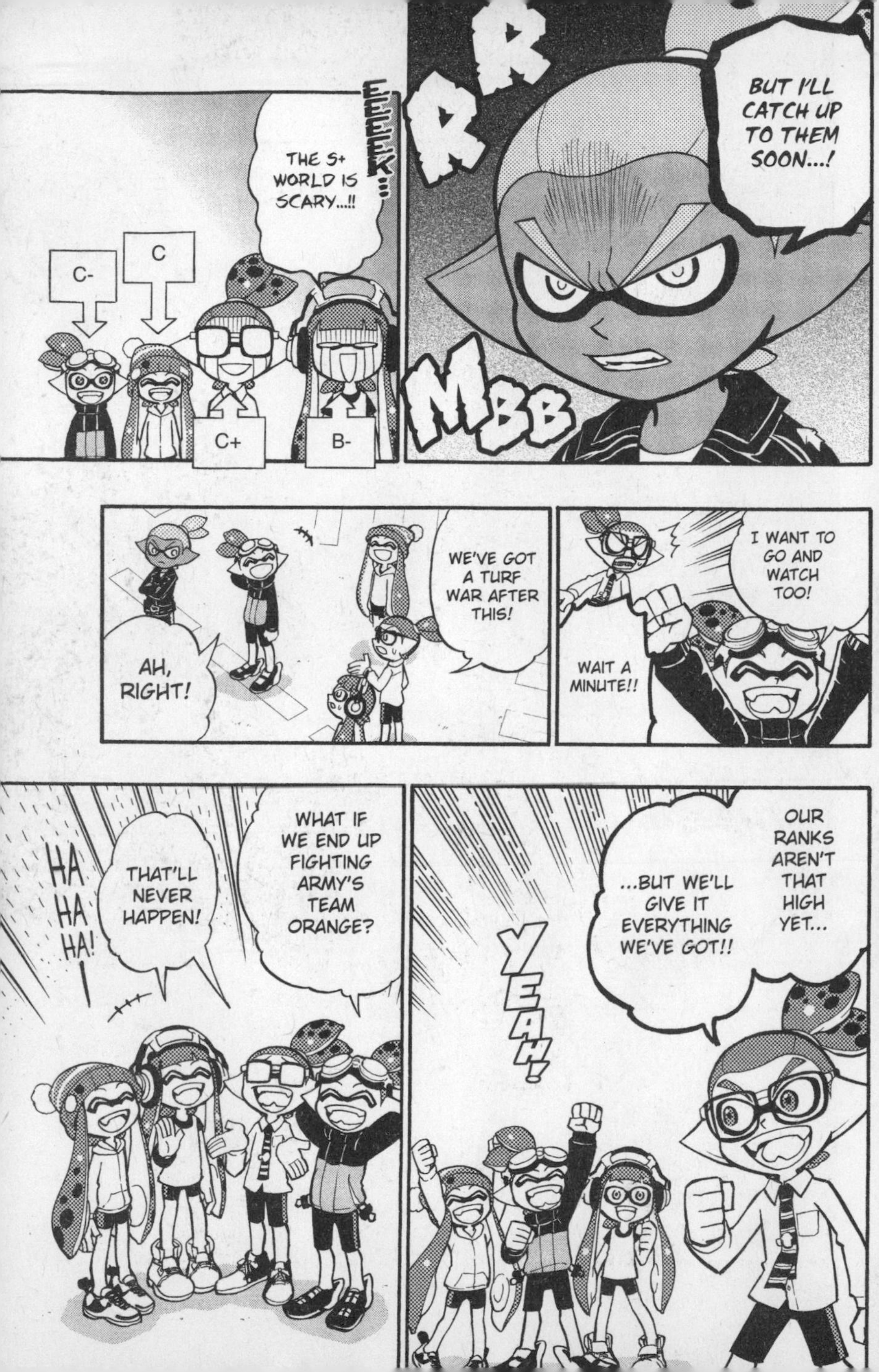
RRR
BUT I'LL CATCH UP TO THEM SOON...!
MBB
THE S+ WORLD IS SCARY...!!
EEEEEK...!
C-
C
C+
B-
I WANT TO GO AND WATCH TOO!
WAIT A MINUTE!!
WE'VE GOT A TURF WAR AFTER THIS!
AH, RIGHT!
OUR RANKS AREN'T THAT HIGH YET...
...BUT WE'LL GIVE IT EVERYTHING WE'VE GOT!!
YEAH!
WHAT IF WE END UP FIGHTING ARMY'S TEAM ORANGE?
THAT'LL NEVER HAPPEN!
HA HA HA!

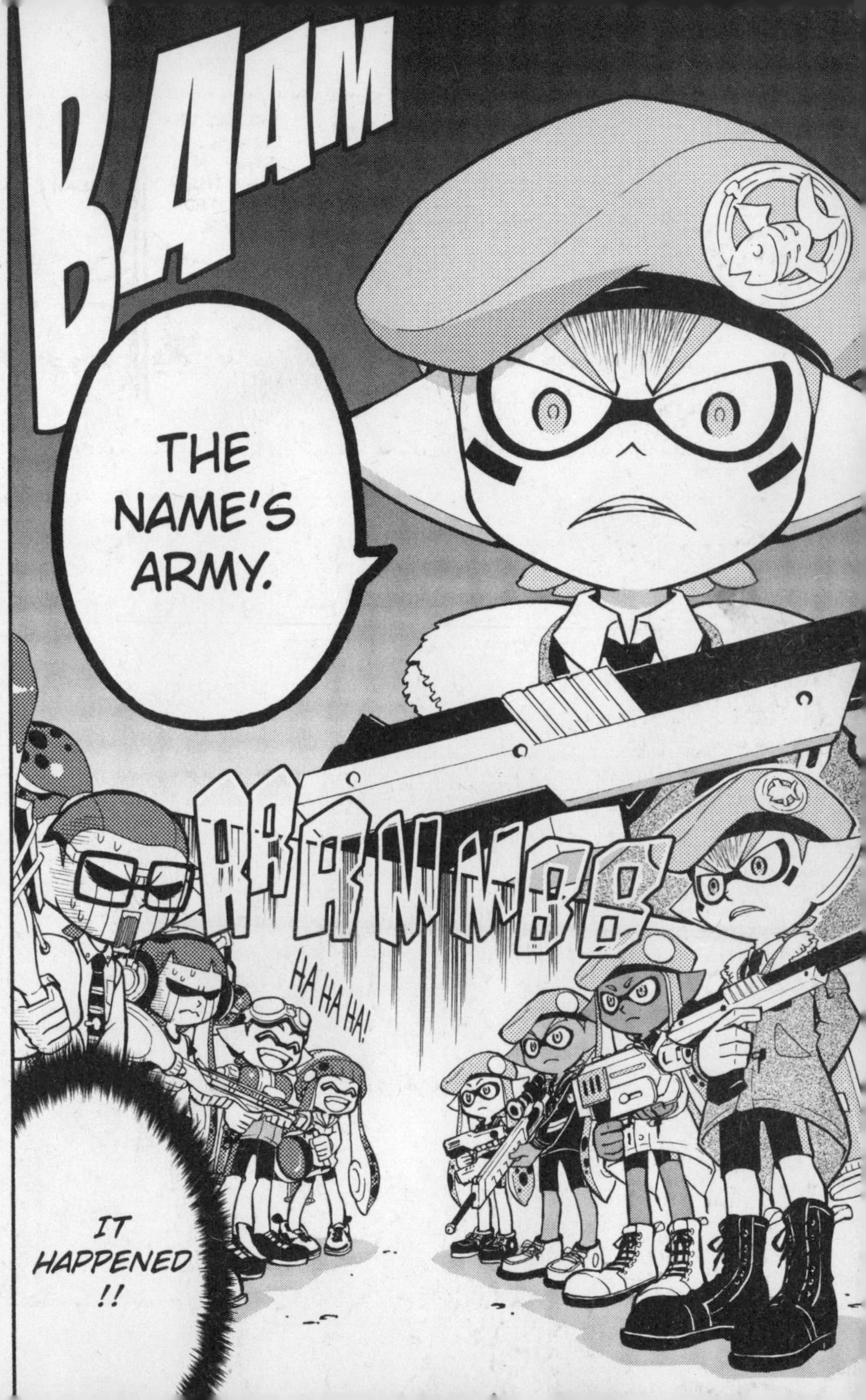
BAAAM
THE NAME'S ARMY.
HA HA HA!
IT HAPPENED !!

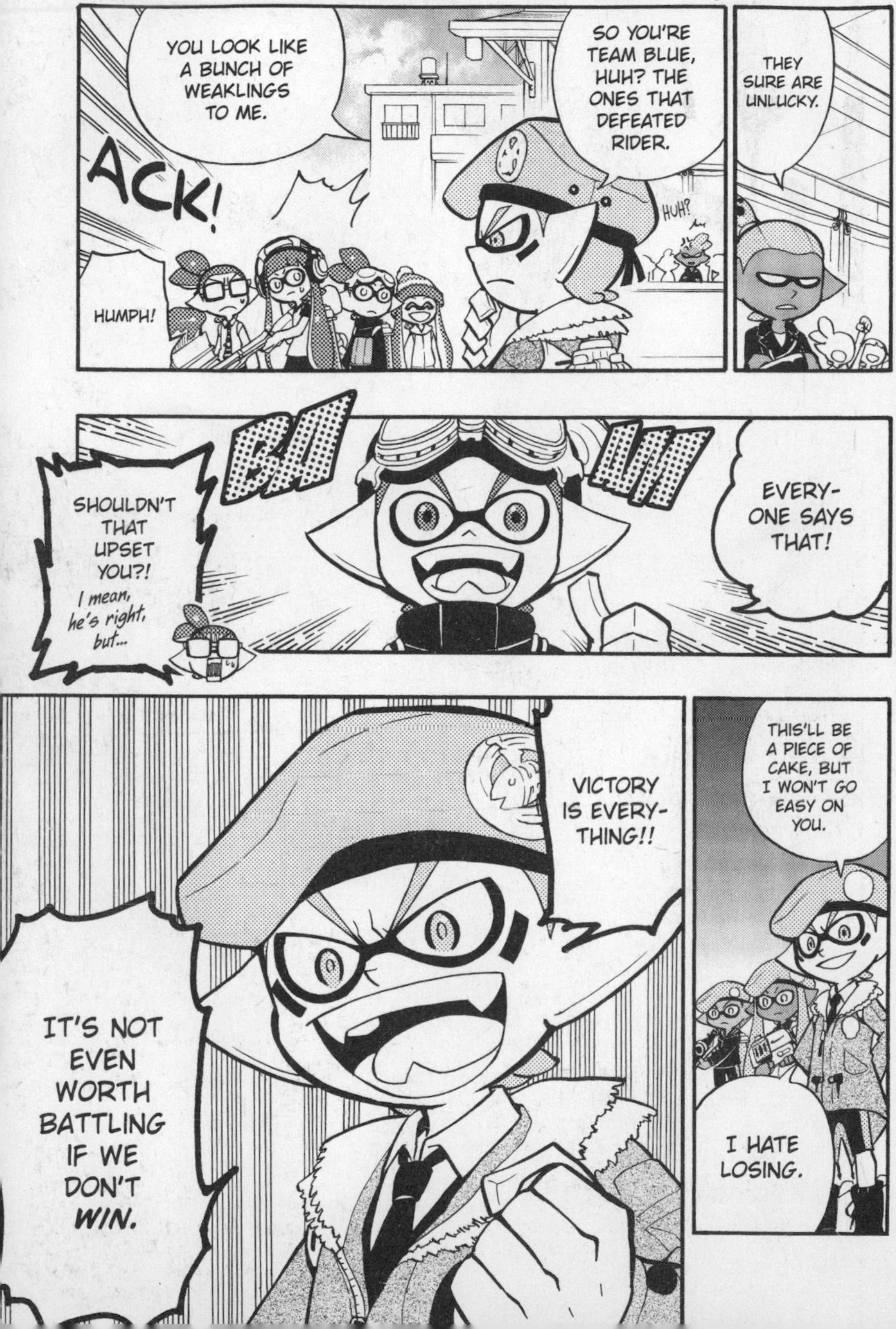
THEY SURE ARE UNLUCKY.
SO YOU'RE TEAM BLUE, HUH? THE ONES THAT DEFEATED RIDER.
HUH?
YOU LOOK LIKE A BUNCH OF WEAKLINGS TO ME.
ACK!
HUMPH!
EVERY-ONE SAYS THAT!
BAM
SHOULDN'T THAT UPSET YOU?!
I mean, he's right, but...
THIS'LL BE A PIECE OF CAKE, BUT I WON'T GO EASY ON YOU.
I HATE LOSING.
VICTORY IS EVERY-THING!!
IT'S NOT EVEN WORTH BATTLING IF WE DON'T ***WIN.***

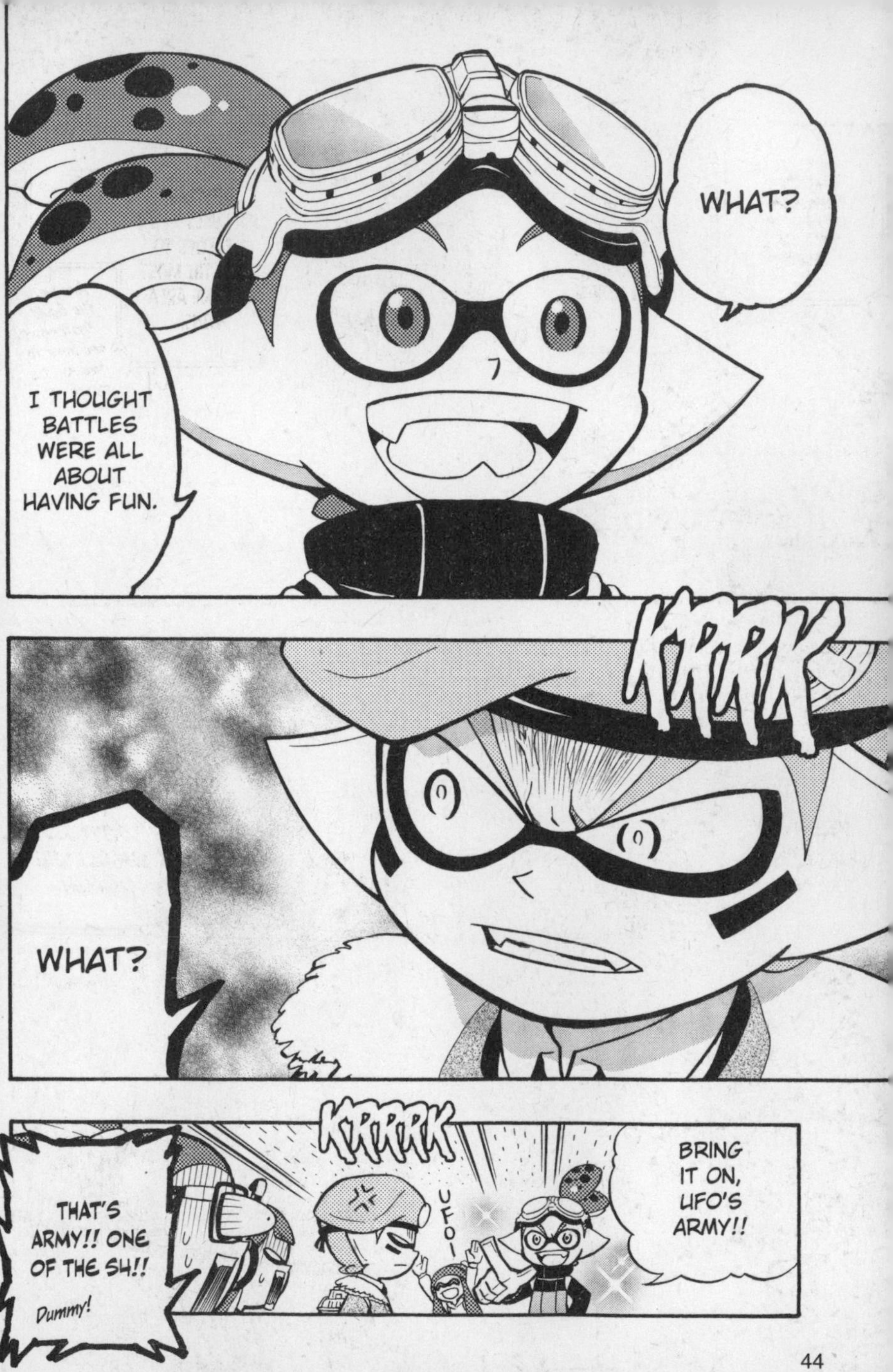
WHAT?
I THOUGHT BATTLES WERE ALL ABOUT HAVING FUN.
KRRRK
WHAT?
KRRRRK
BRING IT ON, UFO'S ARMY!!
UFO!
THAT'S ARMY!! ONE OF THE SH!!
Dummy!

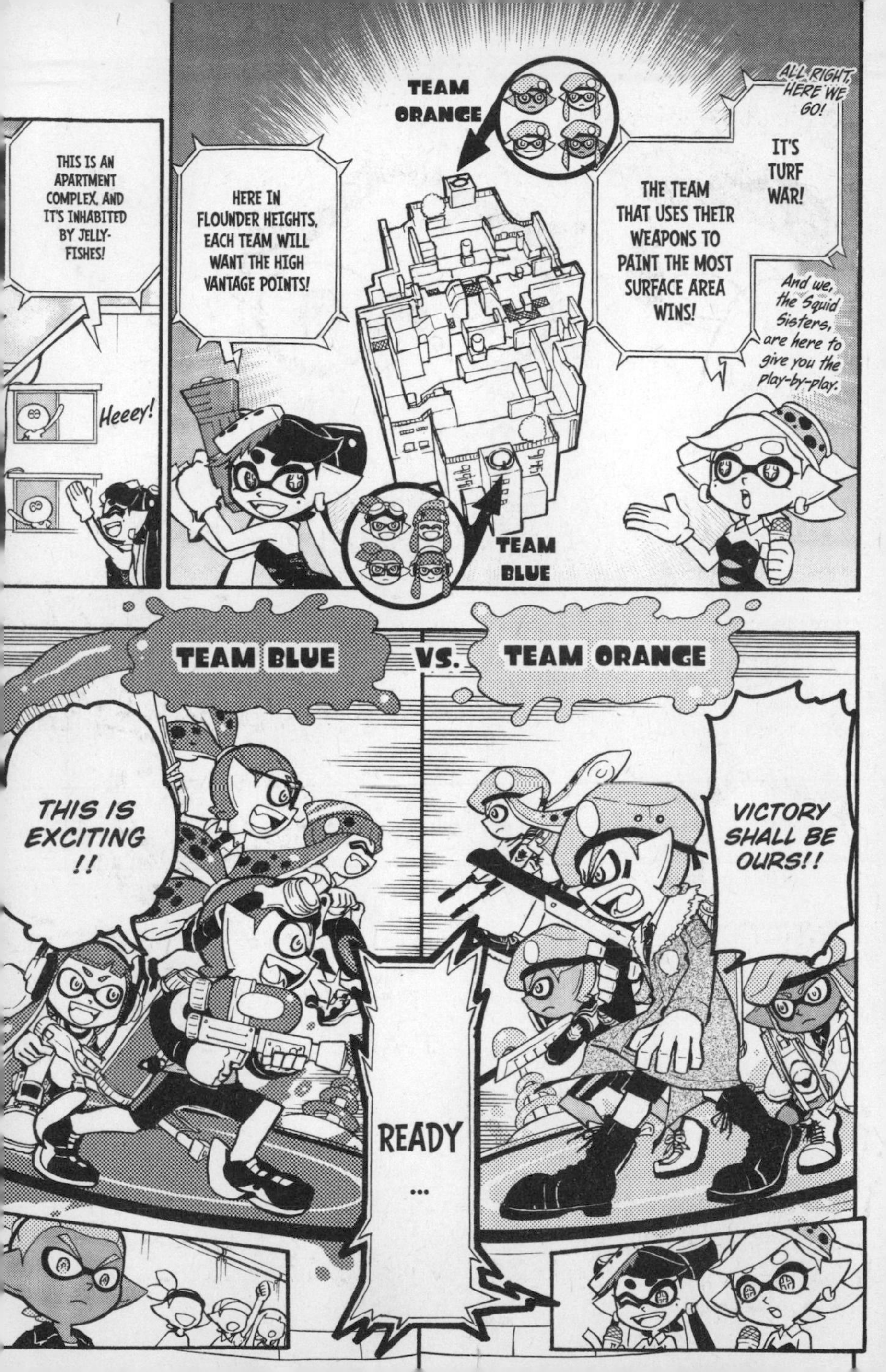
ALL RIGHT, HERE WE GO!
IT'S TURF WAR!
THE TEAM THAT USES THEIR WEAPONS TO PAINT THE MOST SURFACE AREA WINS!
And we, the Squid Sisters, are here to give you the play-by-play.
TEAM ORANGE
HERE IN FLOUNDER HEIGHTS, EACH TEAM WILL WANT THE HIGH VANTAGE POINTS!
TEAM BLUE
THIS IS AN APARTMENT COMPLEX, AND IT'S INHABITED BY JELLY-FISHES!
Heeey!
TEAM BLUE VS. TEAM ORANGE
VICTORY SHALL BE OURS!!
THIS IS EXCITING !!
READY ...

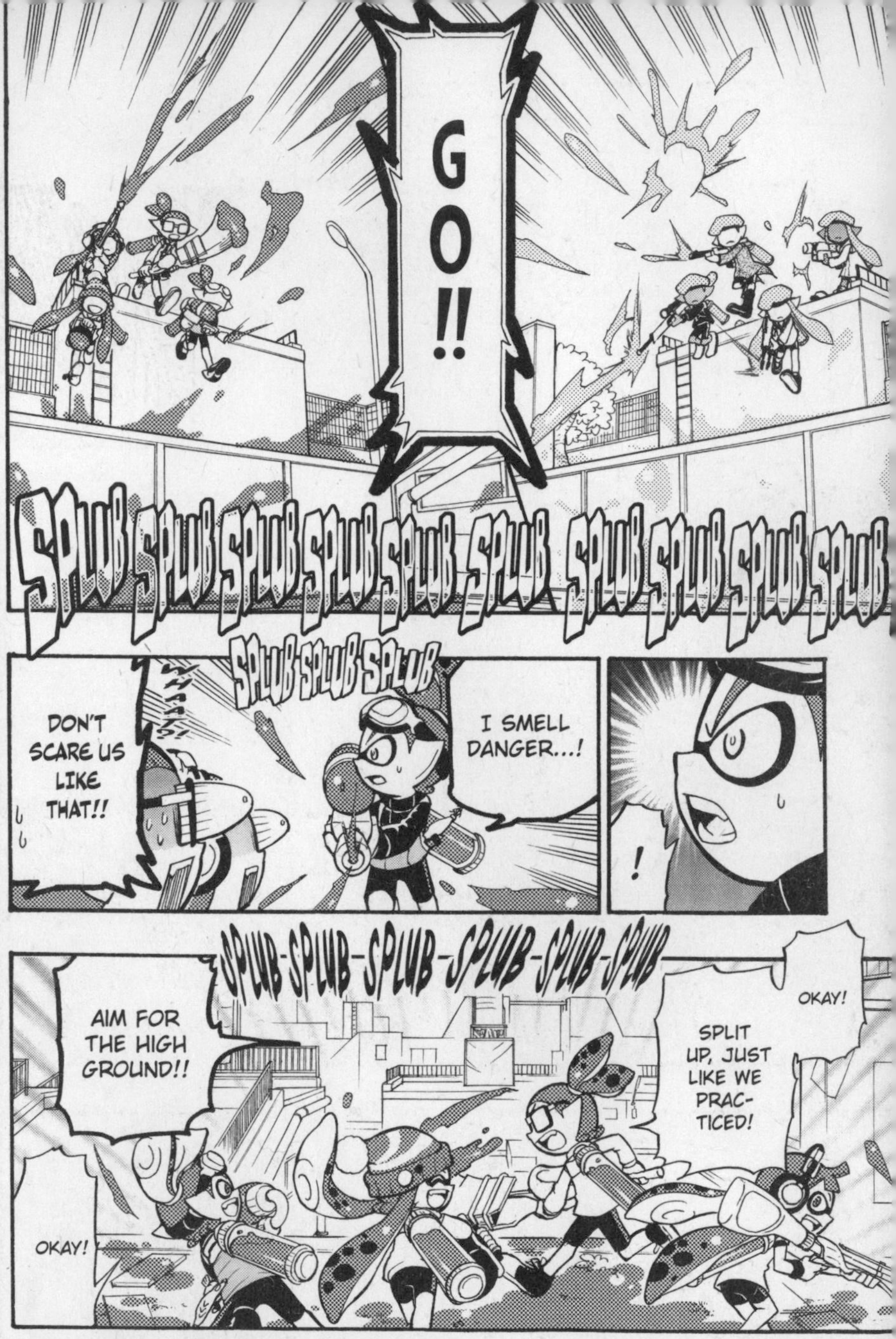
GO!!
SPLUB SPLUB SPLUB SPLUB SPLUB SPLUB SPLUB SPLUB SPLUB SPLUB
!
SPLUB SPLUB SPLUB
I SMELL DANGER...!
DON'T SCARE US LIKE THAT!!
SPLUB-SPLUB-SPLUB-SPLUB-SPLUB-SPLUB
OKAY!
SPLIT UP, JUST LIKE WE PRAC-TICED!
AIM FOR THE HIGH GROUND!!
OKAY!

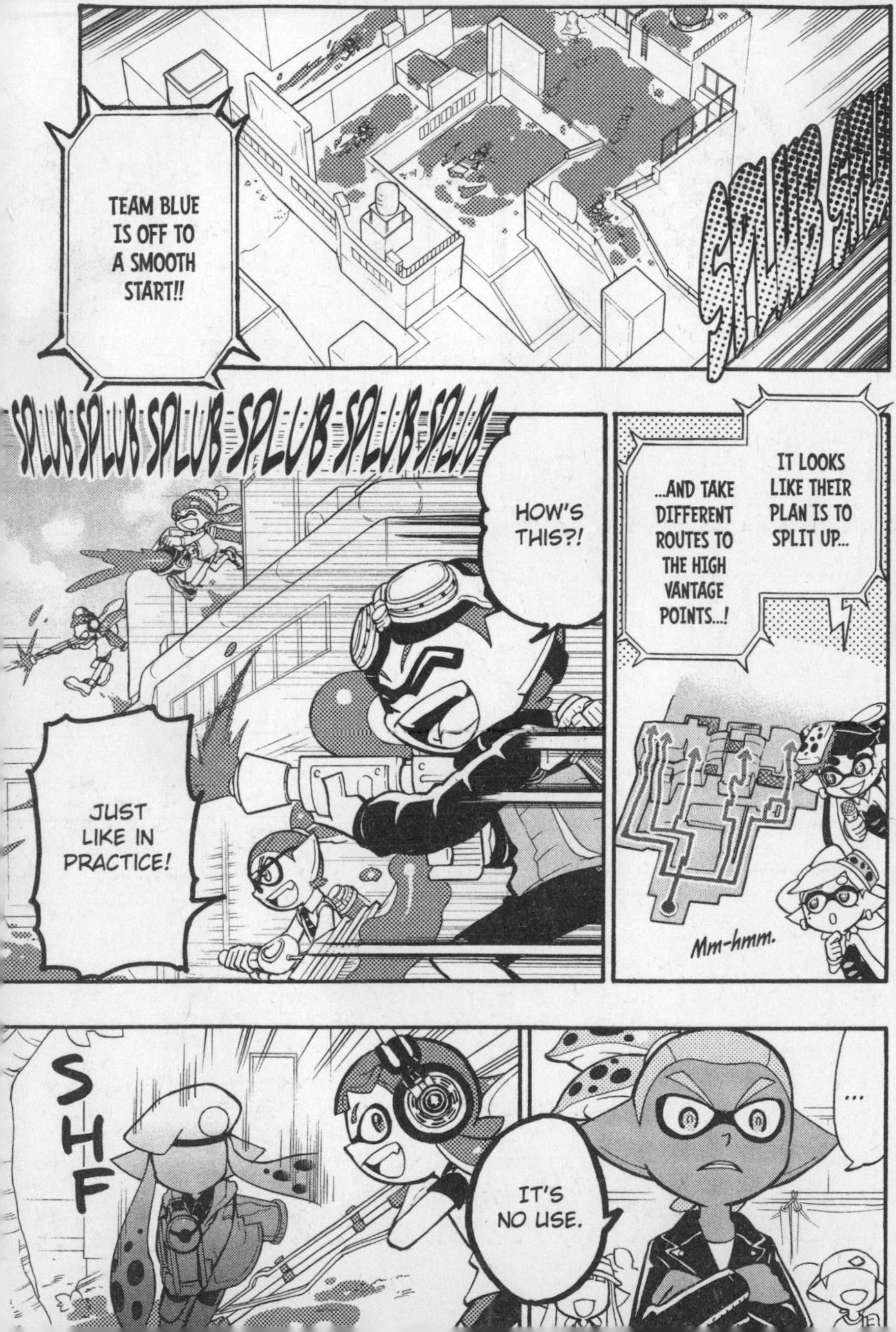
TEAM BLUE IS OFF TO A SMOOTH START!!
IT LOOKS LIKE THEIR PLAN IS TO SPLIT UP...
...AND TAKE DIFFERENT ROUTES TO THE HIGH VANTAGE POINTS...!
Mm-hmm.
SPLUB SPLUB SPLUB SPLUB SPLUB SPLUB
HOW'S THIS?!
JUST LIKE IN PRACTICE!
...
IT'S NO USE.
SHF

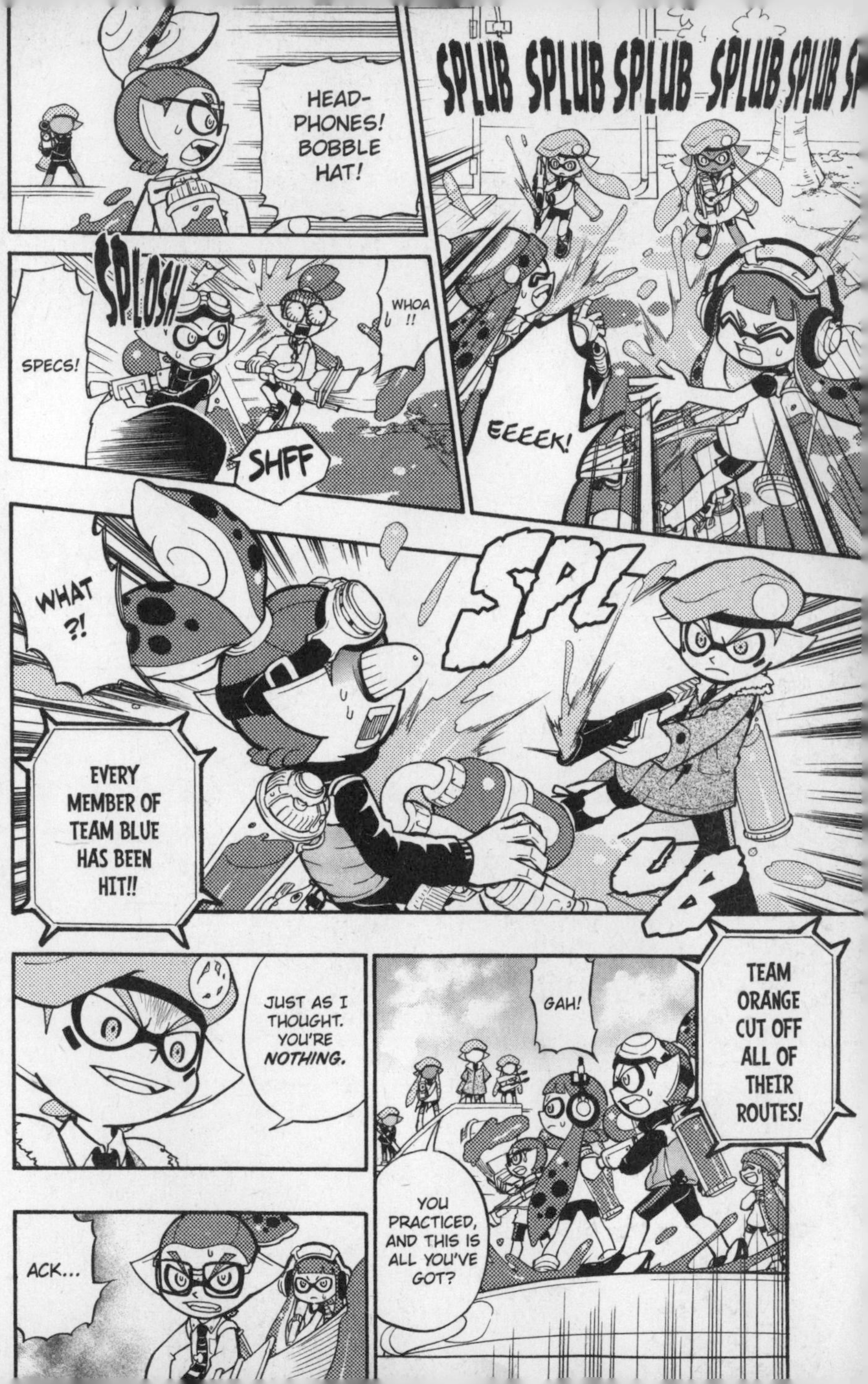
SPLUB SPLUB SPLUB SPLUB SPLUB S
EEEEK!
HEAD-PHONES! BOBBLE HAT!
WHOA!!
SPLOSH
SPECS!
SHFF
SPLUB
WHAT?!
EVERY MEMBER OF TEAM BLUE HAS BEEN HIT!!
TEAM ORANGE CUT OFF ALL OF THEIR ROUTES!
GAH!
YOU PRACTICED, AND THIS IS ALL YOU'VE GOT?
JUST AS I THOUGHT. YOU'RE *NOTHING.*
ACK...

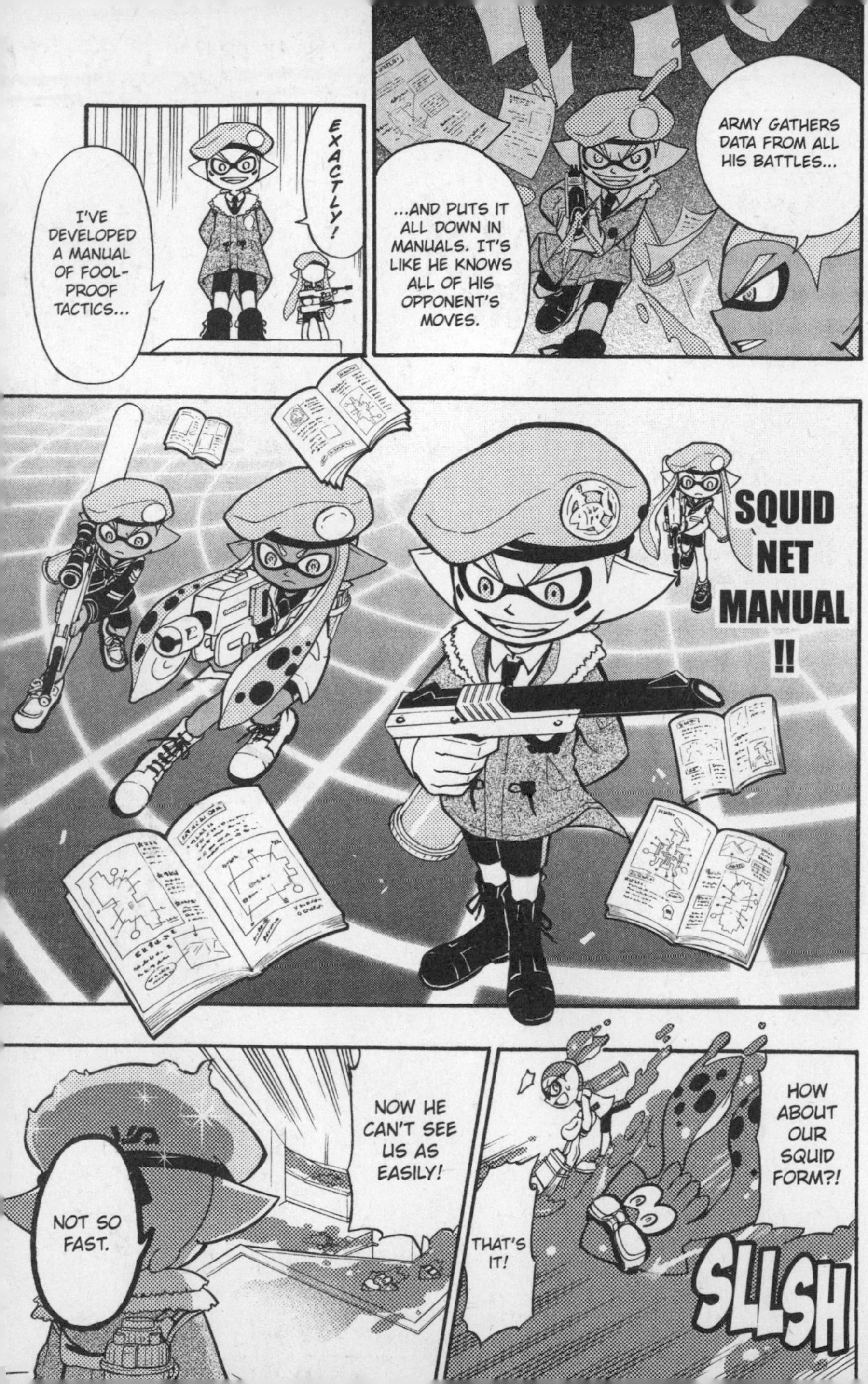
ARMY GATHERS DATA FROM ALL HIS BATTLES...
...AND PUTS IT ALL DOWN IN MANUALS. IT'S LIKE HE KNOWS ALL OF HIS OPPONENT'S MOVES.
EXACTLY!
I'VE DEVELOPED A MANUAL OF FOOL-PROOF TACTICS...
SQUID NET MANUAL!!
HOW ABOUT OUR SQUID FORM?!
SLLSH
THAT'S IT!
NOW HE CAN'T SEE US AS EASILY!
NOT SO FAST.

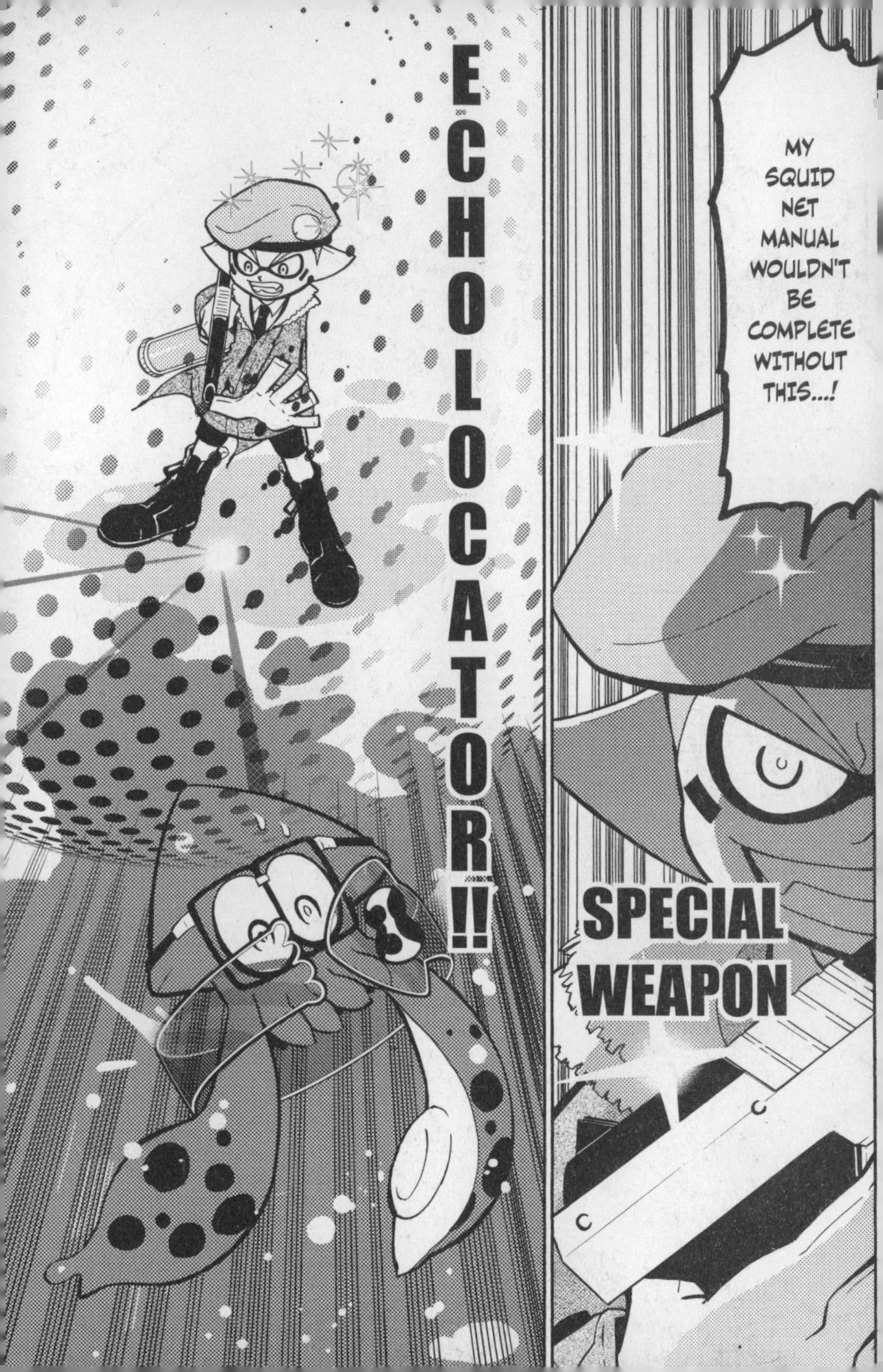
MY SQUID NET MANUAL WOULDN'T BE COMPLETE WITHOUT THIS...!
SPECIAL WEAPON
ECHOLOCATOR!!

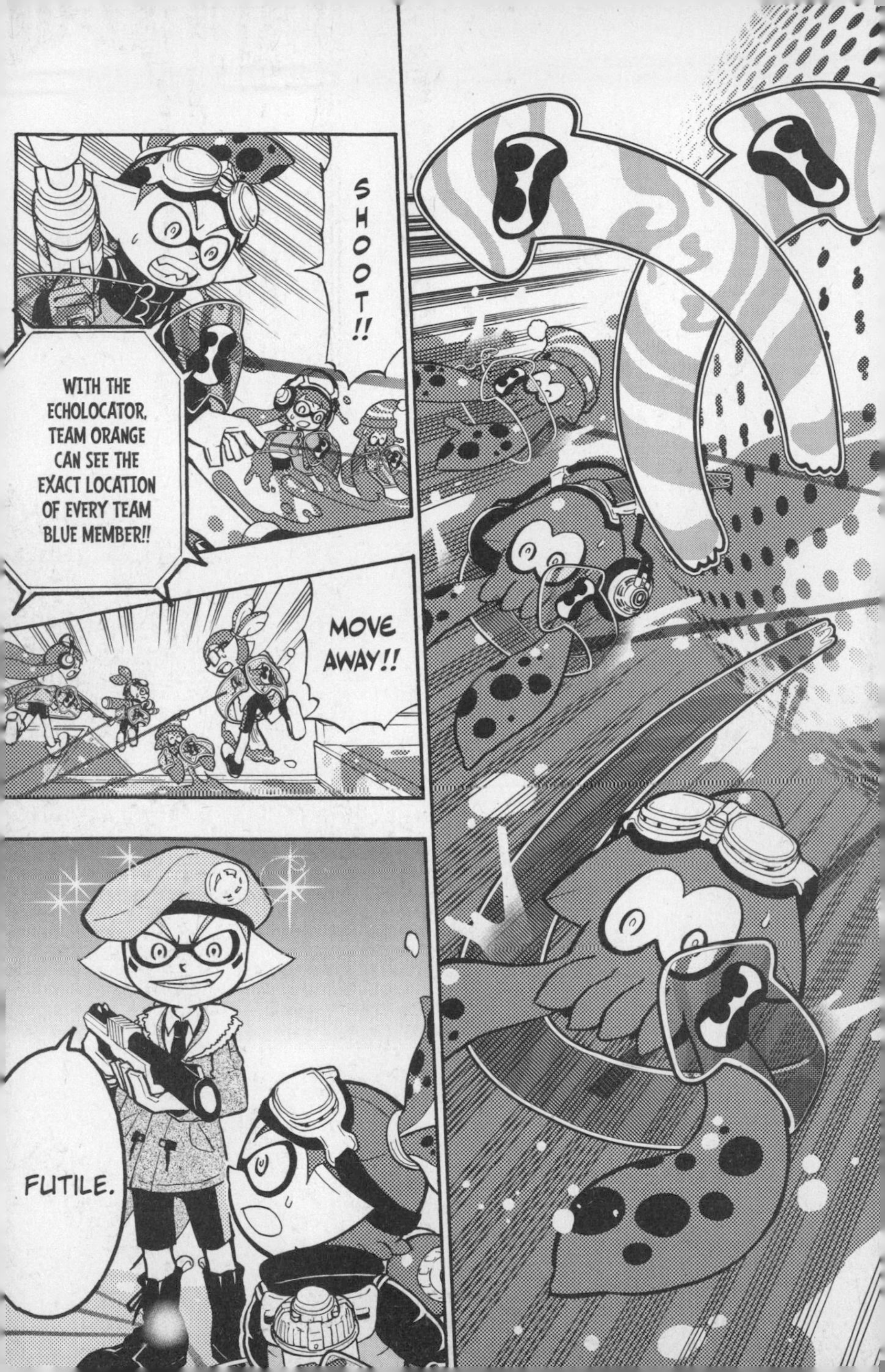
SHOOT!!
WITH THE ECHOLOCATOR, TEAM ORANGE CAN SEE THE EXACT LOCATION OF EVERY TEAM BLUE MEMBER!!
MOVE AWAY!!
FUTILE.

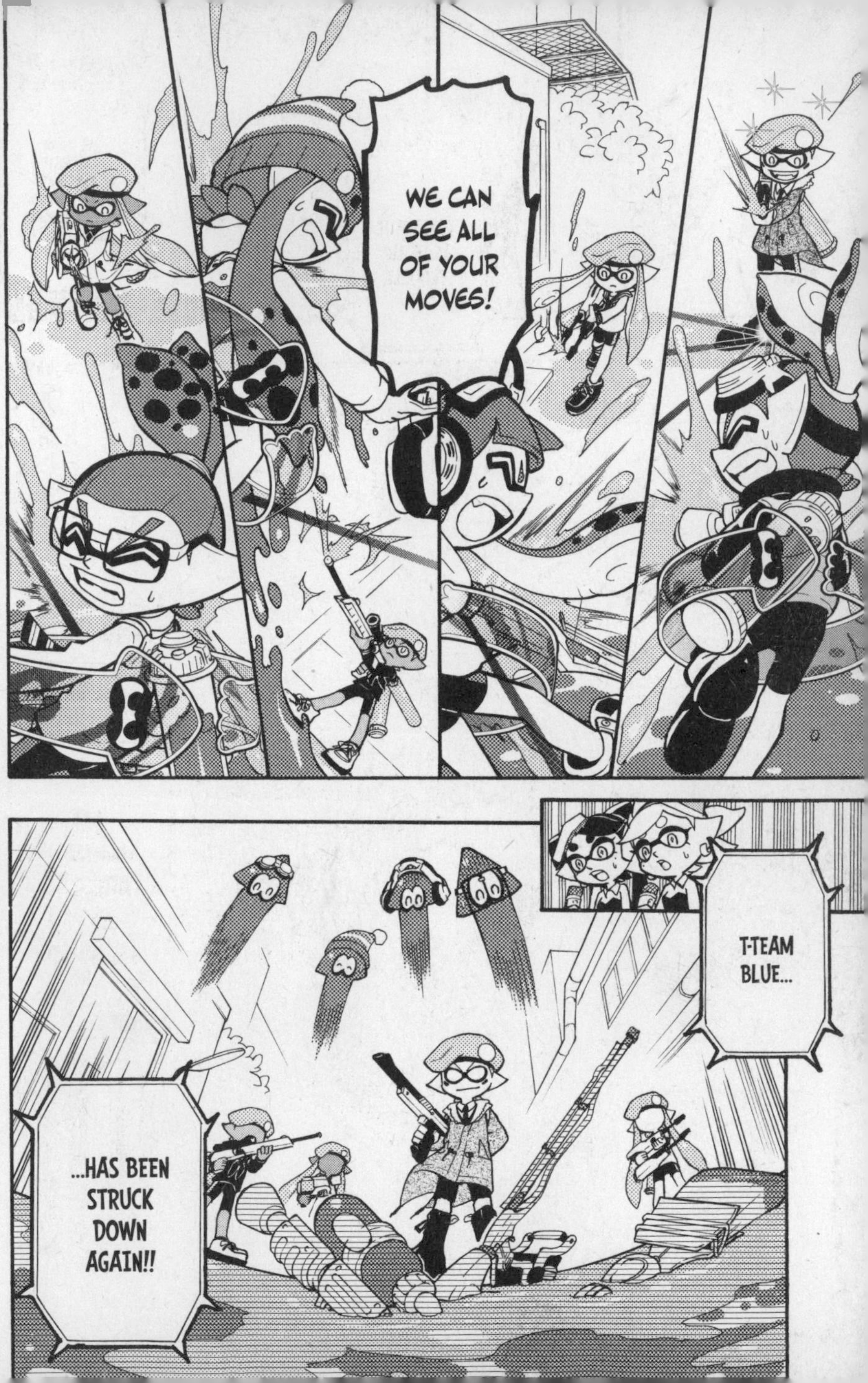
WE CAN SEE ALL OF YOUR MOVES!
T-TEAM BLUE...
...HAS BEEN STRUCK DOWN AGAIN!!

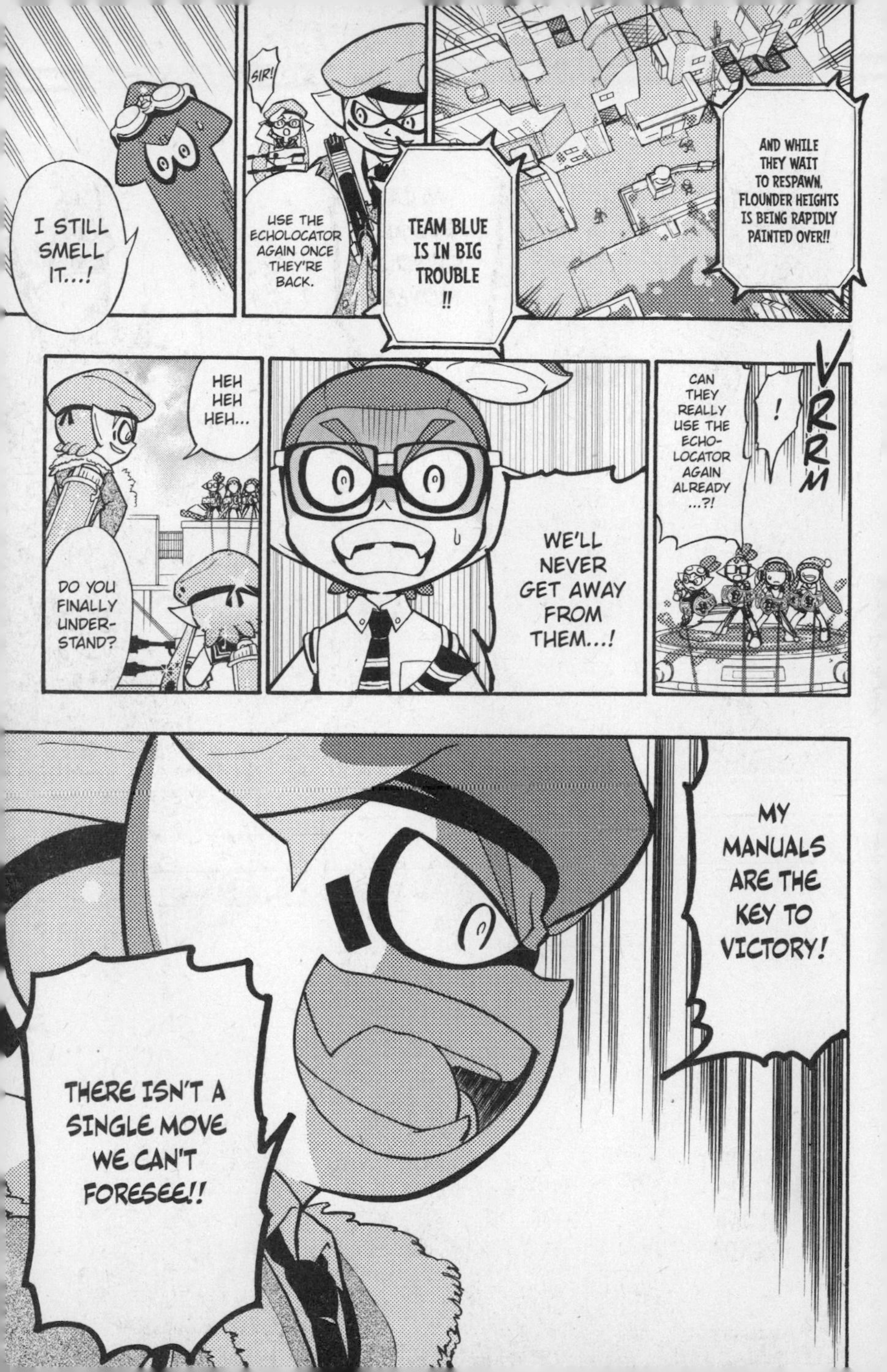
AND WHILE THEY WAIT TO RESPAWN, FLOUNDER HEIGHTS IS BEING RAPIDLY PAINTED OVER!!
TEAM BLUE IS IN BIG TROUBLE !!
SIR!
USE THE ECHOLOCATOR AGAIN ONCE THEY'RE BACK.
I STILL SMELL IT...!
VRRM
!
CAN THEY REALLY USE THE ECHO-LOCATOR AGAIN ALREADY ...?!
WE'LL NEVER GET AWAY FROM THEM...!
HEH HEH HEH...
DO YOU FINALLY UNDER-STAND?
MY MANUALS ARE THE KEY TO VICTORY!
THERE ISN'T A SINGLE MOVE WE CAN'T FORESEE!!

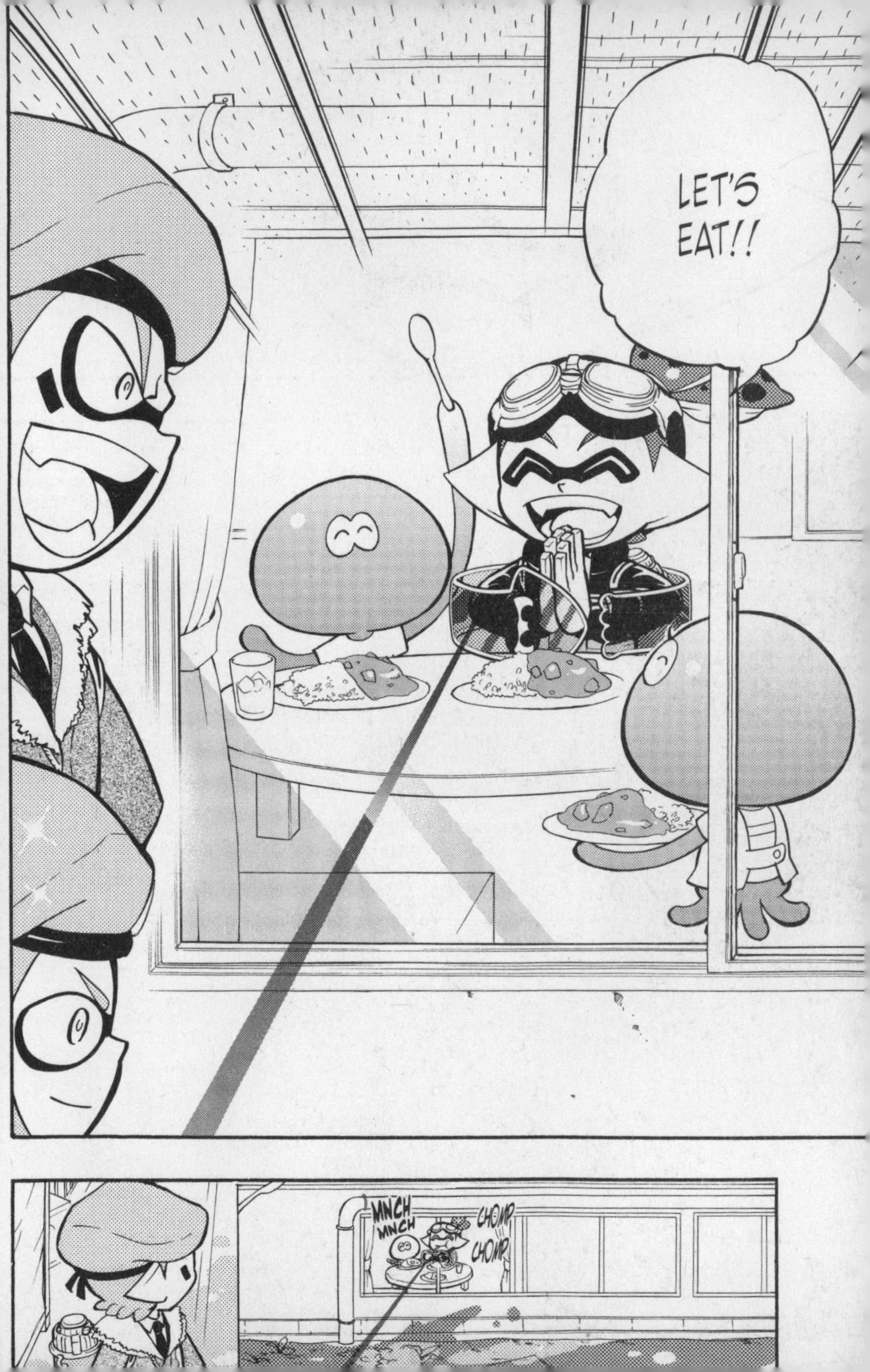
LET'S EAT!!
CHOMP CHOMP
MNCH MNCH

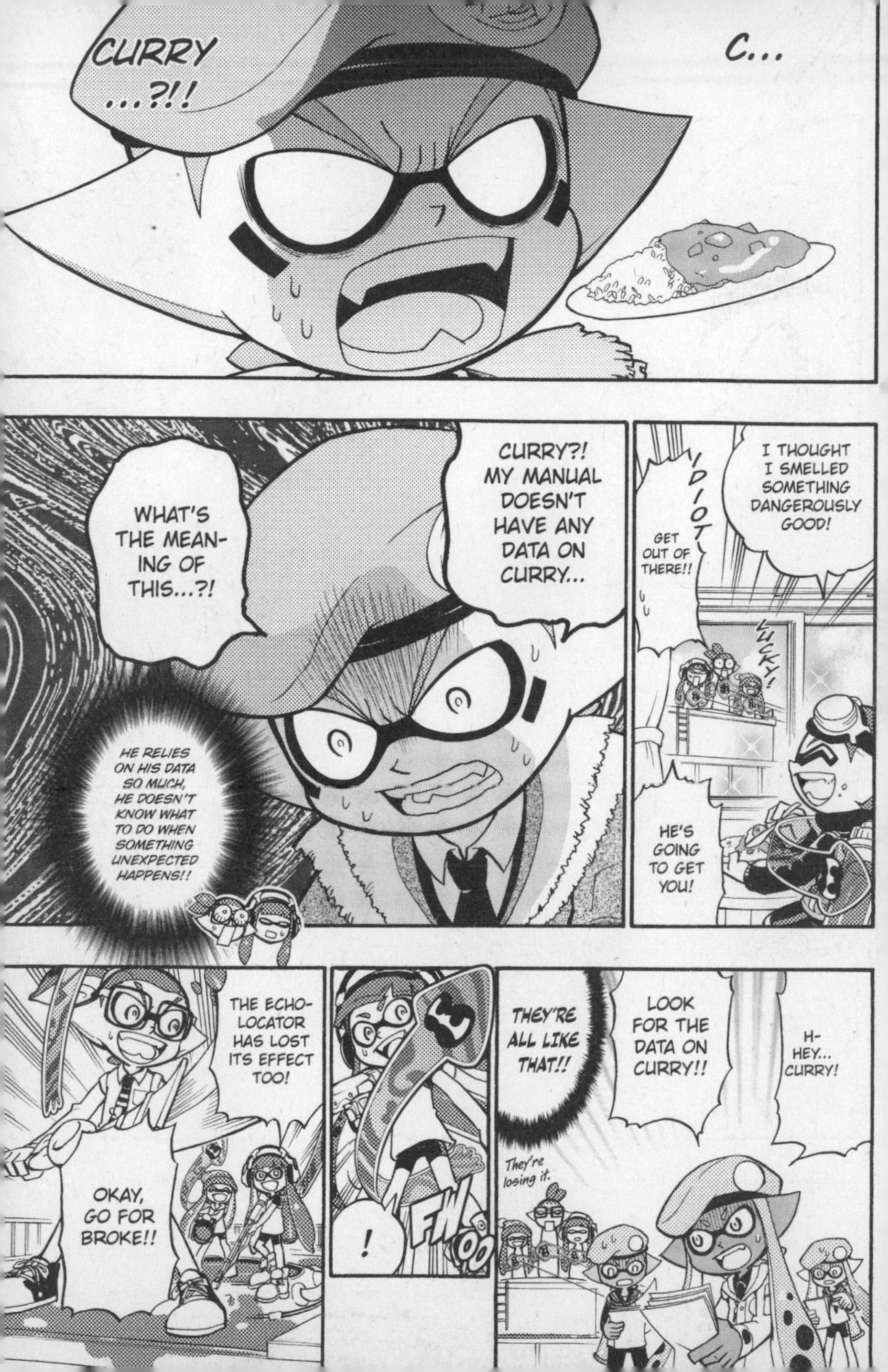
C...
CURRY ...?!!
I THOUGHT I SMELLED SOMETHING DANGEROUSLY GOOD!
IDIOT
GET OUT OF THERE!!
LUCKY!
HE'S GOING TO GET YOU!
CURRY?! MY MANUAL DOESN'T HAVE ANY DATA ON CURRY...
WHAT'S THE MEAN-ING OF THIS...?!
HE RELIES ON HIS DATA SO MUCH, HE DOESN'T KNOW WHAT TO DO WHEN SOMETHING UNEXPECTED HAPPENS!!
H- HEY... CURRY!
LOOK FOR THE DATA ON CURRY!!
They're losing it.
THEY'RE ALL LIKE THAT!!
FWOO
!
THE ECHO-LOCATOR HAS LOST ITS EFFECT TOO!
OKAY, GO FOR BROKE!!

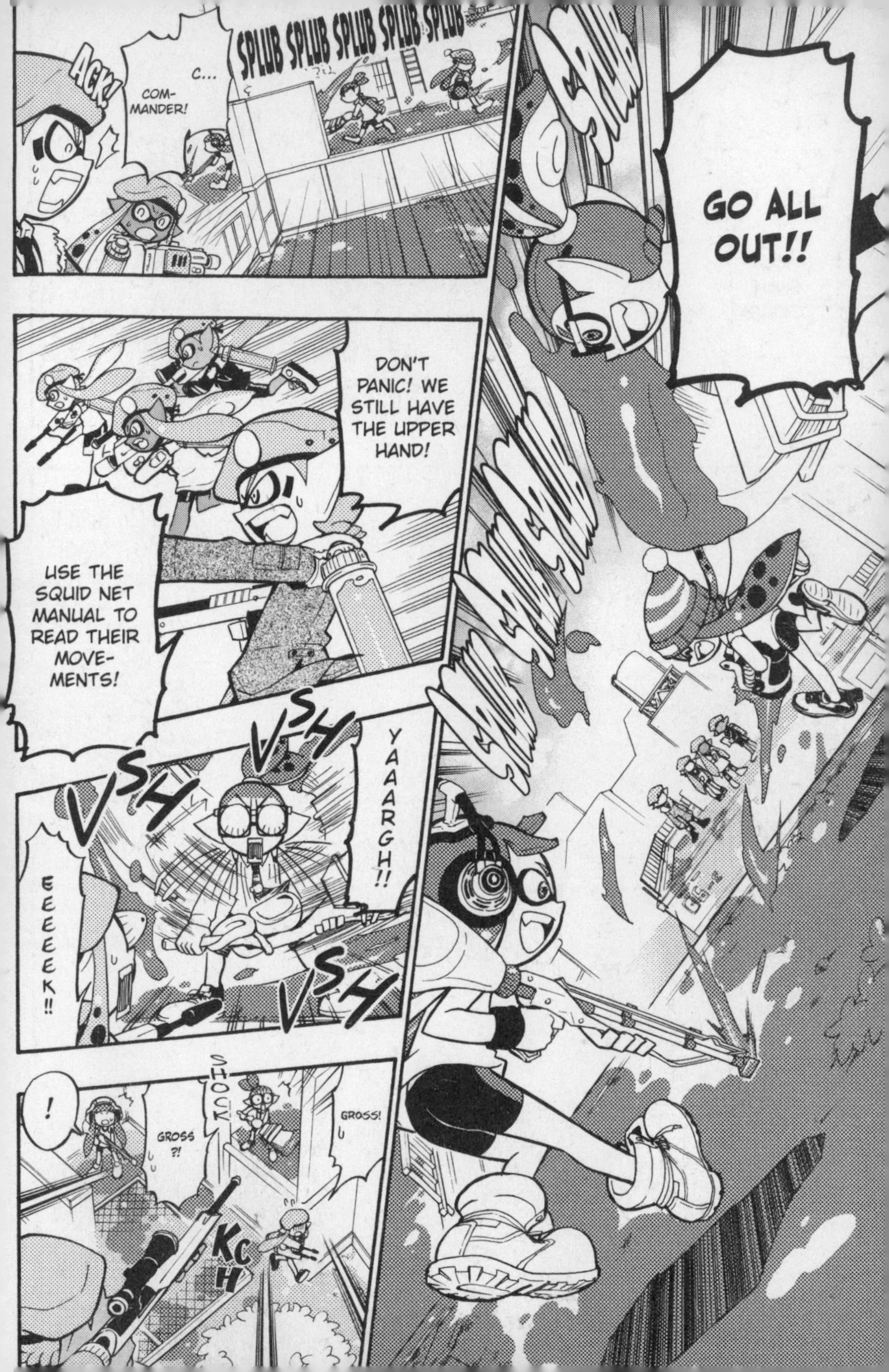
GO ALL OUT!!
SPLUB SPLUB SPLUB SPLUB SPLUB
C... COM-MANDER!
ACK!
DON'T PANIC! WE STILL HAVE THE UPPER HAND!
USE THE SQUID NET MANUAL TO READ THEIR MOVE-MENTS!
YAAARGH!!
VSH
VSH
EEEEEEK!!
VSH
GROSS!
SHOCK
GROSS?!
!
KCH

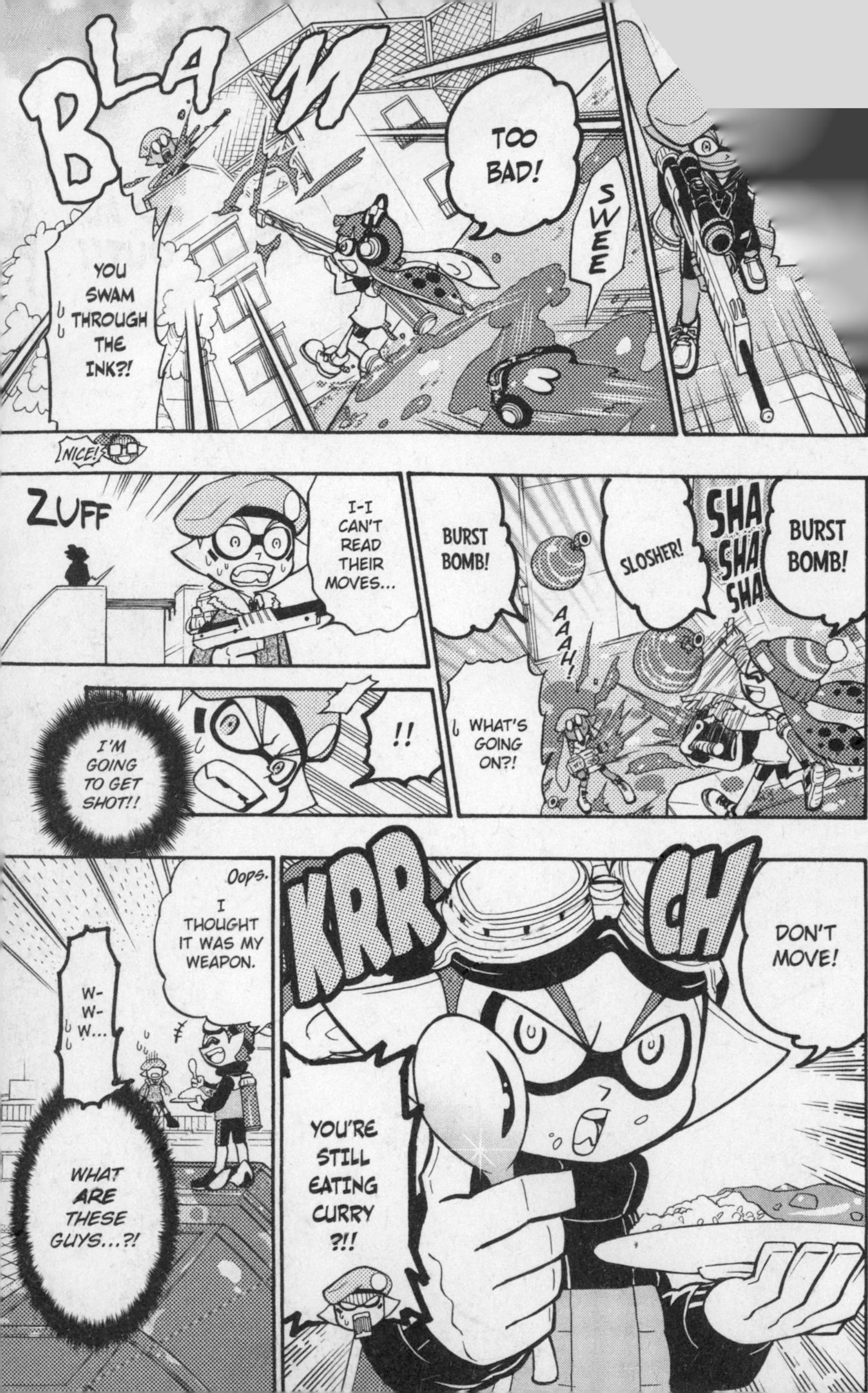
TOO BAD!
SWEE
BLAM
YOU SWAM THROUGH THE INK?!
NICE!
BURST BOMB!
SHA SHA SHA
SLOSHER!
BURST BOMB!
AAAH!
WHAT'S GOING ON?!
I-I CAN'T READ THEIR MOVES...
ZUFF
!!
I'M GOING TO GET SHOT!!
DON'T MOVE!
KRR CH
YOU'RE STILL EATING CURRY ?!!
Oops.
I THOUGHT IT WAS MY WEAPON.
W-W-W...
WHAT ARE THESE GUYS...?!

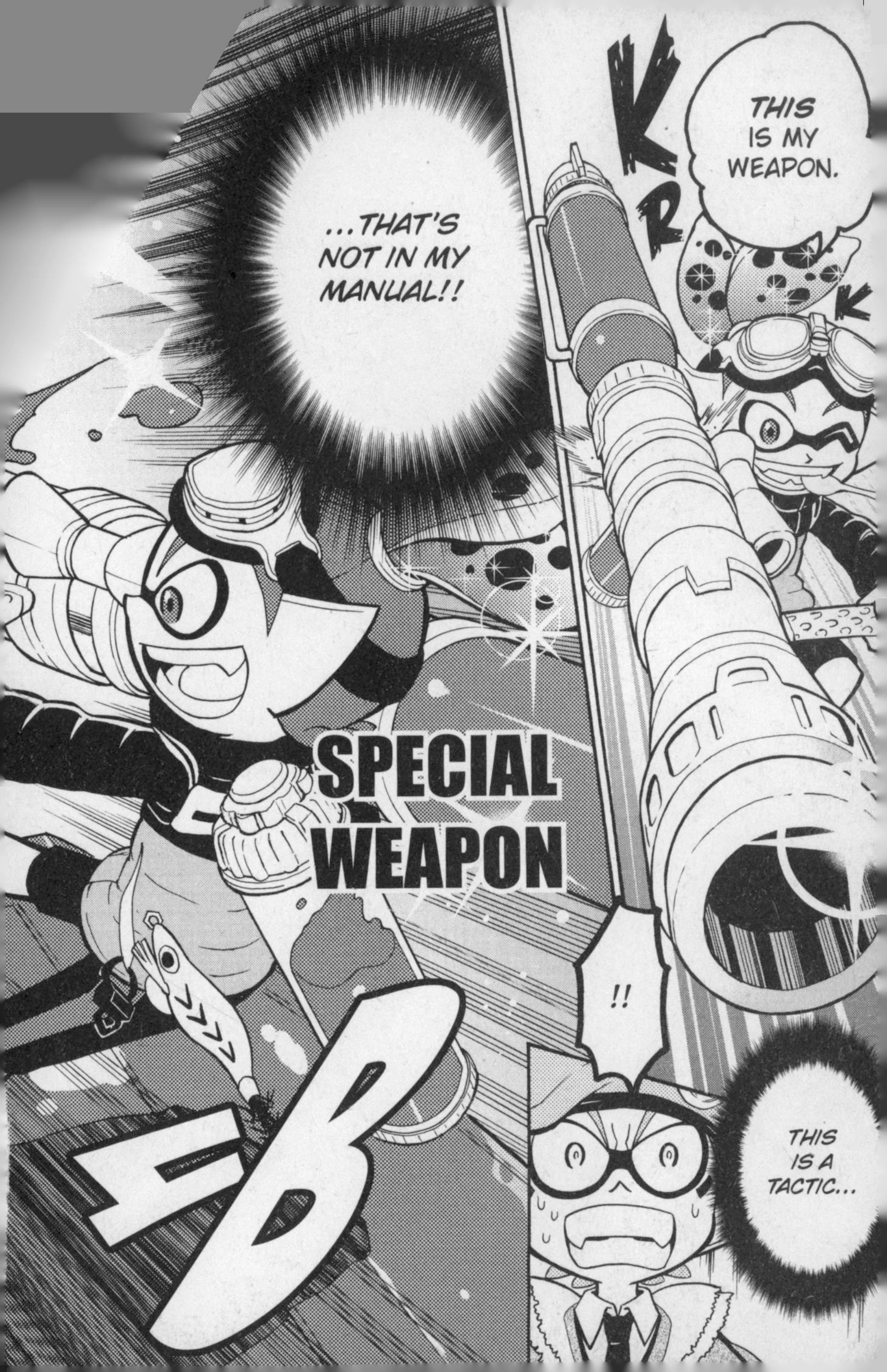
KRK
THIS IS MY WEAPON.
!!
THIS IS A TACTIC...
...THAT'S NOT IN MY MANUAL!!
SPECIAL WEAPON
B

INKZOOKA!!

BEEP

KRA-SPLUU

THAT'S THE GAME!!

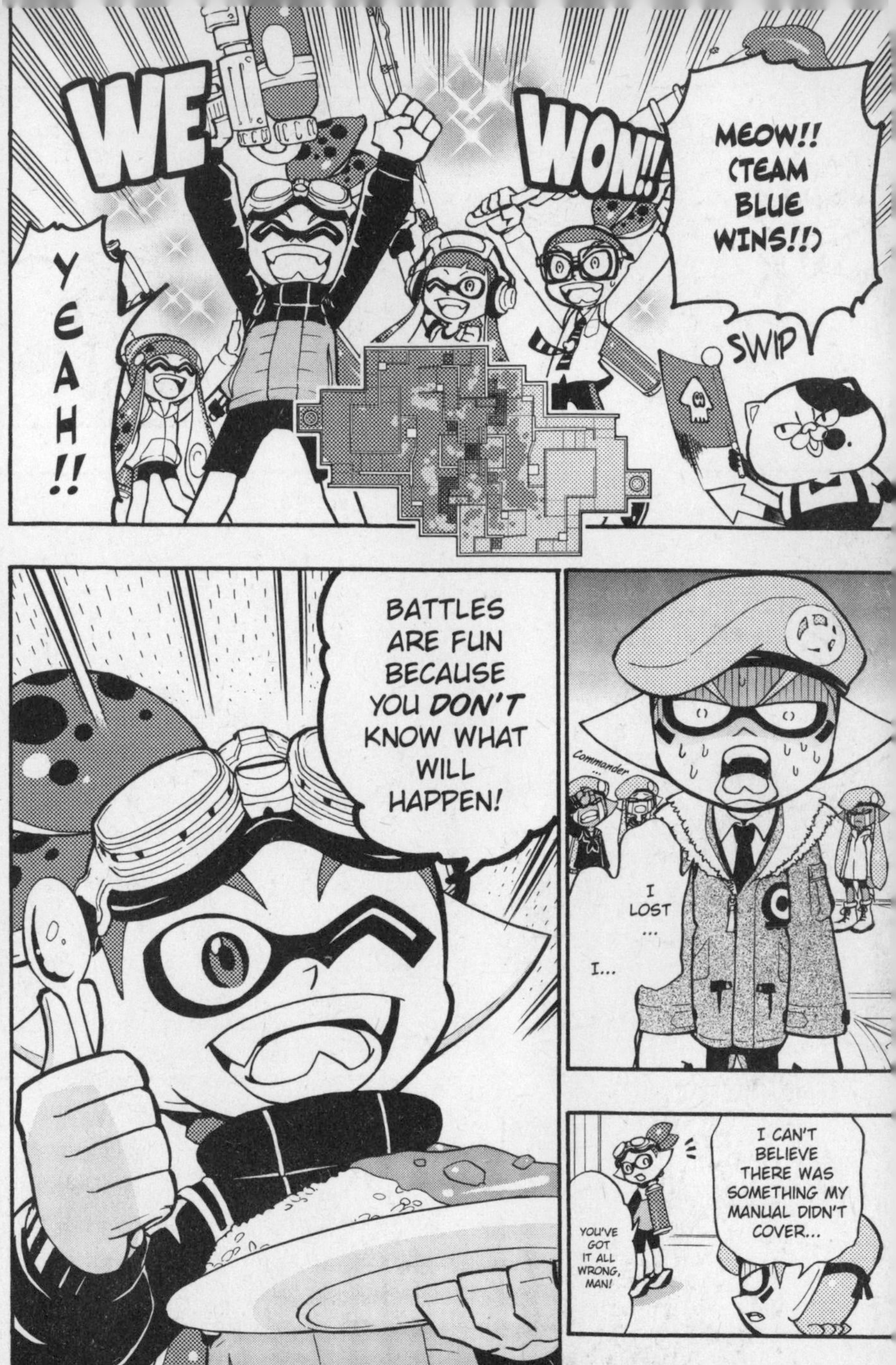
MEOW!! (TEAM BLUE WINS!!)
SWIP
WE WON!!
YEAH!!
Commander...
I LOST...
I...
I CAN'T BELIEVE THERE WAS SOMETHING MY MANUAL DIDN'T COVER...
YOU'VE GOT IT ALL WRONG, MAN!
BATTLES ARE FUN BECAUSE YOU *DON'T* KNOW WHAT WILL HAPPEN!

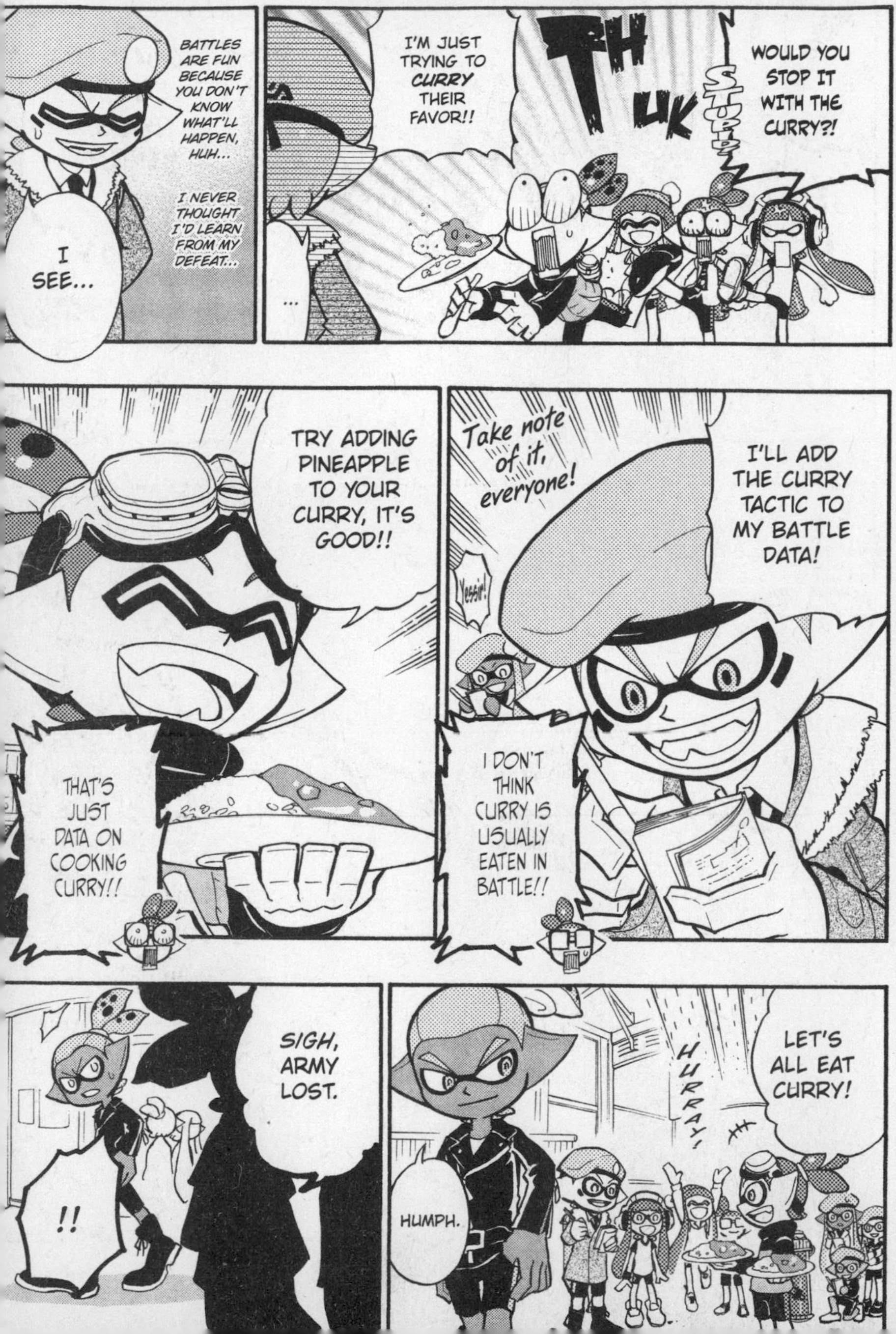
WOULD YOU STOP IT WITH THE CURRY?!
STUPID
THUK
I'M JUST TRYING TO CURRY THEIR FAVOR!!
...
BATTLES ARE FUN BECAUSE YOU DON'T KNOW WHAT'LL HAPPEN, HUH...
I NEVER THOUGHT I'D LEARN FROM MY DEFEAT...
I SEE...
I'LL ADD THE CURRY TACTIC TO MY BATTLE DATA!
Take note of it, everyone!
Yessir!
I DON'T THINK CURRY IS USUALLY EATEN IN BATTLE!!
TRY ADDING PINEAPPLE TO YOUR CURRY, IT'S GOOD!!
THAT'S JUST DATA ON COOKING CURRY!!
LET'S ALL EAT CURRY!
HURRAY!
HUMPH.
SIGH, ARMY LOST.
!!

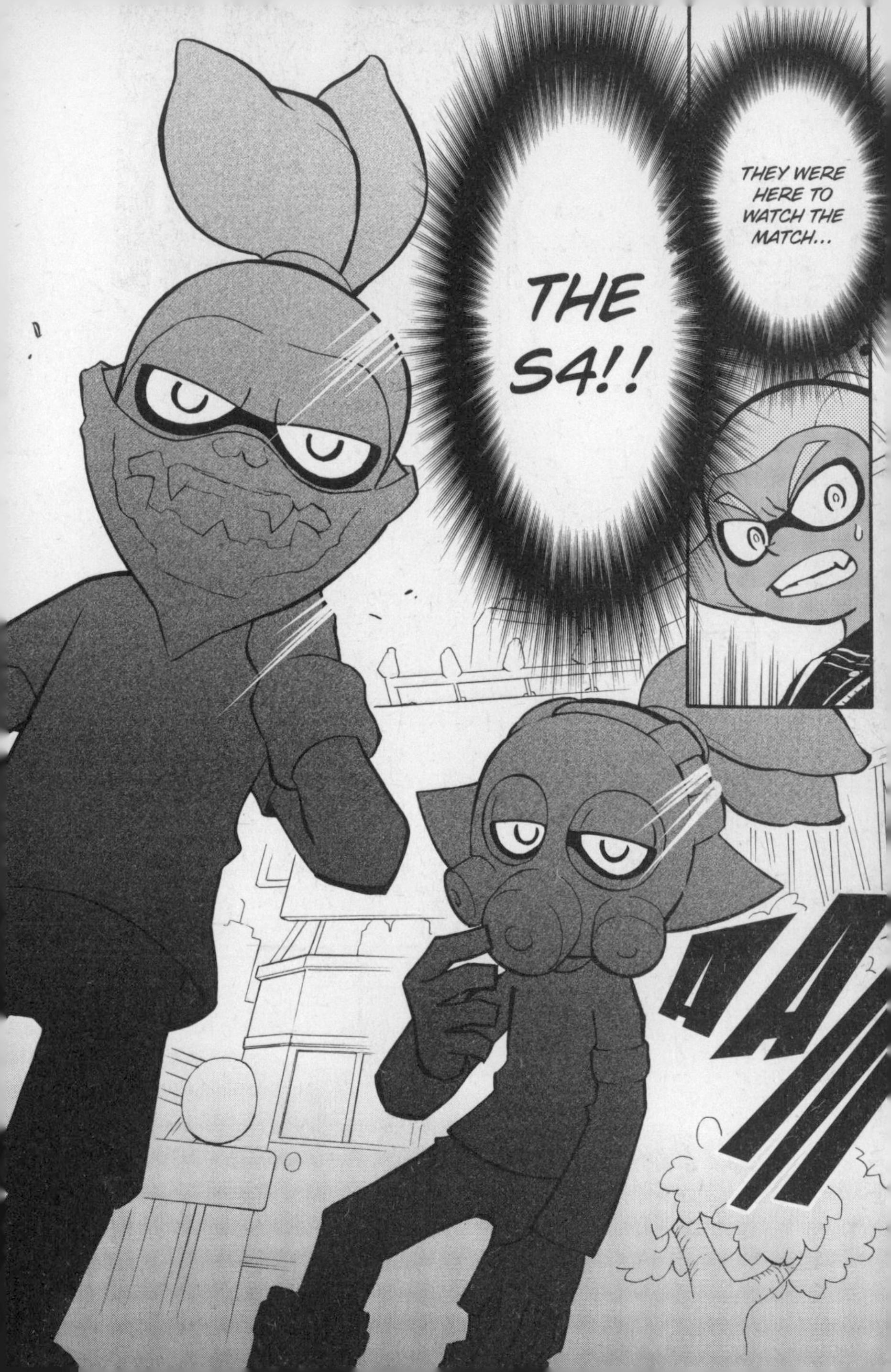
THEY WERE HERE TO WATCH THE MATCH...
THE S4!!

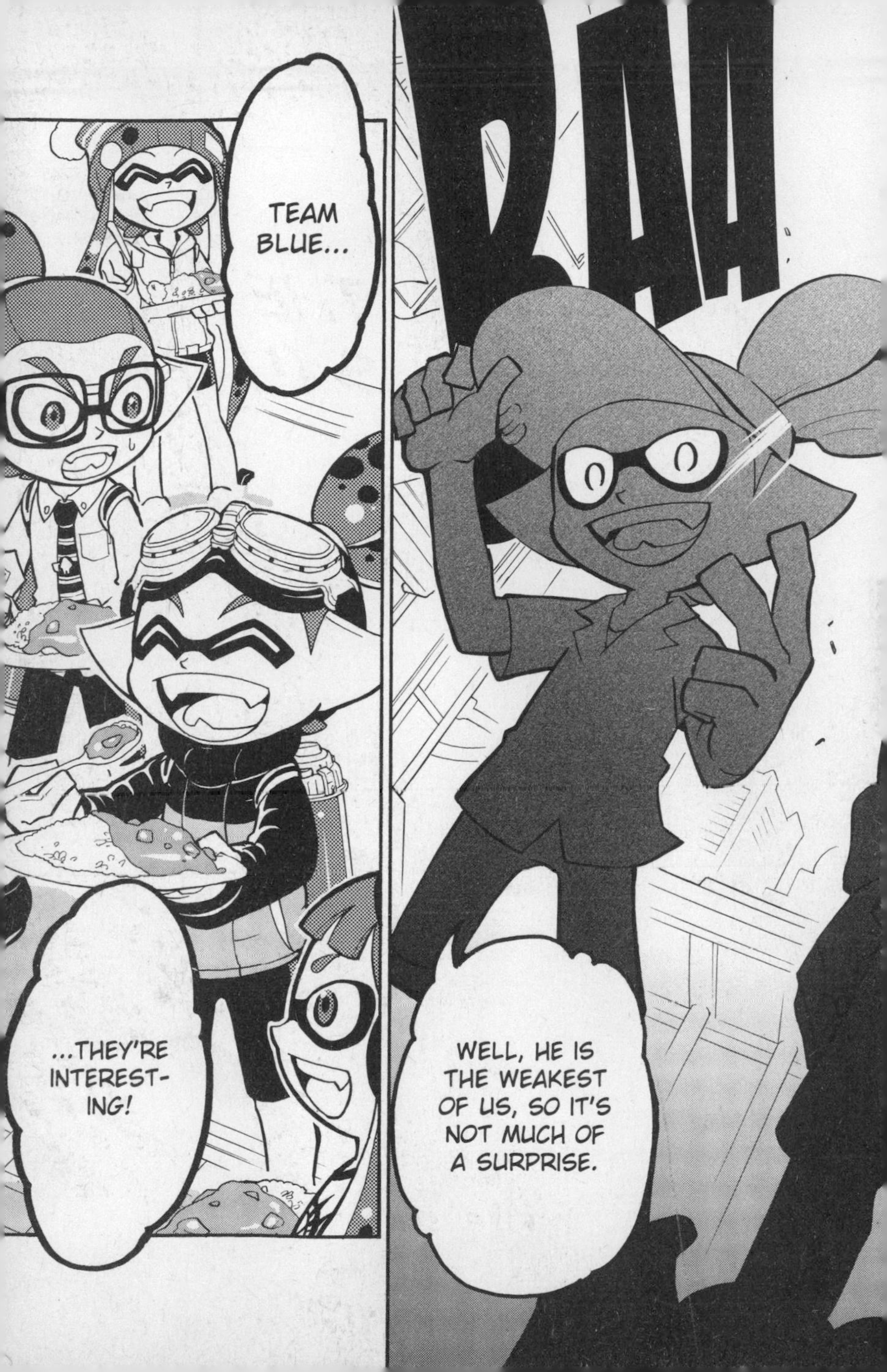
BAM
WELL, HE IS THE WEAKEST OF US, SO IT'S NOT MUCH OF A SURPRISE.
TEAM BLUE...
...THEY'RE INTEREST-ING!

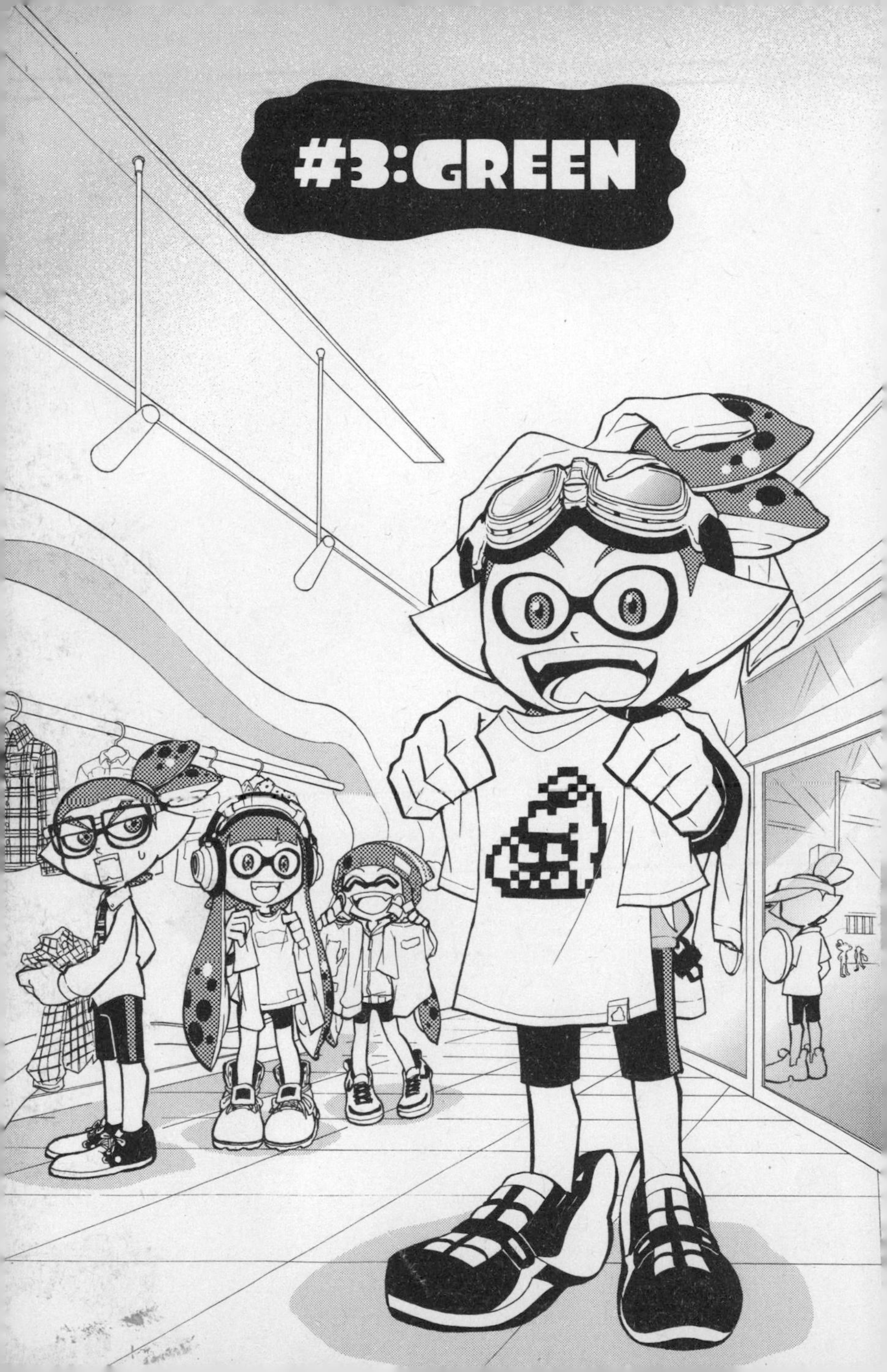
#3:GREEN

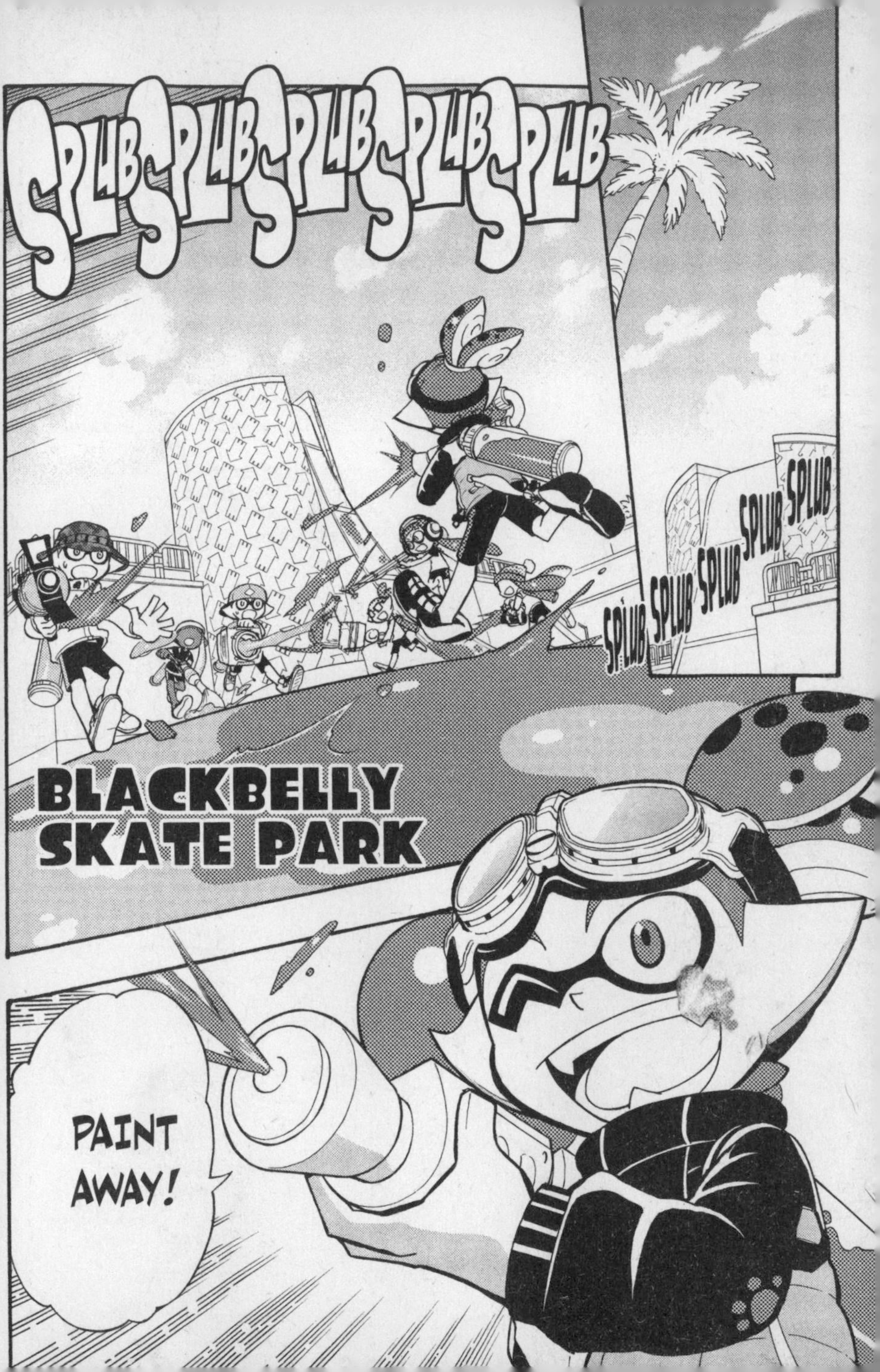
SPLUB SPLUB SPLUB SPLUB SPLUB
SPLUB SPLUB SPLUB SPLUB SPLUB
BLACKBELLY SKATE PARK
PAINT AWAY!

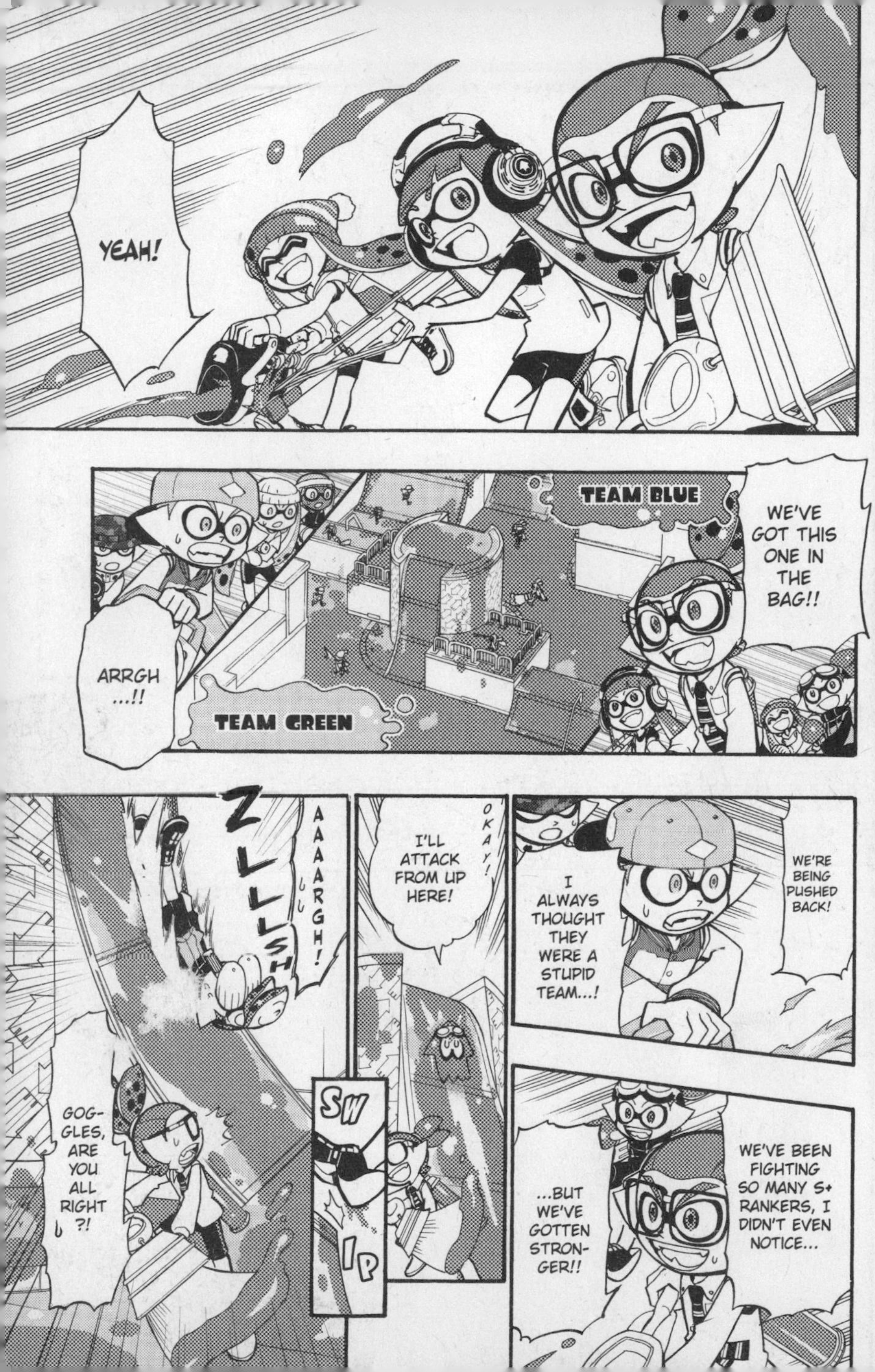
YEAH!
WE'VE GOT THIS ONE IN THE BAG!!
TEAM BLUE
TEAM GREEN
ARRGH ...!!
WE'RE BEING PUSHED BACK!
I ALWAYS THOUGHT THEY WERE A STUPID TEAM...!
WE'VE BEEN FIGHTING SO MANY S+ RANKERS, I DIDN'T EVEN NOTICE...
...BUT WE'VE GOTTEN STRONGER!!
OKAY!
I'LL ATTACK FROM UP HERE!
SWIP
ZZLLLLSH
AAAAARGH!
GOGGLES, ARE YOU ALL RIGHT?!

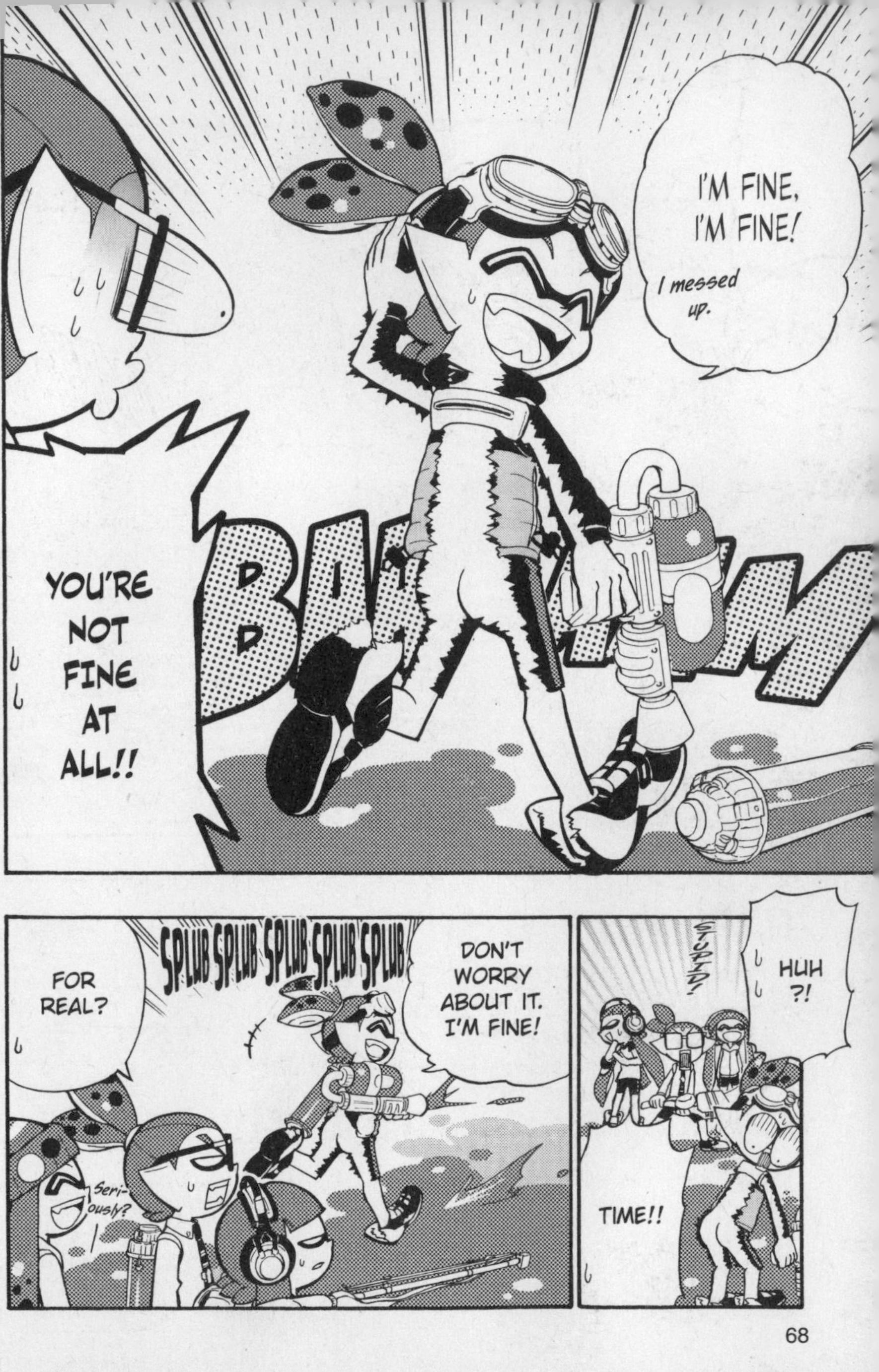
I'M FINE, I'M FINE!
I messed up.
YOU'RE NOT FINE AT ALL!!
HUH?!
STUPID!
TIME!!
SPLUB SPLUB SPLUB SPLUB SPLUB
DON'T WORRY ABOUT IT. I'M FINE!
FOR REAL?
Seri-ously?

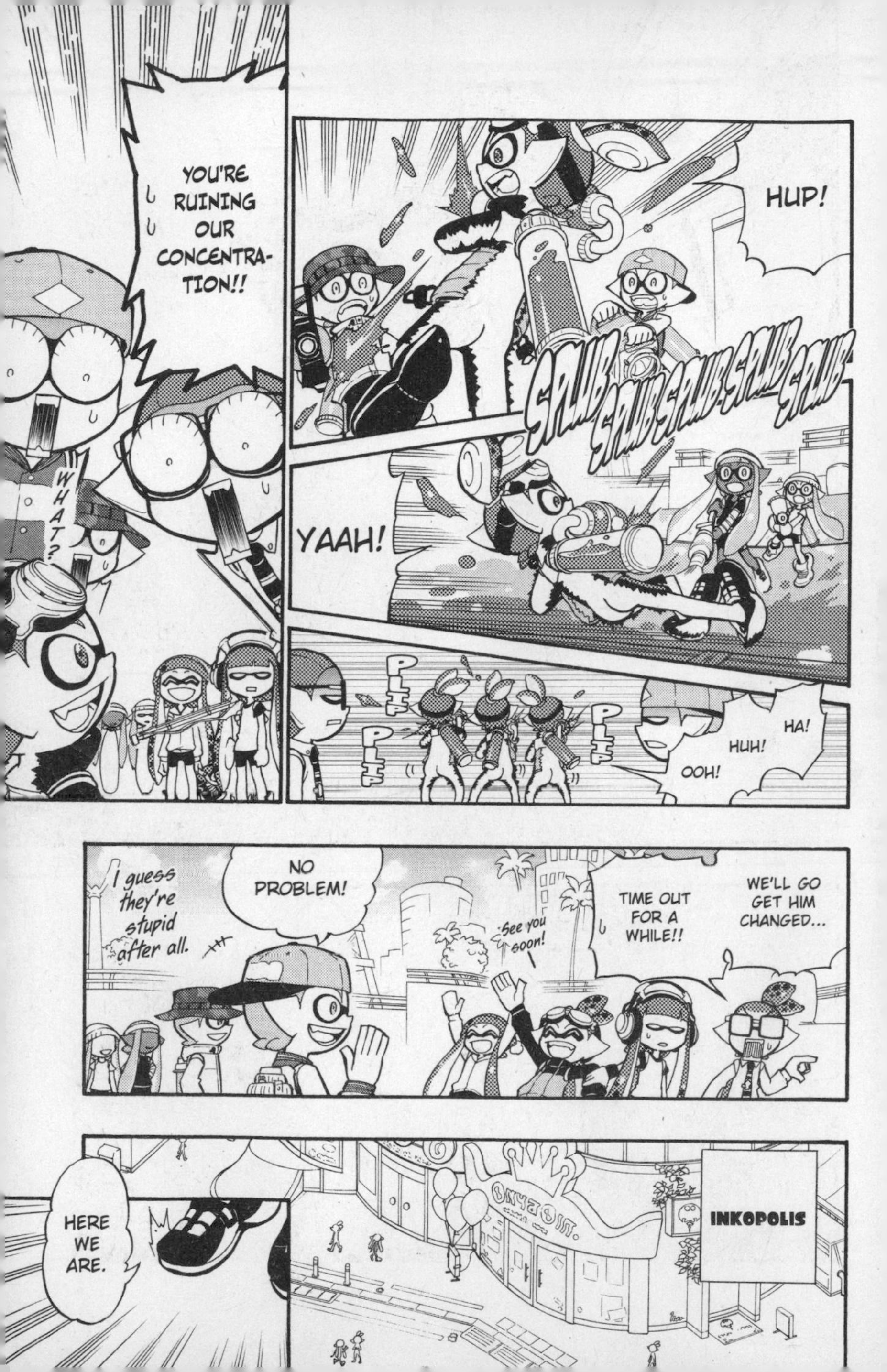
HUP!
SPLUB SPLUB SPLUB SPLUB SPLUB
YAAH!
HA!
HUH!
OOH!
PLIP
PLIP
PLIP
YOU'RE RUINING OUR CONCENTRATION!!
WHAT?
WE'LL GO GET HIM CHANGED...
TIME OUT FOR A WHILE!!
See you soon!
NO PROBLEM!
I guess they're stupid after all.
INKOPOLIS
HERE WE ARE.

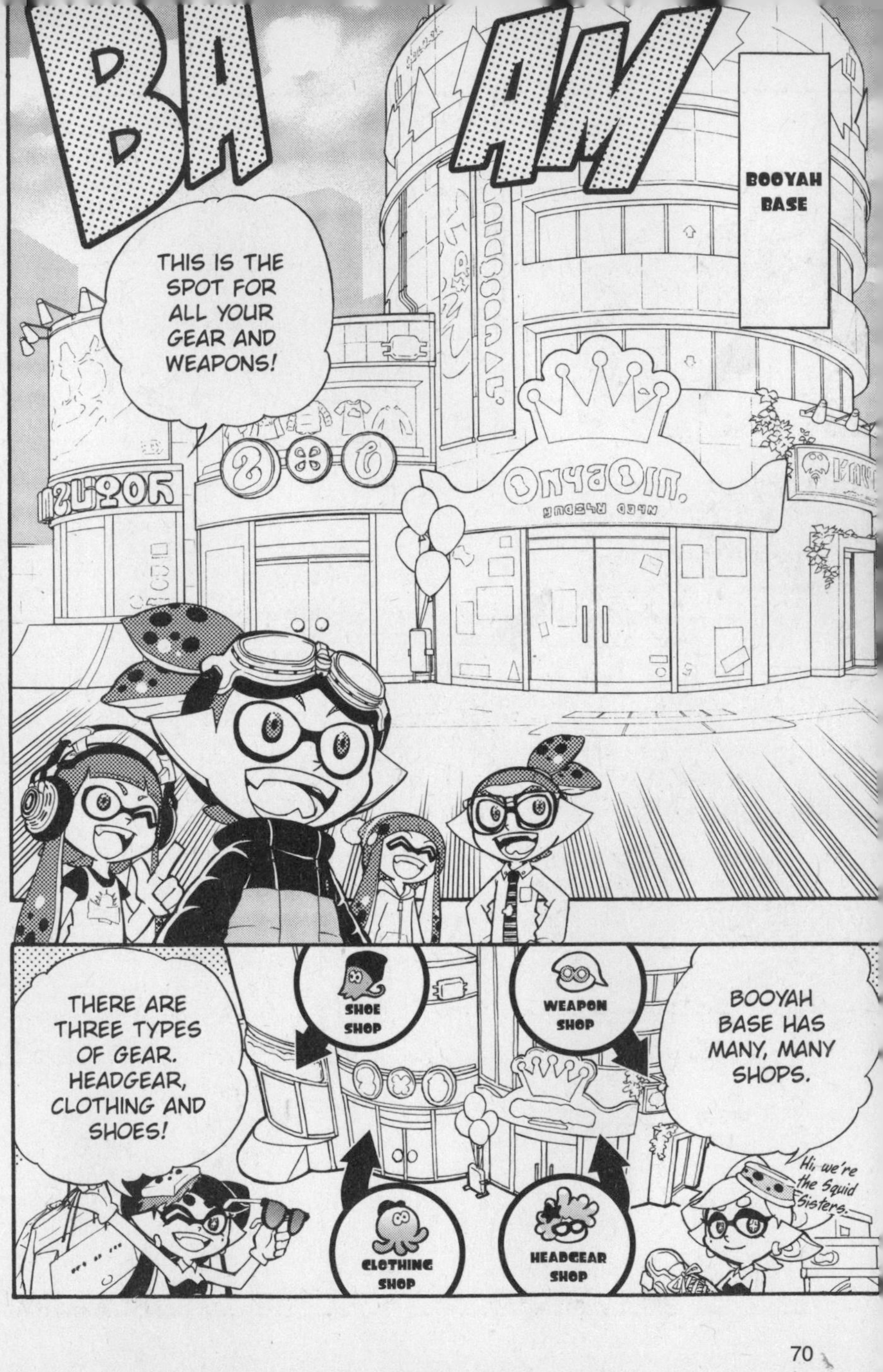
BOOYAH BASE
BAAM
THIS IS THE SPOT FOR ALL YOUR GEAR AND WEAPONS!
BOOYAH BASE HAS MANY, MANY SHOPS.
Hi, we're the Squid Sisters.
WEAPON SHOP
SHOE SHOP
HEADGEAR SHOP
CLOTHING SHOP
THERE ARE THREE TYPES OF GEAR. HEADGEAR, CLOTHING AND SHOES!

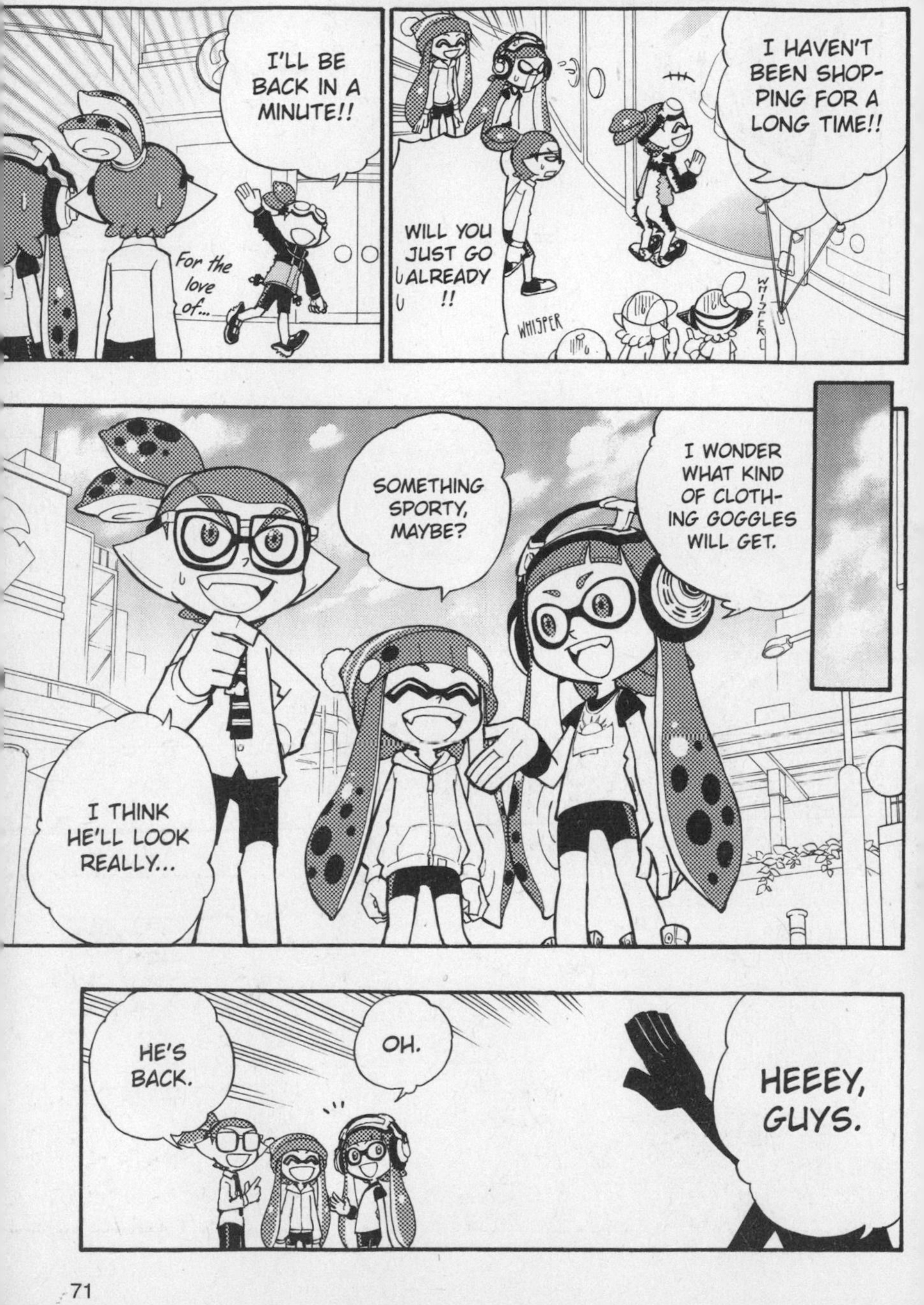
I HAVEN'T BEEN SHOPPING FOR A LONG TIME!!
WILL YOU JUST GO ALREADY!!
WHISPER
WHISPER
I'LL BE BACK IN A MINUTE!!
For the love of...
I WONDER WHAT KIND OF CLOTHING GOGGLES WILL GET.
SOMETHING SPORTY, MAYBE?
I THINK HE'LL LOOK REALLY...
HEEEY, GUYS.
OH.
HE'S BACK.

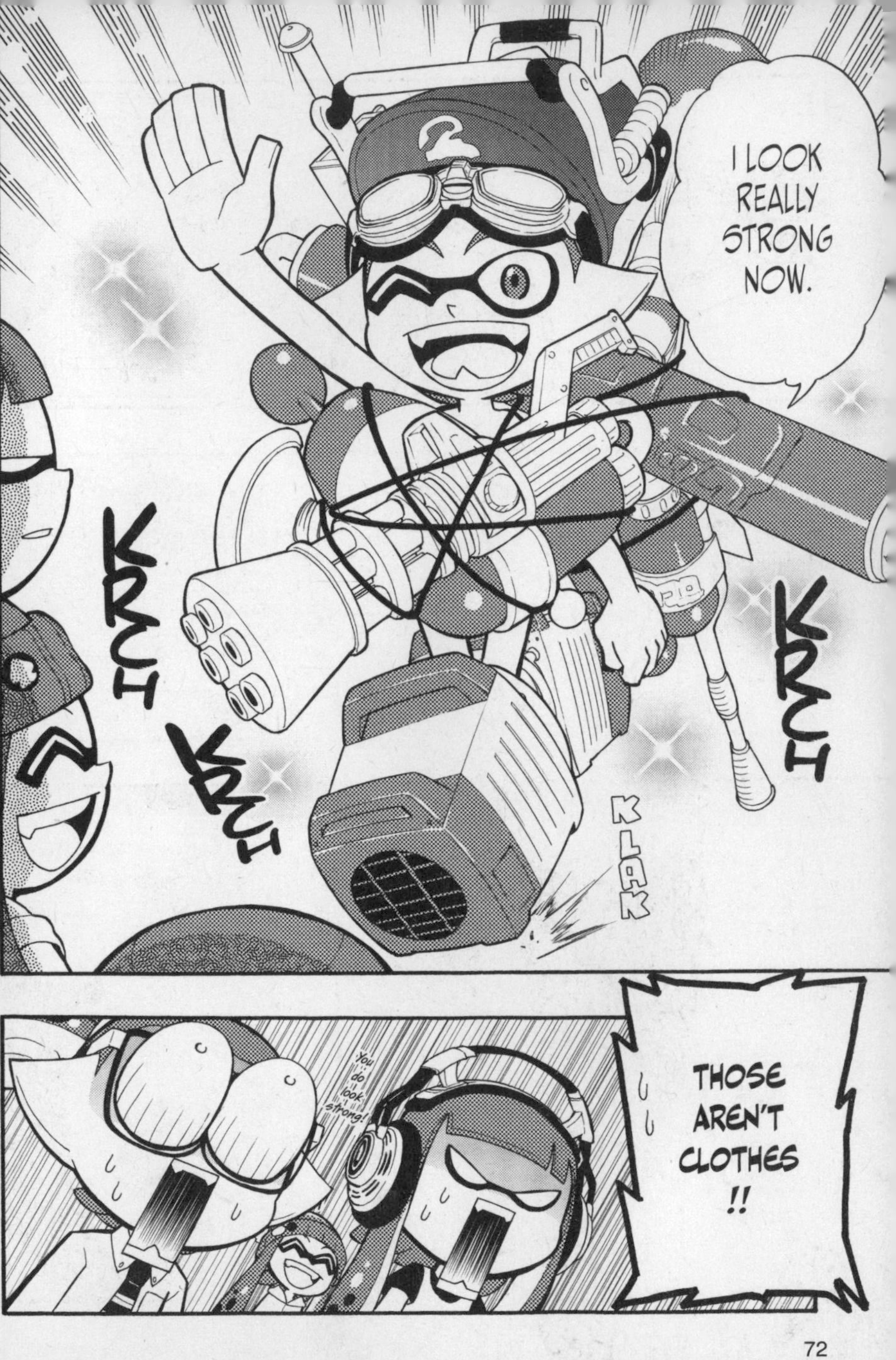
I LOOK REALLY STRONG NOW.
KRCH
KLAK
KRCH
KRCH
THOSE AREN'T CLOTHES !!
You do look strong!

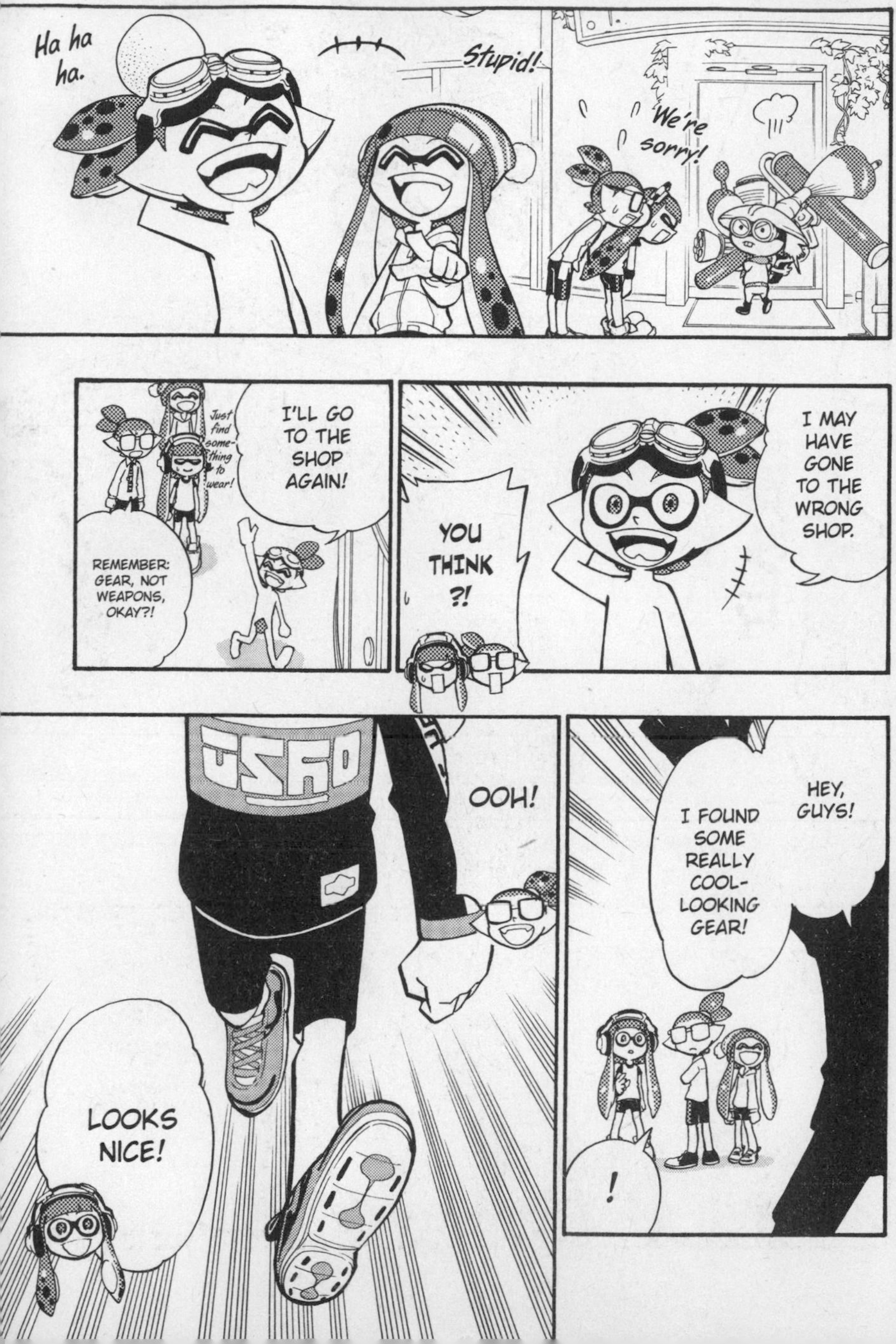
We're sorry!
Stupid!
Ha ha ha.
I MAY HAVE GONE TO THE WRONG SHOP.
YOU THINK ?!
I'LL GO TO THE SHOP AGAIN!
Just find something to wear!
REMEMBER: GEAR, NOT WEAPONS, OKAY?!
HEY, GUYS!
I FOUND SOME REALLY COOL-LOOKING GEAR!
!
OOH!
LOOKS NICE!

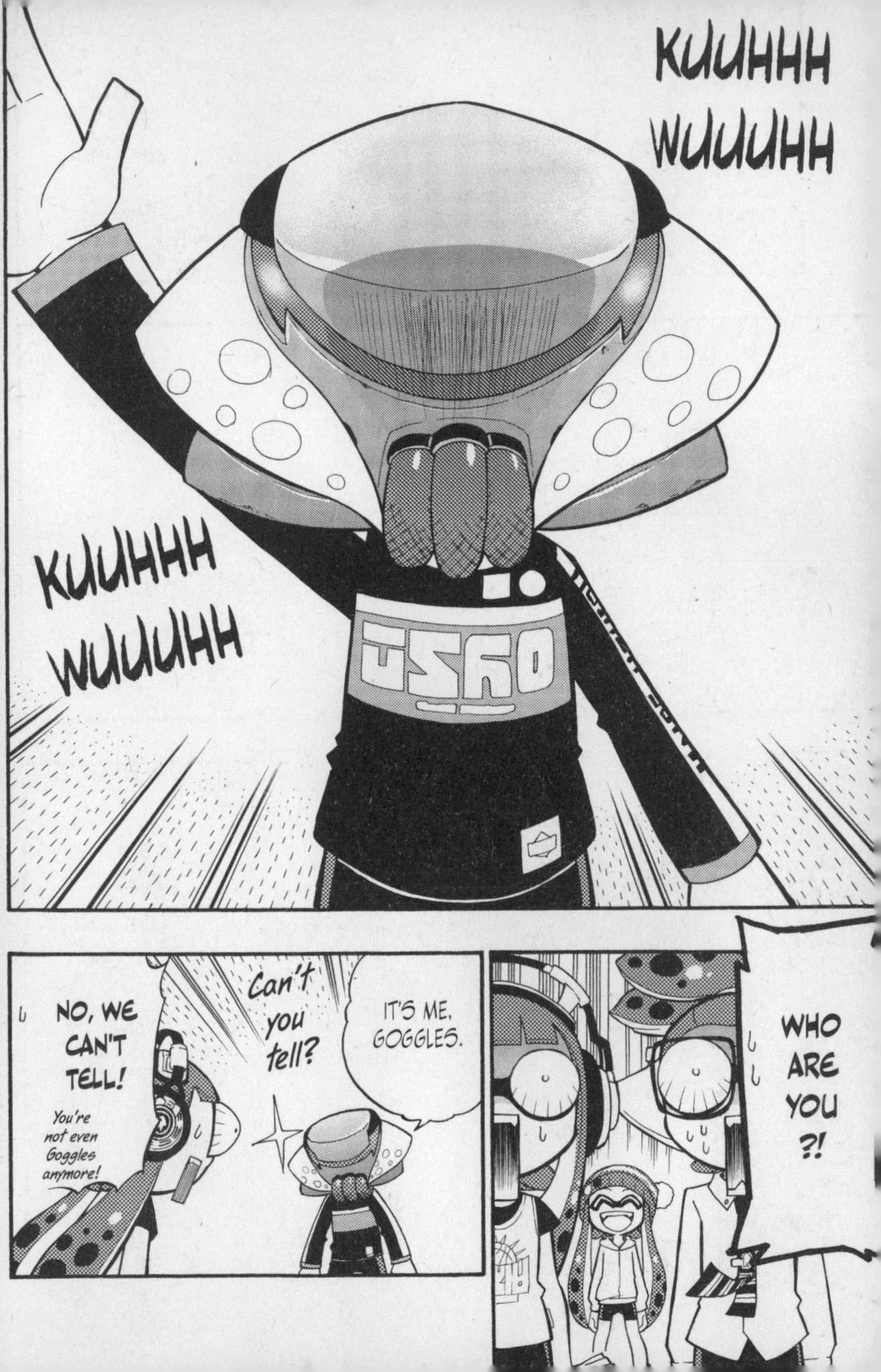
KUUHHH WUUUHH
KUUHHH WUUUHH
WHO ARE YOU ?!
IT'S ME, GOGGLES.
Can't you tell?
NO, WE CAN'T TELL!
You're not even Goggles anymore!

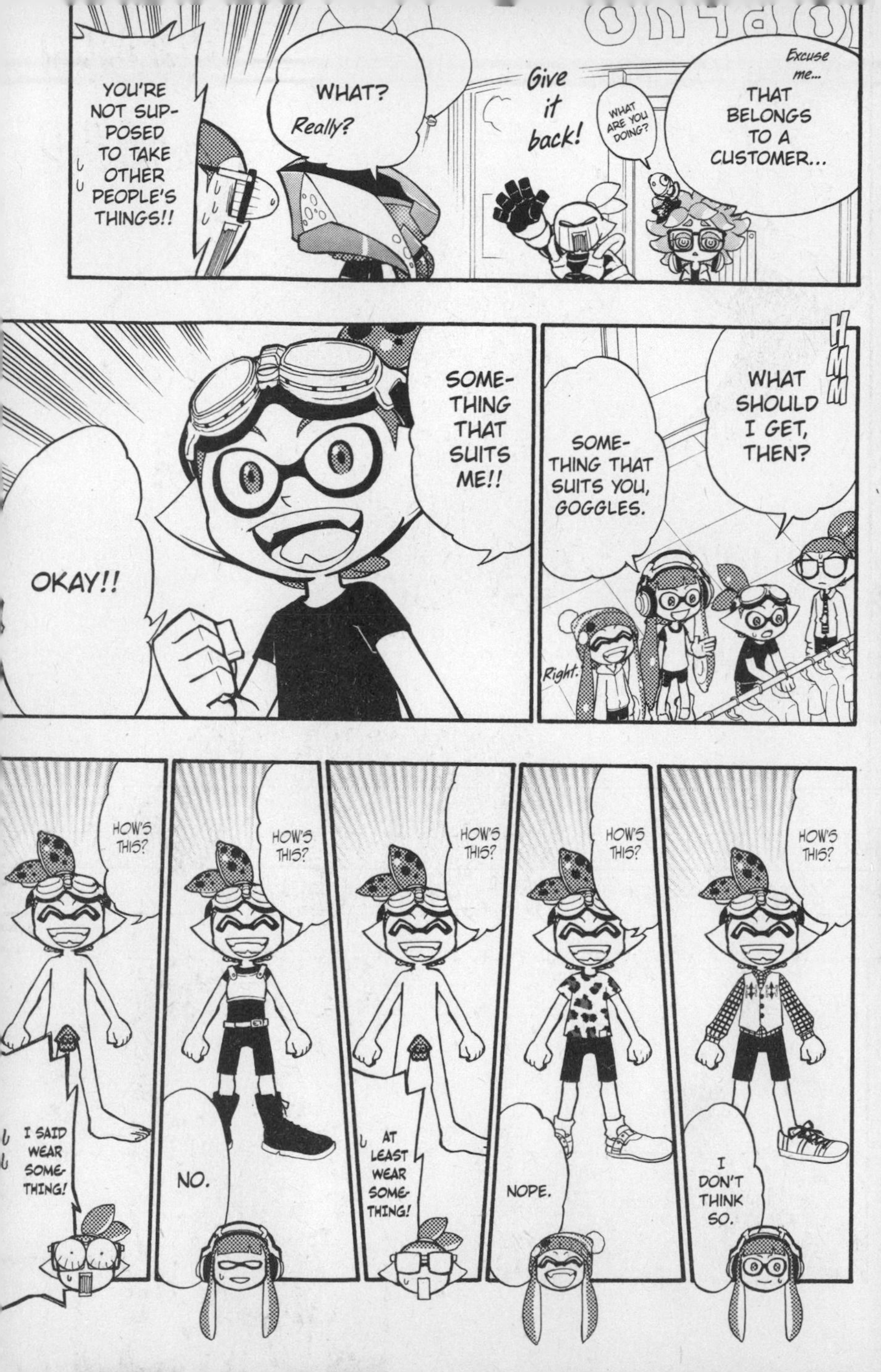
Excuse me... THAT BELONGS TO A CUSTOMER...
WHAT ARE YOU DOING?
Give it back!
WHAT? Really?
YOU'RE NOT SUPPOSED TO TAKE OTHER PEOPLE'S THINGS!!
HMM
WHAT SHOULD I GET, THEN?
SOMETHING THAT SUITS YOU, GOGGLES.
Right.
SOMETHING THAT SUITS ME!!
OKAY!!
HOW'S THIS?
I DON'T THINK SO.
HOW'S THIS?
NOPE.
HOW'S THIS?
AT LEAST WEAR SOMETHING!
HOW'S THIS?
NO.
HOW'S THIS?
I SAID WEAR SOMETHING!

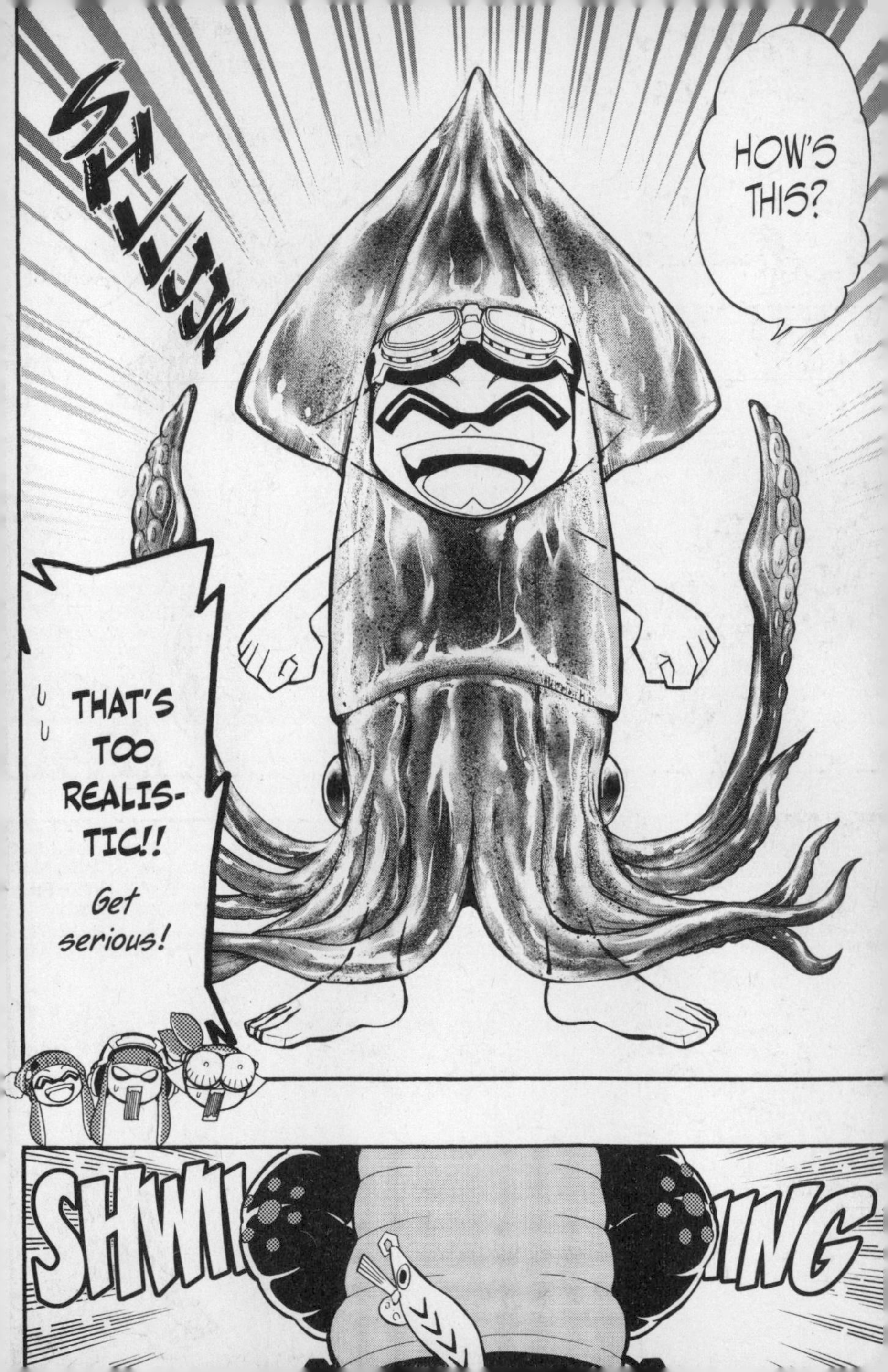
HOW'S THIS?
SHLLUUR
THAT'S TOO REALIS-TIC!!
Get serious!

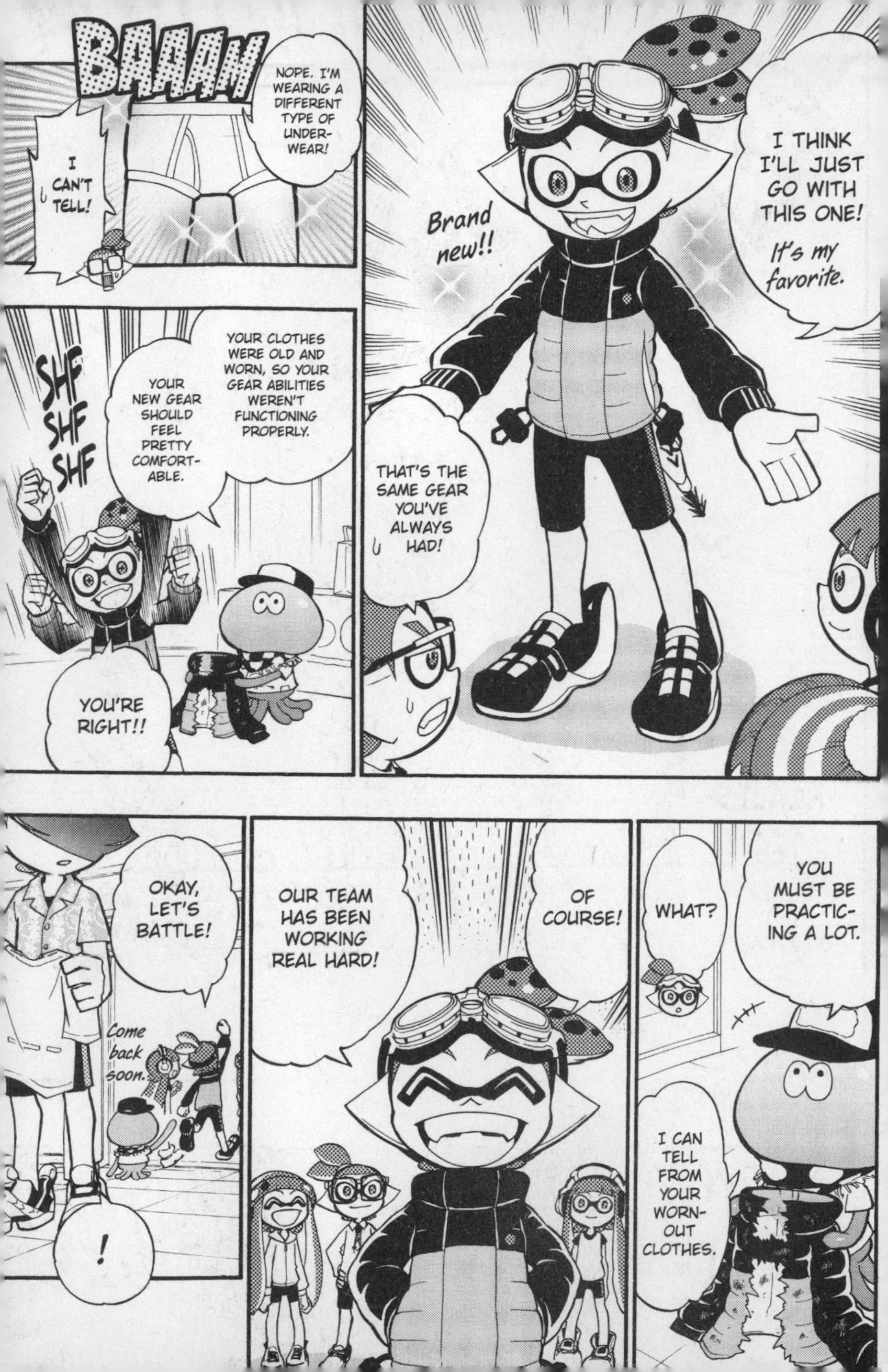
I THINK I'LL JUST GO WITH THIS ONE!
It's my favorite.
Brand new!!
THAT'S THE SAME GEAR YOU'VE ALWAYS HAD!
BAAAM
NOPE. I'M WEARING A DIFFERENT TYPE OF UNDERWEAR!
I CAN'T TELL!
YOUR CLOTHES WERE OLD AND WORN, SO YOUR GEAR ABILITIES WEREN'T FUNCTIONING PROPERLY.
YOUR NEW GEAR SHOULD FEEL PRETTY COMFORTABLE.
SHF SHF SHF
YOU'RE RIGHT!!
YOU MUST BE PRACTICING A LOT.
WHAT?
I CAN TELL FROM YOUR WORN-OUT CLOTHES.
OF COURSE!
OUR TEAM HAS BEEN WORKING REAL HARD!
OKAY, LET'S BATTLE!
Come back soon.
!

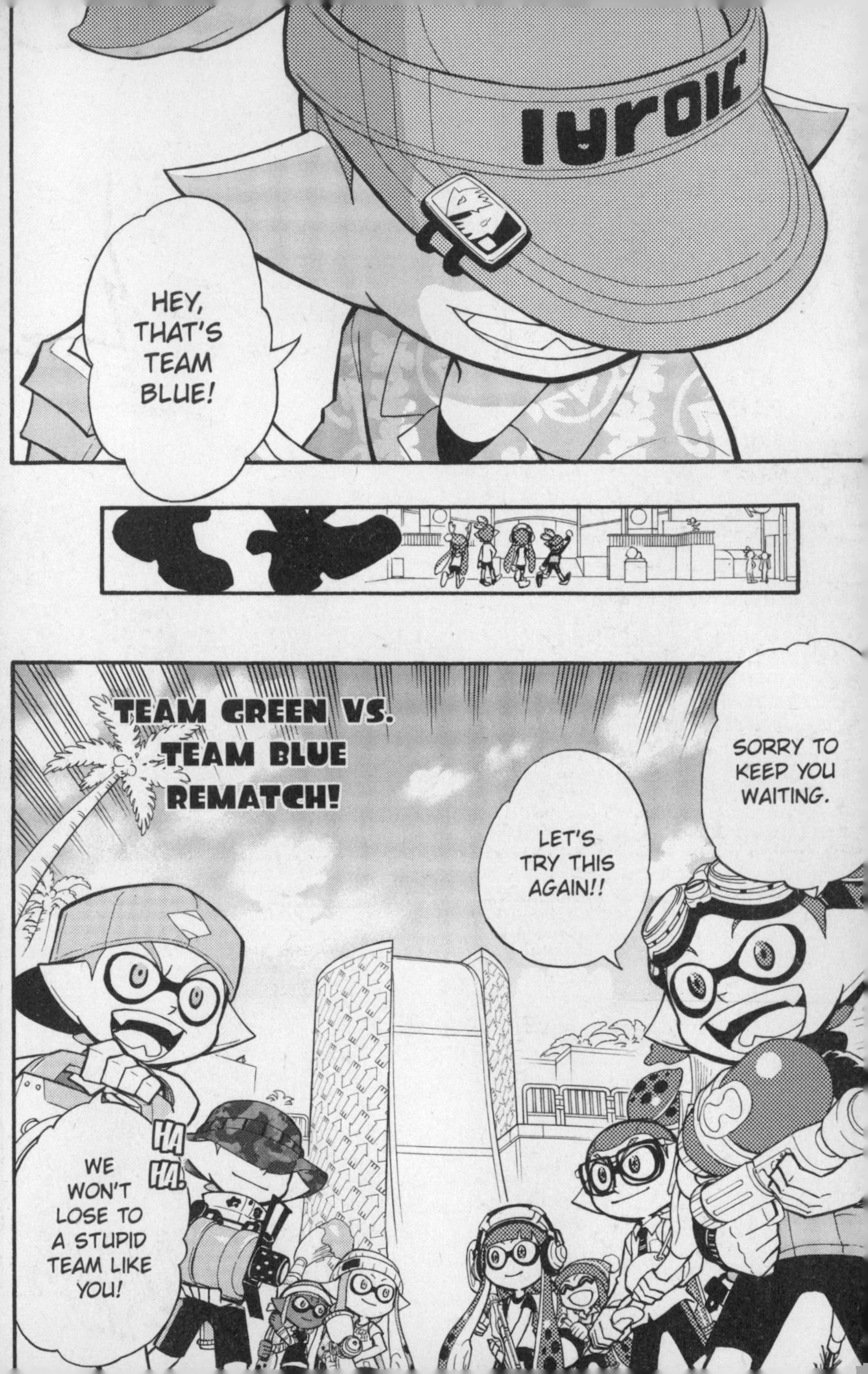
HEY, THAT'S TEAM BLUE!
SORRY TO KEEP YOU WAITING.
LET'S TRY THIS AGAIN!!
TEAM GREEN VS. TEAM BLUE REMATCH!
HA HA.
WE WON'T LOSE TO A STUPID TEAM LIKE YOU!

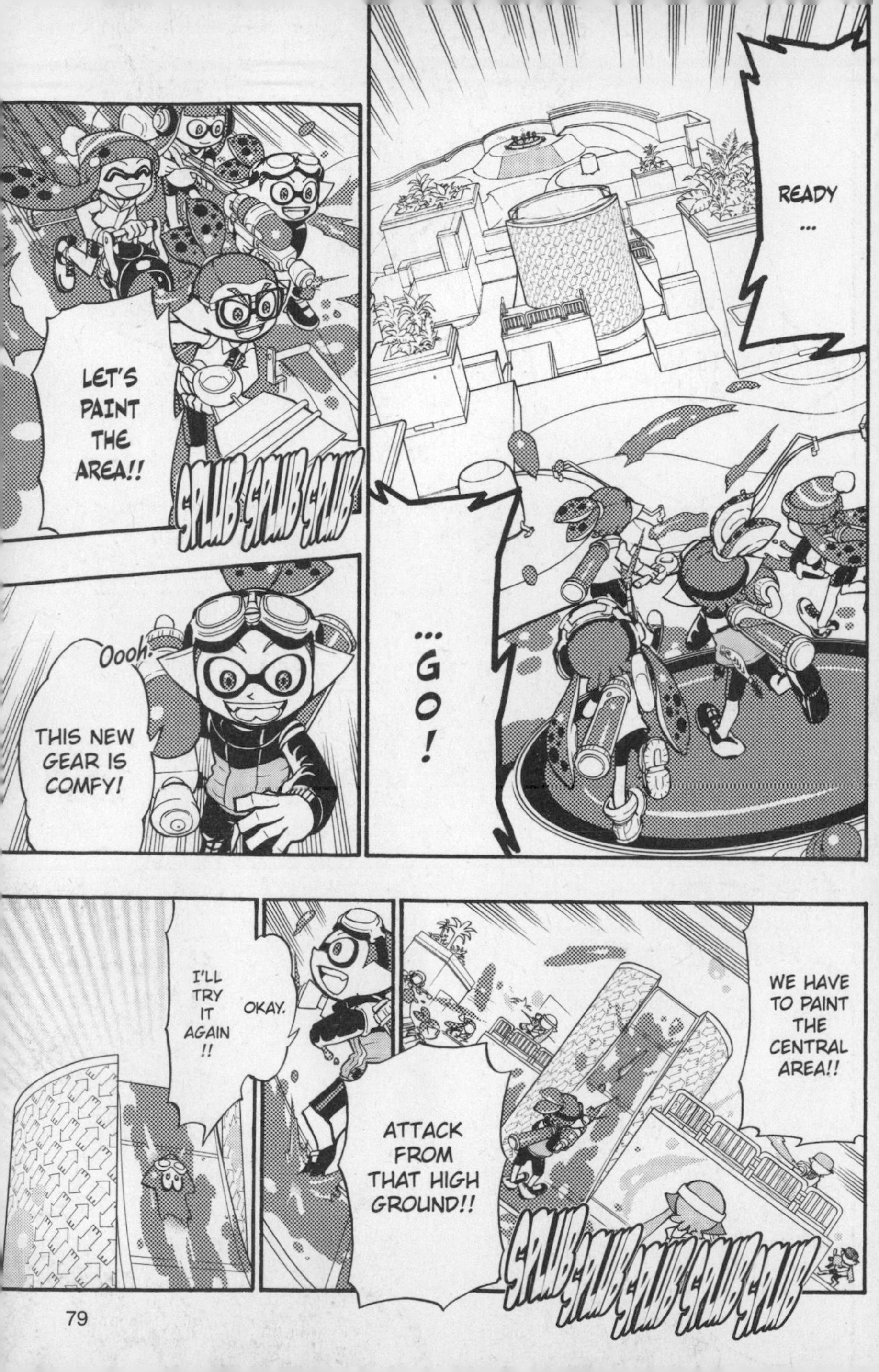
READY ...
...GO!
LET'S PAINT THE AREA!!
SPLUB SPLUB SPLUB
Oooh.
THIS NEW GEAR IS COMFY!
WE HAVE TO PAINT THE CENTRAL AREA!!
SPLUB SPLUB SPLUB SPLUB SPLUB
ATTACK FROM THAT HIGH GROUND!!
OKAY.
I'LL TRY IT AGAIN!!

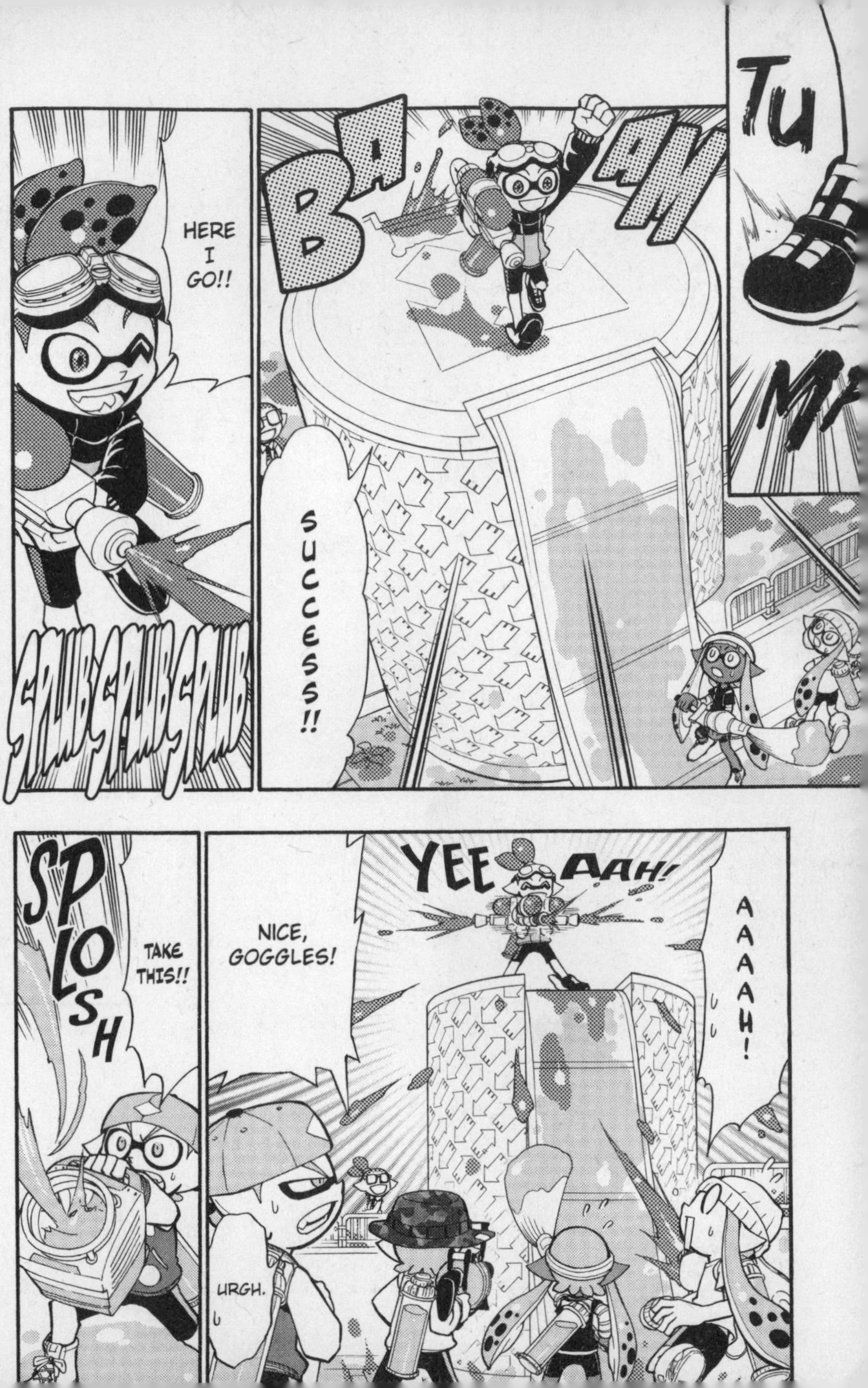

TU
MP
BAAM
SUCCESS!!
HERE I GO!!
SPLUB SPLUB SPLUB
YEE AAH!
AAAAAH!
NICE, GOGGLES!
URGH.
SPLOSH
TAKE THIS!!

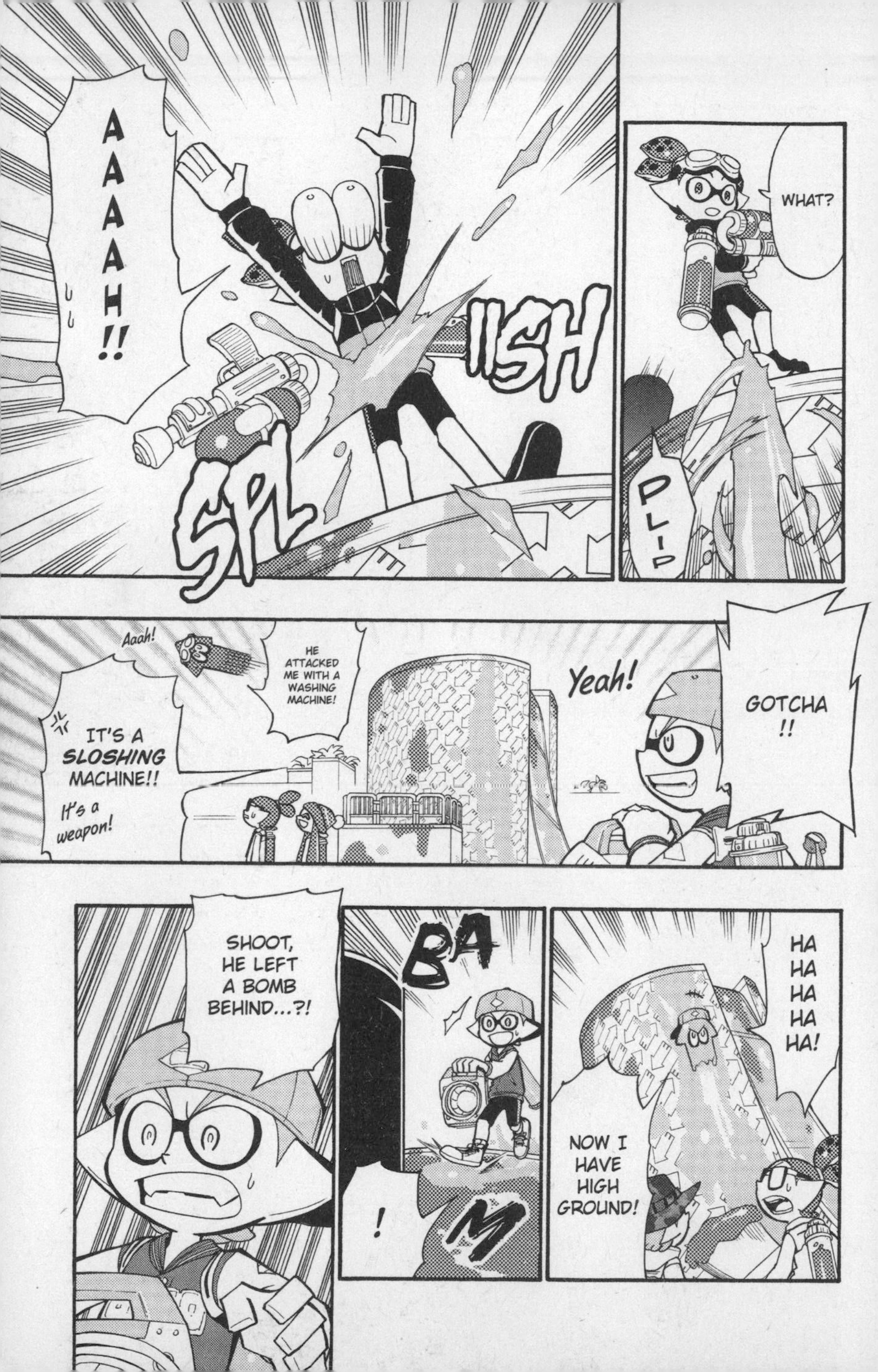
WHAT?
PLIP
AAAAAH!!
SPLISH
GOTCHA !!
Yeah!
HE ATTACKED ME WITH A WASHING MACHINE!
Aaah!
IT'S A SLOSHING MACHINE!!
It's a weapon!
HA HA HA HA HA!
NOW I HAVE HIGH GROUND!
BAM
!
SHOOT, HE LEFT A BOMB BEHIND...?!

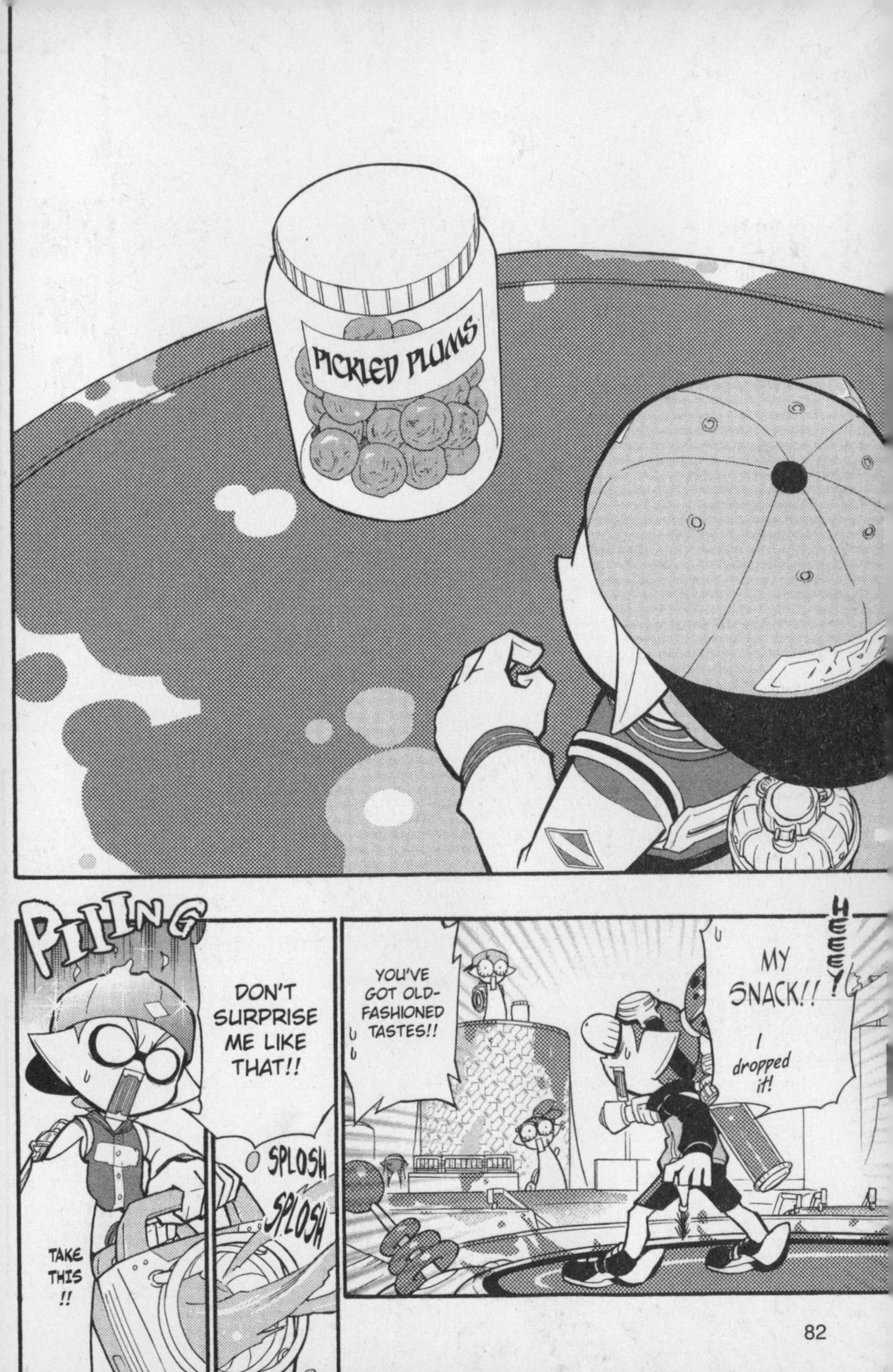
PICKLED PLUMS
HEEEY!
MY SNACK!!
I dropped it!
YOU'VE GOT OLD-FASHIONED TASTES!!
DON'T SURPRISE ME LIKE THAT!!
PIIING
SPLOSH
SPLOSH
TAKE THIS!!

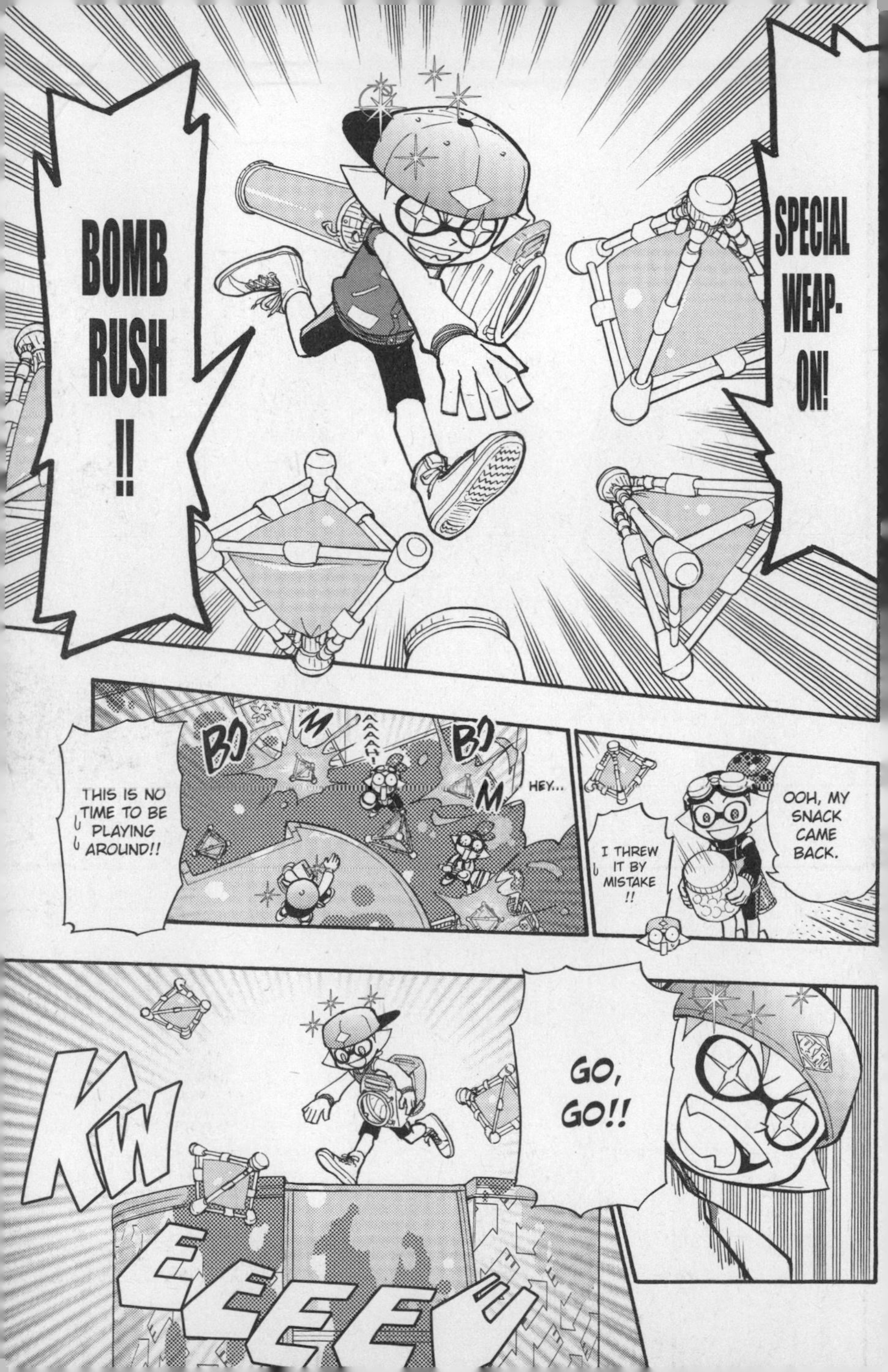
SPECIAL WEAP-ON!
BOMB RUSH !!
OOH, MY SNACK CAME BACK.
I THREW IT BY MISTAKE !!
BOM
AAAAH!
BOM
HEY...
THIS IS NO TIME TO BE PLAYING AROUND!!
GO, GO!!
KWEEEEE

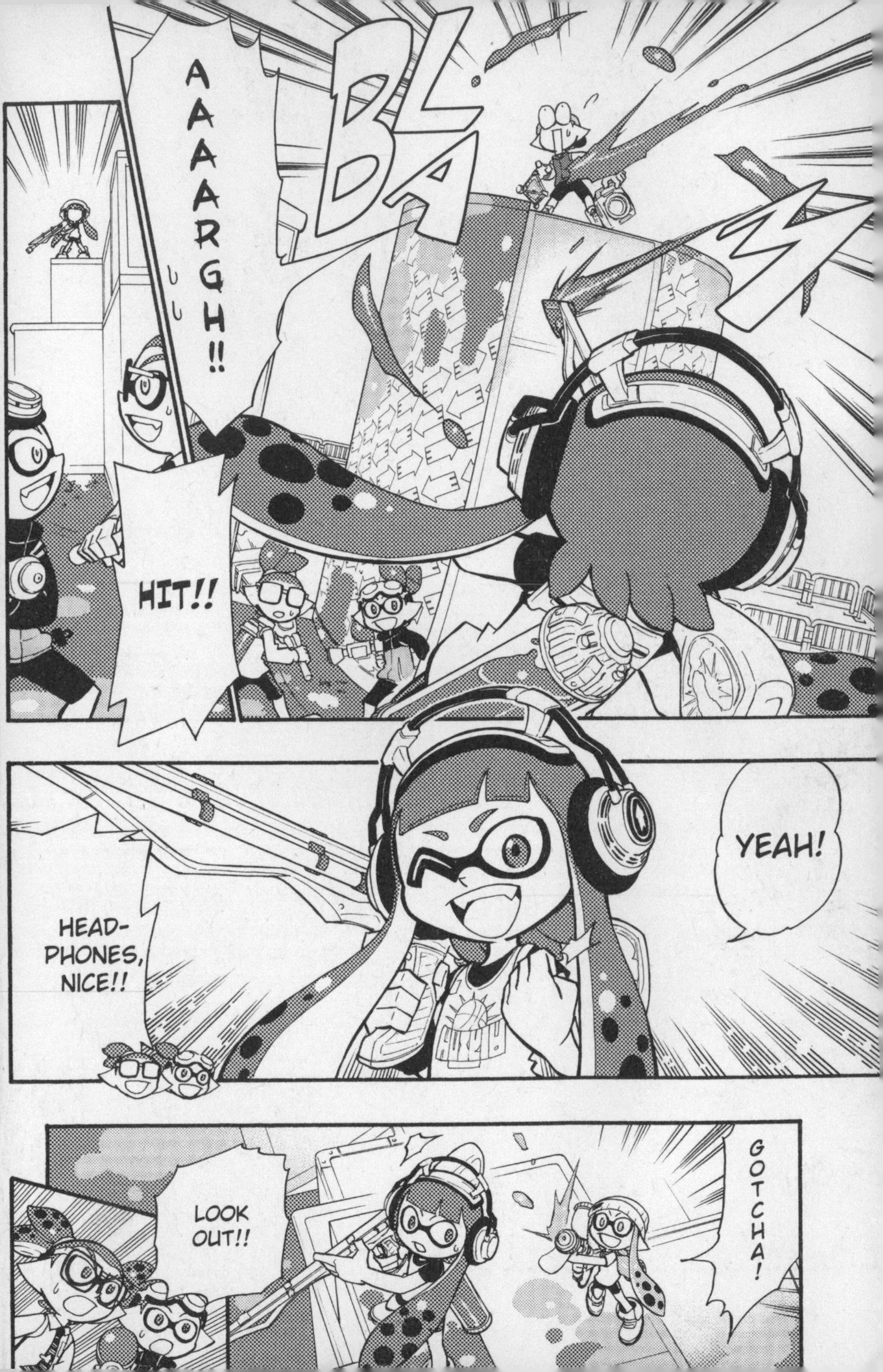
BLAM
AAAARGH!!
HIT!!
YEAH!
HEAD-PHONES, NICE!!
GOTCHA!
LOOK OUT!!

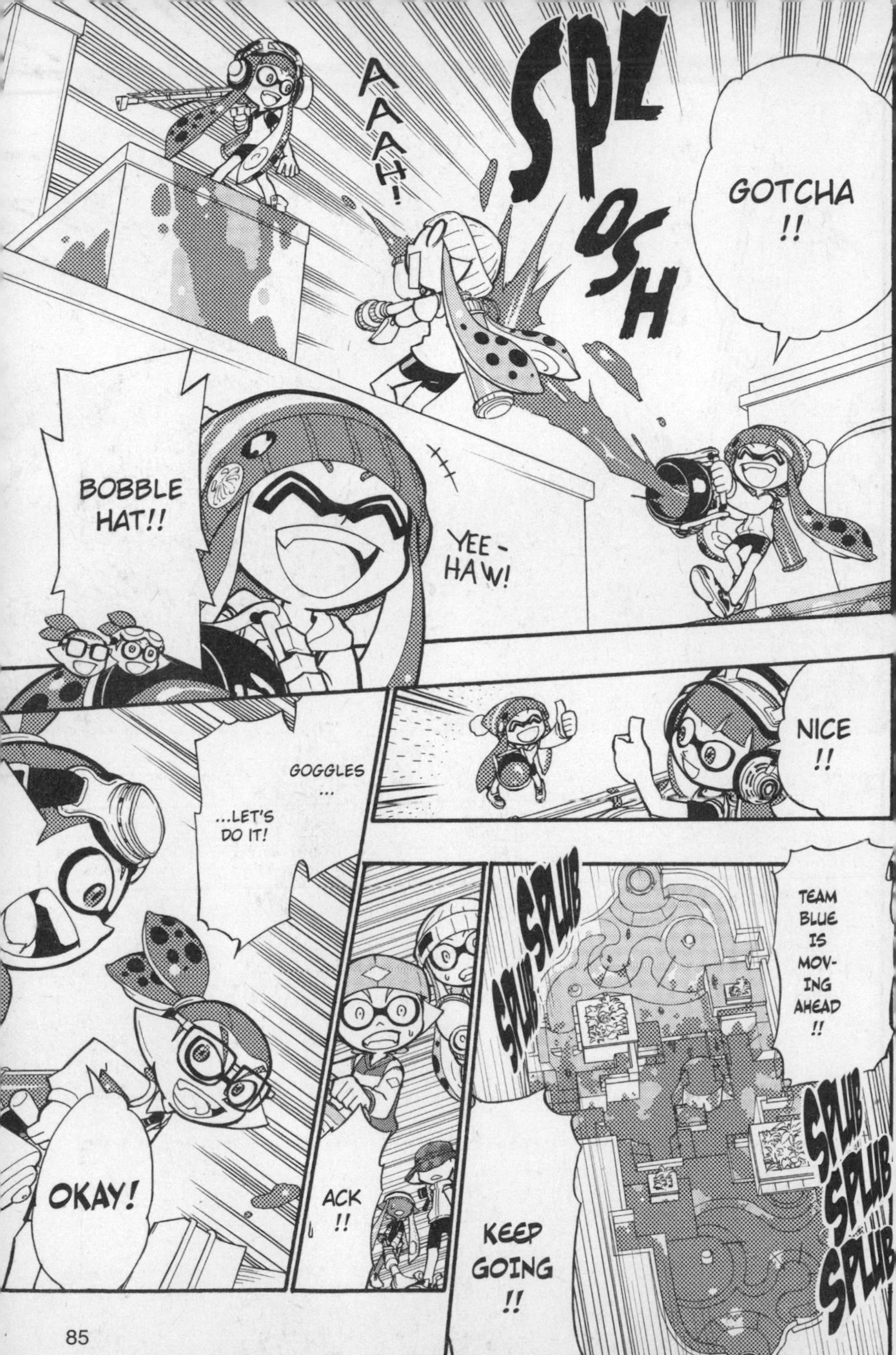
GOTCHA!!
SPLOSH
AAAAH!
YEE-HAW!
BOBBLE HAT!!
NICE!!
TEAM BLUE IS MOVING AHEAD!!
SPLUB SPLUB SPLUB
SPLUB SPLUB SPLUB
KEEP GOING!!
ACK!!
GOGGLES...
...LET'S DO IT!
OKAY!

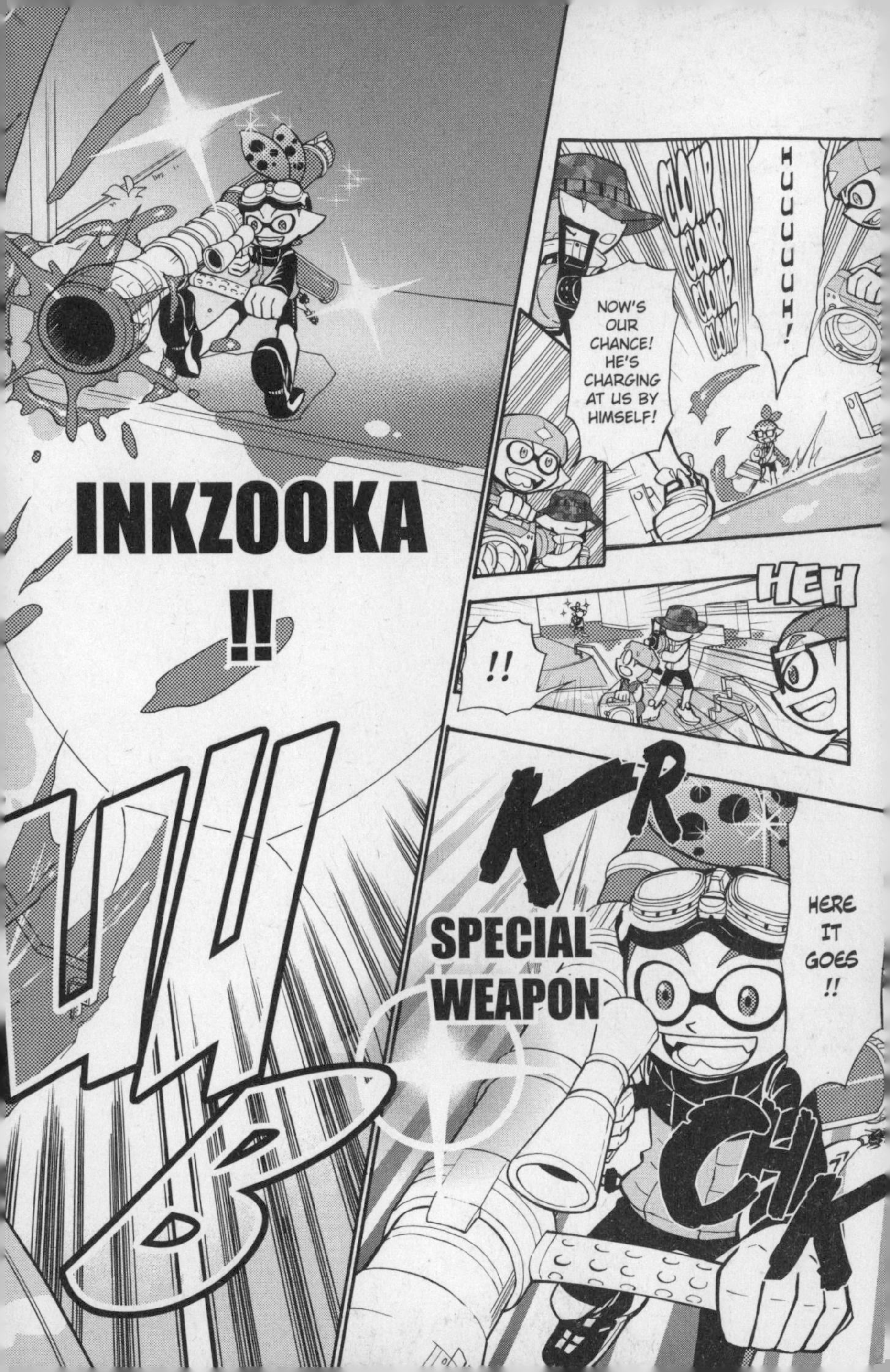
HUUUUUH!
GLOMP GLOMP GLOMP GLOMP
NOW'S OUR CHANCE! HE'S CHARGING AT US BY HIMSELF!
HEH
!!
HERE IT GOES !!
KR
SPECIAL WEAPON
CHK
INKZOOKA
!!

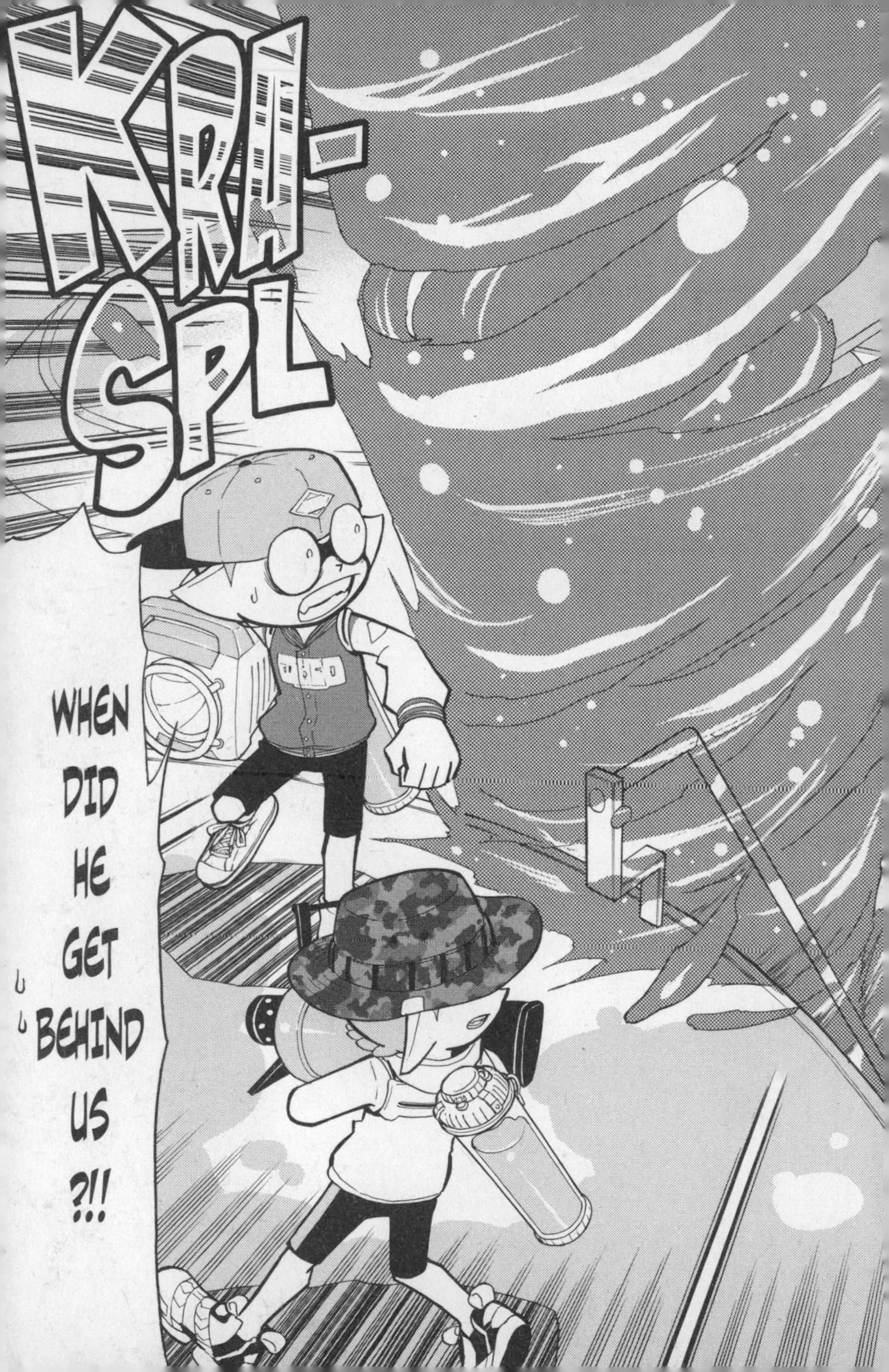
KRA-SPL
WHEN DID HE GET BEHIND US ?!!

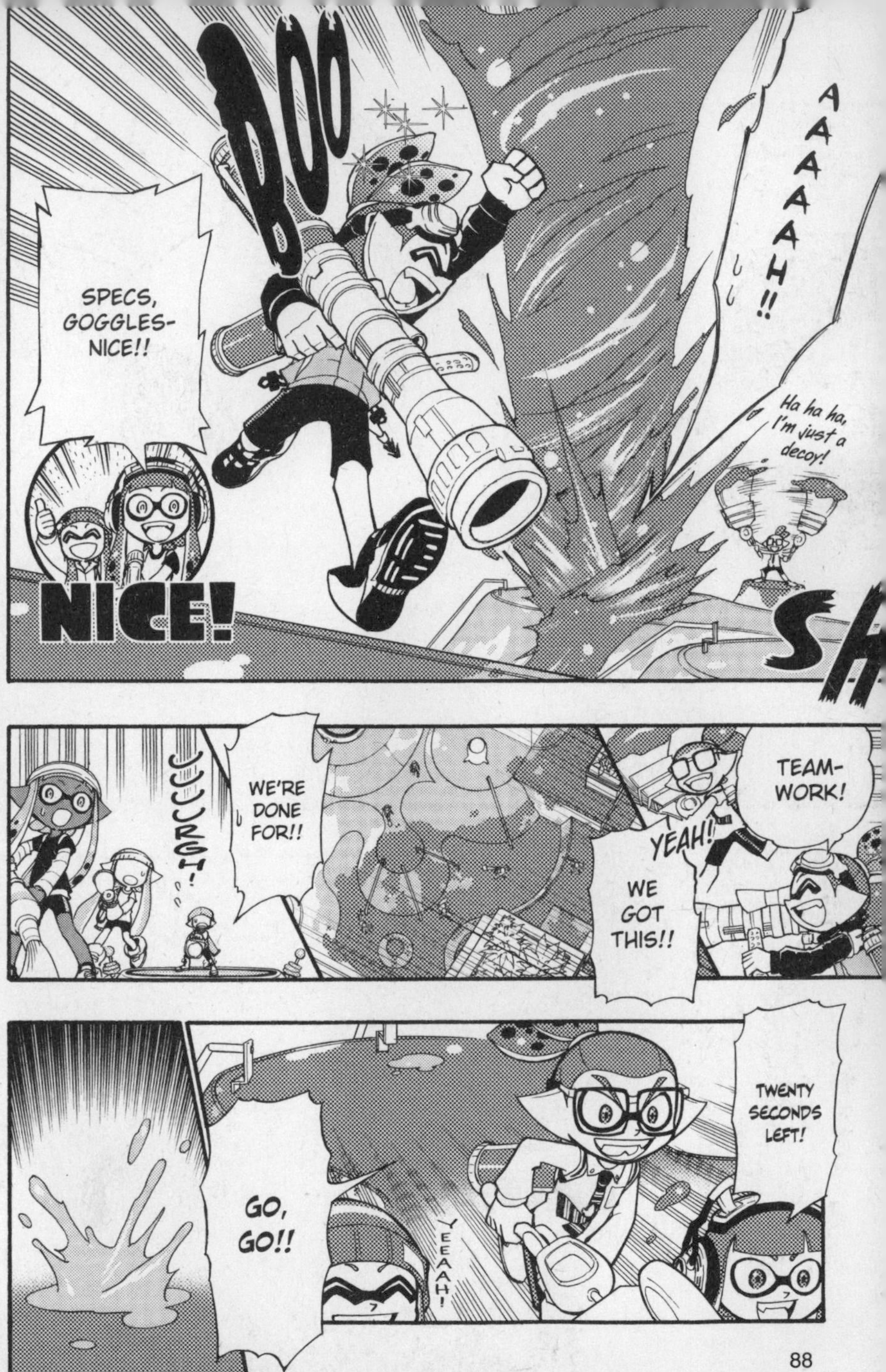

AAAAAH!!
Ha ha ha, I'm just a decoy!
BOO
SPECS, GOGGLES-NICE!!
NICE!
SH
TEAM-WORK!
YEAH!
WE GOT THIS!!
WE'RE DONE FOR!!
UUURGH!
TWENTY SECONDS LEFT!
YEEAAAH!
GO, GO!!

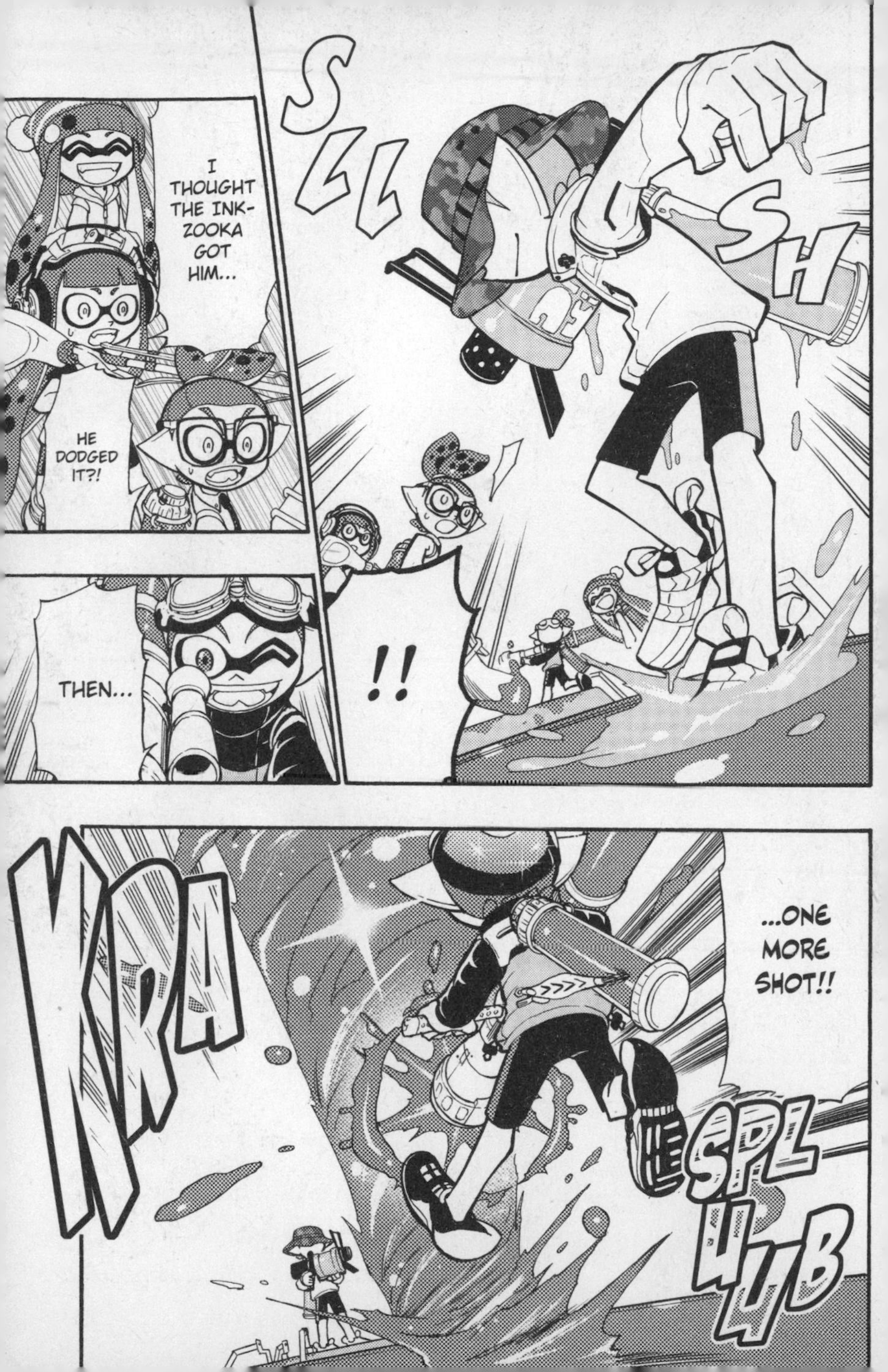
SLLSH
!!
I THOUGHT THE INK-ZOOKA GOT HIM...
HE DODGED IT?!
THEN...
...ONE MORE SHOT!!
KRA
SPLUUB

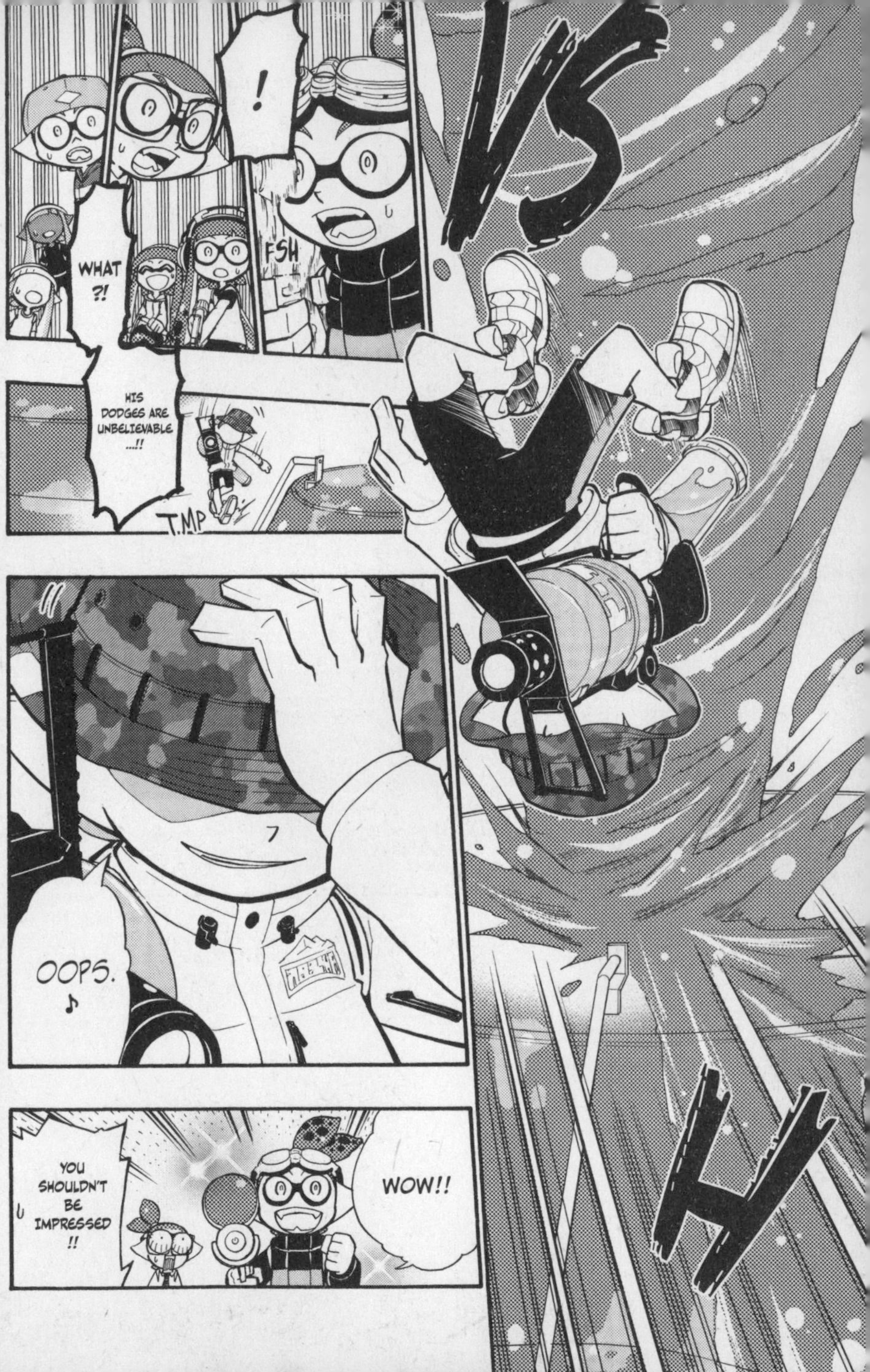
!
FSH
WHAT ?!
HIS DODGES ARE UNBELIEVABLE ...!!
T.MP
OOPS. ♪
WOW!!
YOU SHOULDN'T BE IMPRESSED !!

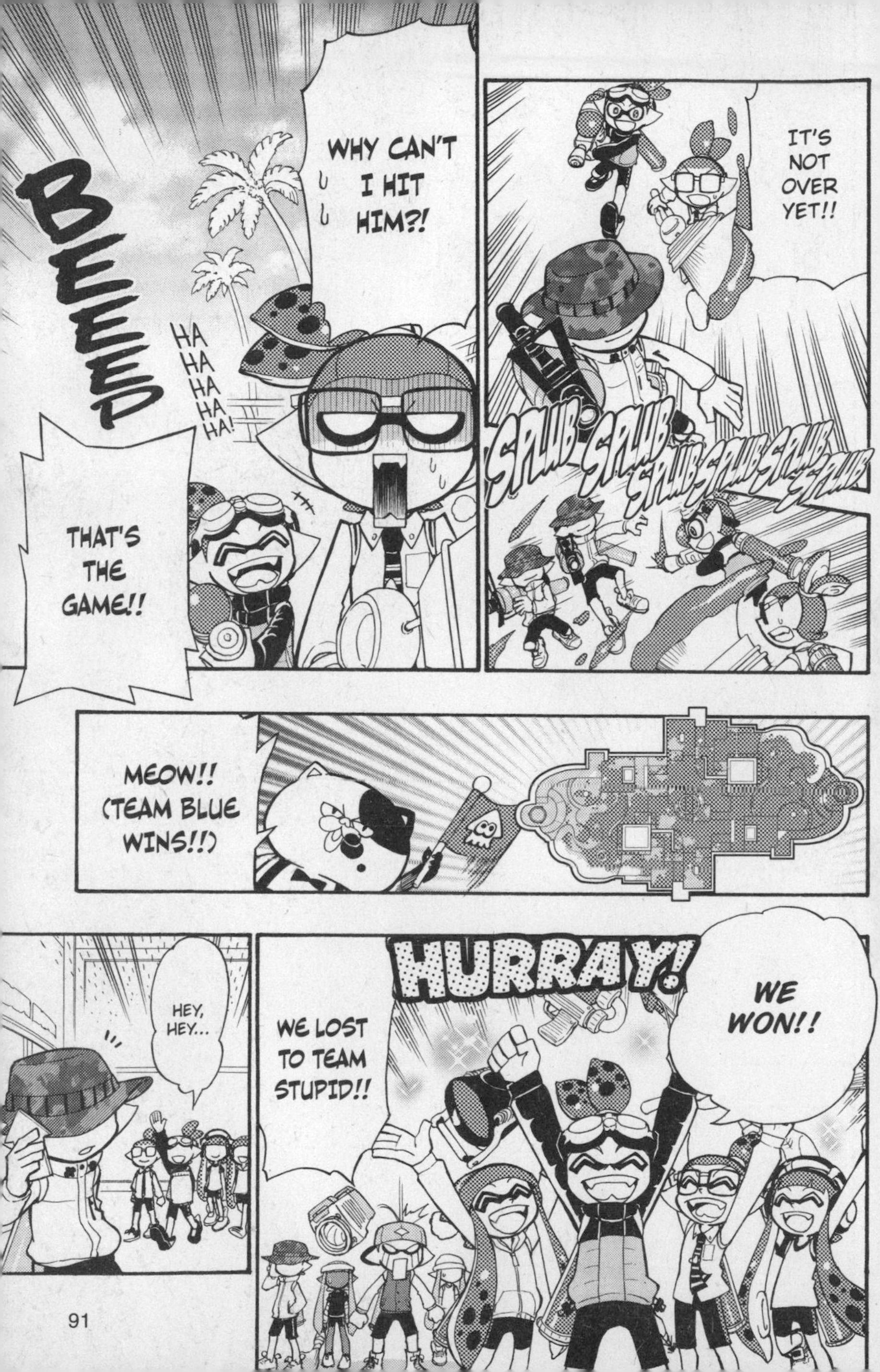
IT'S NOT OVER YET!!
SPLUB SPLUB SPLUB SPLUB SPLUB SPLUB SPLUB
WHY CAN'T I HIT HIM?!
BEEEP
HA HA HA HA HA!
THAT'S THE GAME!!
MEOW!! (TEAM BLUE WINS!!)
HURRAY!
WE WON!!
WE LOST TO TEAM STUPID!!
HEY, HEY...

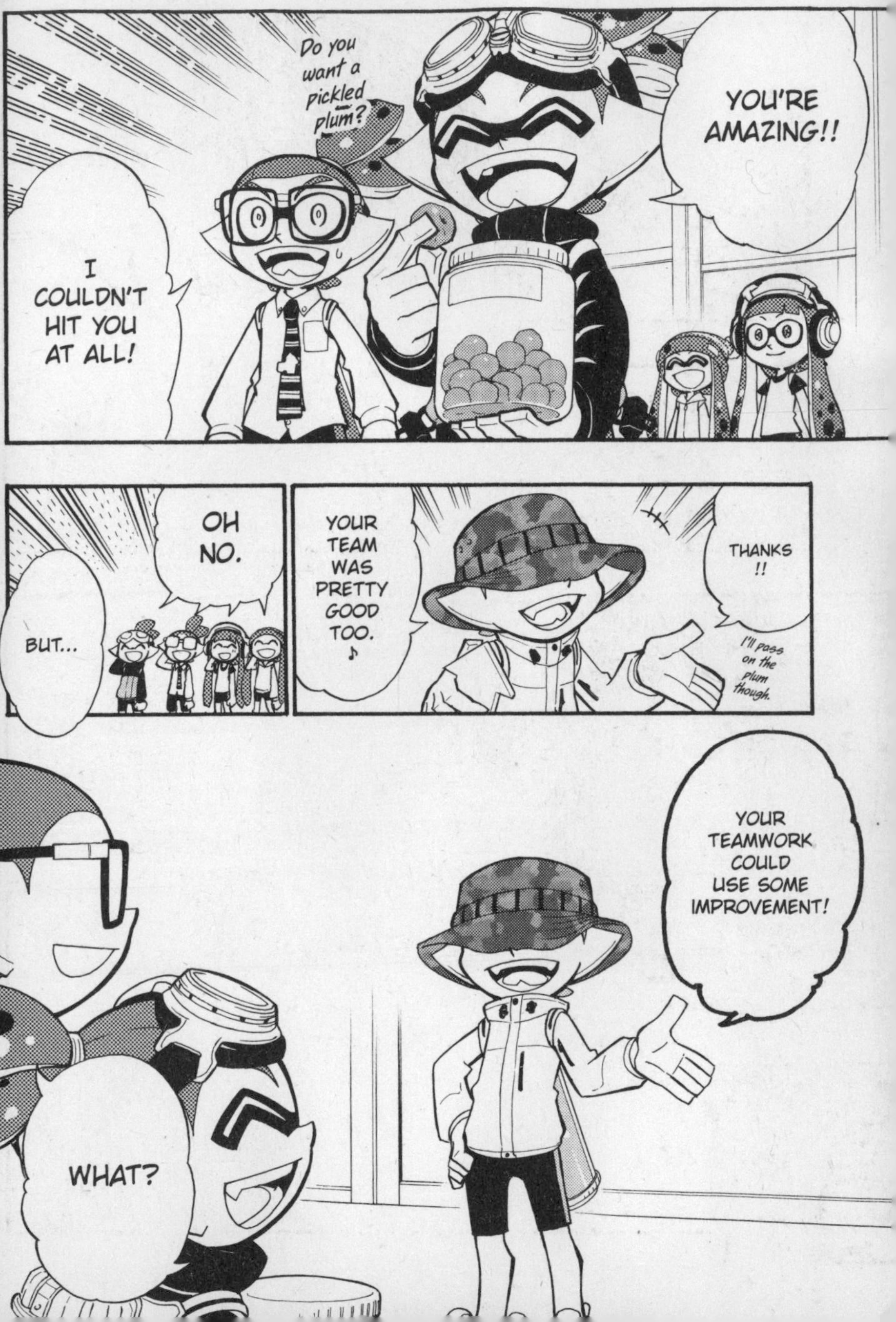
YOU'RE AMAZING!!
Do you want a pickled plum?
I COULDN'T HIT YOU AT ALL!
THANKS !!
I'll pass on the plum though.
YOUR TEAM WAS PRETTY GOOD TOO. ♪
OH NO.
BUT...
YOUR TEAMWORK COULD USE SOME IMPROVEMENT!
WHAT?

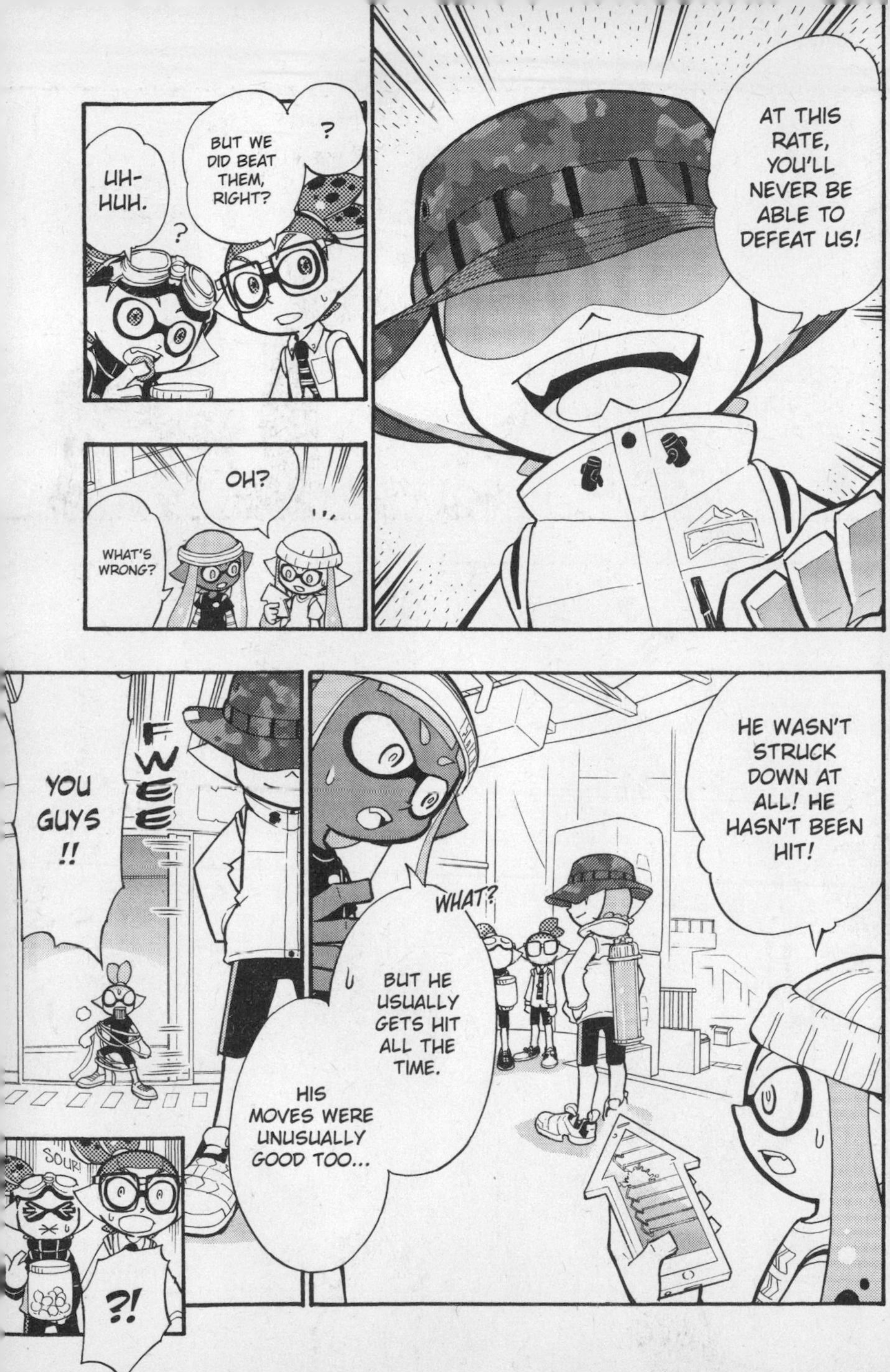
AT THIS RATE, YOU'LL NEVER BE ABLE TO DEFEAT US!
?
BUT WE DID BEAT THEM, RIGHT?
UH-HUH.
?
OH?
WHAT'S WRONG?
HE WASN'T STRUCK DOWN AT ALL! HE HASN'T BEEN HIT!
WHAT?
BUT HE USUALLY GETS HIT ALL THE TIME.
HIS MOVES WERE UNUSUALLY GOOD TOO...
FWEE
YOU GUYS!!
SOUR!
?!

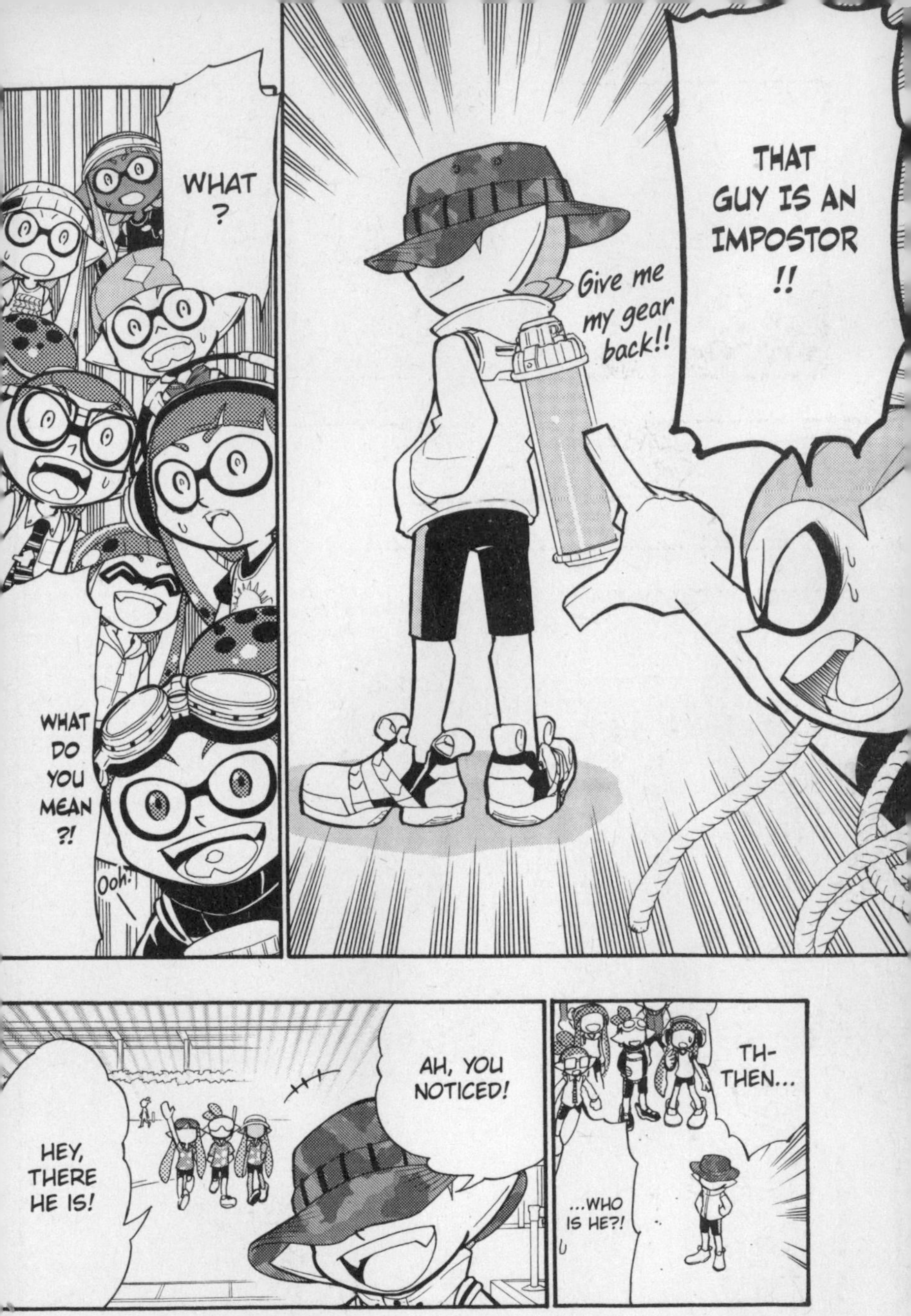
THAT GUY IS AN IMPOSTOR !!
Give me my gear back!!
WHAT ?
WHAT DO YOU MEAN ?!
Ooh!
TH- THEN...
...WHO IS HE?!
AH, YOU NOTICED!
HEY, THERE HE IS!

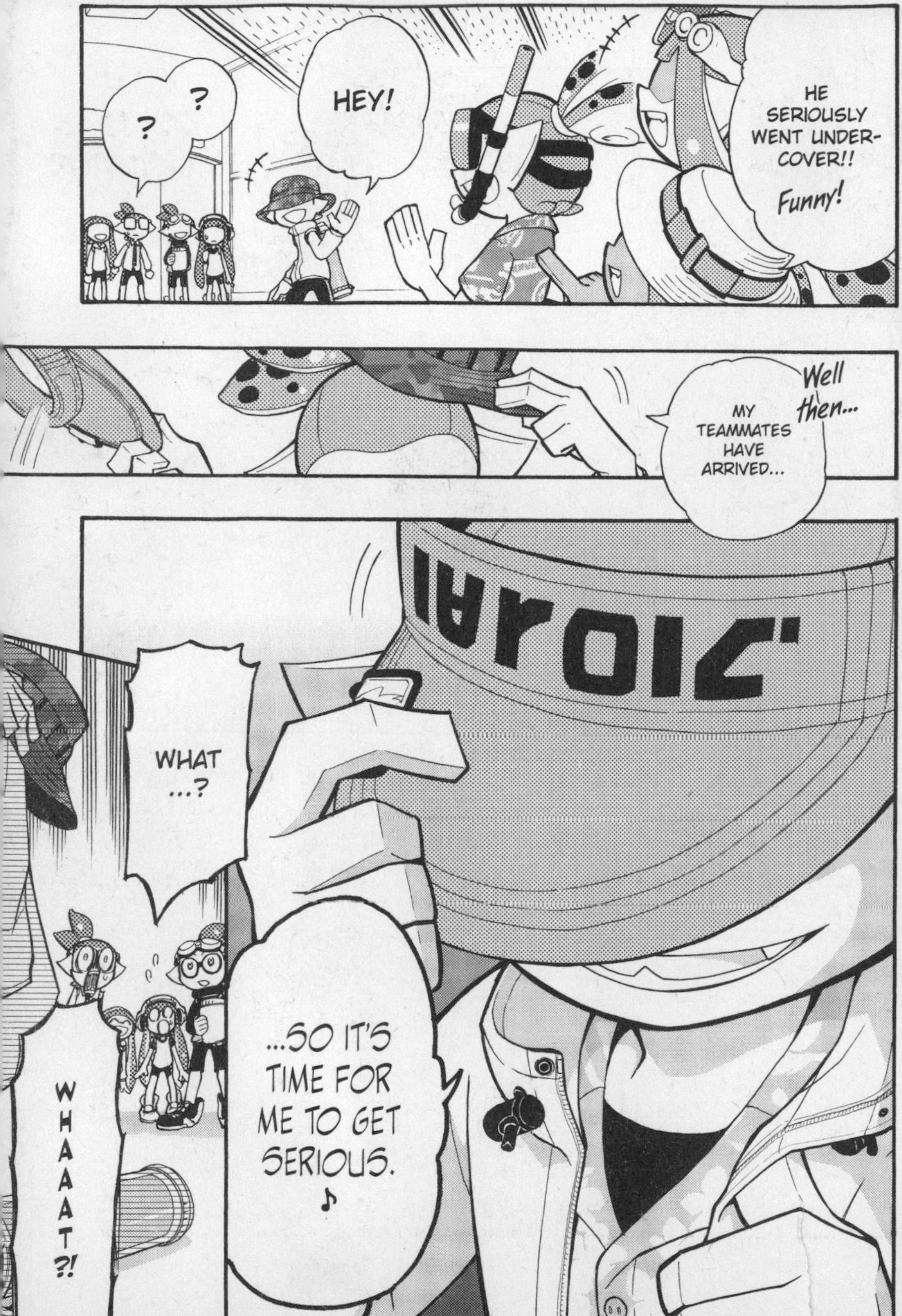
HE SERIOUSLY WENT UNDER-COVER!!
Funny!
HEY!
? ?
Well then...
MY TEAMMATES HAVE ARRIVED...
...SO IT'S TIME FOR ME TO GET SERIOUS. ♪
WHAT ...?
WHAAAAT?!

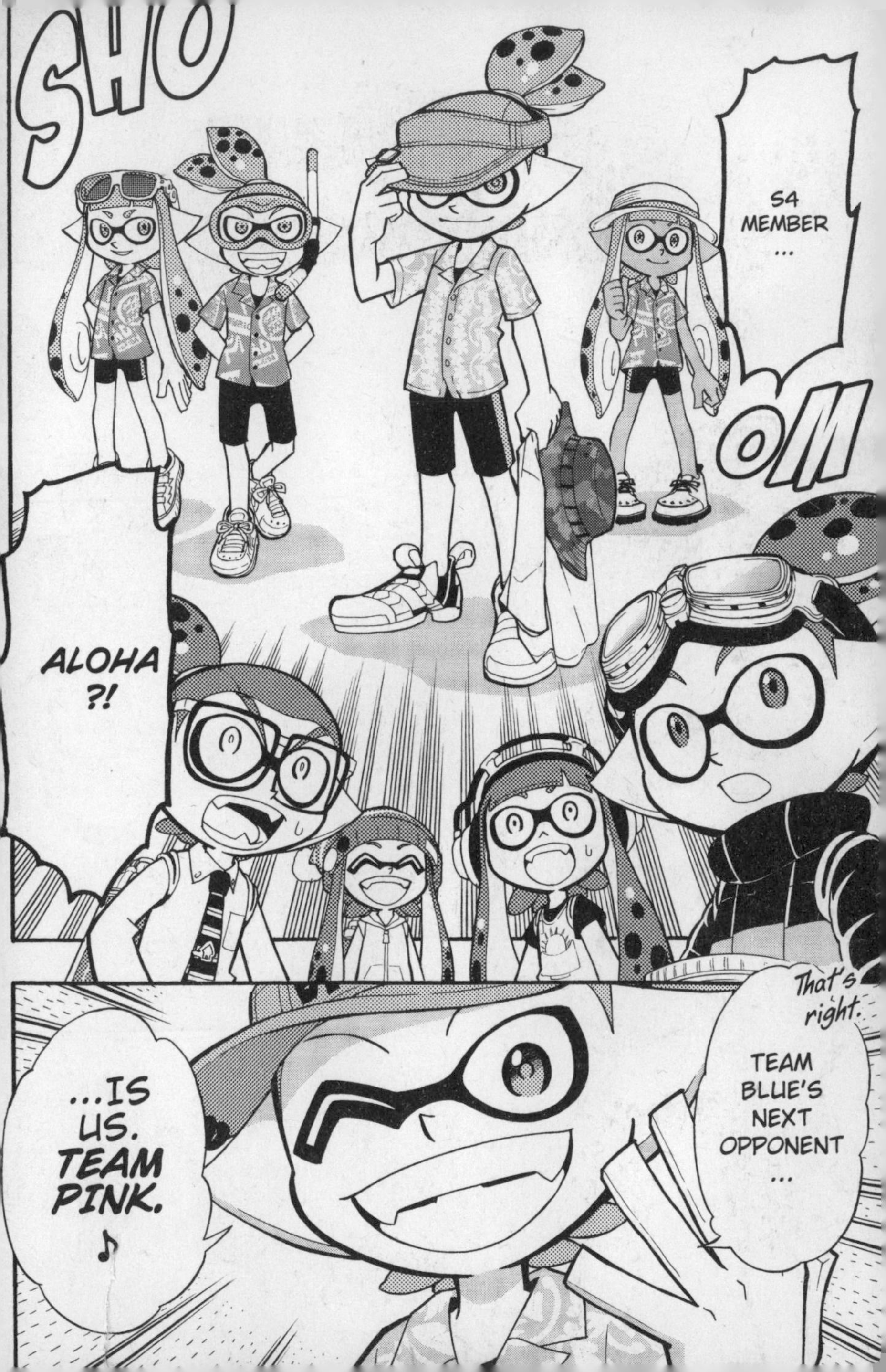
S4 MEMBER ...
SHO
OM
ALOHA ?!
That's right.
TEAM BLUE'S NEXT OPPONENT ...
...IS US. TEAM PINK. ♪

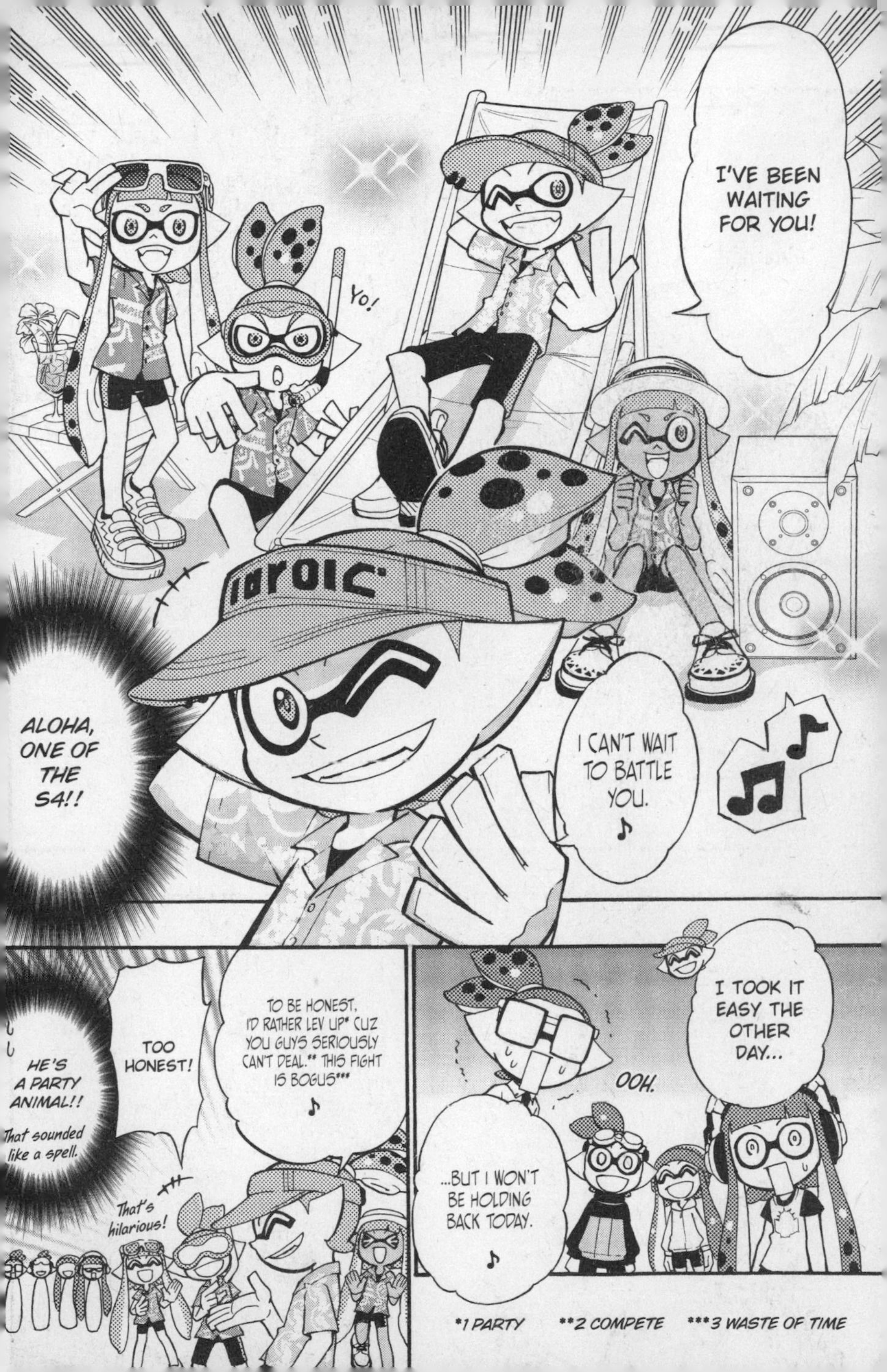
I'VE BEEN WAITING FOR YOU!
Yo!
I CAN'T WAIT TO BATTLE YOU. ♪
ALOHA, ONE OF THE S4!!
I TOOK IT EASY THE OTHER DAY...
OOH.
...BUT I WON'T BE HOLDING BACK TODAY. ♪
TO BE HONEST, I'D RATHER LEV UP* CUZ YOU GUYS SERIOUSLY CAN'T DEAL.** THIS FIGHT IS BOGUS*** ♪
TOO HONEST!
HE'S A PARTY ANIMAL!!
That sounded like a spell.
That's hilarious!
*1 PARTY **2 COMPETE ***3 WASTE OF TIME

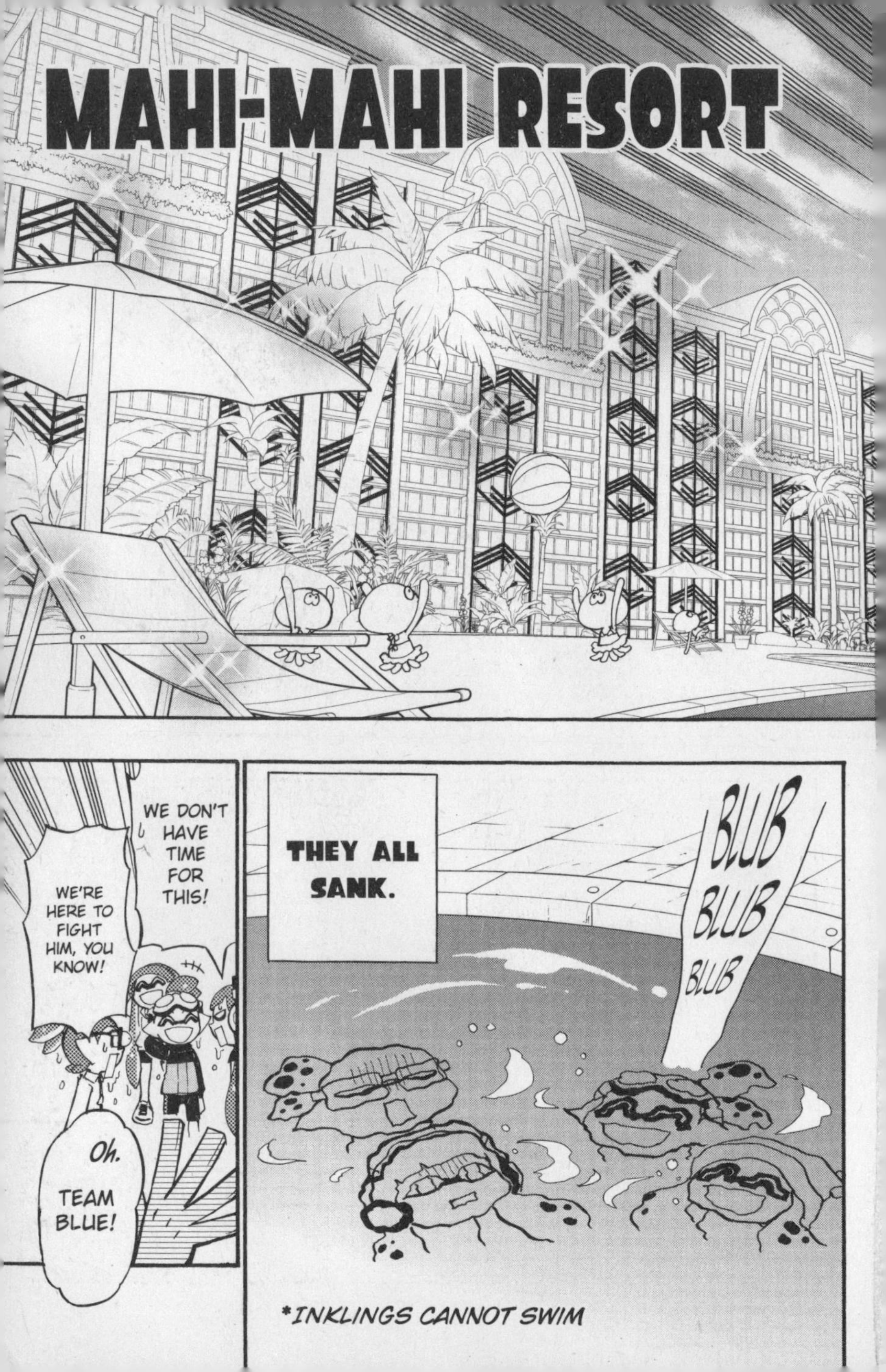
MAHI-MAHI RESORT
THEY ALL SANK.
BLUB BLUB BLUB
*INKLINGS CANNOT SWIM
WE DON'T HAVE TIME FOR THIS!
WE'RE HERE TO FIGHT HIM, YOU KNOW!
Oh.
TEAM BLUE!

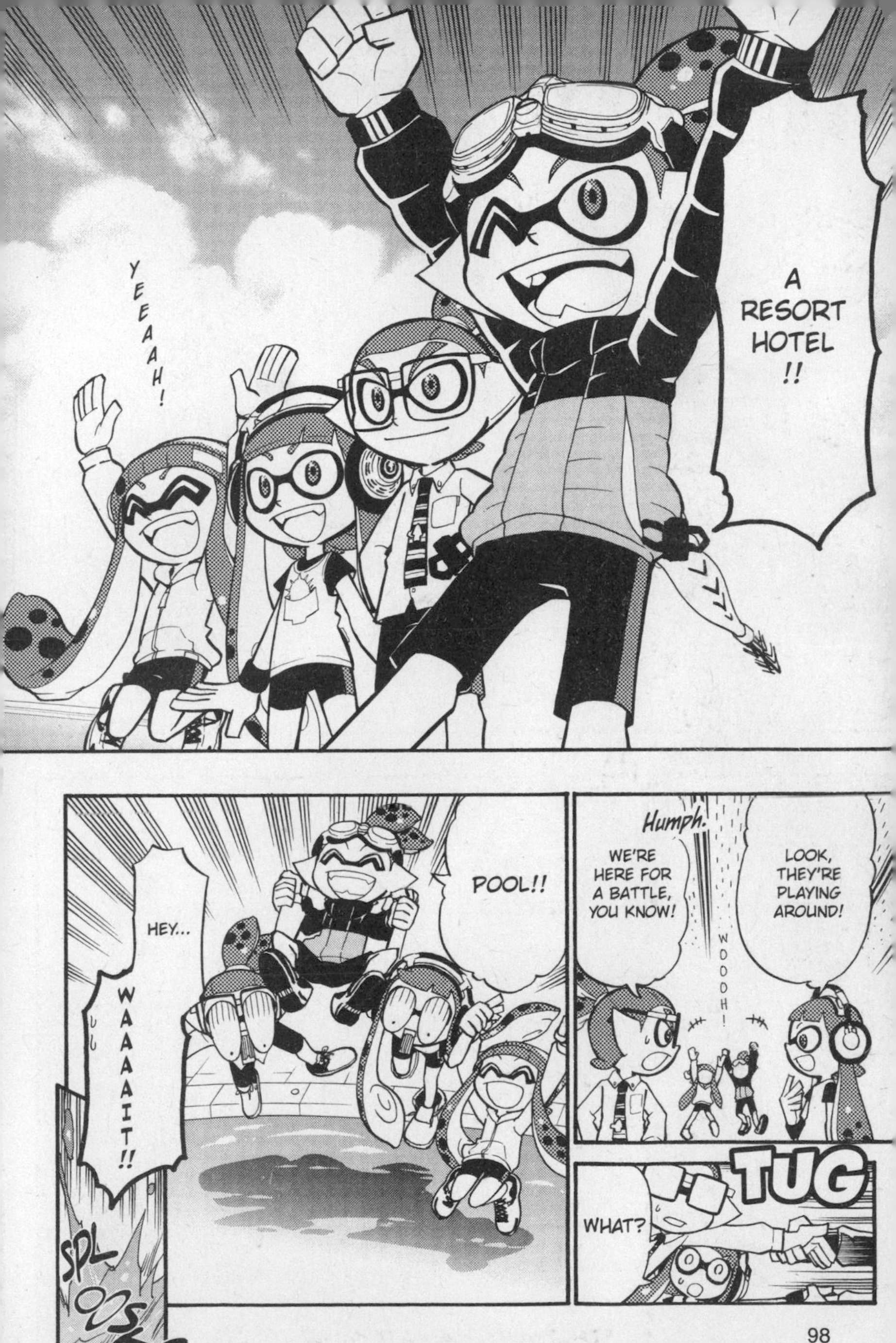
A RESORT HOTEL !!
YEEAAAH!
LOOK, THEY'RE PLAYING AROUND!
WOOOH!
Humph.
WE'RE HERE FOR A BATTLE, YOU KNOW!
TUG
WHAT?
POOL!!
HEY...
WAAAAAIT!!
SPLOOSH

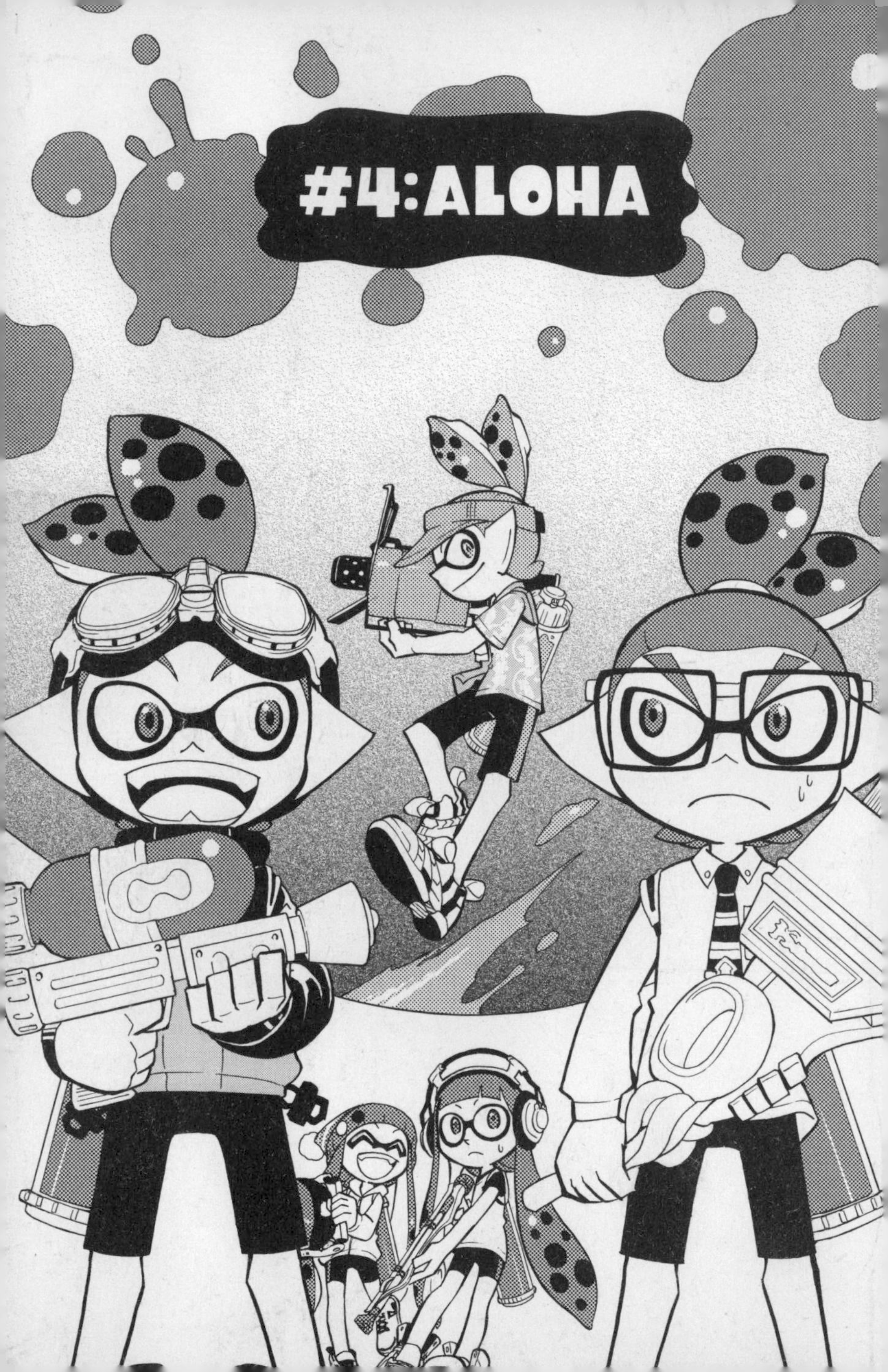
#4: ALOHA

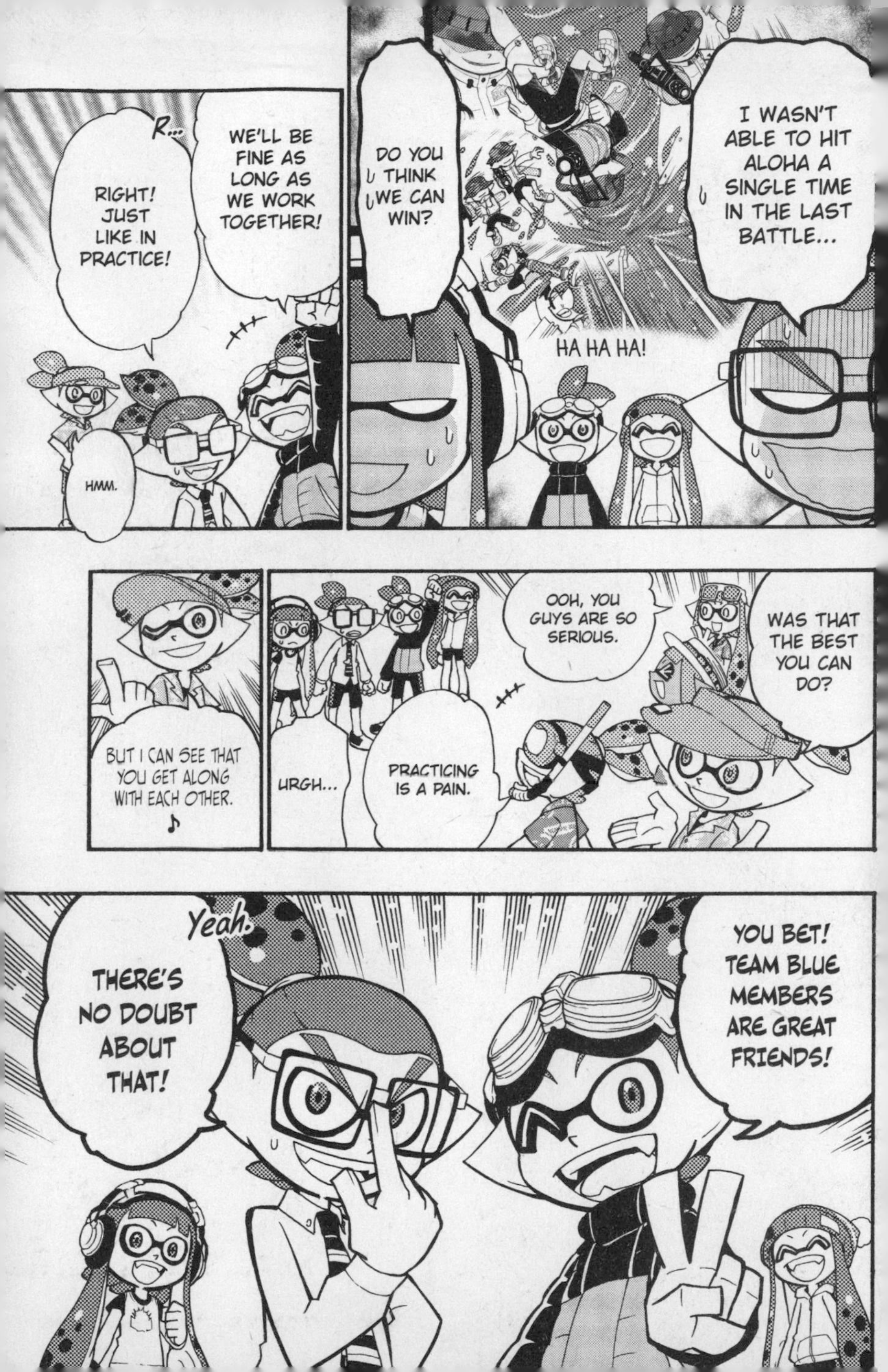
I WASN'T ABLE TO HIT ALOHA A SINGLE TIME IN THE LAST BATTLE...
HA HA HA!
DO YOU THINK WE CAN WIN?
WE'LL BE FINE AS LONG AS WE WORK TOGETHER!
R...
RIGHT! JUST LIKE IN PRACTICE!
HMM.
WAS THAT THE BEST YOU CAN DO?
OOH, YOU GUYS ARE SO SERIOUS.
PRACTICING IS A PAIN.
URGH...
BUT I CAN SEE THAT YOU GET ALONG WITH EACH OTHER. ♪
YOU BET! TEAM BLUE MEMBERS ARE GREAT FRIENDS!
Yeah.
THERE'S NO DOUBT ABOUT THAT!

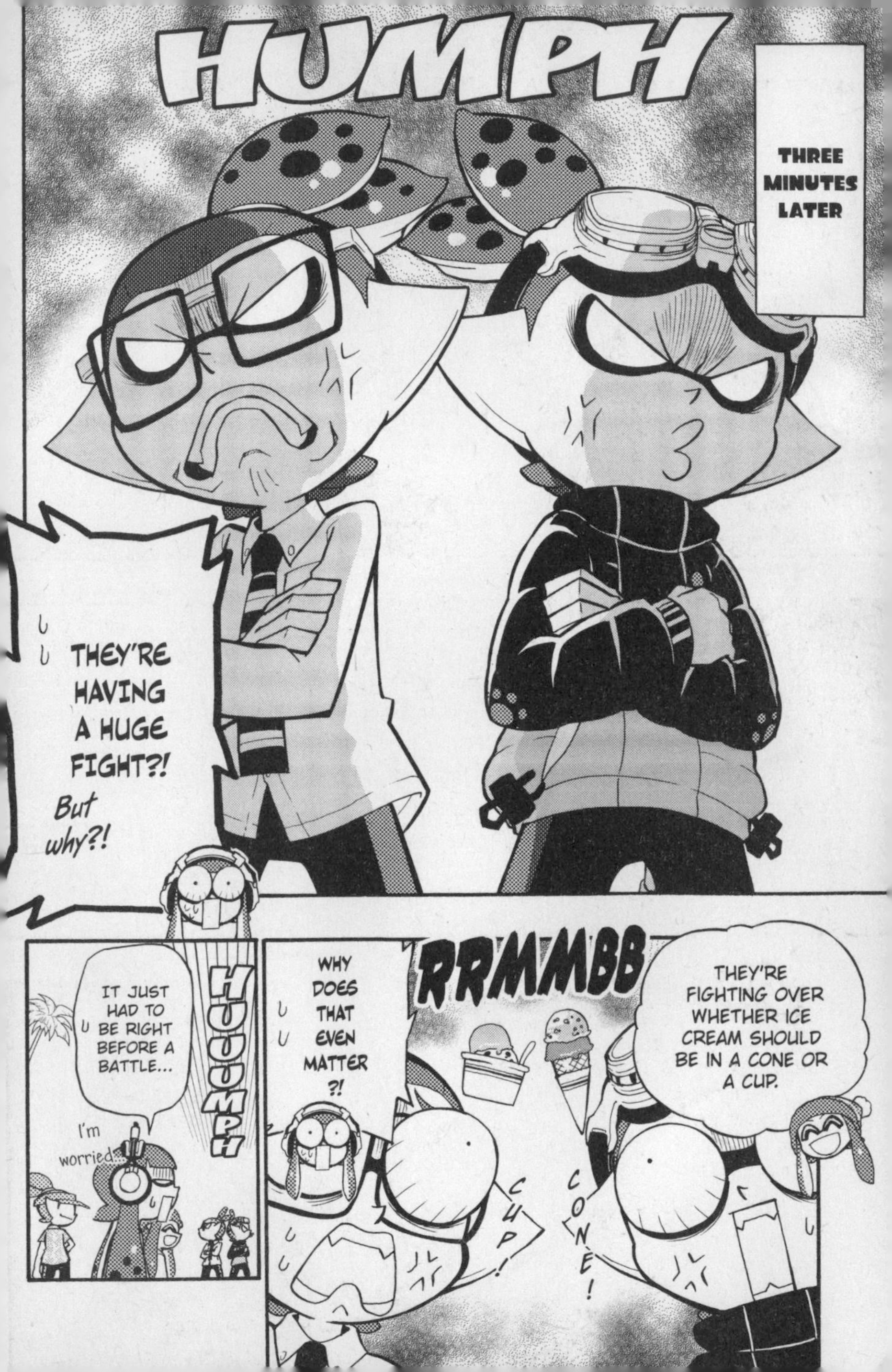
HUMPH
THREE MINUTES LATER
THEY'RE HAVING A HUGE FIGHT?!
But why?!
RRMMBB
THEY'RE FIGHTING OVER WHETHER ICE CREAM SHOULD BE IN A CONE OR A CUP.
WHY DOES THAT EVEN MATTER?!
CONE!
CUP!
HUUUUMPH
IT JUST HAD TO BE RIGHT BEFORE A BATTLE...
I'm worried...

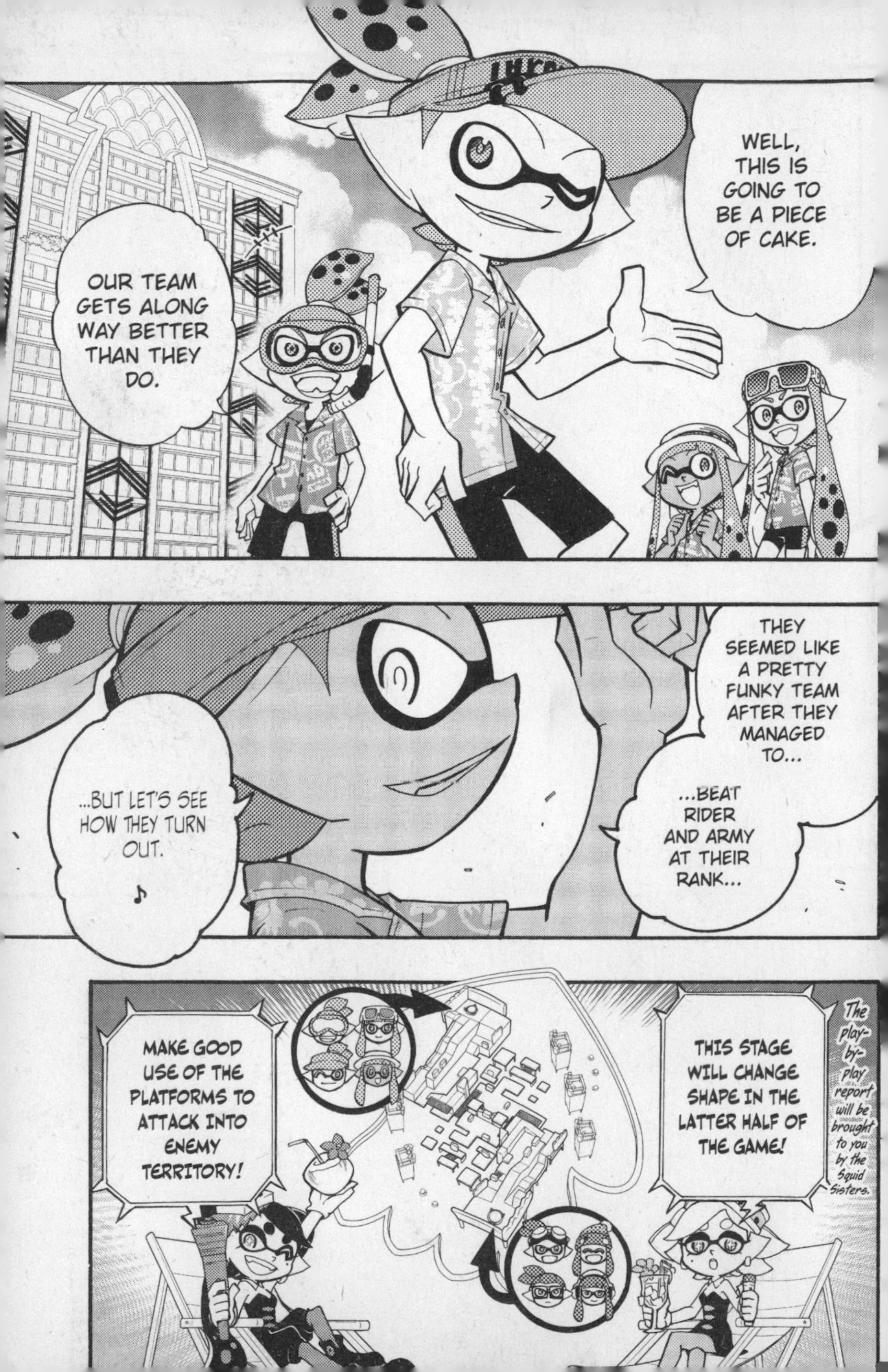
WELL, THIS IS GOING TO BE A PIECE OF CAKE.
OUR TEAM GETS ALONG WAY BETTER THAN THEY DO.
THEY SEEMED LIKE A PRETTY FUNKY TEAM AFTER THEY MANAGED TO...
...BEAT RIDER AND ARMY AT THEIR RANK...
...BUT LET'S SEE HOW THEY TURN OUT. ♪
The play-by-play report will be brought to you by the Squid Sisters.
THIS STAGE WILL CHANGE SHAPE IN THE LATTER HALF OF THE GAME!
MAKE GOOD USE OF THE PLATFORMS TO ATTACK INTO ENEMY TERRITORY!

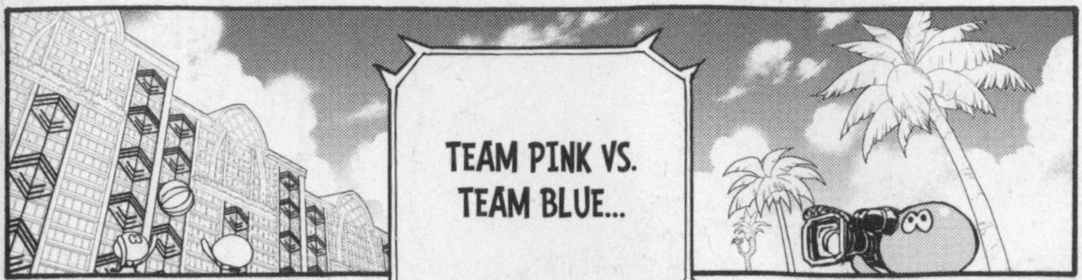
TEAM PINK VS.
TEAM BLUE...
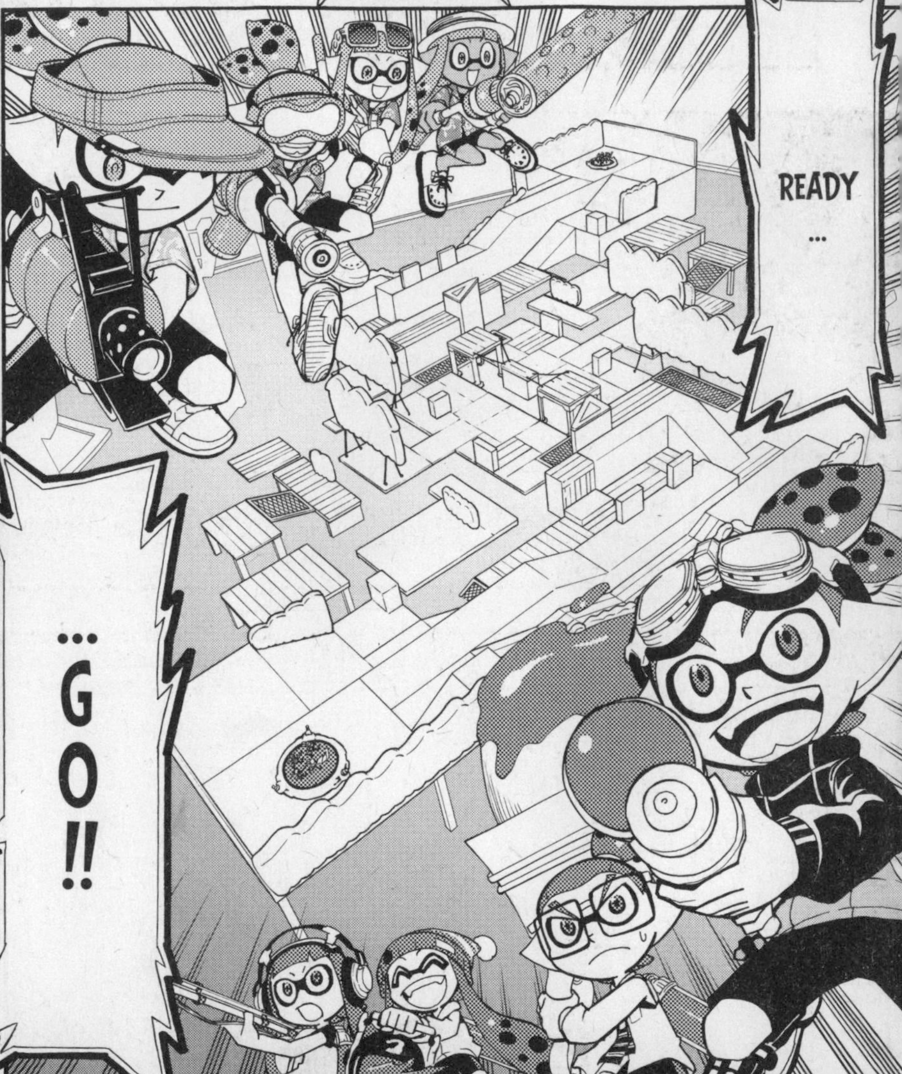
READY
...
...GO!!

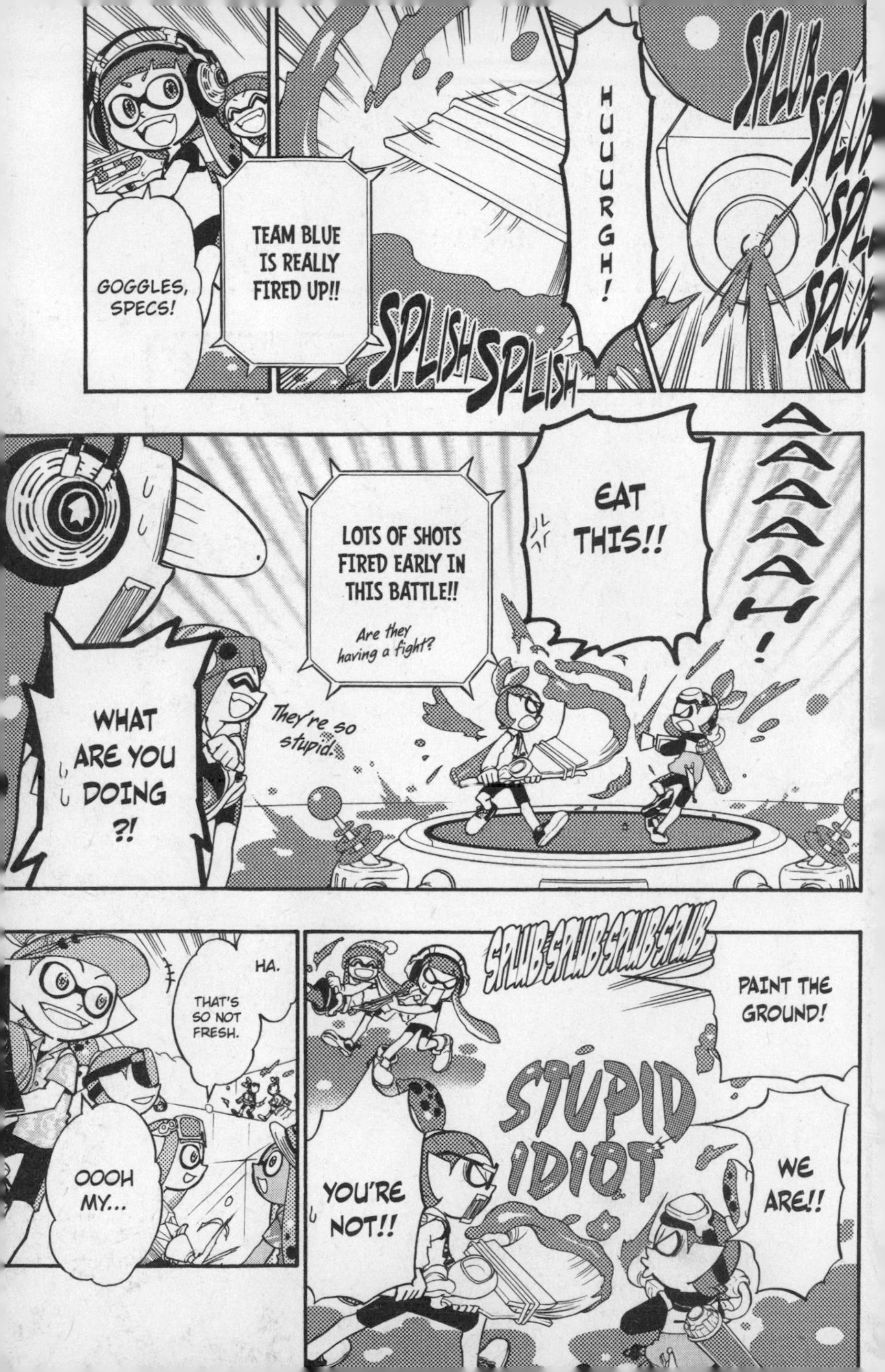
SPLUB SPLUB SPLUB SPLUB
HUUURGH!
SPLISH SPLISH
TEAM BLUE IS REALLY FIRED UP!!
GOGGLES, SPECS!
AAAAAH!
EAT THIS!!
LOTS OF SHOTS FIRED EARLY IN THIS BATTLE!!
Are they having a fight?
They're so stupid.
WHAT ARE YOU DOING ?!
SPLUB SPLUB SPLUB SPLUB
PAINT THE GROUND!
WE ARE!!
STUPID IDIOT
YOU'RE NOT!!
HA.
THAT'S SO NOT FRESH.
OOOH MY...

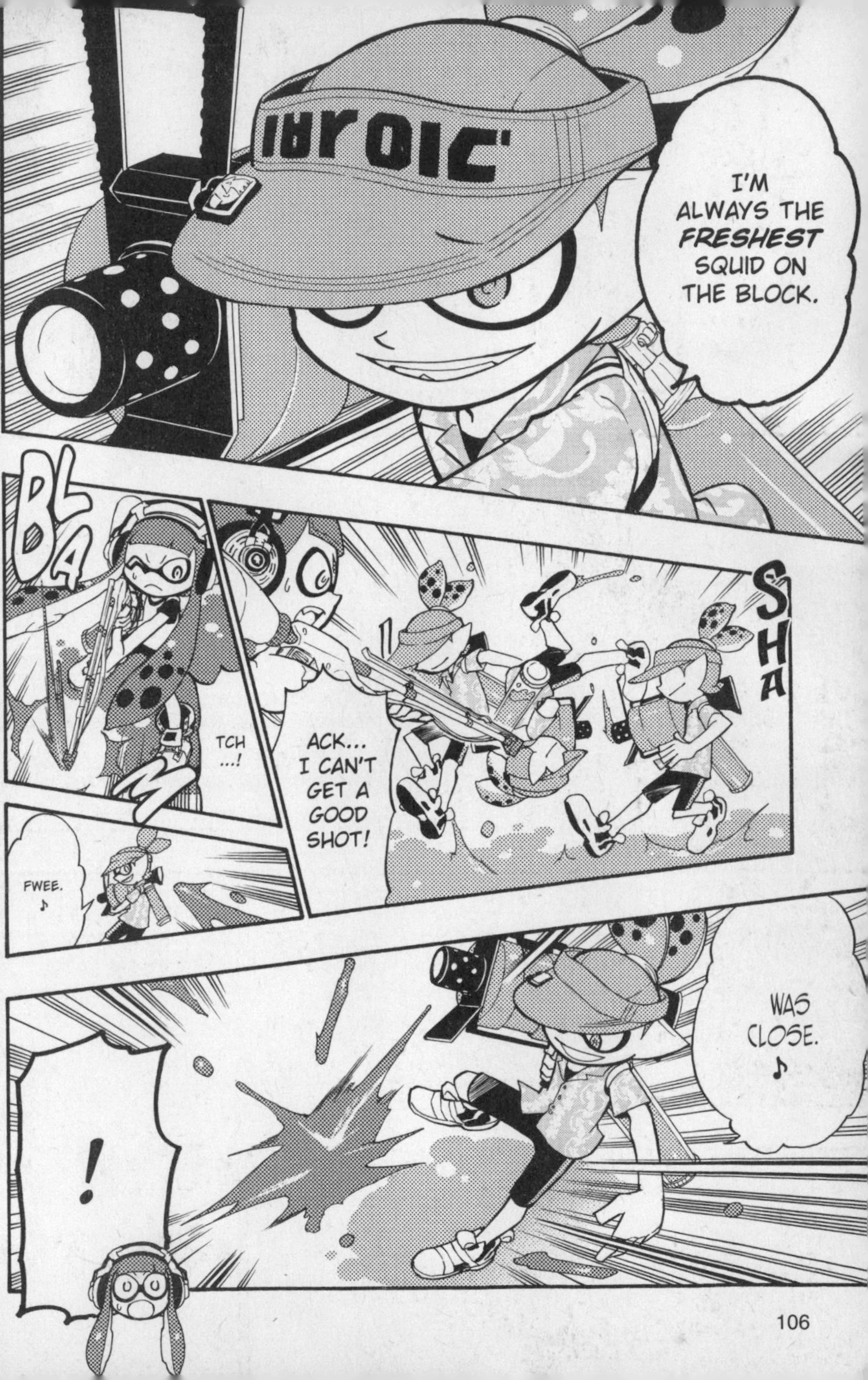
I'M ALWAYS THE FRESHEST SQUID ON THE BLOCK.
SHA
ACK... I CAN'T GET A GOOD SHOT!
BLAM
TCH ...!
FWEE. ♪
WAS CLOSE. ♪
!

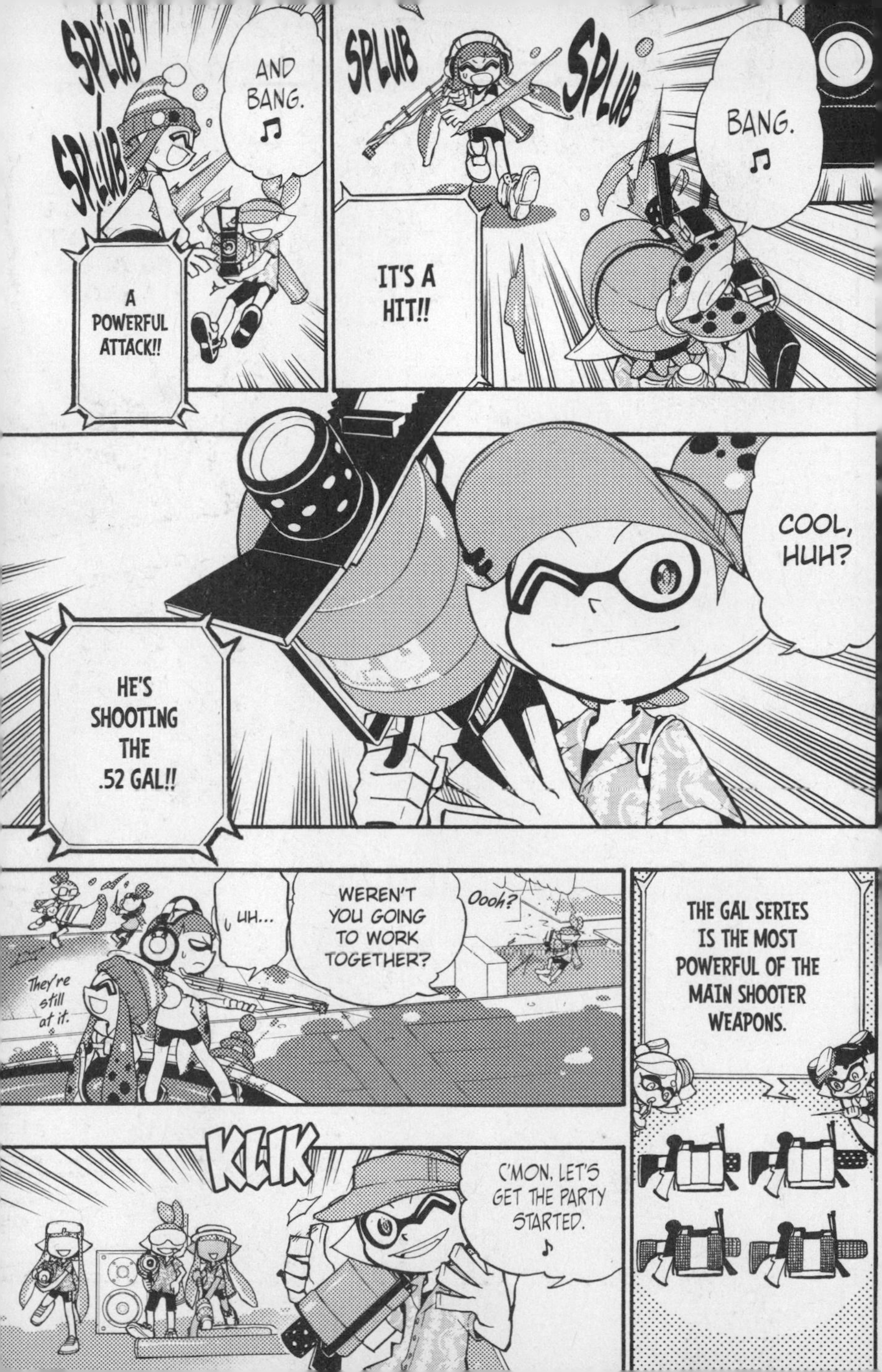
SPLUB
BANG. ♫
SPLUB
IT'S A HIT!!
SPLUB
SPLUB
AND BANG. ♫
A POWERFUL ATTACK!!
COOL, HUH?
HE'S SHOOTING THE .52 GAL!!
THE GAL SERIES IS THE MOST POWERFUL OF THE MAIN SHOOTER WEAPONS.
Oooh?
WEREN'T YOU GOING TO WORK TOGETHER?
UH...
They're still at it.
KLIK
C'MON, LET'S GET THE PARTY STARTED. ♪

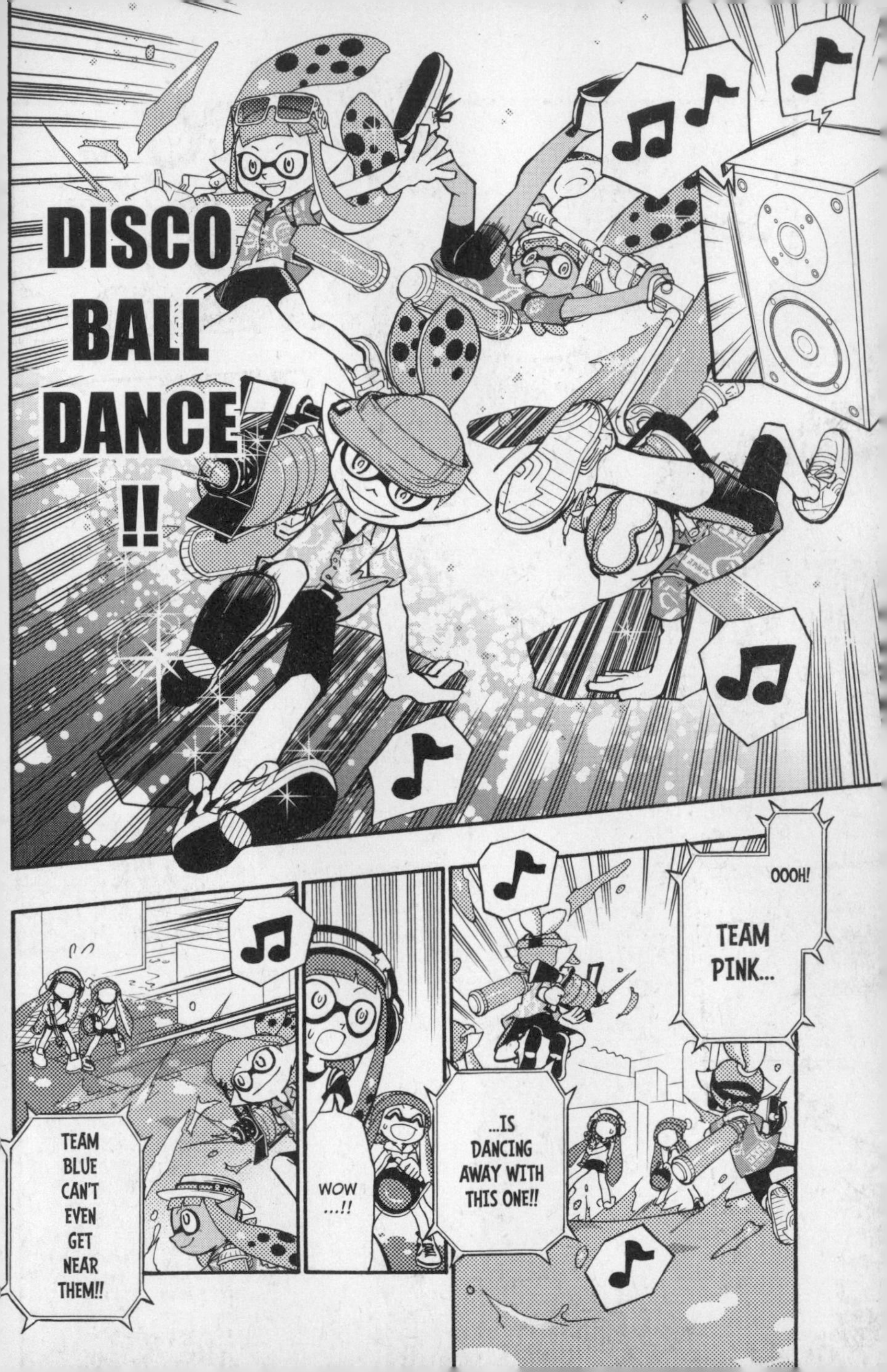
DISCO BALL DANCE !!
OOOH!
TEAM PINK...
...IS DANCING AWAY WITH THIS ONE!!
WOW ...!!
TEAM BLUE CAN'T EVEN GET NEAR THEM!!

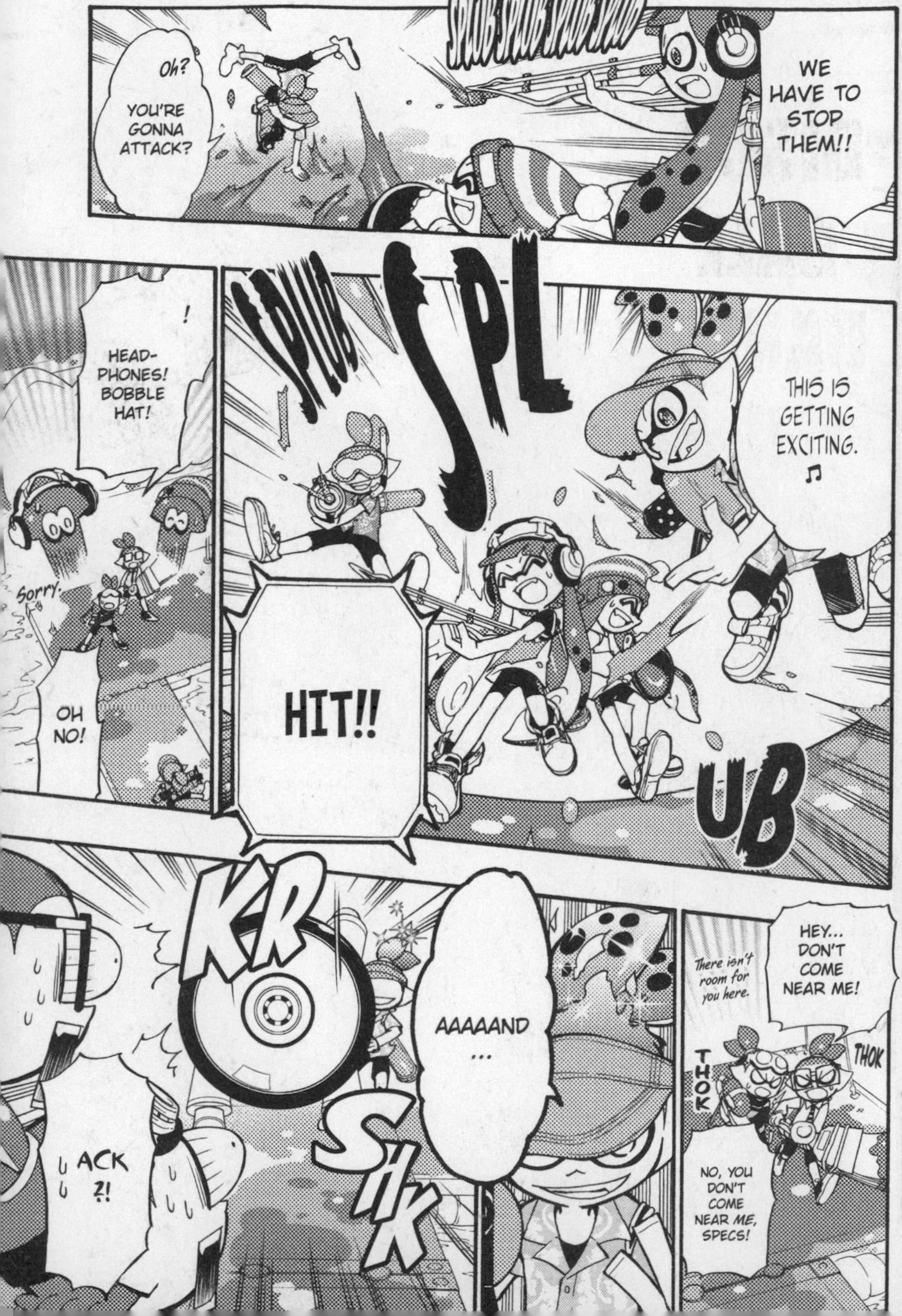
WE HAVE TO STOP THEM!!
SPLUB SPLUB SPLUB SPLUB
Oh?
YOU'RE GONNA ATTACK?
THIS IS GETTING EXCITING. ♪
SPL
UB
SPLUB
HIT!!
!
HEAD-PHONES! BOBBLE HAT!
Sorry.
OH NO!
HEY... DON'T COME NEAR ME!
There isn't room for you here.
THOK
THOK
NO, YOU DON'T COME NEAR ME, SPECS!
AAAAAND ...
KR
SHK
ACK ?!

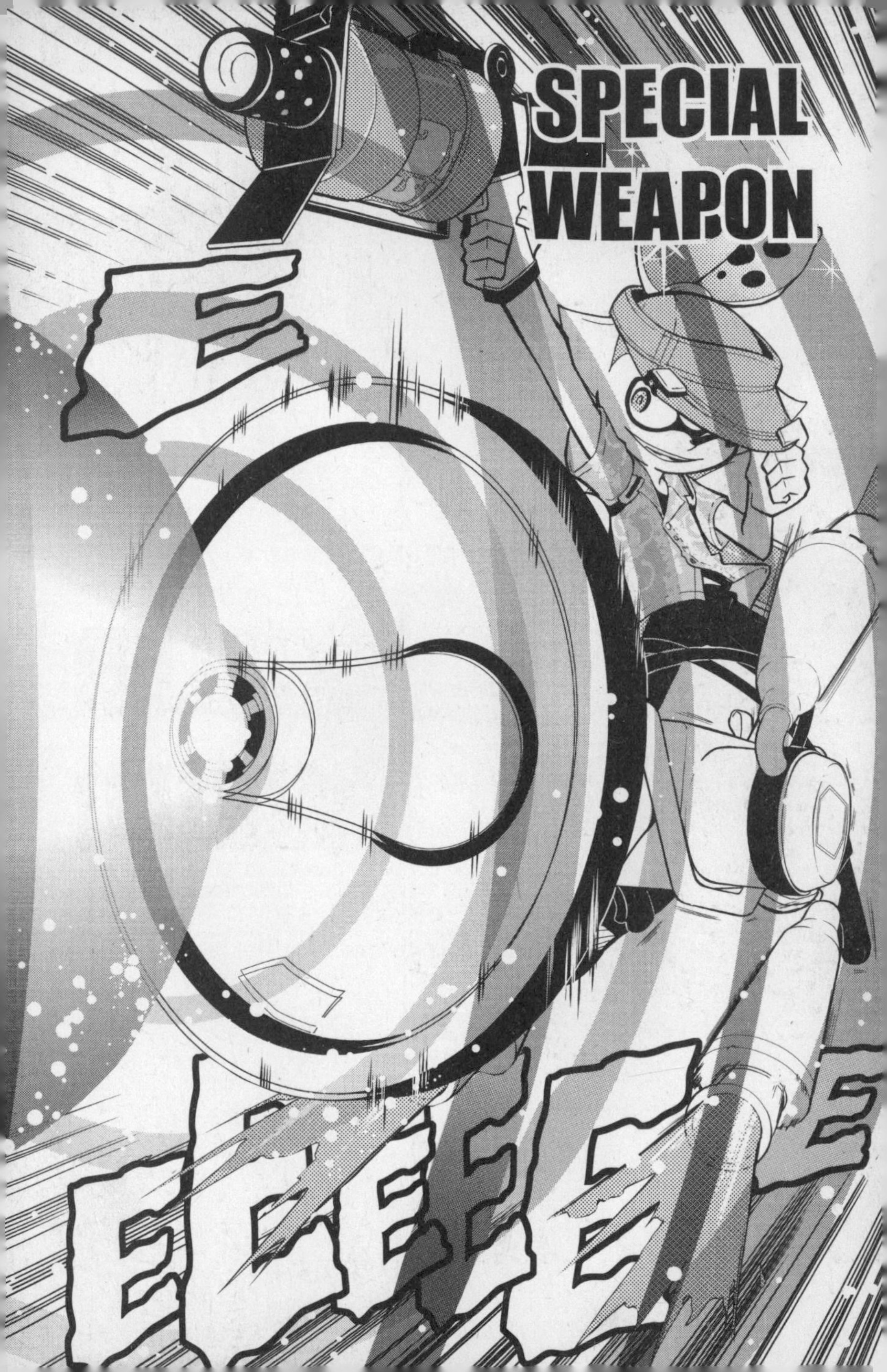
SPECIAL WEAPON
EEEEEE

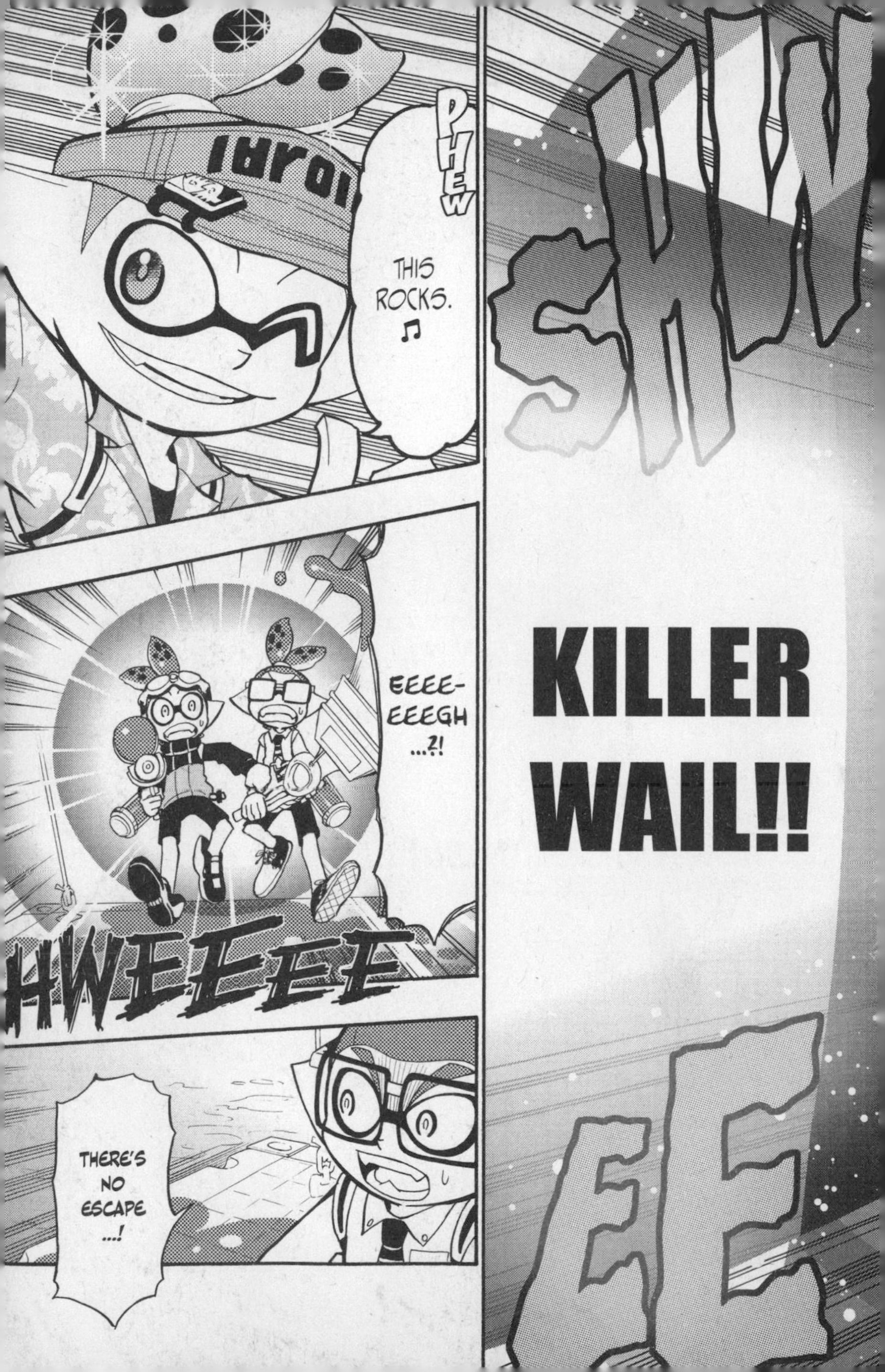
KILLER WAIL!!
EE
PHEW
THIS ROCKS. ♫
EEEE-EEEGH ...?!
HWEEEEE
THERE'S NO ESCAPE ...!

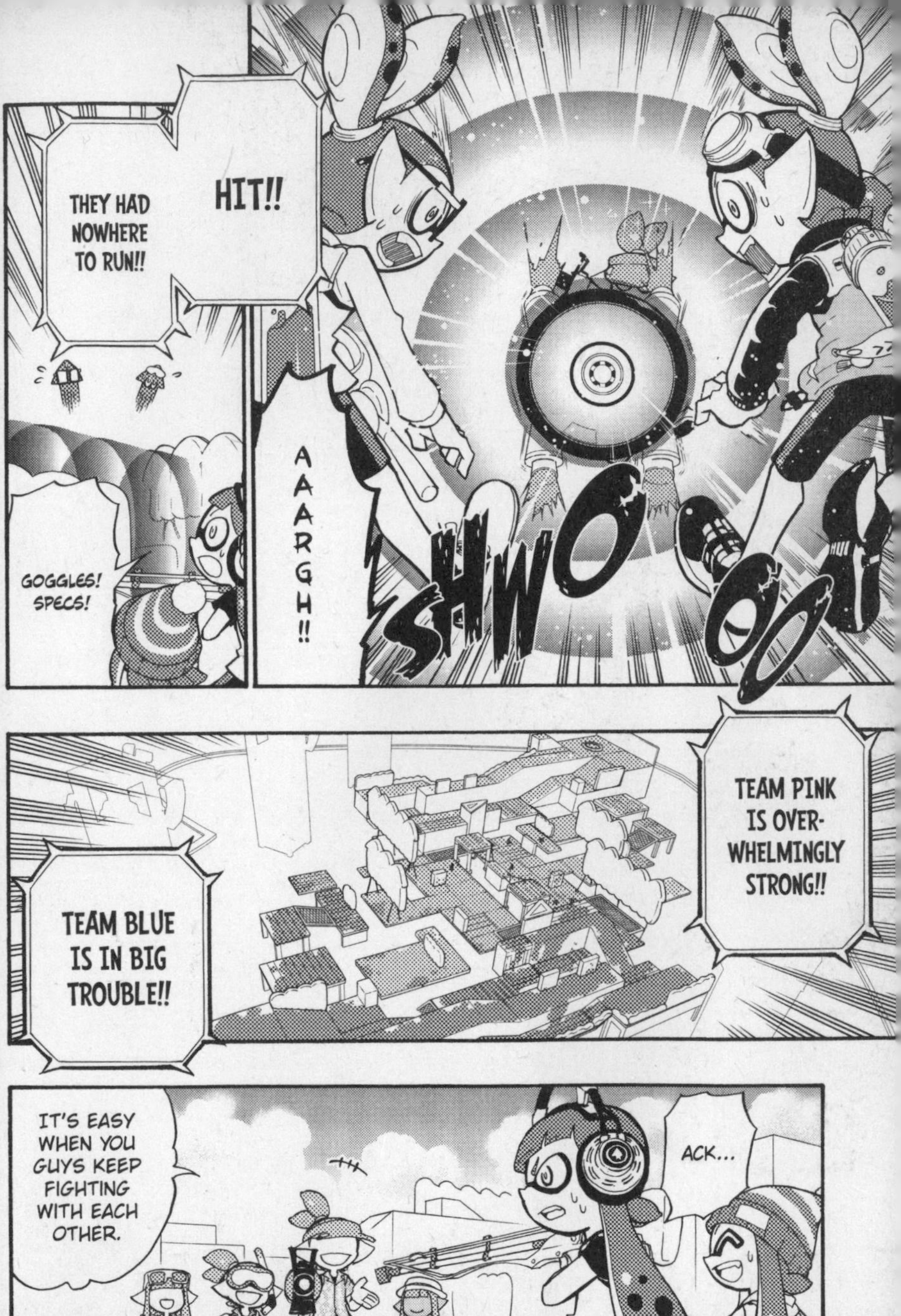
THEY HAD NOWHERE TO RUN!! HIT!!
AAARGH!!
SHWOOO
GOGGLES! SPECS!
TEAM PINK IS OVER-WHELMINGLY STRONG!!
TEAM BLUE IS IN BIG TROUBLE!!
ACK...
IT'S EASY WHEN YOU GUYS KEEP FIGHTING WITH EACH OTHER.

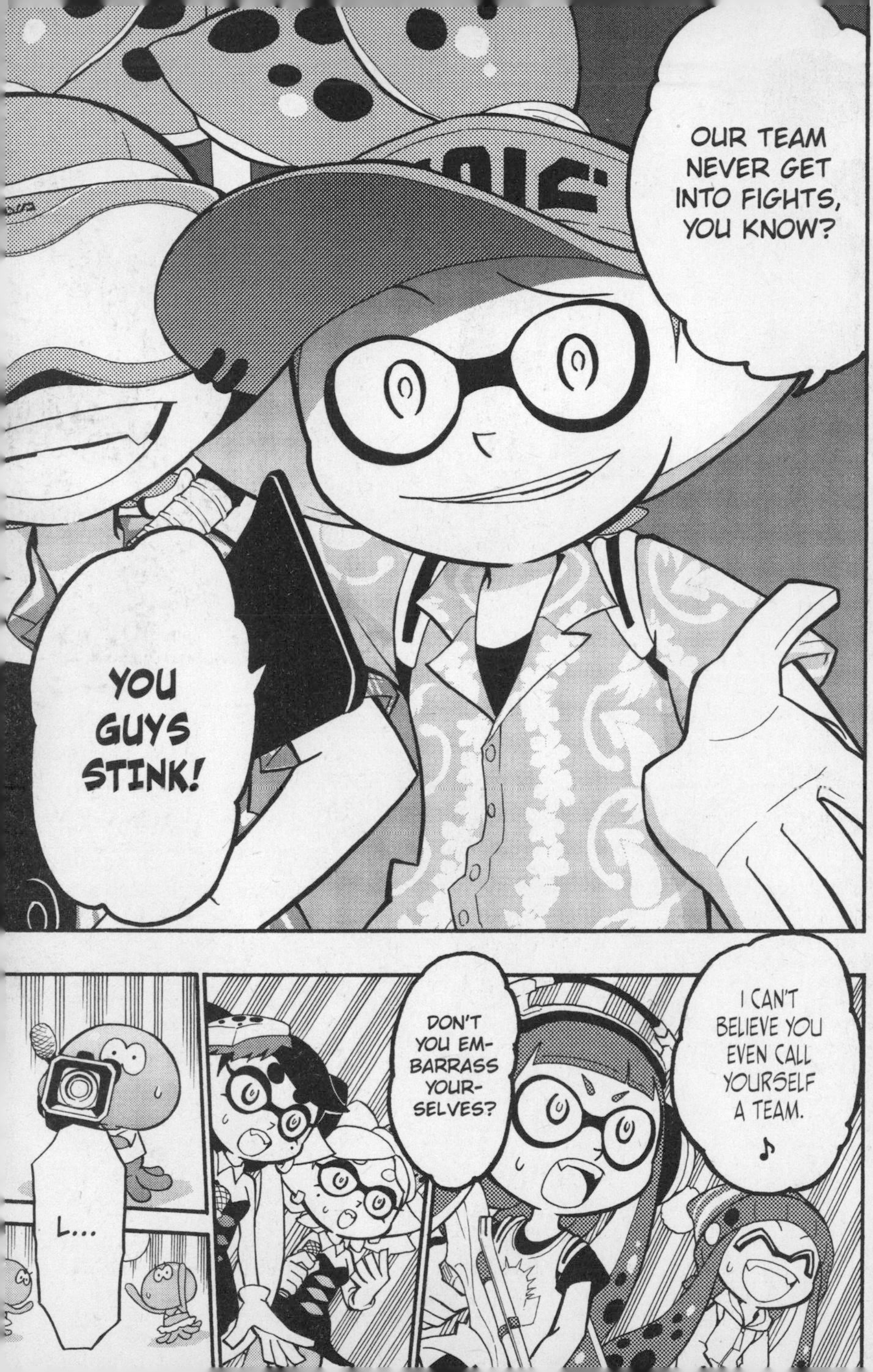
OUR TEAM NEVER GET INTO FIGHTS, YOU KNOW?
YOU GUYS STINK!
I CAN'T BELIEVE YOU EVEN CALL YOURSELF A TEAM. ♪
DON'T YOU EM-BARRASS YOUR-SELVES?
L...

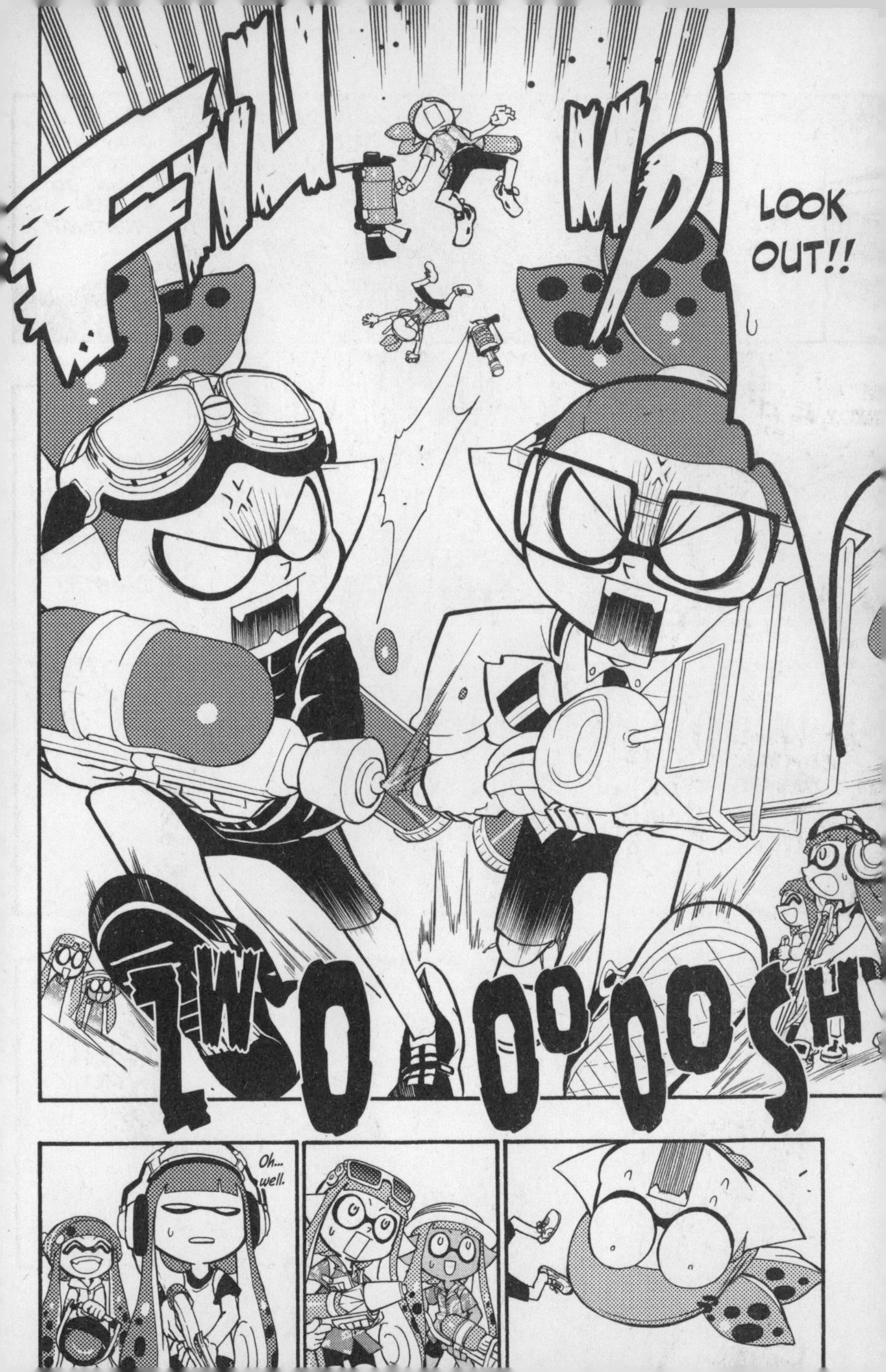
LOOK OUT!!
Oh... well.

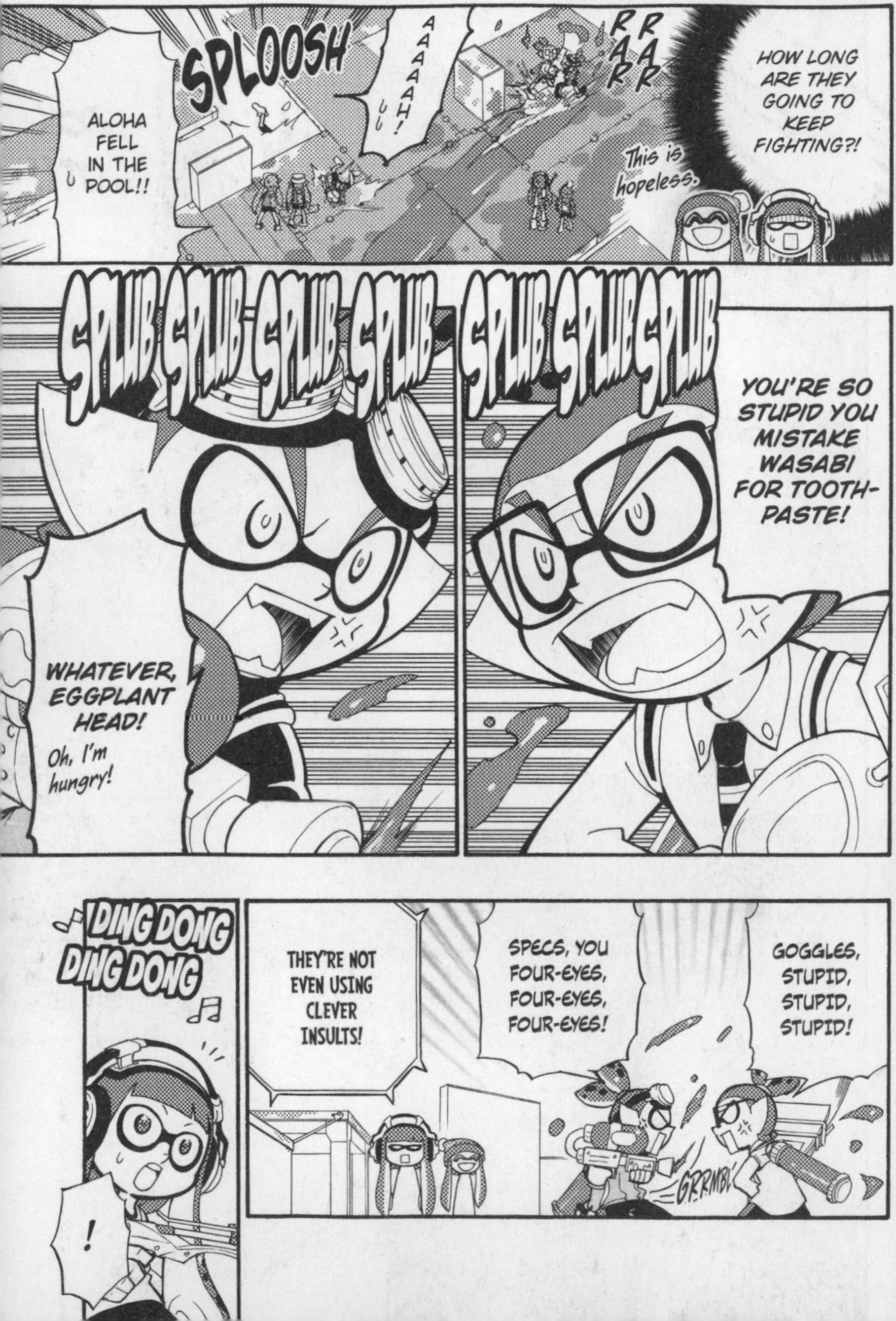
HOW LONG ARE THEY GOING TO KEEP FIGHTING?!
RAR RAR
This is hopeless.
AAAAAAH!
SPLOOSH
ALOHA FELL IN THE POOL!!
SPLUB SPLUB SPLUB
YOU'RE SO STUPID YOU MISTAKE WASABI FOR TOOTH-PASTE!
SPLUB SPLUB SPLUB SPLUB
WHATEVER, EGGPLANT HEAD!
Oh, I'm hungry!
GOGGLES, STUPID, STUPID, STUPID!
SPECS, YOU FOUR-EYES, FOUR-EYES, FOUR-EYES!
THEY'RE NOT EVEN USING CLEVER INSULTS!
GRRMBL
DING DONG DING DONG
!

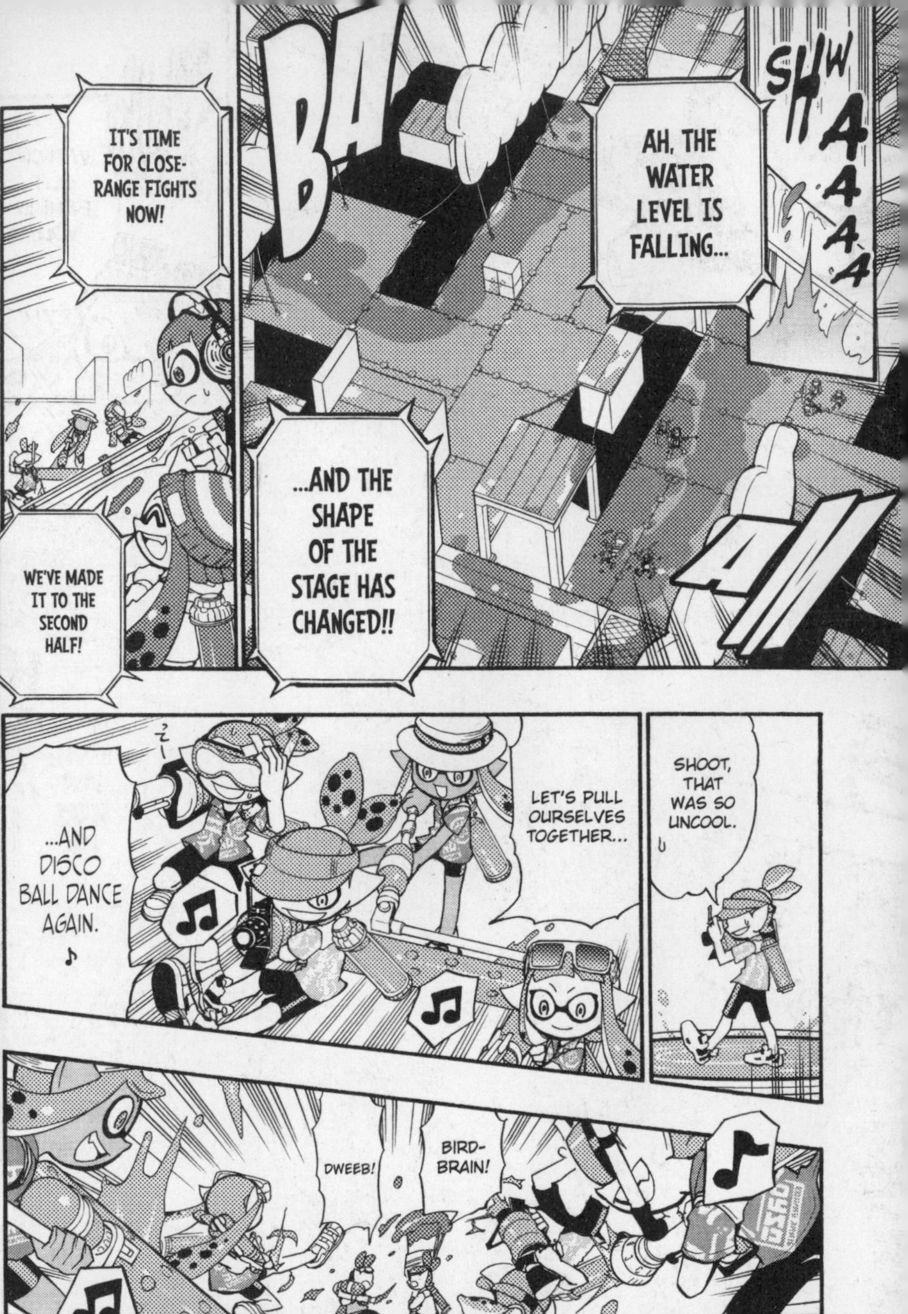
SHWAAAA
AH, THE WATER LEVEL IS FALLING...
BA-
...AND THE SHAPE OF THE STAGE HAS CHANGED!!
IT'S TIME FOR CLOSE-RANGE FIGHTS NOW!
WE'VE MADE IT TO THE SECOND HALF!
SHOOT, THAT WAS SO UNCOOL.
LET'S PULL OURSELVES TOGETHER...
...AND DISCO BALL DANCE AGAIN. ♪
BIRD-BRAIN!
DWEEB!

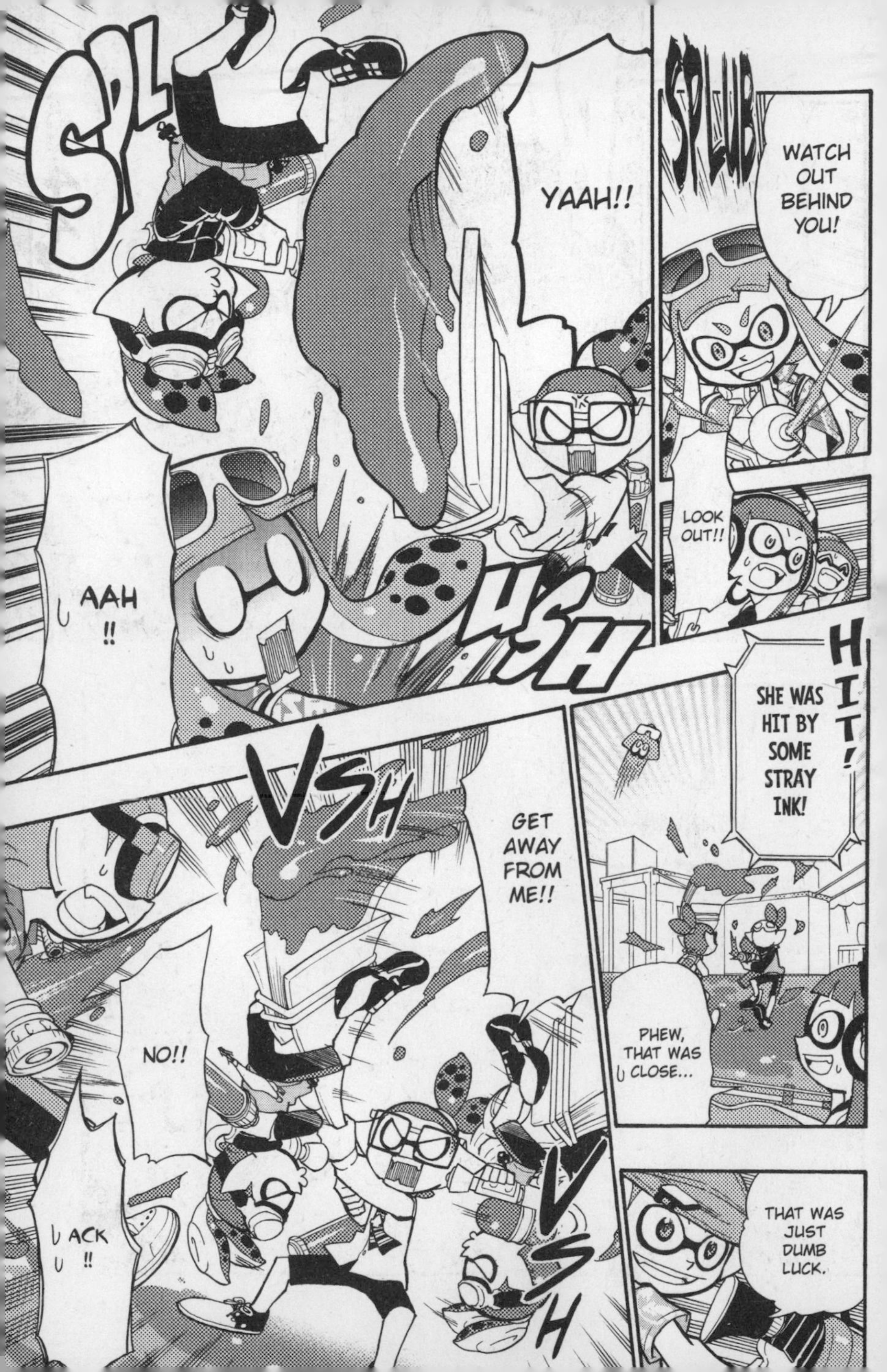
SPLUB
WATCH OUT BEHIND YOU!
LOOK OUT!!
SPL
YAAH!!
USH
AAH!!
HIT!
SHE WAS HIT BY SOME STRAY INK!
PHEW, THAT WAS CLOSE...
THAT WAS JUST DUMB LUCK.
VSH
GET AWAY FROM ME!!
NO!!
VSH
ACK!!

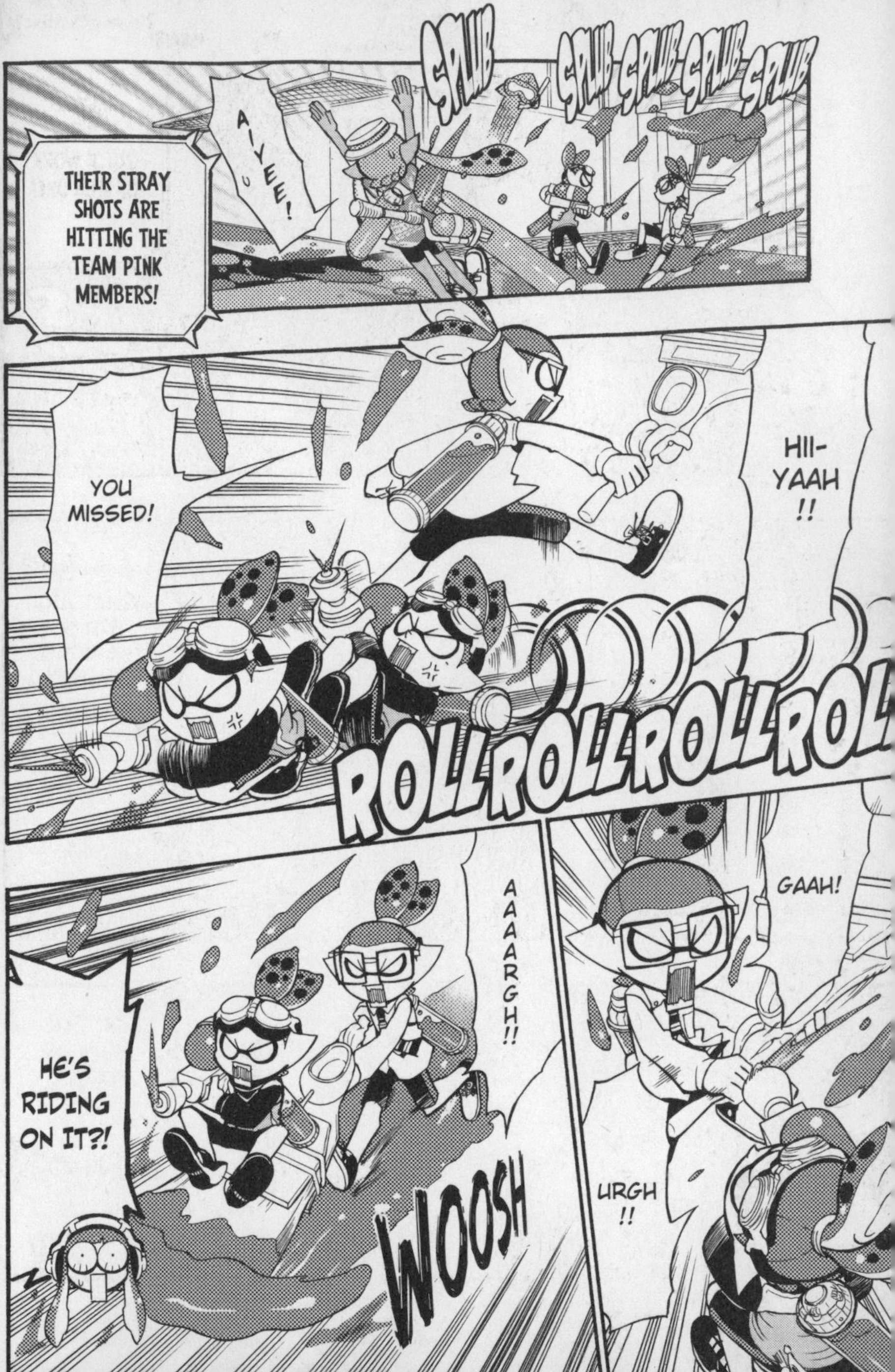
SPLUB SPLUB SPLUB SPLUB SPLUB
AIYEE!
THEIR STRAY SHOTS ARE HITTING THE TEAM PINK MEMBERS!
HII-YAAH!!
YOU MISSED!
ROLLROLLROLLROL
GAAH!
URGH!!
AAAAARGH!!
HE'S RIDING ON IT?!
WOOSH

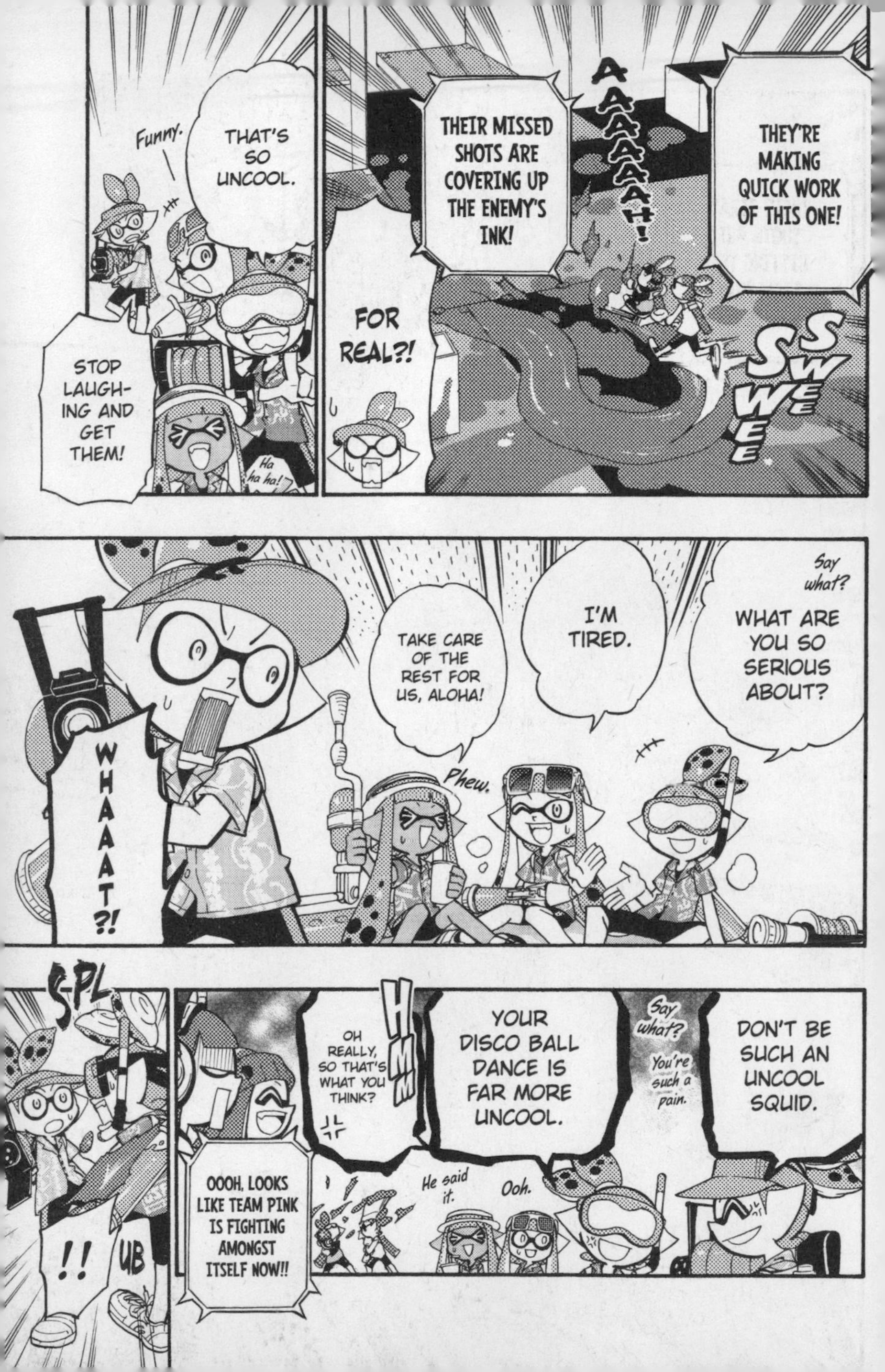
THEY'RE MAKING QUICK WORK OF THIS ONE!
AAAAAAAH!
SWEE SWEE
THEIR MISSED SHOTS ARE COVERING UP THE ENEMY'S INK!
FOR REAL?!
THAT'S SO UNCOOL.
Funny.
STOP LAUGH-ING AND GET THEM!
Ha ha ha!
Say what?
WHAT ARE YOU SO SERIOUS ABOUT?
I'M TIRED.
TAKE CARE OF THE REST FOR US, ALOHA!
Phew.
WHAAAAT?!
DON'T BE SUCH AN UNCOOL SQUID.
Say what?
You're such a pain.
YOUR DISCO BALL DANCE IS FAR MORE UNCOOL.
HMM
OH REALLY, SO THAT'S WHAT YOU THINK?
Ooh.
He said it.
OOOH, LOOKS LIKE TEAM PINK IS FIGHTING AMONGST ITSELF NOW!!
S-PL
!!
UB

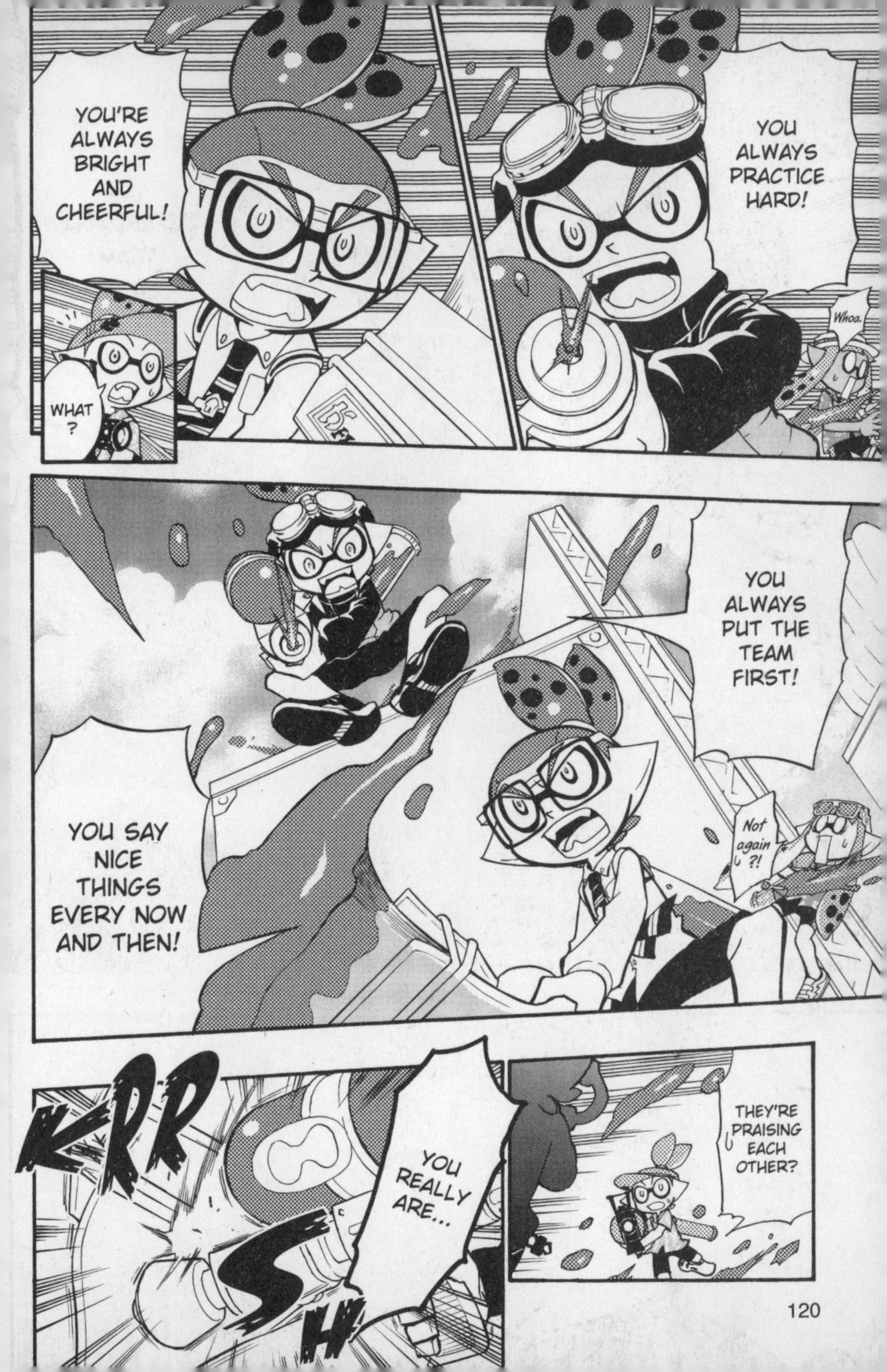
YOU ALWAYS PRACTICE HARD!
Whoa.
YOU'RE ALWAYS BRIGHT AND CHEERFUL!
WHAT ?
YOU ALWAYS PUT THE TEAM FIRST!
Not again ?!
YOU SAY NICE THINGS EVERY NOW AND THEN!
THEY'RE PRAISING EACH OTHER?
YOU REALLY ARE...
KRRSH

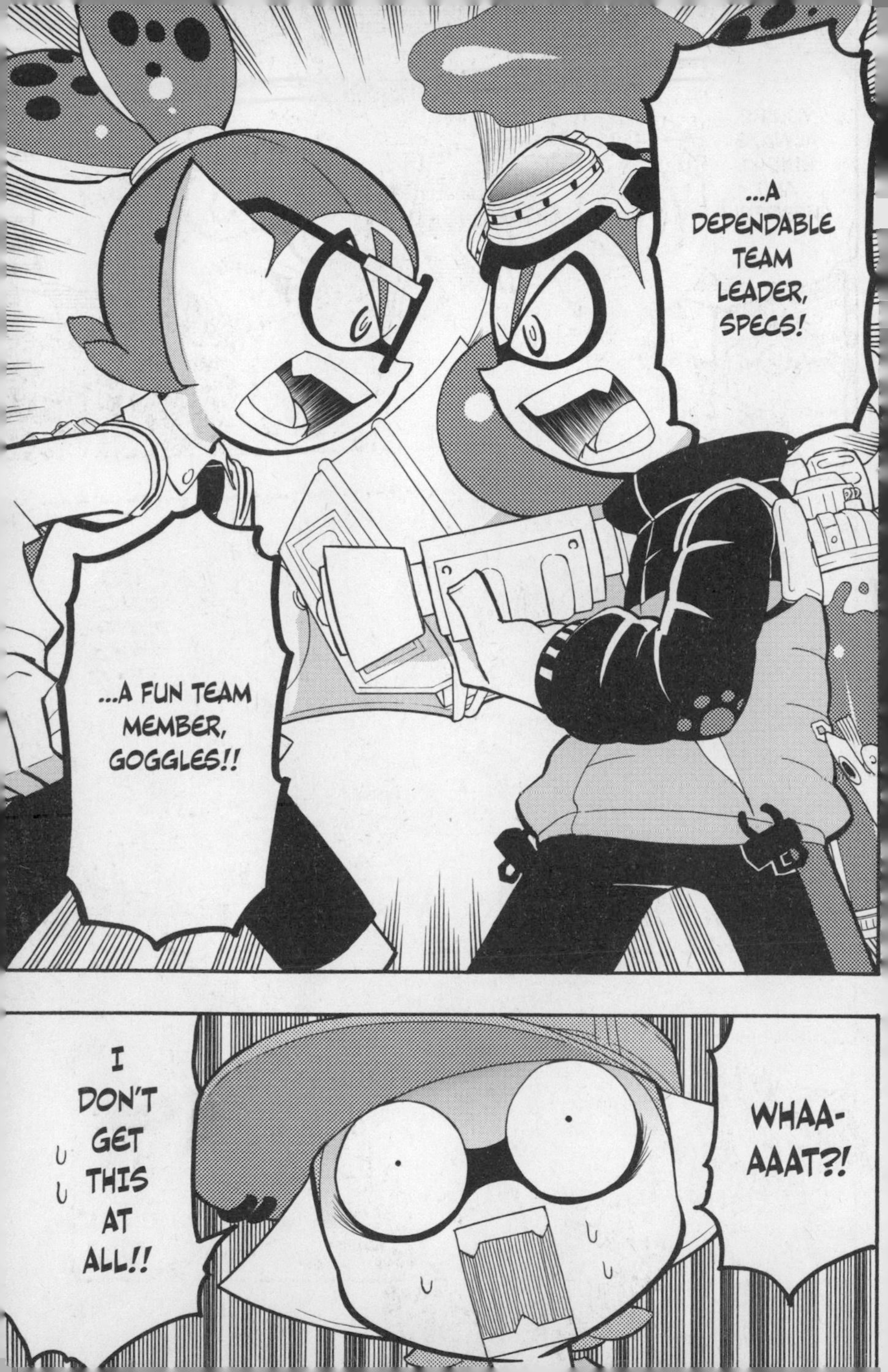
...A DEPENDABLE TEAM LEADER, SPECS!
...A FUN TEAM MEMBER, GOGGLES!!
WHAA-AAAT?!
I DON'T GET THIS AT ALL!!

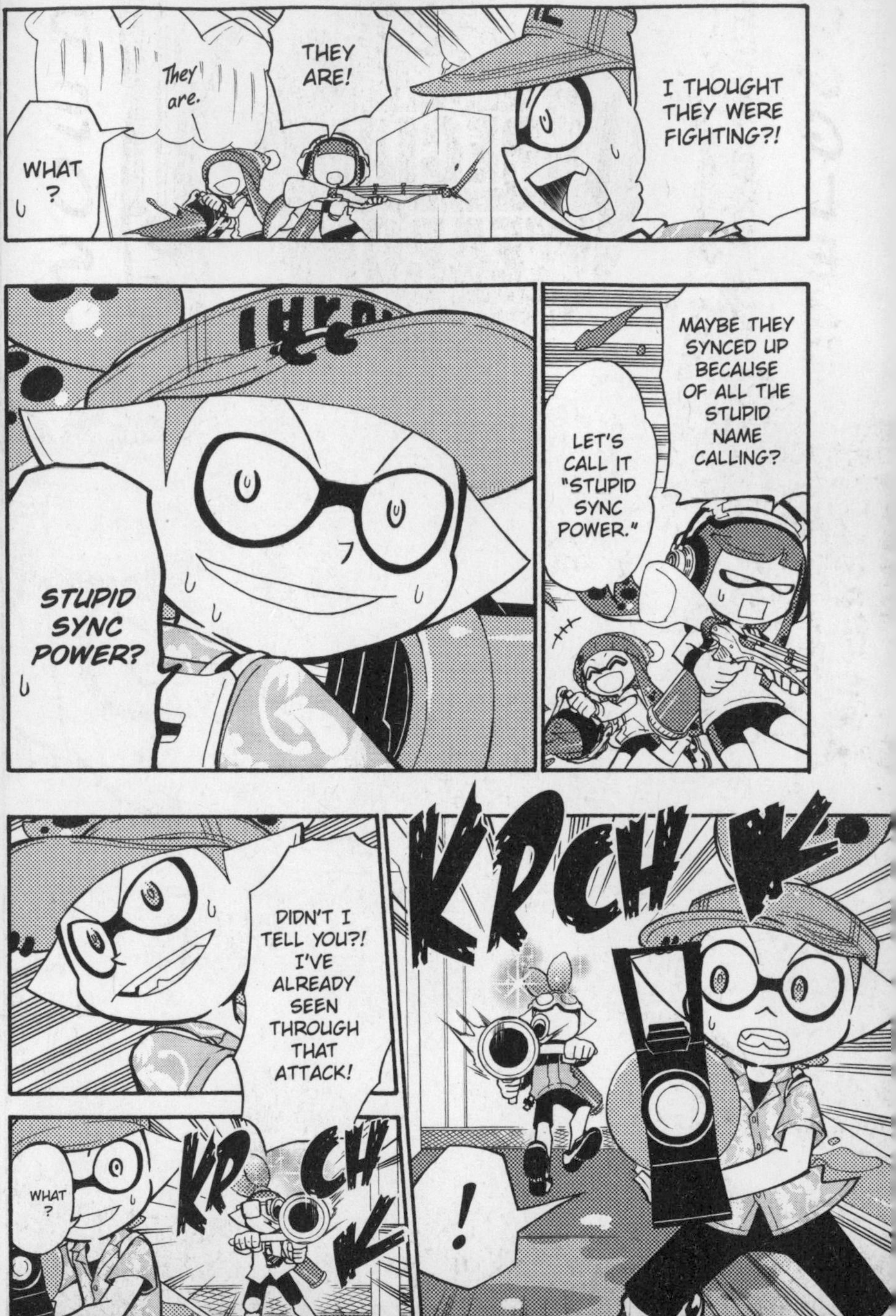
I THOUGHT THEY WERE FIGHTING?!
THEY ARE!
They are.
WHAT?
MAYBE THEY SYNCED UP BECAUSE OF ALL THE STUPID NAME CALLING?
LET'S CALL IT "STUPID SYNC POWER."
STUPID SYNC POWER?
KRCHK
!
DIDN'T I TELL YOU?! I'VE ALREADY SEEN THROUGH THAT ATTACK!
KRCHK
WHAT?

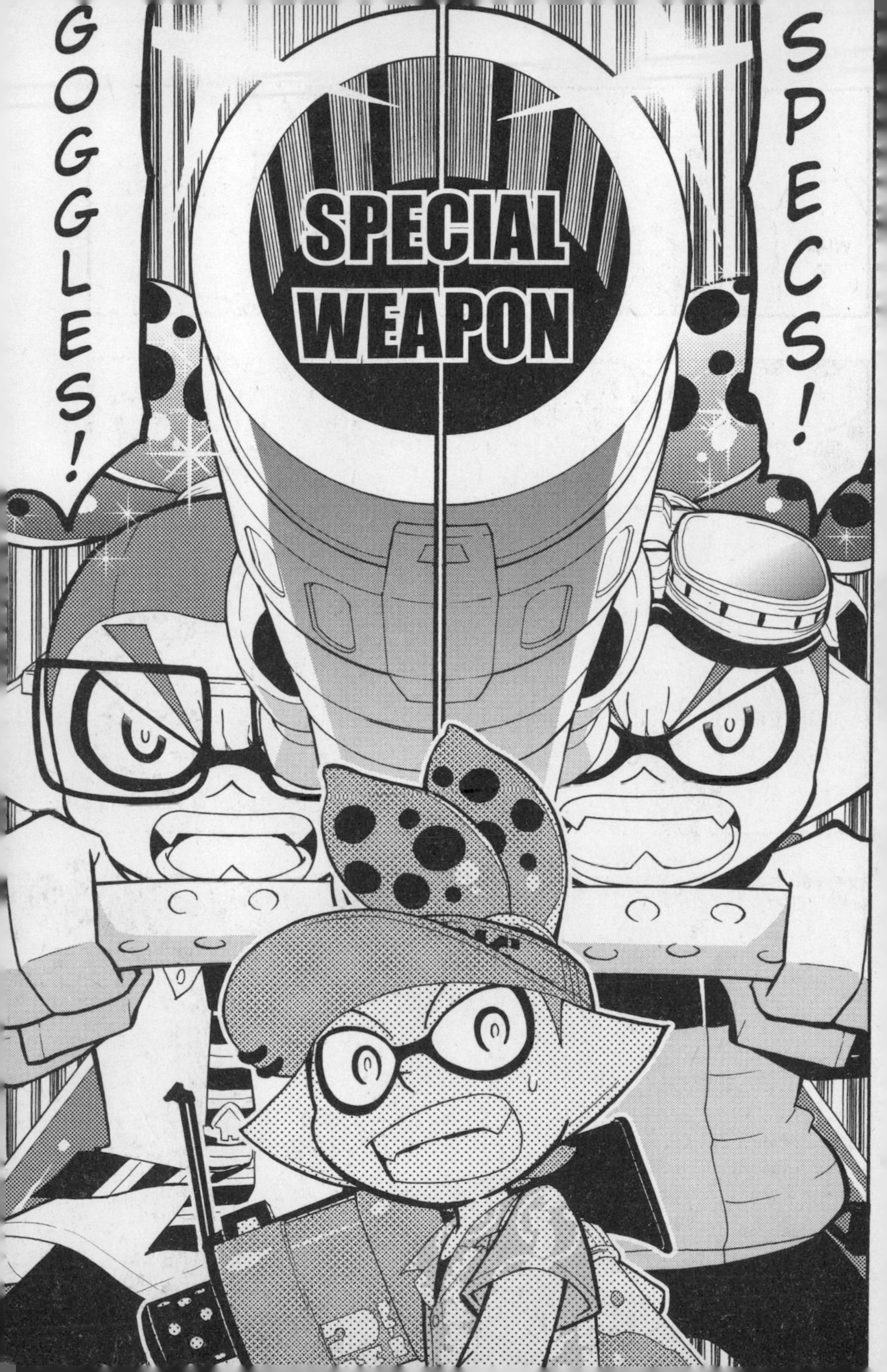
SPECS!
SPECIAL WEAPON
GOGGLES!

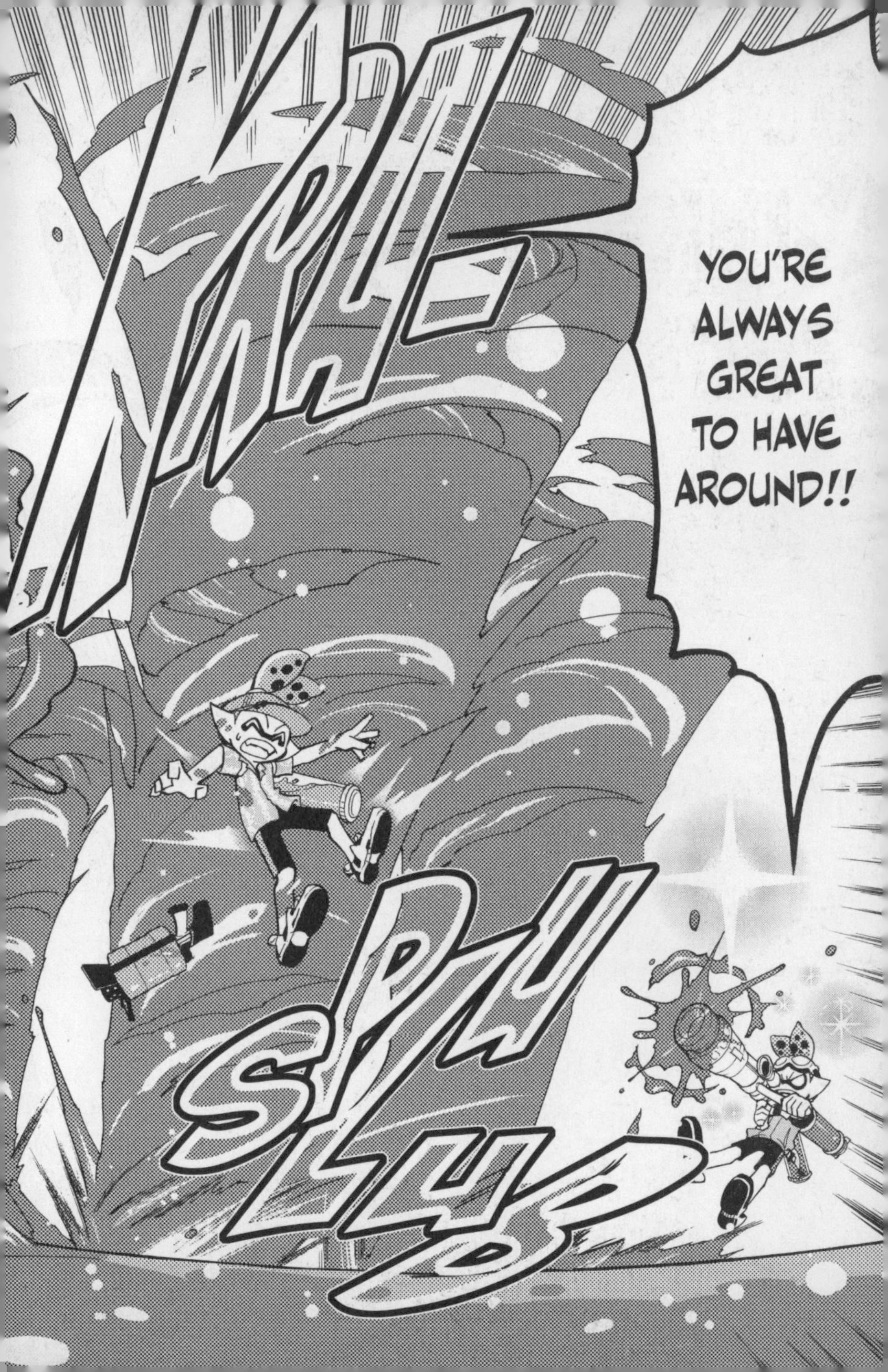
YOU'RE ALWAYS GREAT TO HAVE AROUND!!

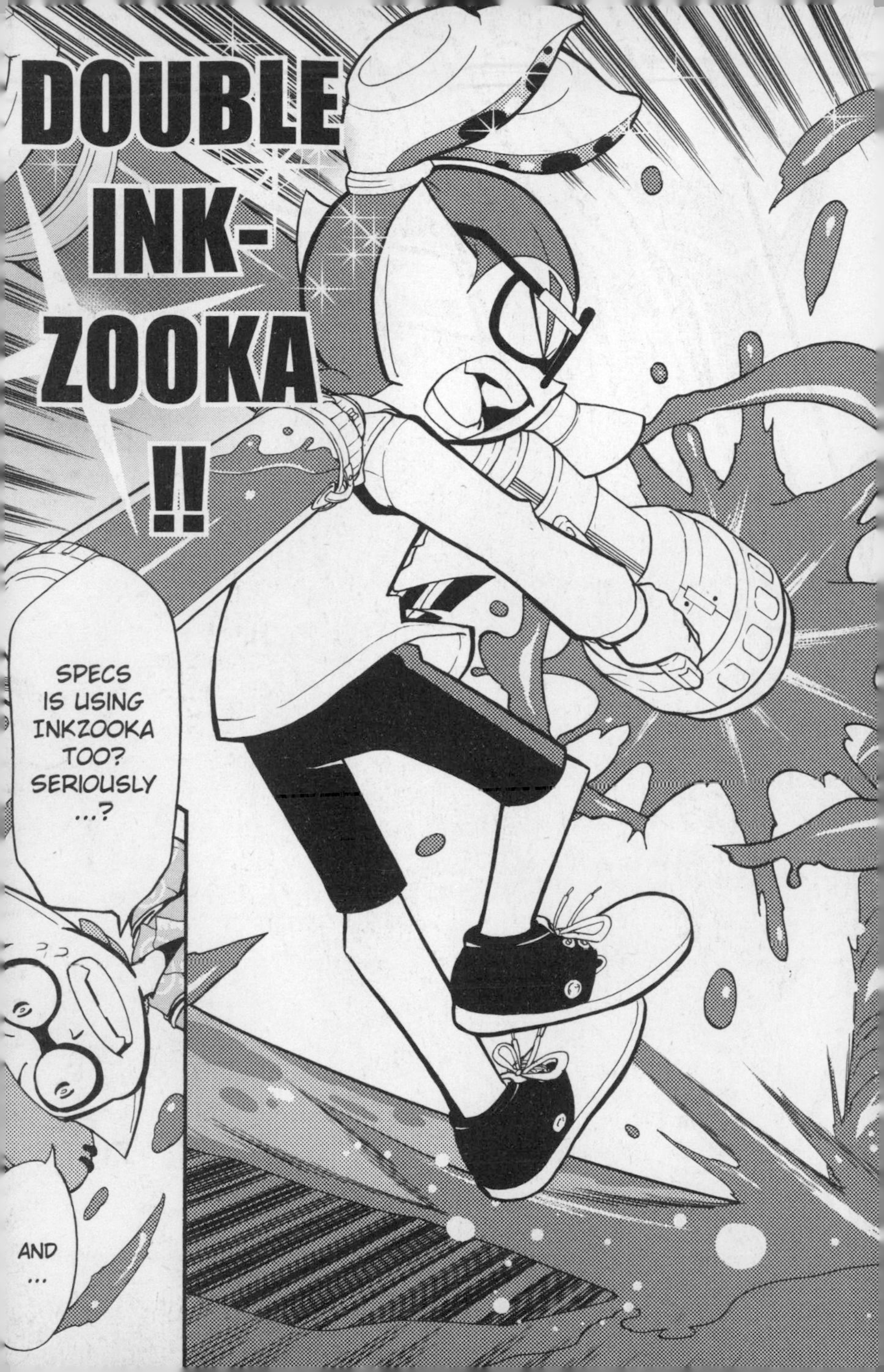
DOUBLE INK-ZOOKA !!
SPECS IS USING INKZOOKA TOO? SERIOUSLY ...?
AND ...

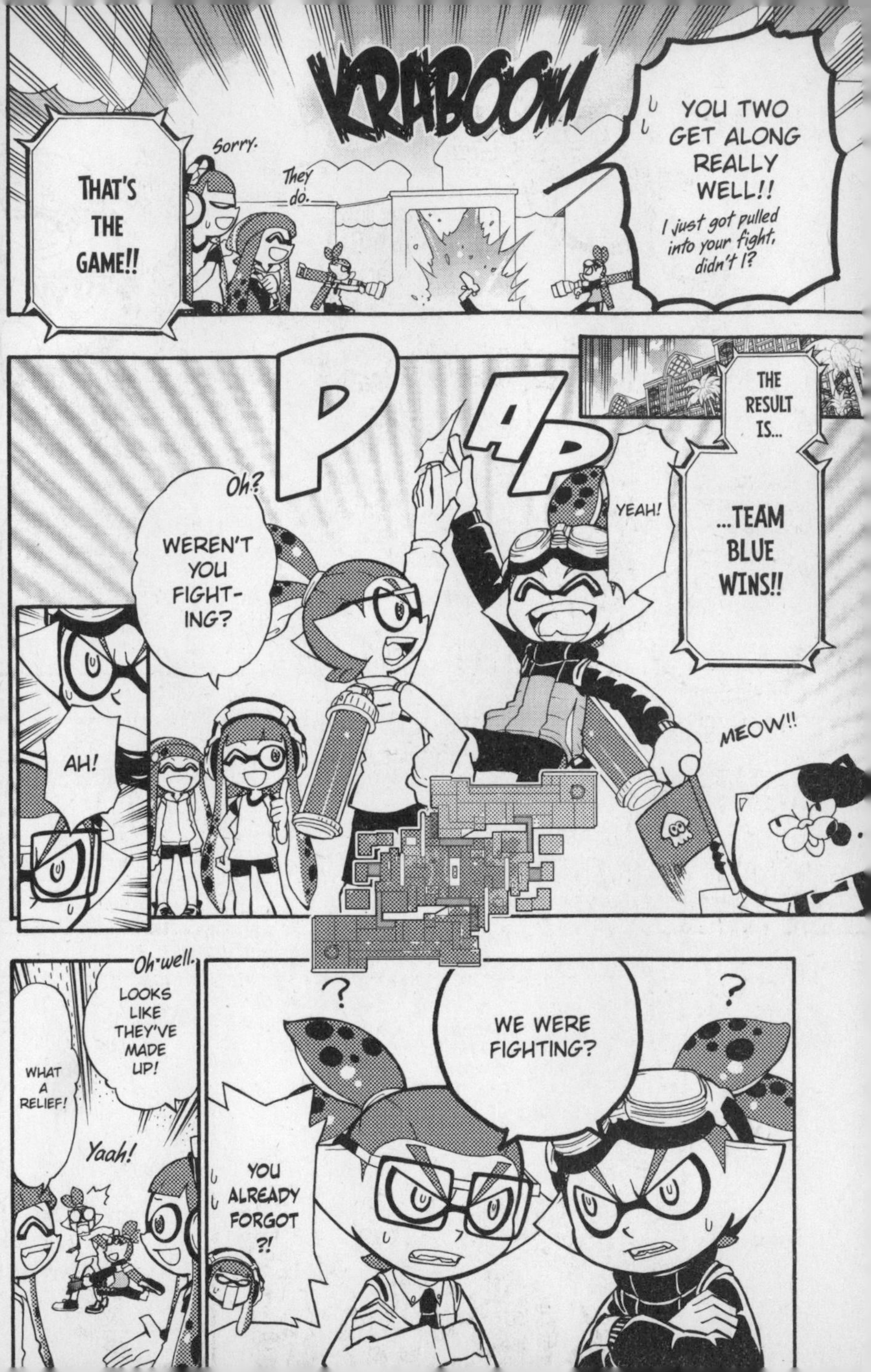
KRABOOM
YOU TWO GET ALONG REALLY WELL!!
I just got pulled into your fight, didn't I?
Sorry.
They do.
THAT'S THE GAME!!
THE RESULT IS...
...TEAM BLUE WINS!!
PAP
YEAH!
MEOW!!
Oh?
WEREN'T YOU FIGHT-ING?
AH!
WE WERE FIGHTING?
YOU ALREADY FORGOT?!
Oh well.
LOOKS LIKE THEY'VE MADE UP!
WHAT A RELIEF!
Yaah!

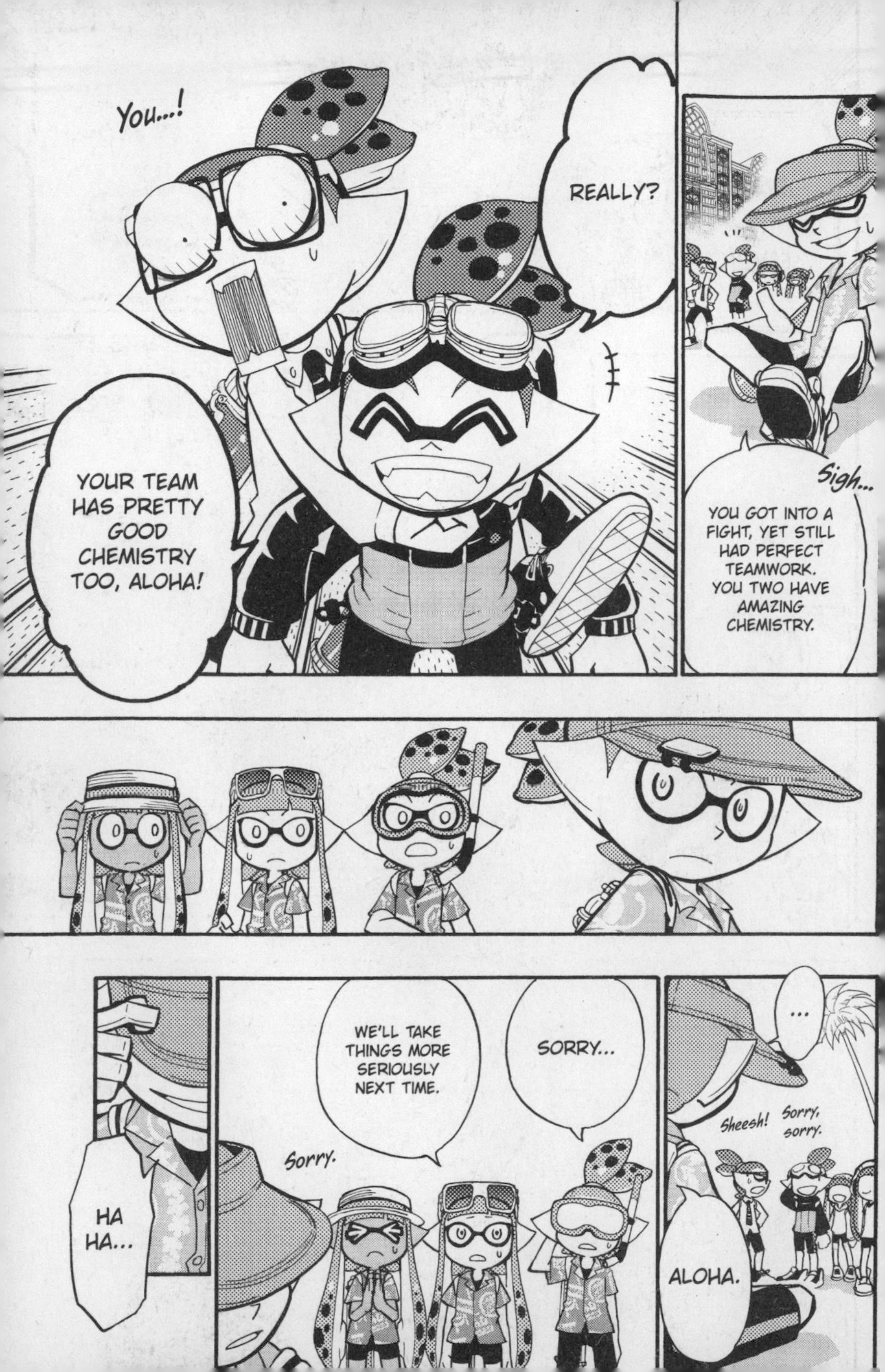
Sigh...
YOU GOT INTO A FIGHT, YET STILL HAD PERFECT TEAMWORK. YOU TWO HAVE AMAZING CHEMISTRY.
REALLY?
You...!
YOUR TEAM HAS PRETTY GOOD CHEMISTRY TOO, ALOHA!
...
Sheesh!
Sorry, sorry.
ALOHA.
SORRY...
WE'LL TAKE THINGS MORE SERIOUSLY NEXT TIME.
Sorry.
HA HA...

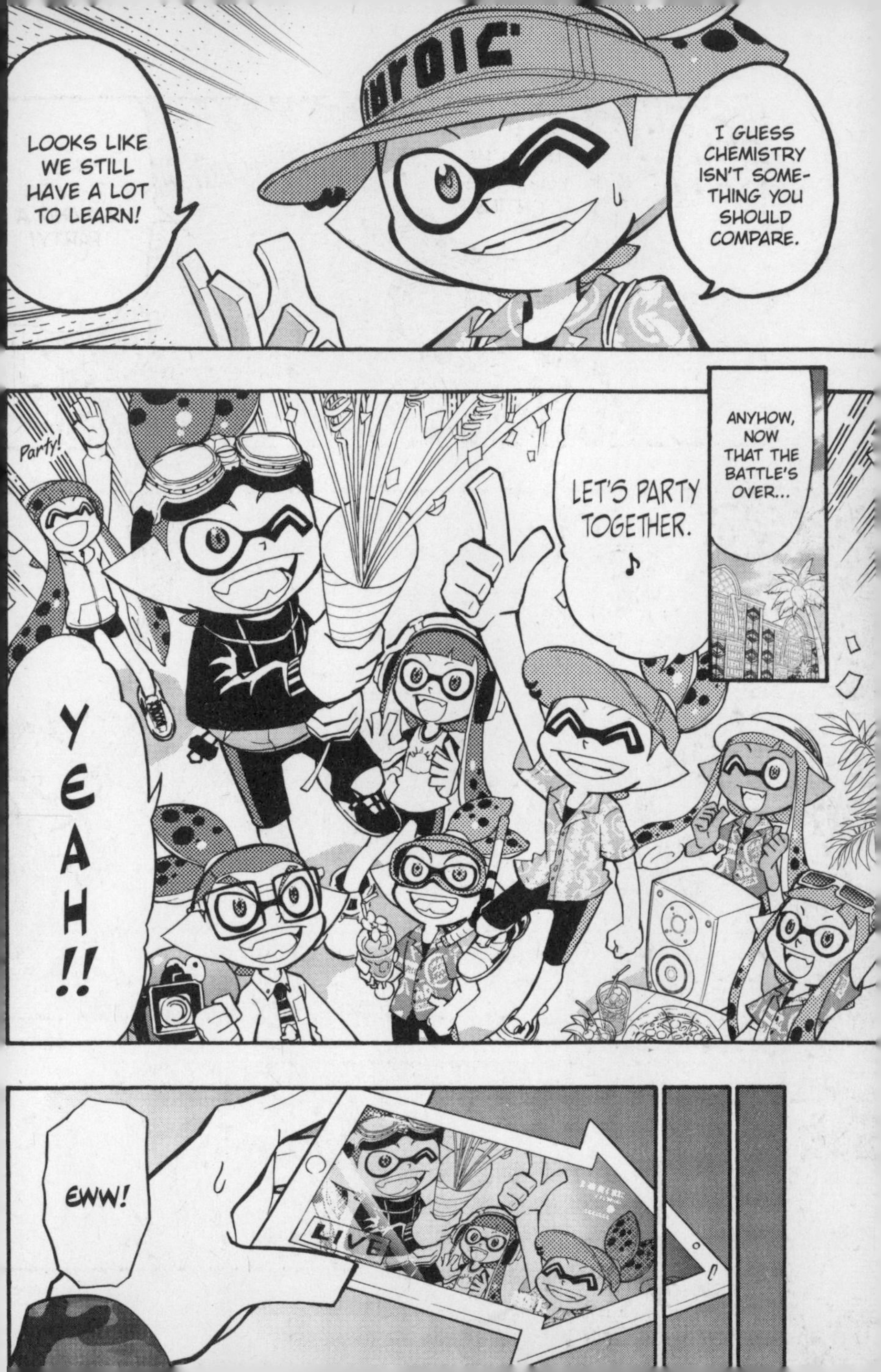
I GUESS CHEMISTRY ISN'T SOME-THING YOU SHOULD COMPARE.
LOOKS LIKE WE STILL HAVE A LOT TO LEARN!
ANYHOW, NOW THAT THE BATTLE'S OVER...
LET'S PARTY TOGETHER. ♪
Party!
YEAH!!
LIVE
EWW!

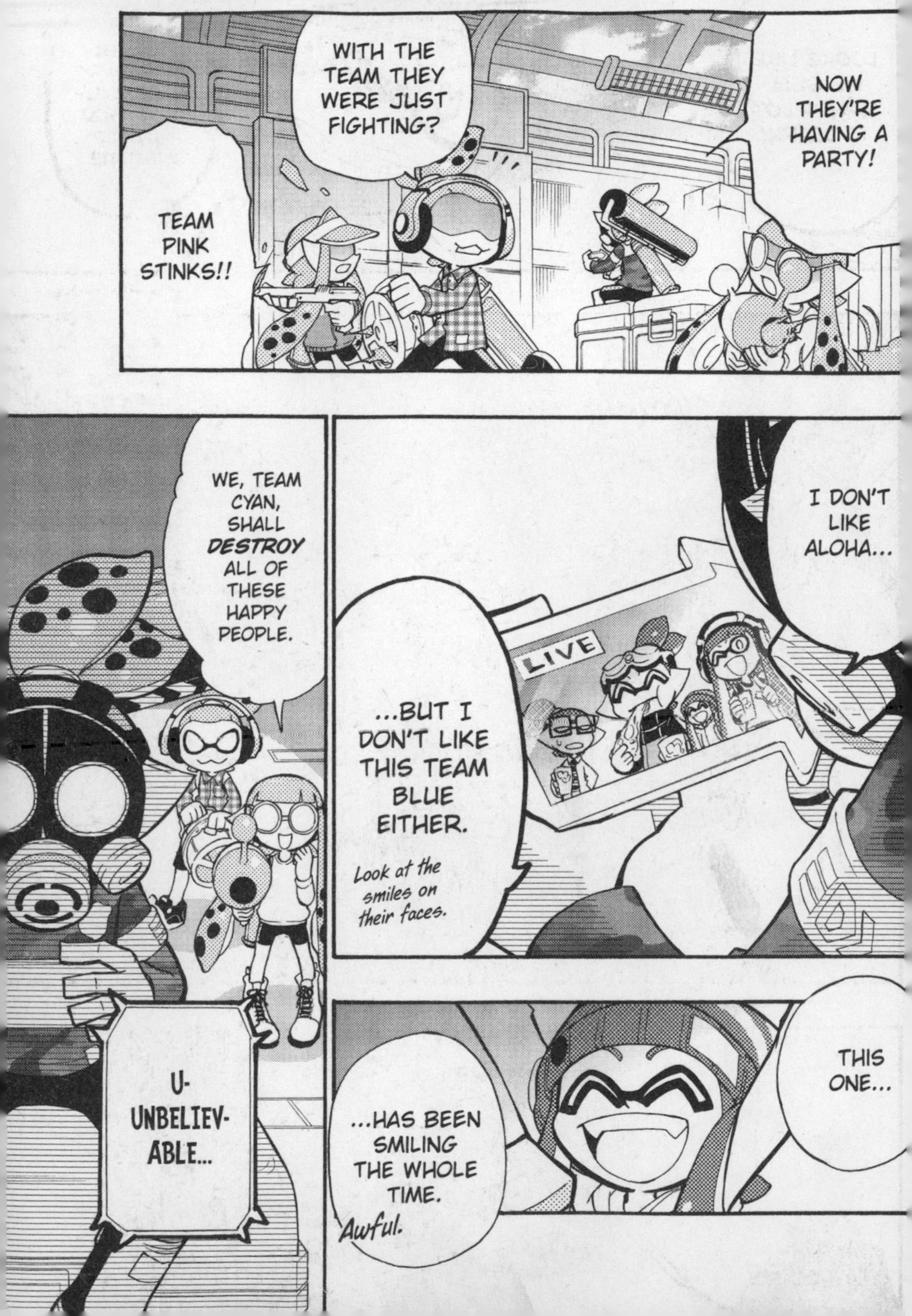
NOW THEY'RE HAVING A PARTY!
WITH THE TEAM THEY WERE JUST FIGHTING?
TEAM PINK STINKS!!
I DON'T LIKE ALOHA...
LIVE
...BUT I DON'T LIKE THIS TEAM BLUE EITHER.
Look at the smiles on their faces.
THIS ONE...
...HAS BEEN SMILING THE WHOLE TIME.
Awful.
WE, TEAM CYAN, SHALL DESTROY ALL OF THESE HAPPY PEOPLE.
U-UNBELIEV-ABLE...

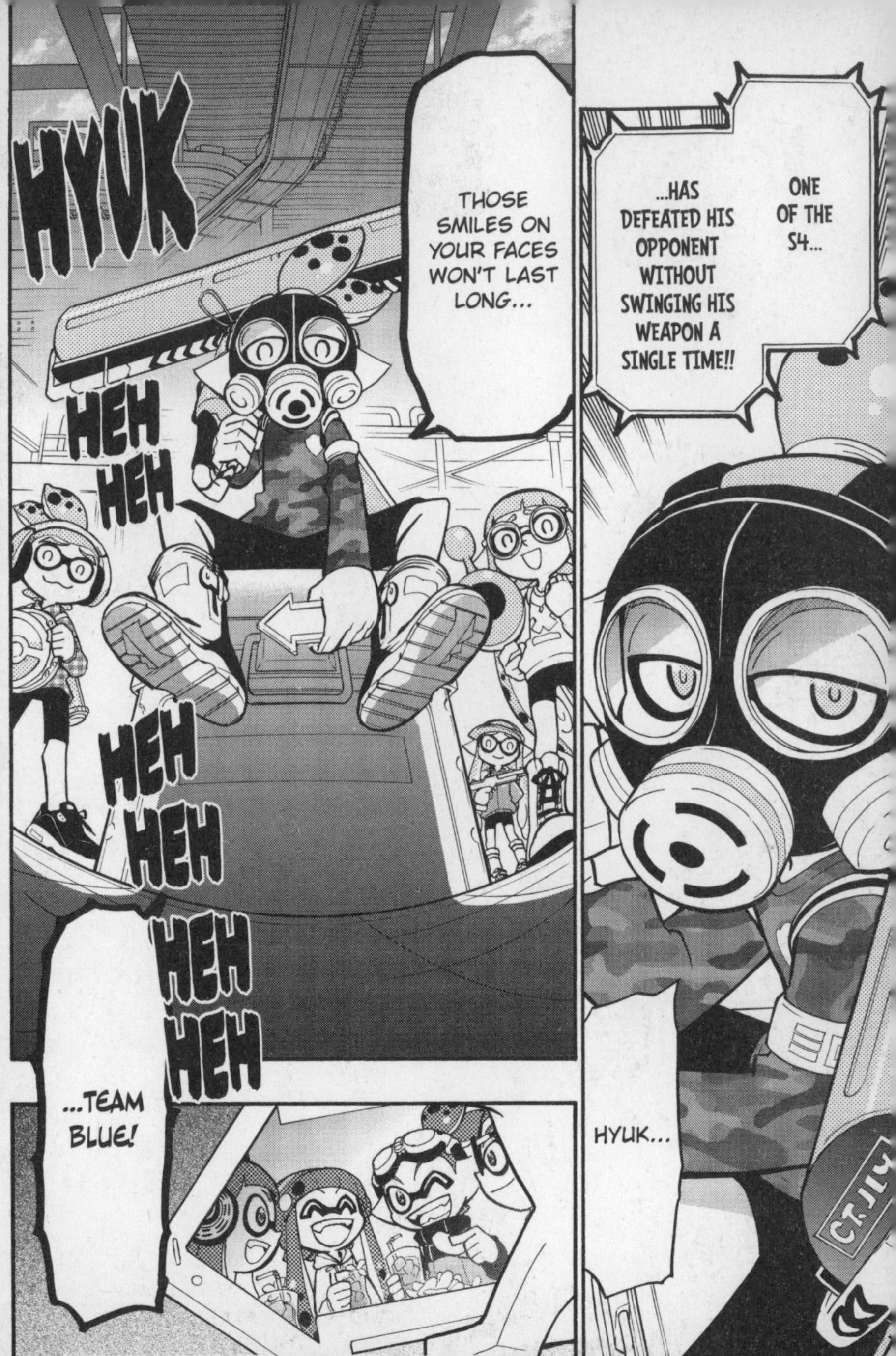
ONE OF THE S4...
...HAS DEFEATED HIS OPPONENT WITHOUT SWINGING HIS WEAPON A SINGLE TIME!!
HYUK...
THOSE SMILES ON YOUR FACES WON'T LAST LONG...
HYUK
HEH HEH
HEH HEH
HEH HEH
...TEAM BLUE!

SPLATOON VOLUME 1 END / CONTINUED IN VOLUME 2

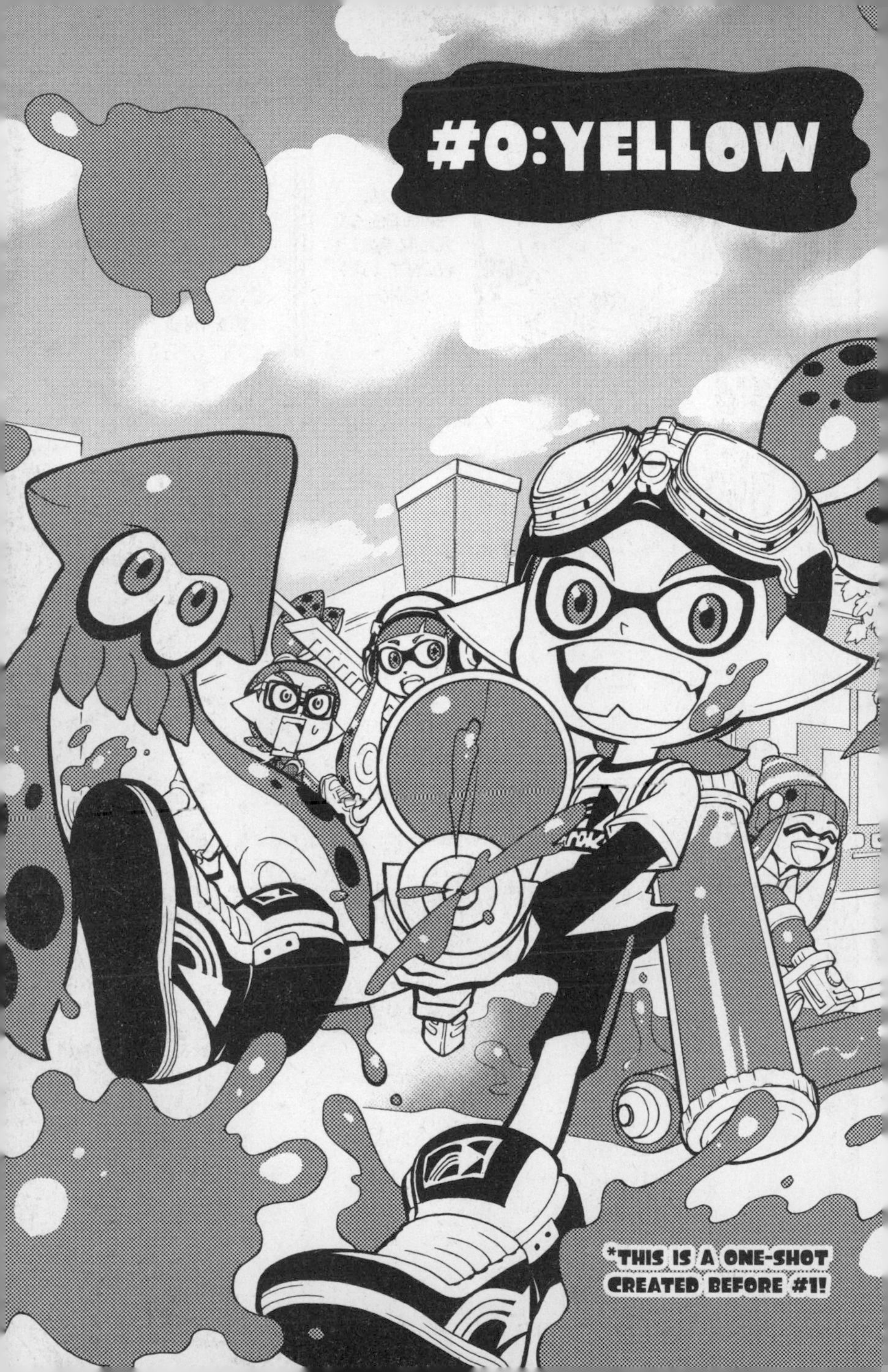
#0:YELLOW
*THIS IS A ONE-SHOT CREATED BEFORE #1!

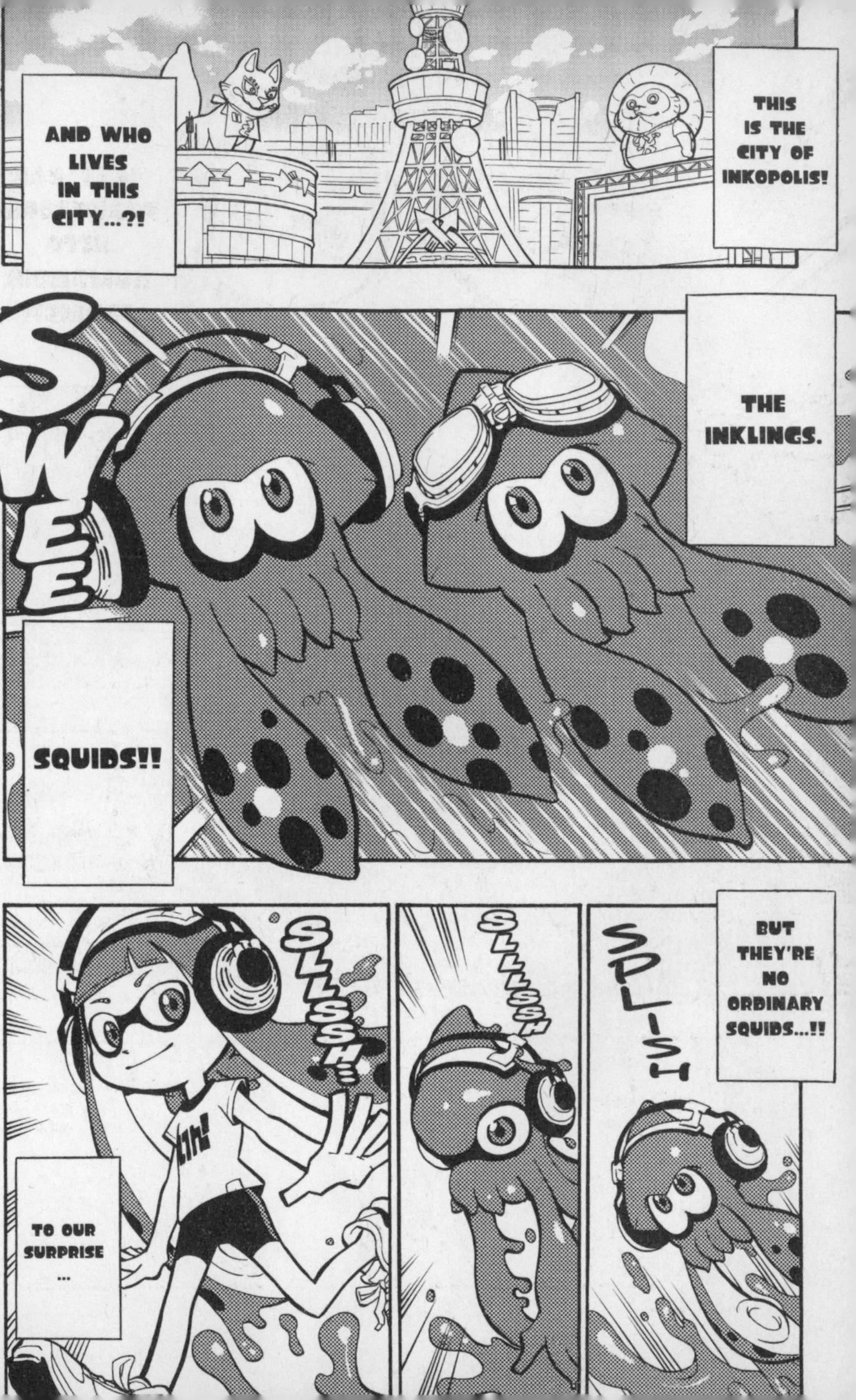
THIS IS THE CITY OF INKOPOLIS!
AND WHO LIVES IN THIS CITY...?!
THE INKLINGS.
SWEE
SQUIDS!!
BUT THEY'RE NO ORDINARY SQUIDS...!!
SPLISH
SLLLSSH
SLLSSH!!
TO OUR SURPRISE ...

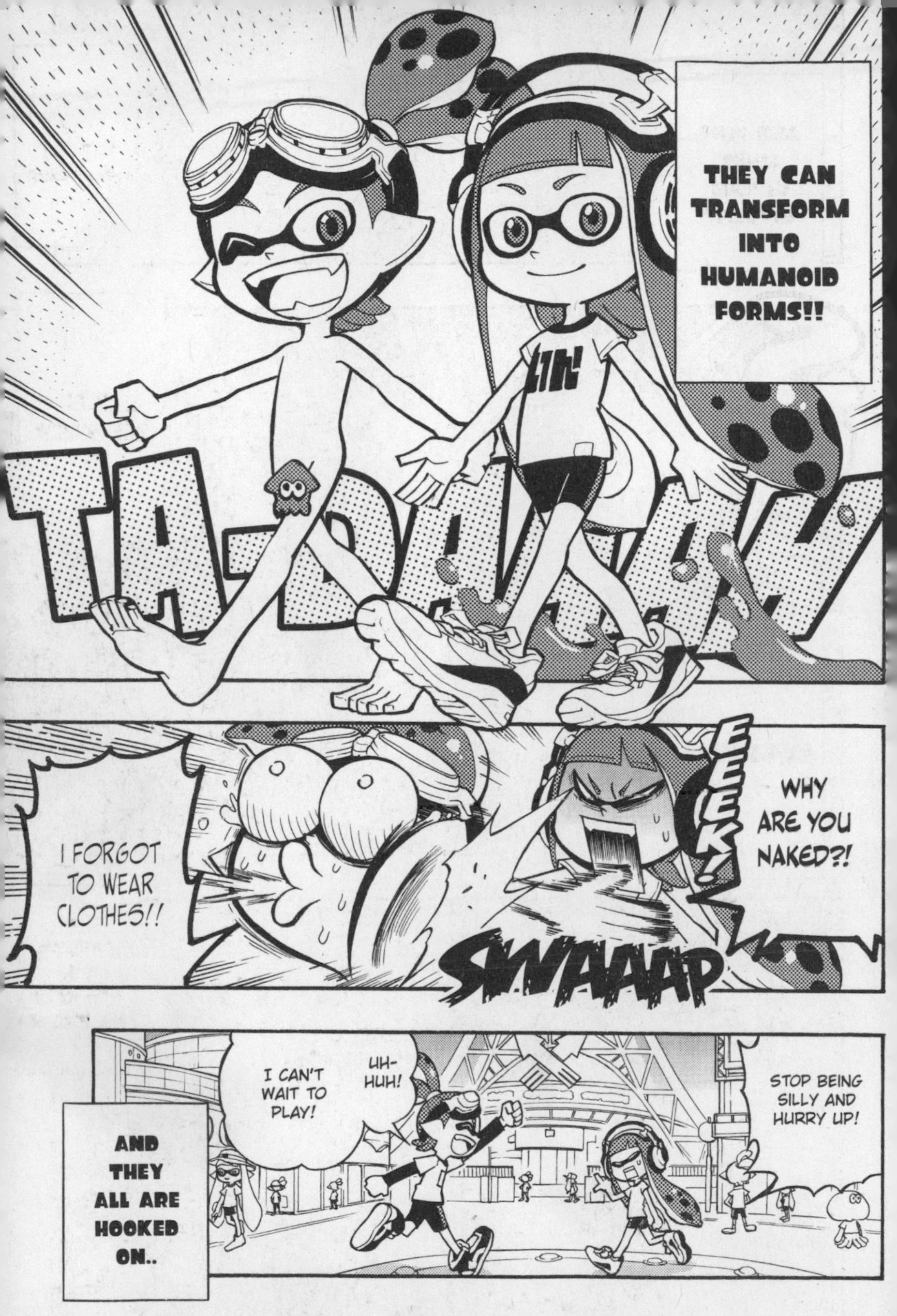
THEY CAN TRANSFORM INTO HUMANOID FORMS!!
TA-
WHY ARE YOU NAKED?!
EEEEK!
SWAAAP
I FORGOT TO WEAR CLOTHES!!
STOP BEING SILLY AND HURRY UP!
UH-HUH!
I CAN'T WAIT TO PLAY!
AND THEY ALL ARE HOOKED ON..

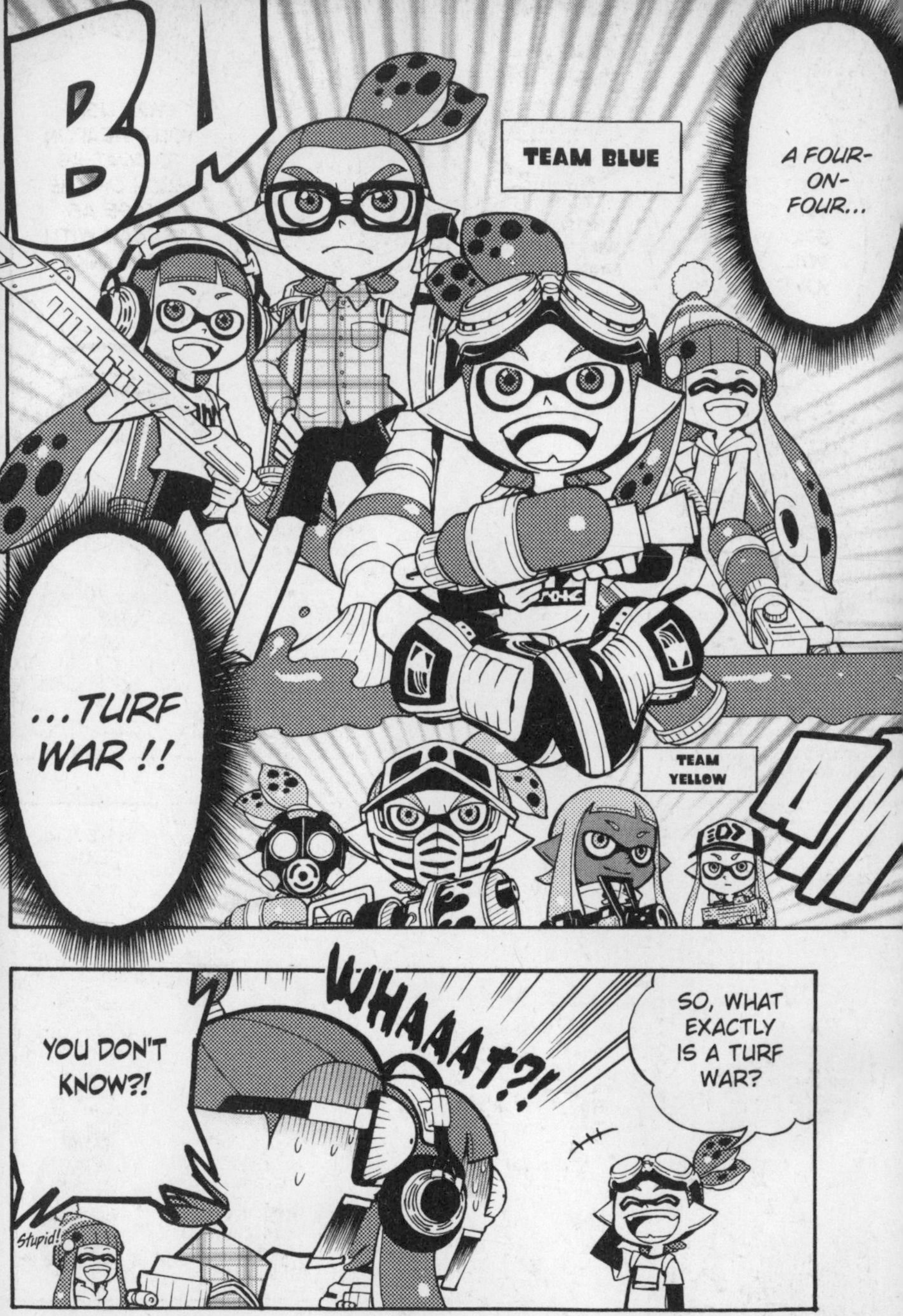
A FOUR-ON-FOUR...
TEAM BLUE
...TURF WAR!!
TEAM YELLOW
SO, WHAT EXACTLY IS A TURF WAR?
WHAAAT?!
YOU DON'T KNOW?!
Stupid!

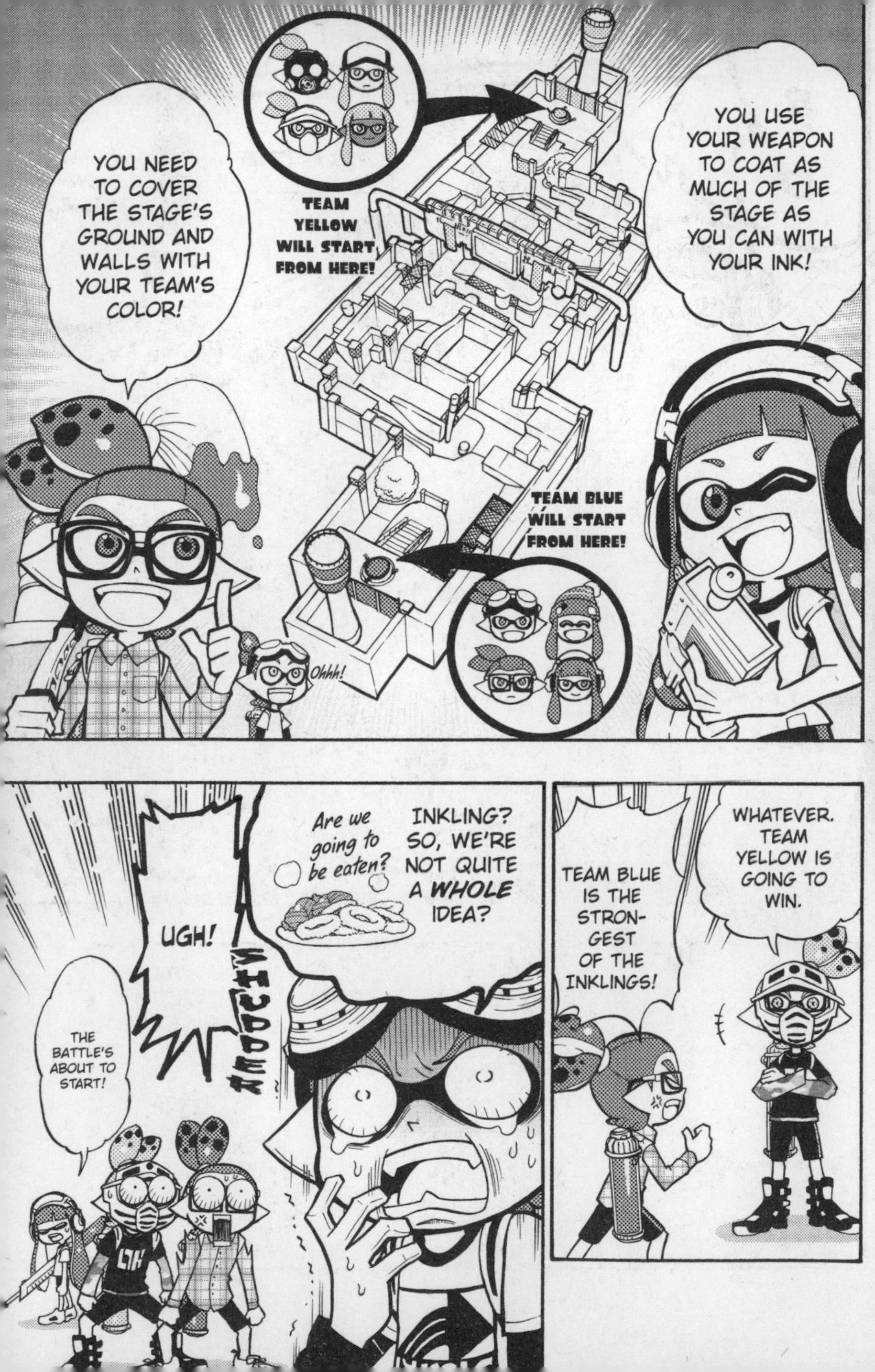
YOU USE YOUR WEAPON TO COAT AS MUCH OF THE STAGE AS YOU CAN WITH YOUR INK!
TEAM YELLOW WILL START FROM HERE!
YOU NEED TO COVER THE STAGE'S GROUND AND WALLS WITH YOUR TEAM'S COLOR!
TEAM BLUE WILL START FROM HERE!
Ohhh!
WHATEVER. TEAM YELLOW IS GOING TO WIN.
TEAM BLUE IS THE STRON-GEST OF THE INKLINGS!
INKLING? SO, WE'RE NOT QUITE A WHOLE IDEA?
Are we going to be eaten?
UGH!
SHUDDER
THE BATTLE'S ABOUT TO START!

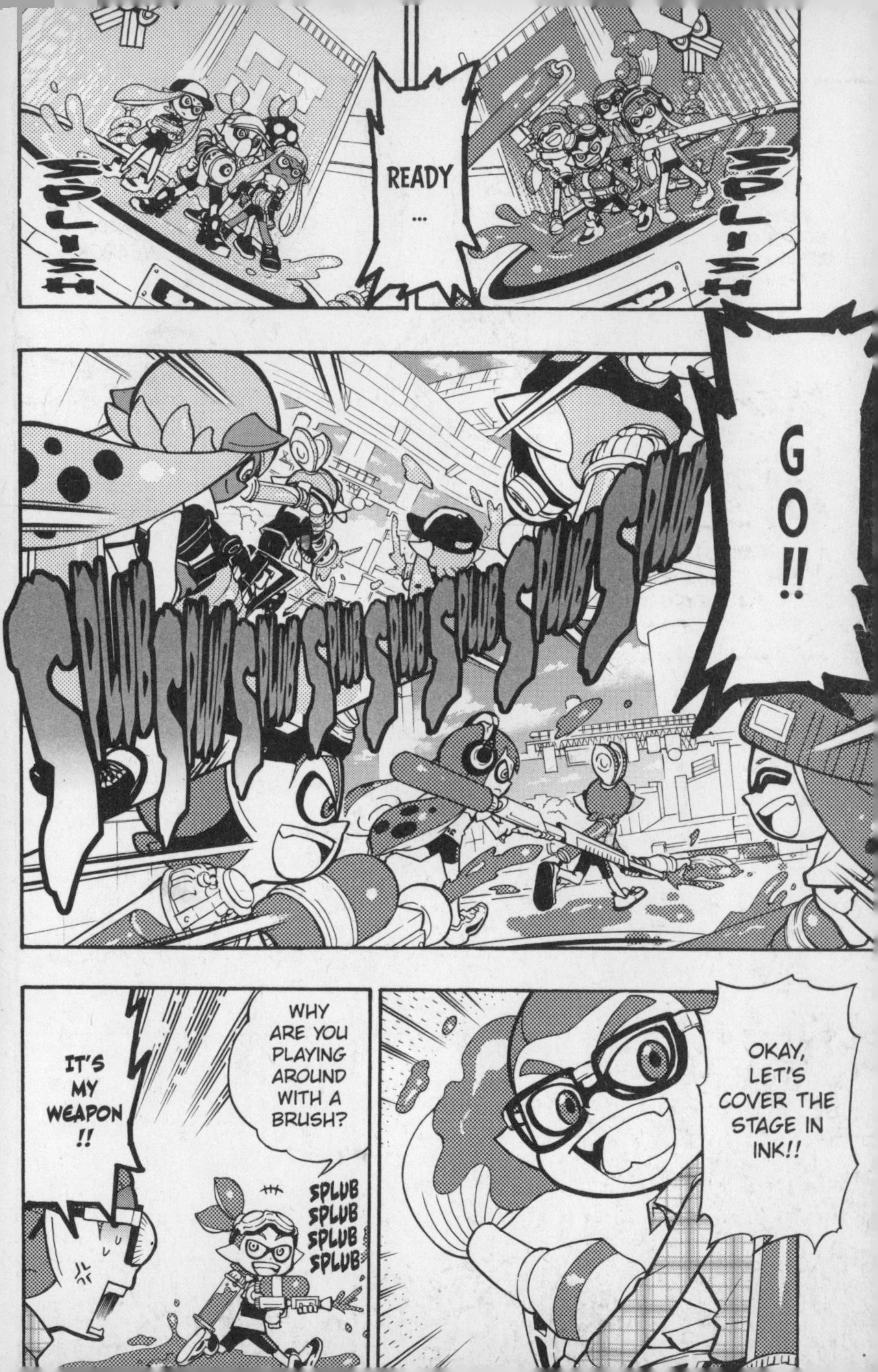
SPLISH!!
READY ...
SPLISH!!
GO!!
SPLUB SPLUB SPLUB SPLUB SPLUB SPLUB SPLUB SPLUB
OKAY, LET'S COVER THE STAGE IN INK!!
WHY ARE YOU PLAYING AROUND WITH A BRUSH?
IT'S MY WEAPON!!
SPLUB SPLUB SPLUB SPLUB

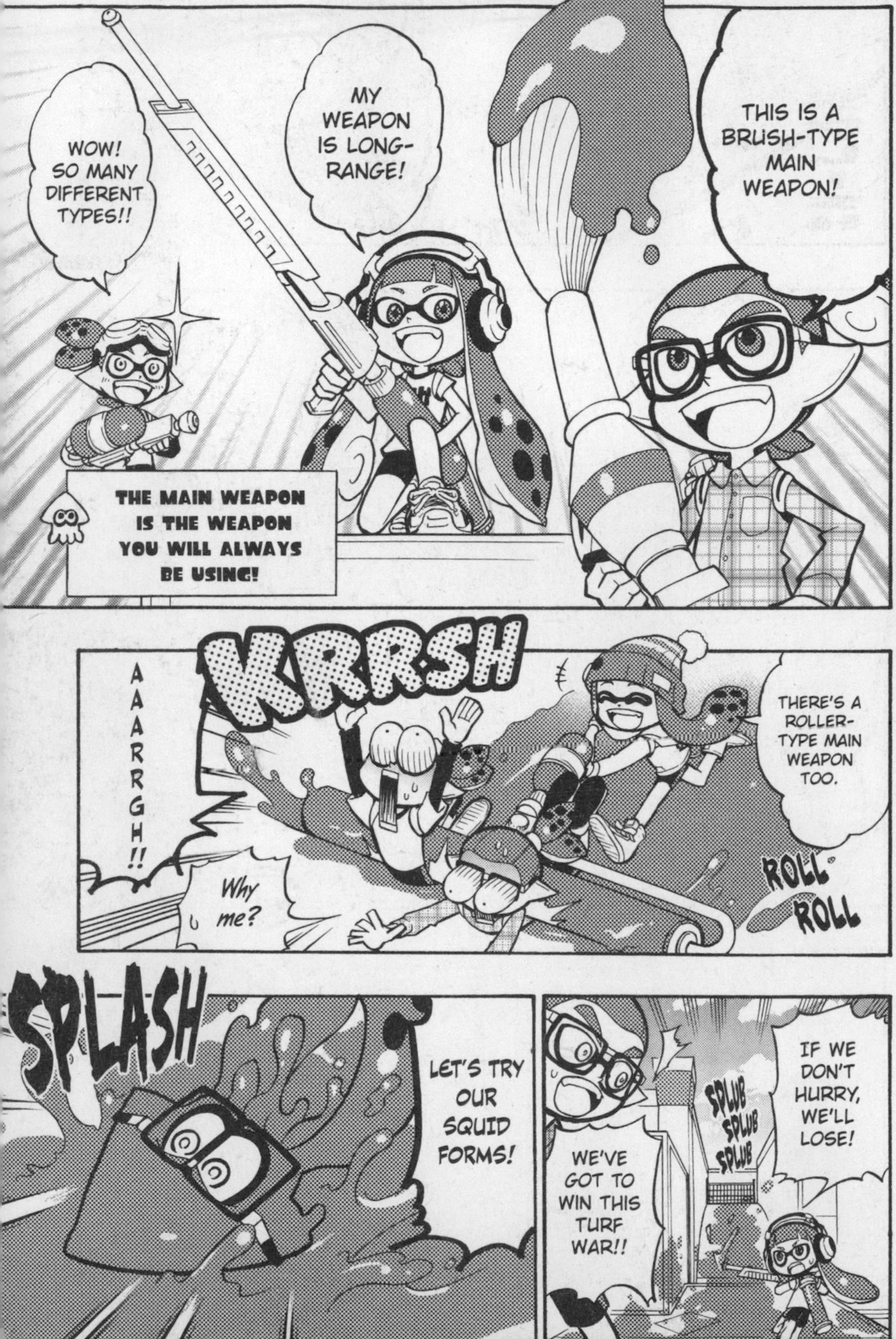

THIS IS A BRUSH-TYPE MAIN WEAPON!
MY WEAPON IS LONG-RANGE!
WOW! SO MANY DIFFERENT TYPES!!
THE MAIN WEAPON IS THE WEAPON YOU WILL ALWAYS BE USING!
THERE'S A ROLLER-TYPE MAIN WEAPON TOO.
ROLL ROLL
KRRSH
AAAARRGH!!
Why me?
IF WE DON'T HURRY, WE'LL LOSE!
SPLUB SPLUB SPLUB
WE'VE GOT TO WIN THIS TURF WAR!!
LET'S TRY OUR SQUID FORMS!
SPLASH

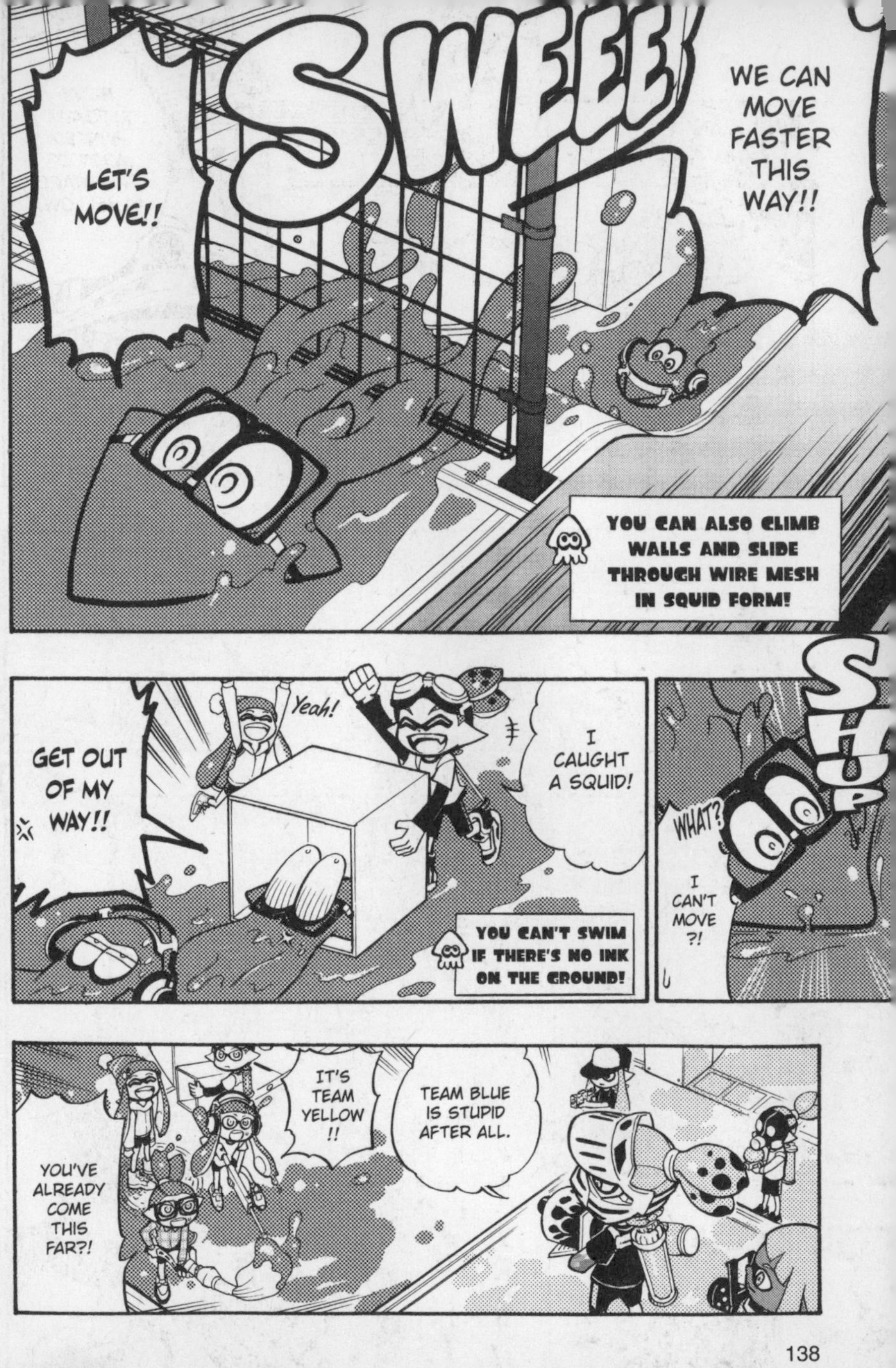
SWEEE
WE CAN MOVE FASTER THIS WAY!!
LET'S MOVE!!
YOU CAN ALSO CLIMB WALLS AND SLIDE THROUGH WIRE MESH IN SQUID FORM!
SHUP
WHAT?
I CAN'T MOVE?!
I CAUGHT A SQUID!
Yeah!
GET OUT OF MY WAY!!
YOU CAN'T SWIM IF THERE'S NO INK ON THE GROUND!
TEAM BLUE IS STUPID AFTER ALL.
IT'S TEAM YELLOW!!
YOU'VE ALREADY COME THIS FAR?!

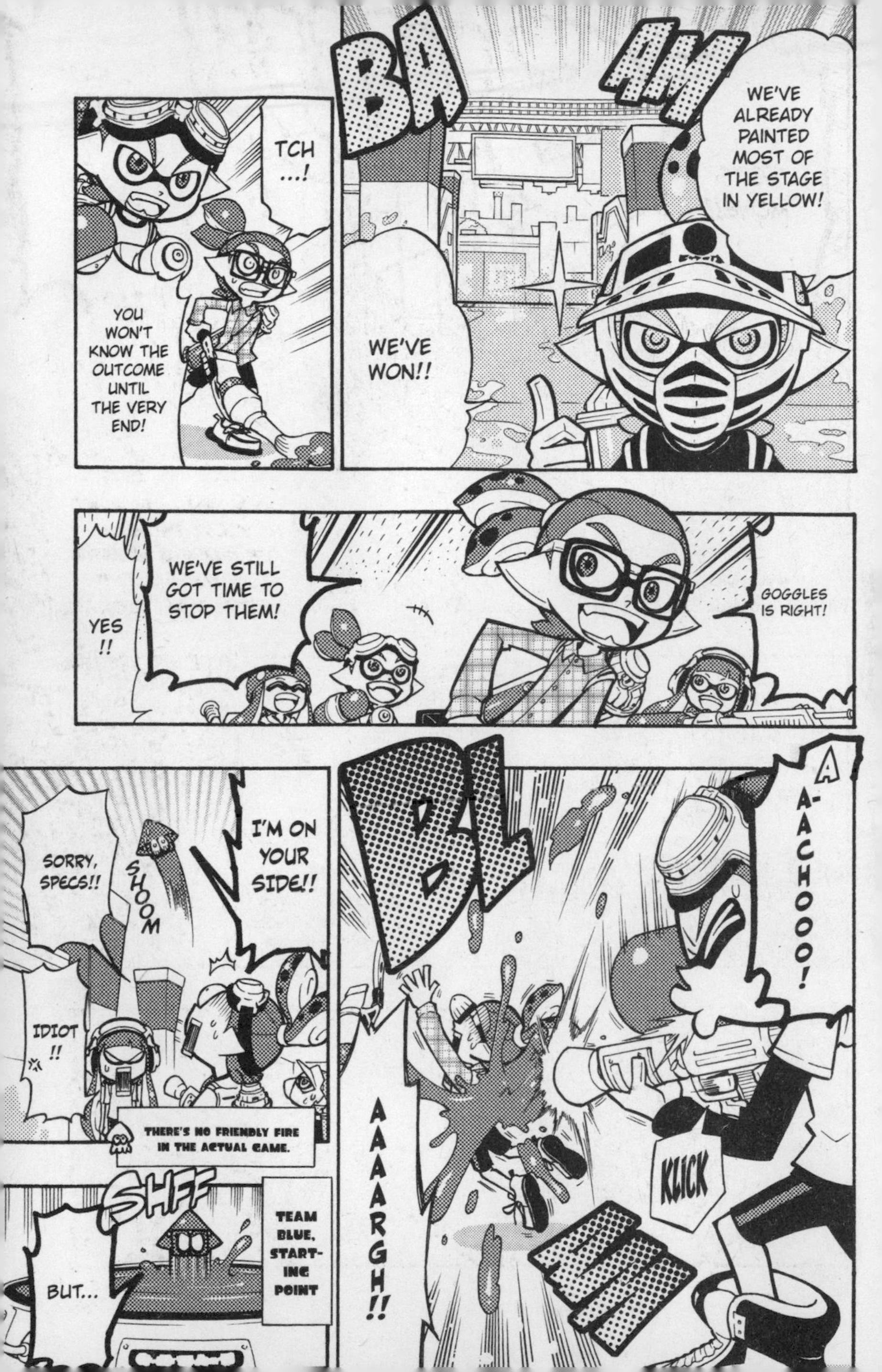
BAAM
WE'VE ALREADY PAINTED MOST OF THE STAGE IN YELLOW!
WE'VE WON!!
TCH ...!
YOU WON'T KNOW THE OUTCOME UNTIL THE VERY END!
GOGGLES IS RIGHT!
WE'VE STILL GOT TIME TO STOP THEM!
YES !!
A A-AACHOOOO!
BL
KLICK
AAAARGH!!
I'M ON YOUR SIDE!!
SORRY, SPECS!!
SHOOM
IDIOT !!
THERE'S NO FRIENDLY FIRE IN THE ACTUAL GAME.
TEAM BLUE, START-ING POINT
SHFF
BUT...

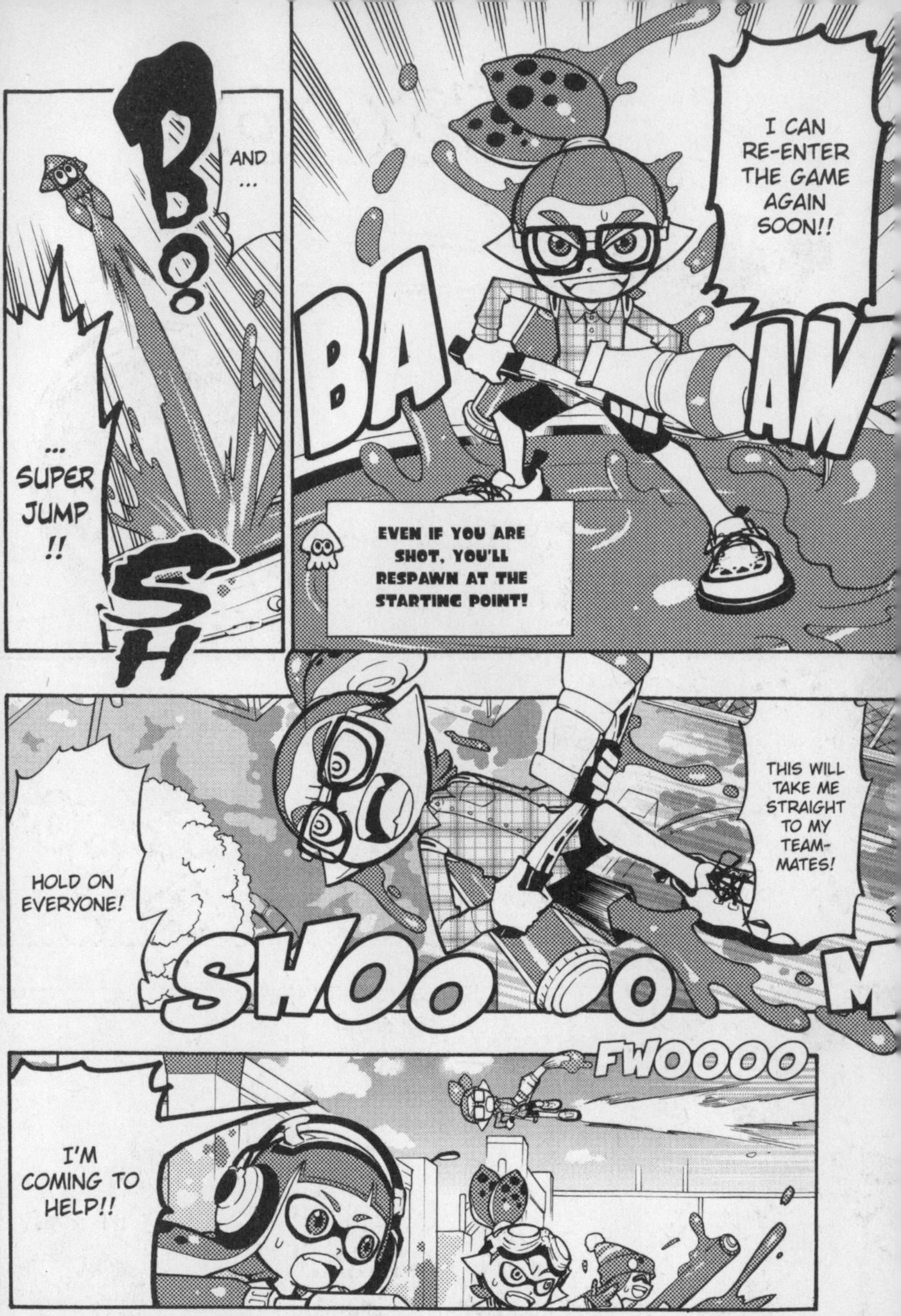
I CAN RE-ENTER THE GAME AGAIN SOON!!
BA
AM
EVEN IF YOU ARE SHOT, YOU'LL RESPAWN AT THE STARTING POINT!
AND ...
BOOO
... SUPER JUMP !!
SH
THIS WILL TAKE ME STRAIGHT TO MY TEAM-MATES!
HOLD ON EVERYONE!
SHOO
O
M
FWOOOO
I'M COMING TO HELP!!

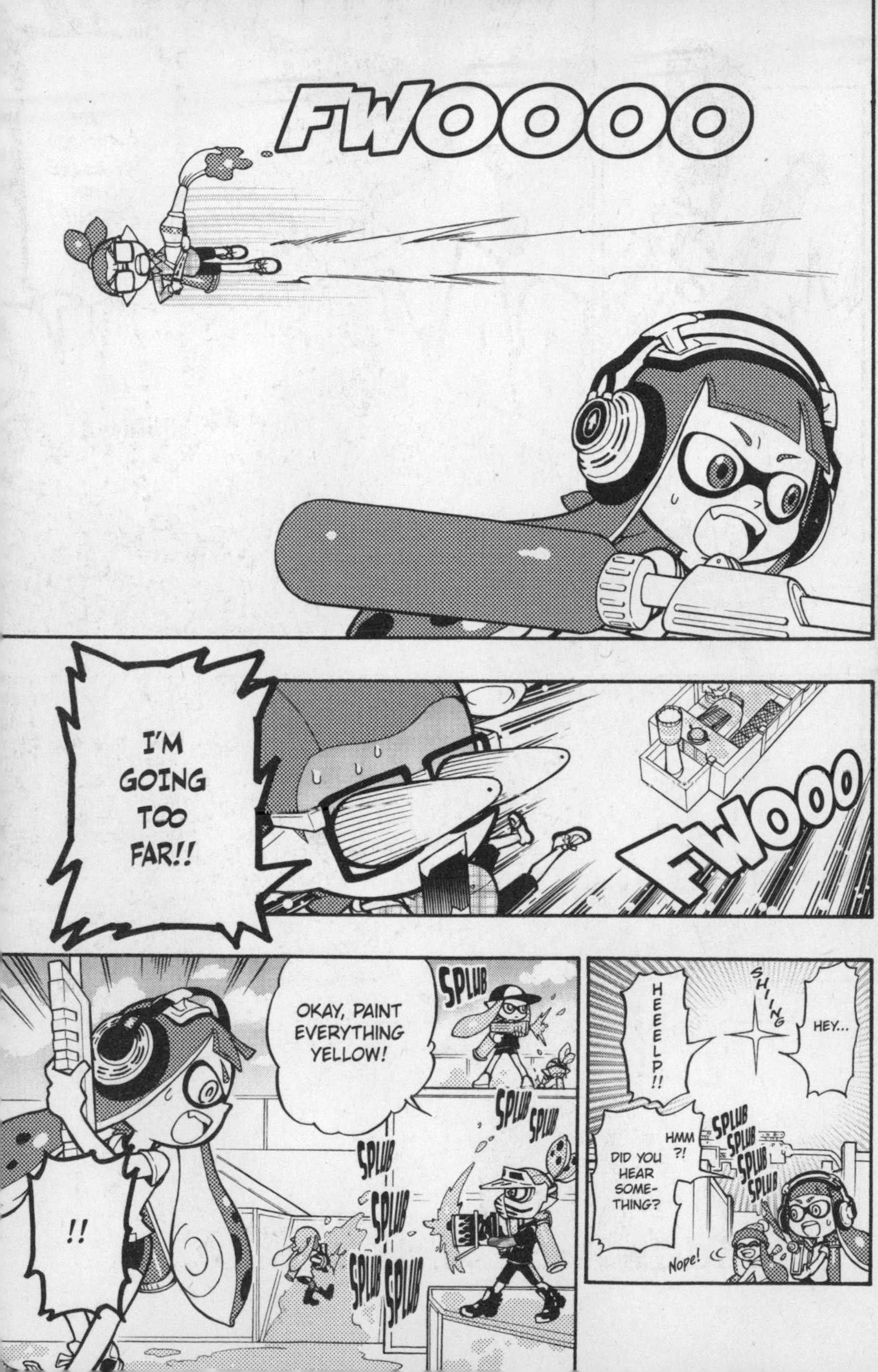
FWOOOO
FWOOO
I'M GOING TOO FAR!!
HEY...
SHING
HEEEELP!!
HMM ?!
DID YOU HEAR SOME-THING?
SPLUB SPLUB SPLUB SPLUB
Nope!
SPLUB
OKAY, PAINT EVERYTHING YELLOW!
SPLUB SPLUB
SPLUB SPLUB SPLUB SPLUB
!!

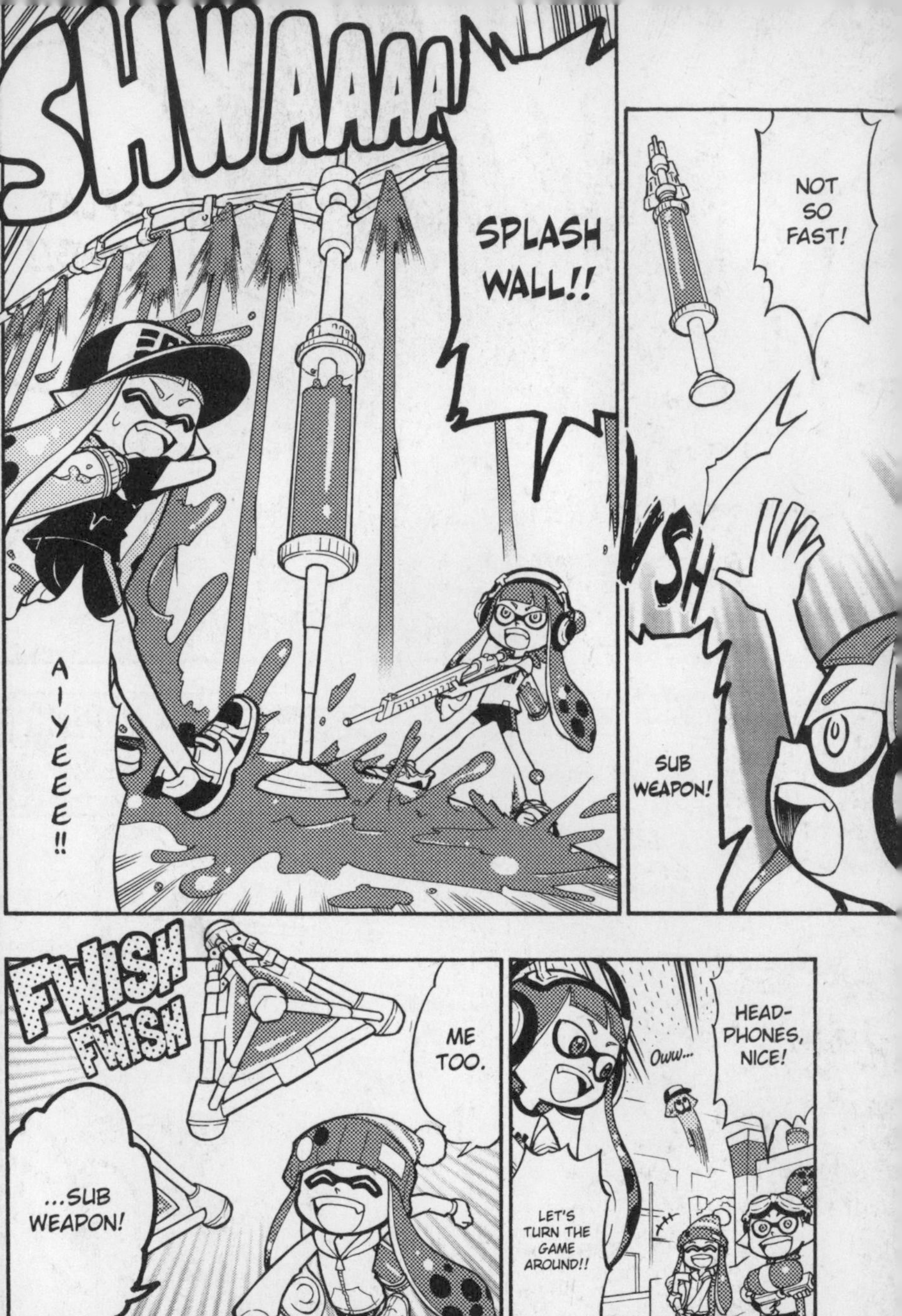
NOT SO FAST!
VSH
SUB WEAPON!
SHWAAAA
SPLASH WALL!!
AIYEEE!!
HEAD-PHONES, NICE!
Oww...
LET'S TURN THE GAME AROUND!!
FWISH FWISH
ME TOO.
...SUB WEAPON!

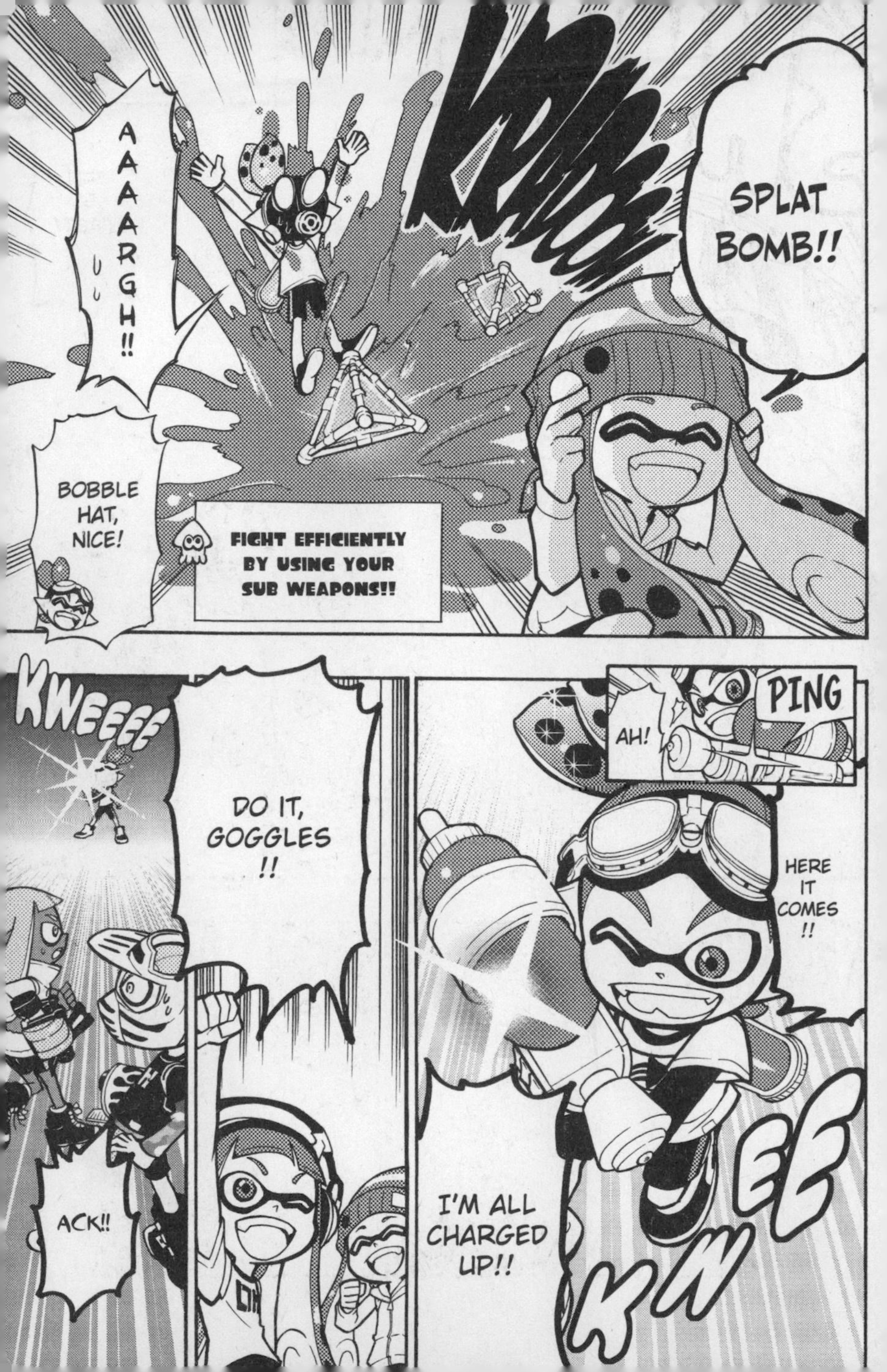
SPLAT BOMB!!
AAAARGH!!
FIGHT EFFICIENTLY BY USING YOUR SUB WEAPONS!!
BOBBLE HAT, NICE!
PING
AH!
HERE IT COMES!!
I'M ALL CHARGED UP!!
DO IT, GOGGLES!!
KWEEEE
ACK!!

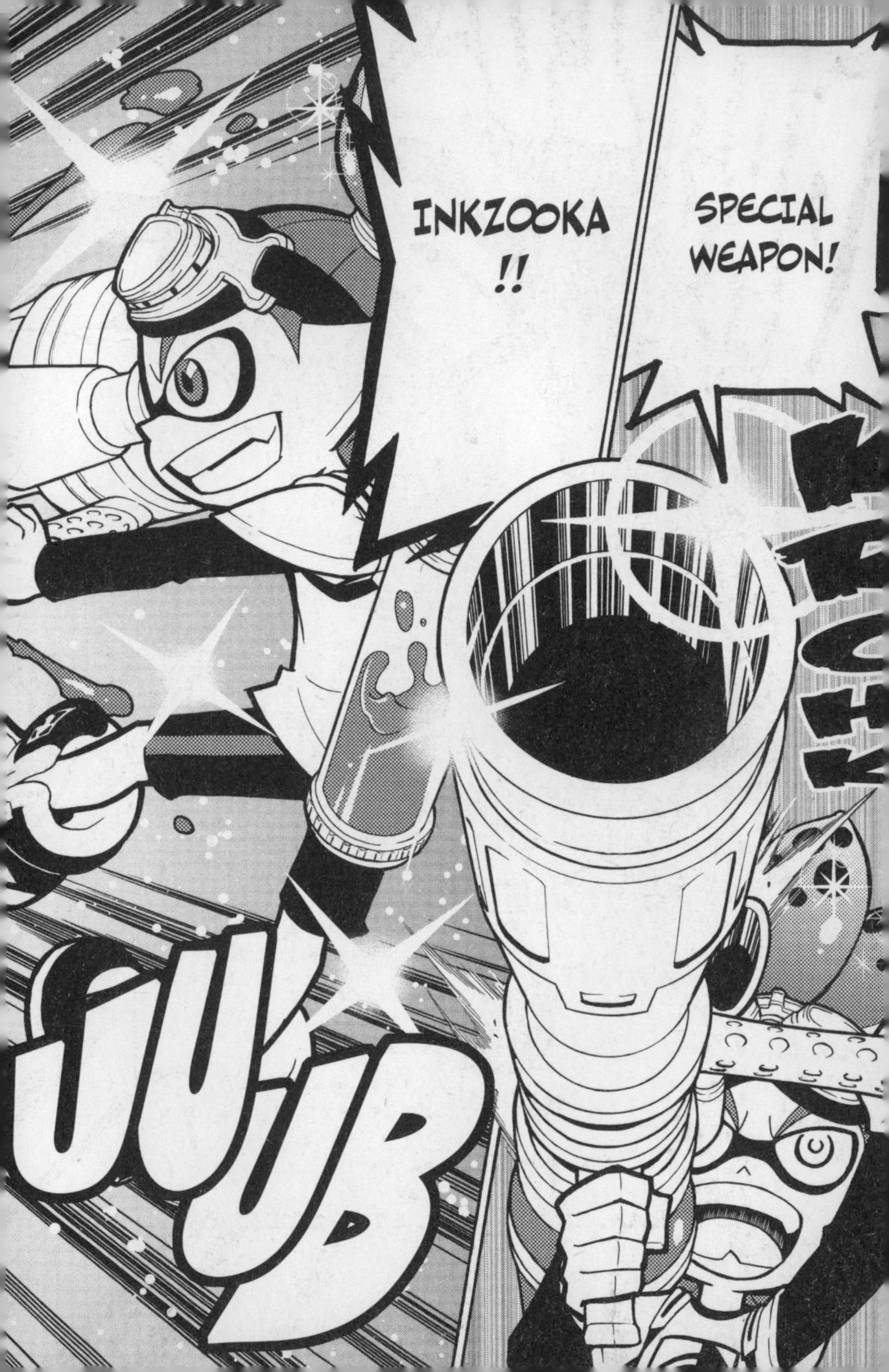
SPECIAL WEAPON!
INKZOOKA !!

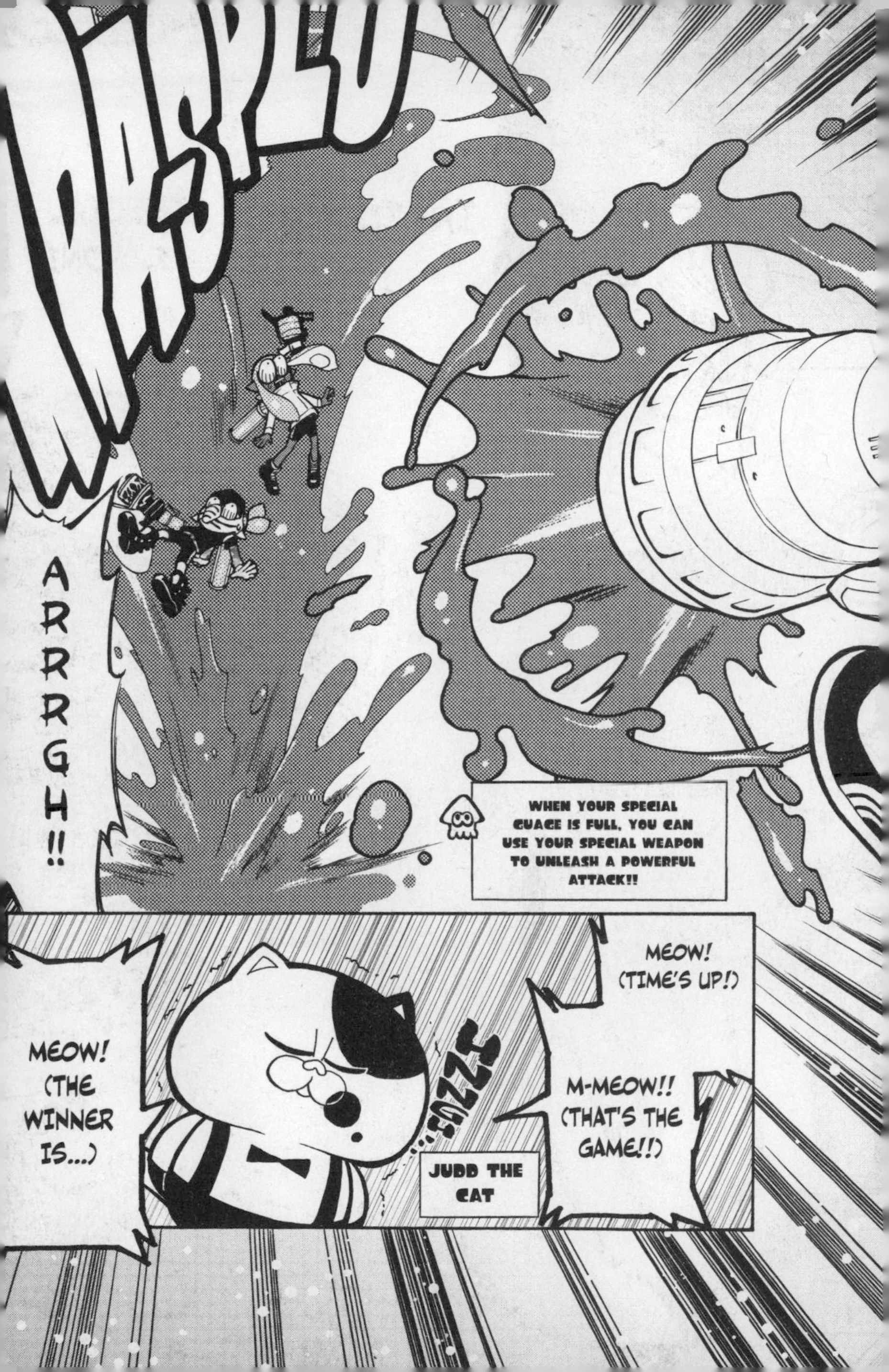
ARRRGH!!
WHEN YOUR SPECIAL GUAGE IS FULL, YOU CAN USE YOUR SPECIAL WEAPON TO UNLEASH A POWERFUL ATTACK!!
MEOW! (TIME'S UP!)
M-MEOW!! (THAT'S THE GAME!!)
JUDD THE CAT
MEOW! (THE WINNER IS...)

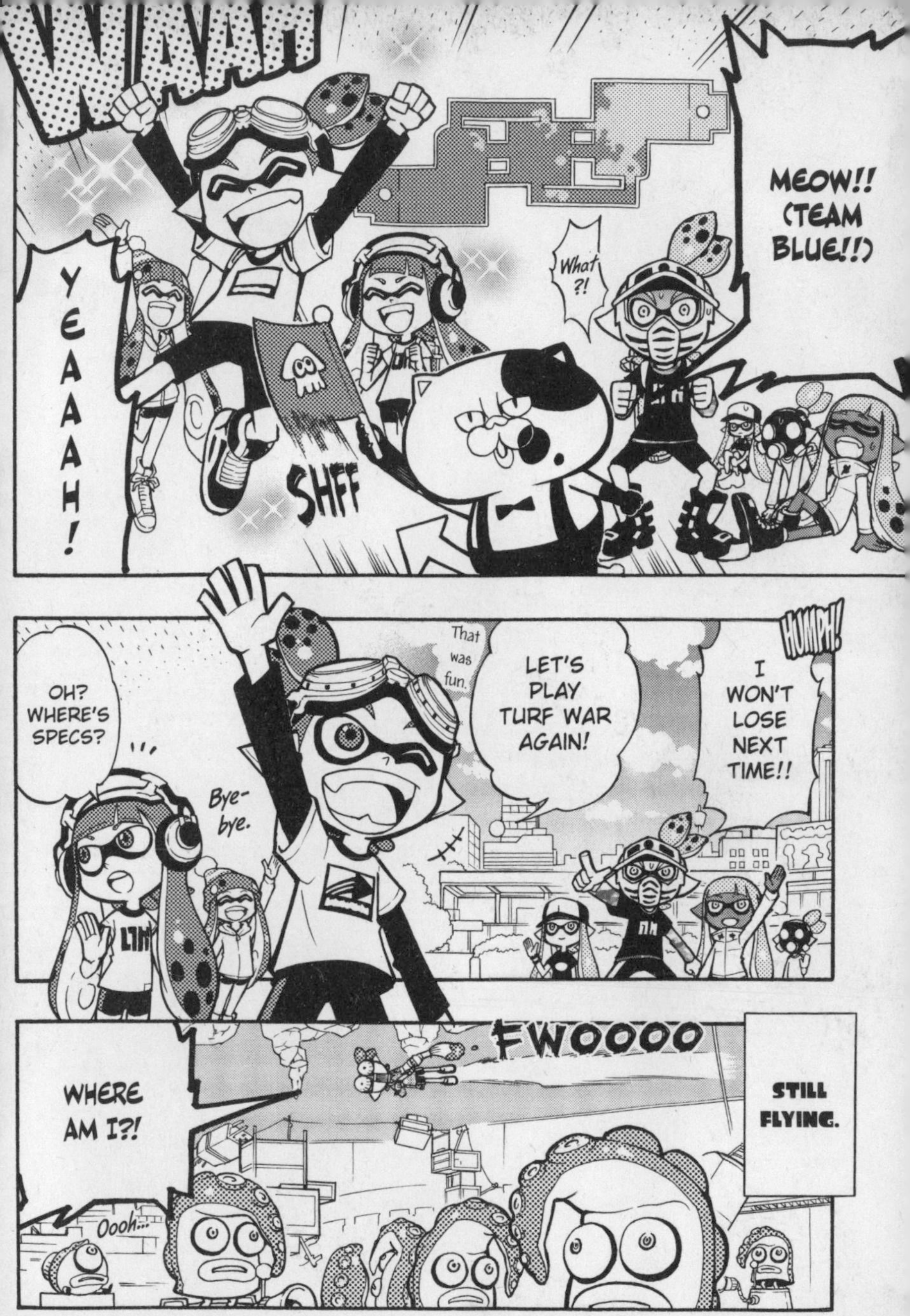
MEOW!! (TEAM BLUE!!)
What ?!
WAAH
YEAAAAH!
SHFF
HUMPH!
I WON'T LOSE NEXT TIME!!
LET'S PLAY TURF WAR AGAIN!
That was fun.
Bye-bye.
OH? WHERE'S SPECS?
STILL FLYING.
FWOOOO
WHERE AM I?!
Oooh...

#0:YELLOW / END

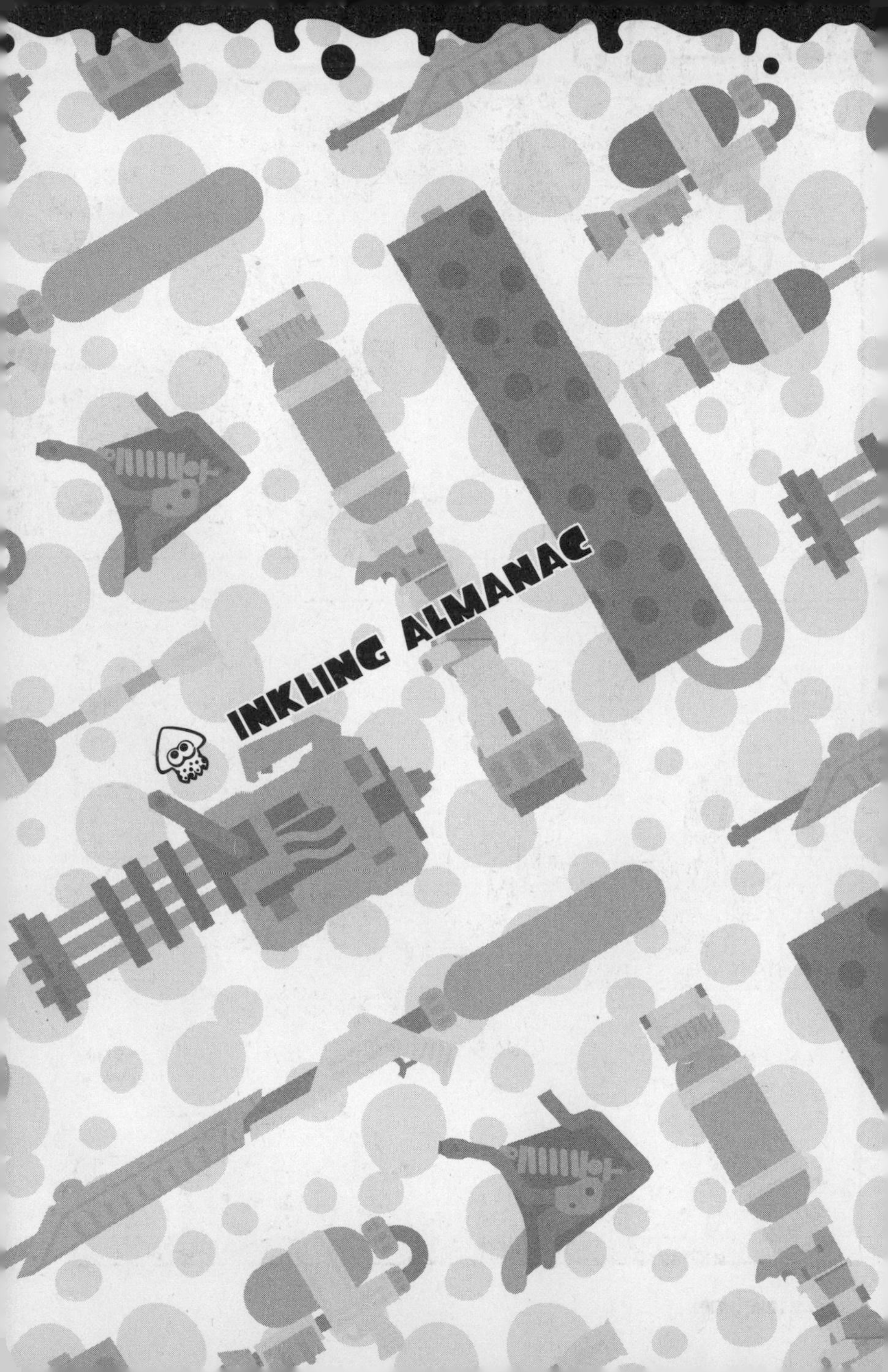
INKLING ALMANAC

GOGGLES

Weapon: Tentatek Splattershot
Headgear: Pilot Goggles
Clothing: Armor Jacket Replica
Shoes: Hero Runner Replicas

INFO

•He's such a restless sleeper that he often rolls out of bed in his sleep and can't hear his alarm clock.

•The pickled plums he snacks on are handmade by his grandmother.

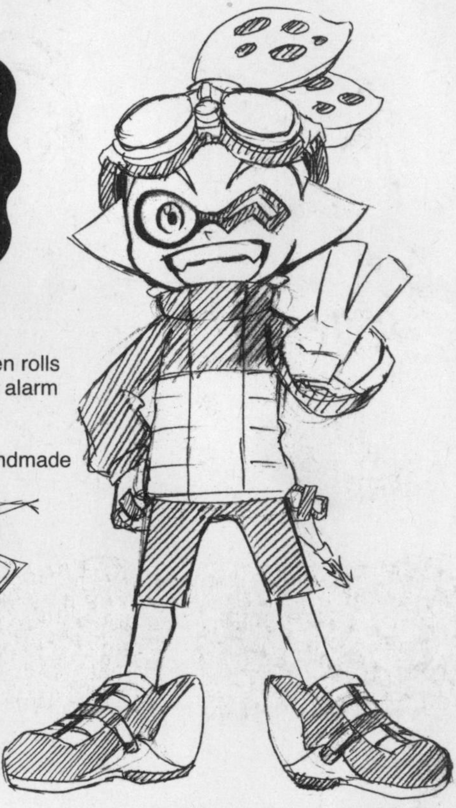

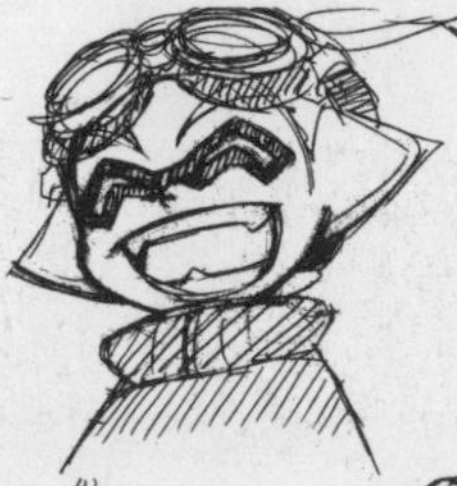

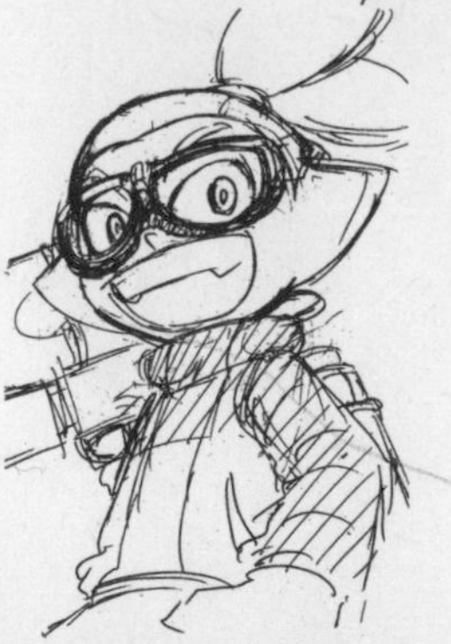

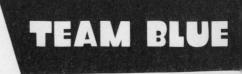

TEAM BLUE

BOBBLE HAT   HEADPHONES   SPECS

Weapon: Slosher
Headgear: Bobble Hat
Clothing: Green Zip Hoodie
Shoes: Purple Sea Slugs

Weapon: Classic Squiffer
Headgear: Studio
          Headphones
Clothing: B-ball Jersey (Away)
Shoes: Red Work Boots

Weapon: Octobrush
          (and others)
Headgear: Retro Specs
Clothing: Shirt & Tie
Shoes: Plum Casuals

INFO

•They always bring boxed lunches to their daily practices.
(Goggles loves rice balls, but he often forgets to bring them.)

TEAM YELLOW-GREEN

RIDER

Weapon: Gold Dynamo Roller
Headgear: Fake Contacts
Clothing: Black Inky Rider
Shoes: Octoling Boots

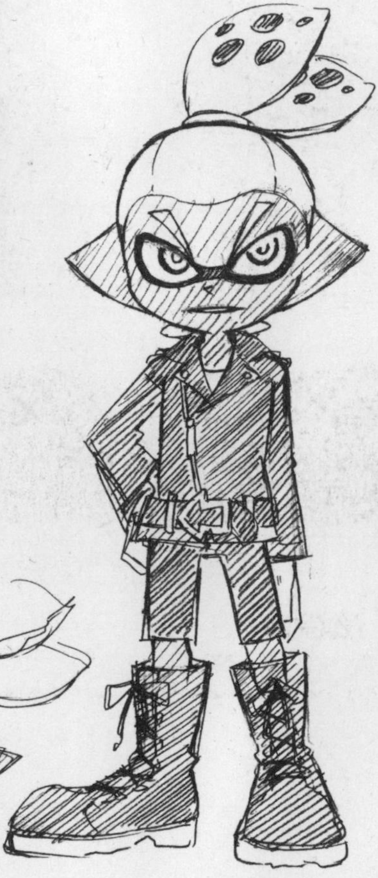

INFO

•He comes up with his own training program and practices diligently.

•He takes good care of his weapon too.

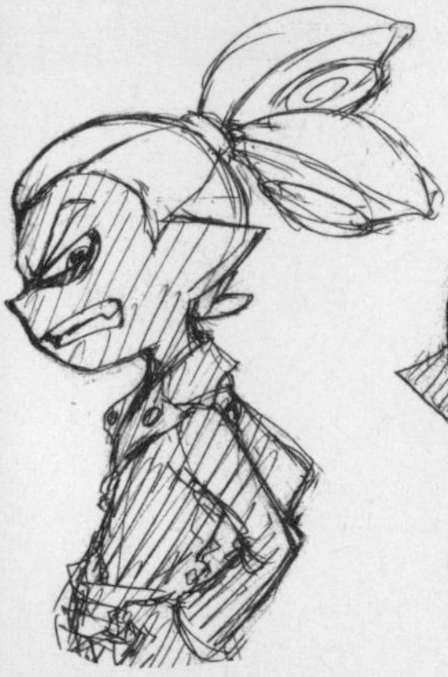

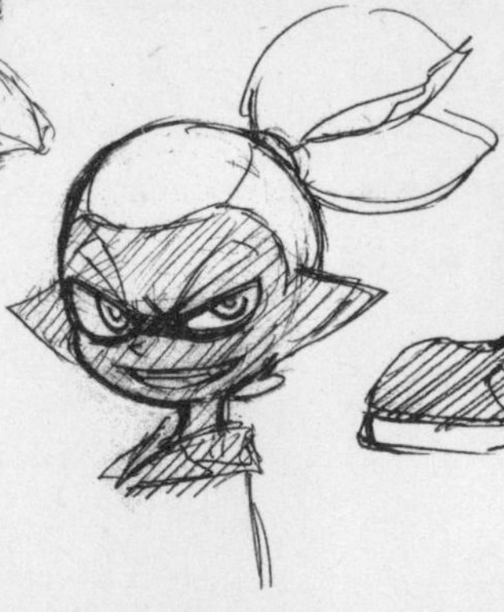

BAMBOO HAT

SCHOOL UNIFORM

STEALTH GOGGLES

Weapon: Heavy Splatling
Headgear: Bamboo Hat
Clothing: Navy Striped LS
Shoes: Blue Slip-Ons

Weapon: .52 Gal Deco
Headgear: Squid Hairclips
Clothing: School Uniform
Shoes: School Shoes

Weapon: Jet Squelcher
Headgear: Stealth Goggles
Clothing: Camo Zip Hoodie
Shoes: Pro Trail Boots

INFO

•They had never battled together before this tournament.

ARMY

Weapon: N-ZAP '85
Headgear: Special Forces Beret
Clothing: Forge Inkling Parka
Shoes: Punk Cherries

INFO

- He does his face camo himself.
- He's actually from a rich family.
- One of the S4.

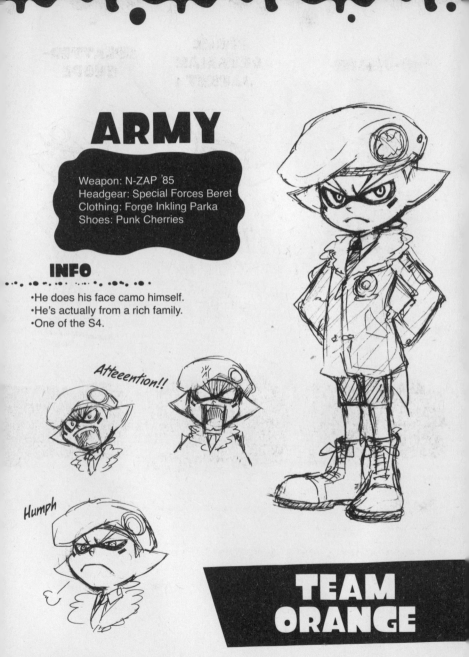

Atteeention!!

Humph

TEAM ORANGE

W-SAILOR

Weapon: Dual Squelcher
Headgear: Special Forces Beret
Clothing: White Sailor Suit
Shoes: Mawcasins

FORGE OCTARIAN JACKET

Weapon: Rapid Blaster
Headgear: Special Forces Beret
Clothing: Forge Octarian Jacket
Shoes: Punk Whites

SPLATTER-SCOPE

Headgear: Special Forces Beret
Clothing: Blue Sailor Suit
Shoes: Shark Moccasins

INFO

- They always clean up after themselves, whether it's practice or battles.
- They always arrive precisely on time.

TEAM PINK

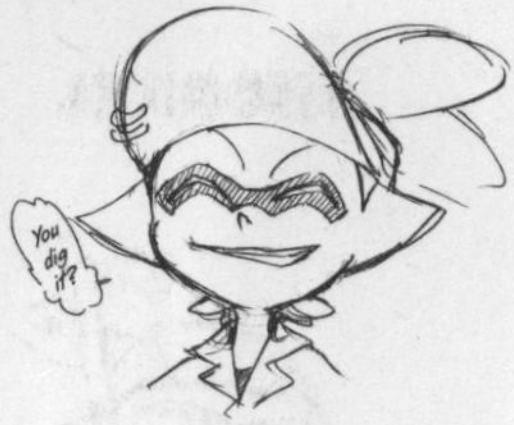
You dig it?

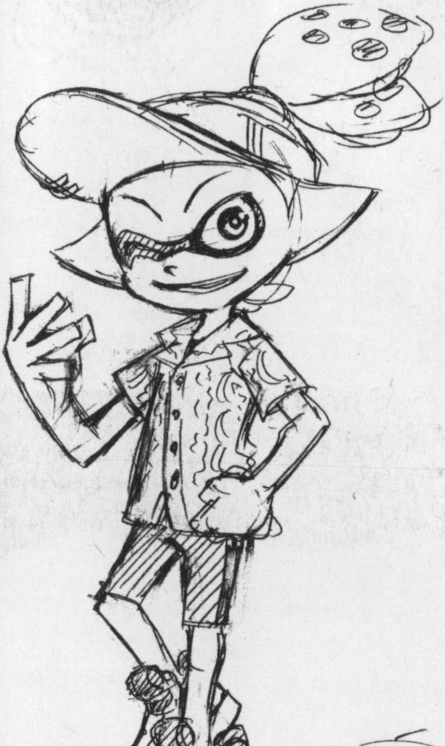

ALOHA

Weapon:.52 Gal
Headgear: Golf Visor
Clothing: Aloha Shirt
Shoes: Crazy Arrows

INFO

•He's an Inkling so he can't swim, but he can surf.

•He has a huge address list of his party friends.

•One of the S4.

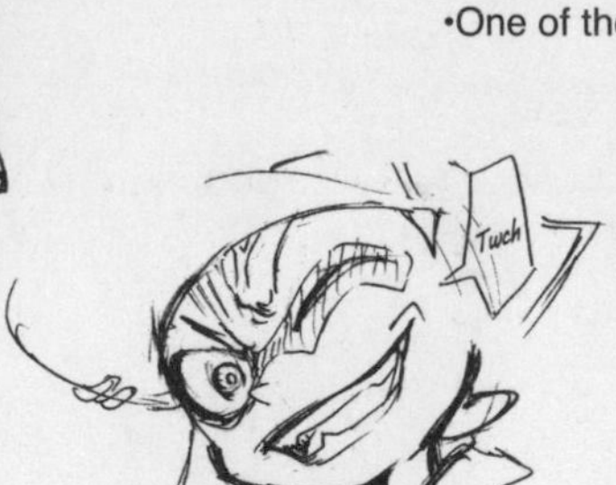
Twch

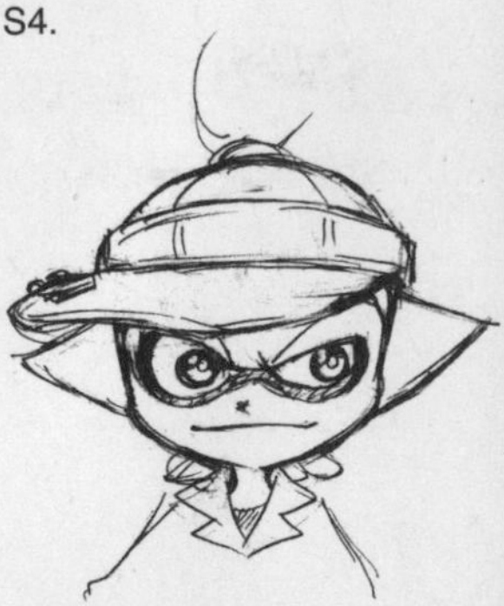

STRAW

OCTOGLASSES

SNORKEL

Weapon: Krak-On Splat
    Roller
Headgear: Straw Boater
Clothing: Logo Aloha Shirt
Shoes: Cherry Kicks

Weapon: Berry Splattershot
    Pro
Headgear: Octoglasses
Clothing: Logo Aloha Shirt
Shoes: Strapping Reds

Weapon: H-3 Nozzlenose
Headgear: Snorkel Mask
Clothing: Logo Aloha Shirt
Shoes: White Seahorses

INFO

•Their social media is full of photos from their parties and events.

BACKWARDS

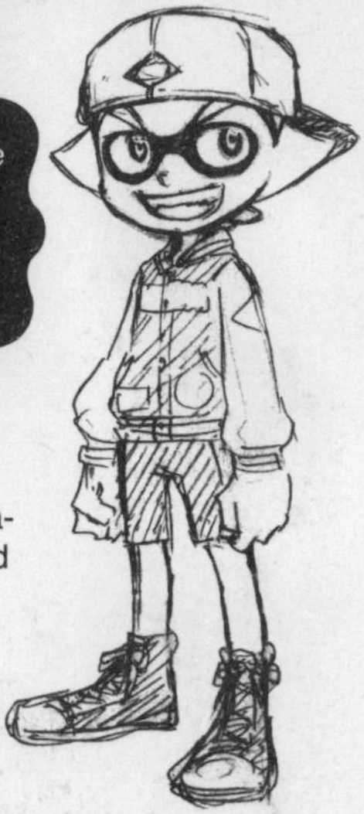

Weapon: Sloshing Machine
Headgear: Backwards Cap
Clothing: Varsity Jacket
Shoes: Hunter Hi-Tops

INFO

•He doesn't like people calling his weapon a washing machine. Once, he checked to see if his Sloshing Machine could wash clothes, and ended up with ink stains everywhere.

JUNGLE HAT

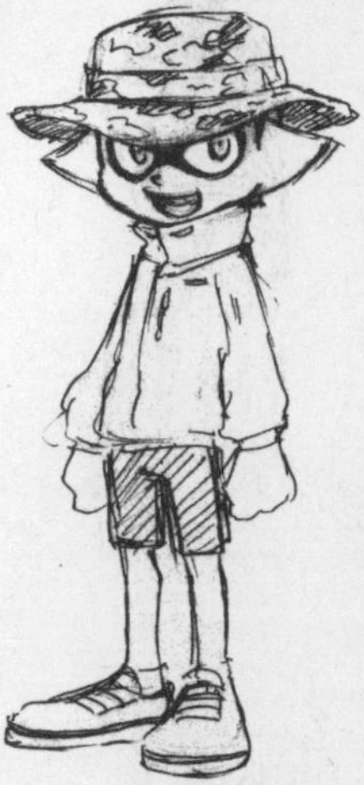

Weapon: .52 Gal
Headgear: Safari Hat
Clothing: Olive Ski Jacket
Shoes: Strapping Whites

BEANIE

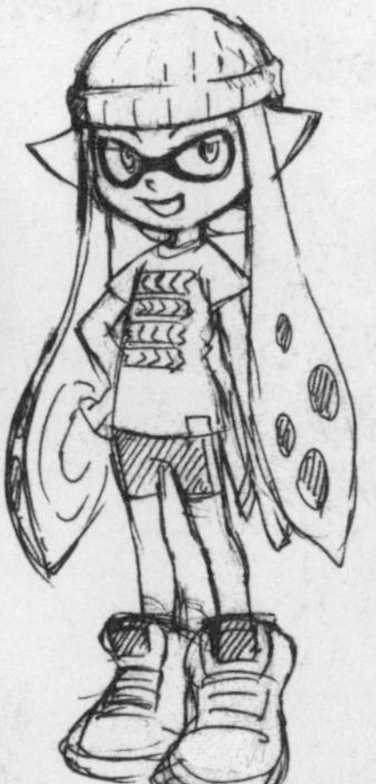

Weapon: Aerospray MG
Headgear: Short Beanie
Clothing: Gray Vector Tee
Shoes: Red Hi-Horses

CLEATS

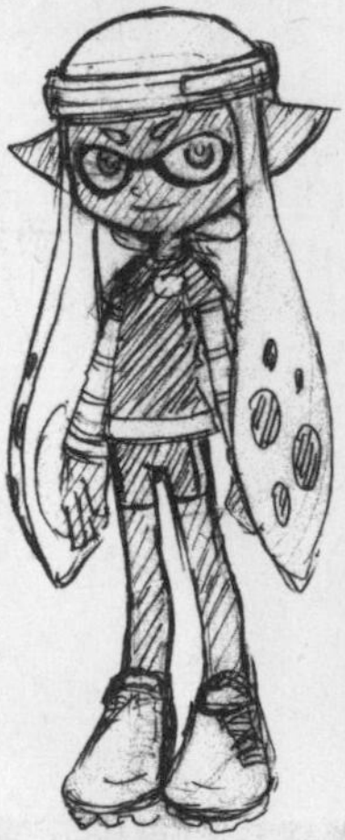

Weapon: Inkbrush Nouveau
Headgear: White Headband
Clothing: Part-Time Pirate
Shoes: Soccer Cleats

INFO

•After the battle against Team Blue, they started double-checking themselves for impostors before every battle.

TEAM GREEN

TEAM YELLOW

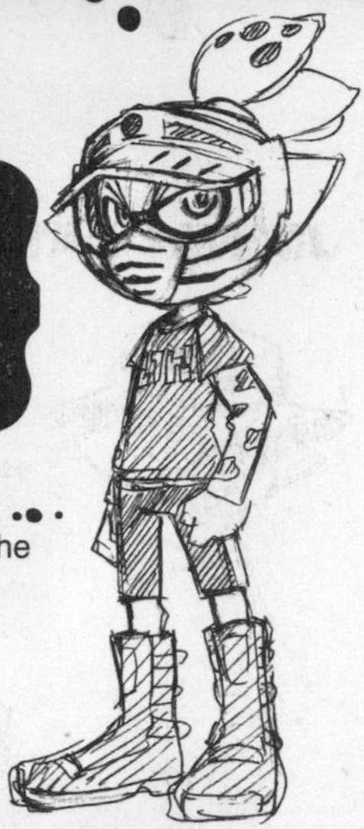

PAINTBALL MASK

Weapon: Blaster
Headgear: Paintball Mask
Clothing: Camo Layered LS black T-shirt for some reason.
Shoes: Moto Boots

INFO

•Often helps out with the household chores.

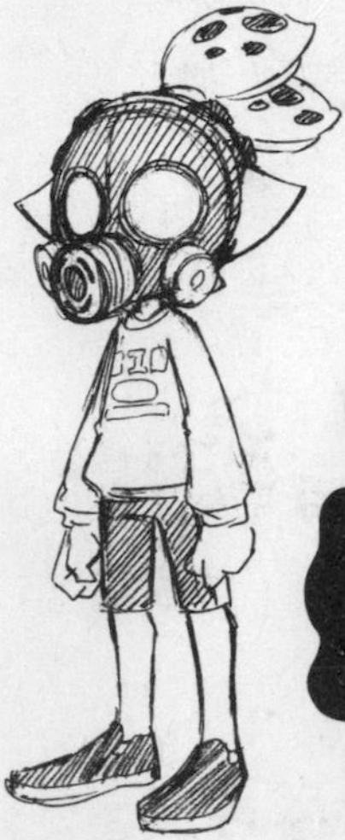

GAS MASK

Weapon: Splattershot
Headgear: Gas Mask
Clothing: Gray College Sweat
Shoes: Blue Slip-Ons

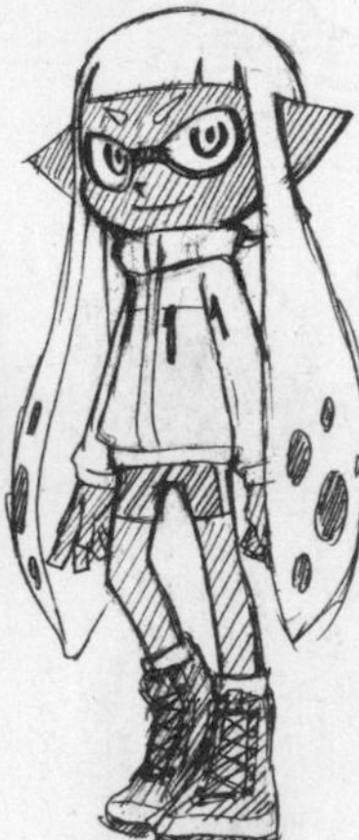

OLIVE

Weapon: .52 Gal
Headgear: Fake Contacts
Clothing: Olive Ski Jacket
Shoes: Pro Trail Boots

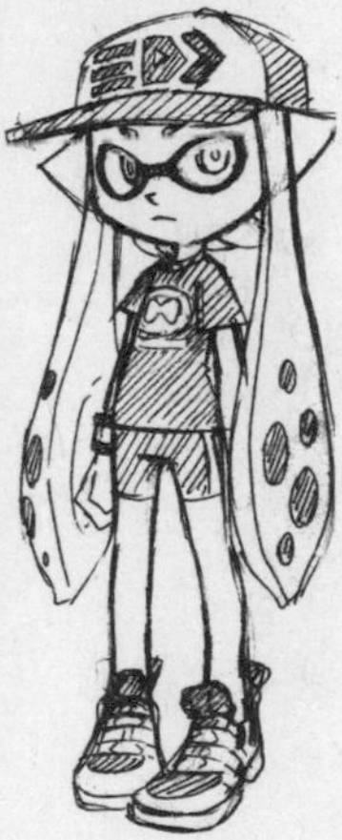

TAKO

Weapon: Splattershot Jr.
Headgear: Takoroka Mesh black for some reason.
Clothing: Black Squideye
Shoes: Orange Arrows

INFO

•Often holds practice matches against Team Blue.
•Gas Mask is not the same person as Mask from the S4.

TEAM BLUE #0

#0 Team Blue is slightly different from the current Team Blue.

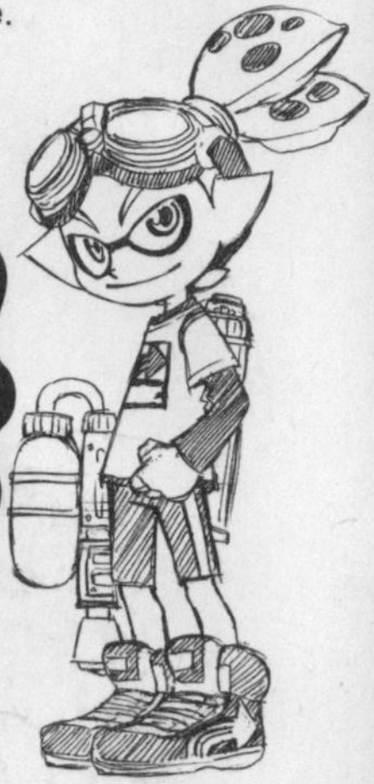

GOGGLES

Weapon: Splattershot
(but his Special Weapon is Inkzooka for some reason)
Headgear: Pilot Goggles
Clothing: Zink Layered LS
Shoes: Purple Hi-Horses

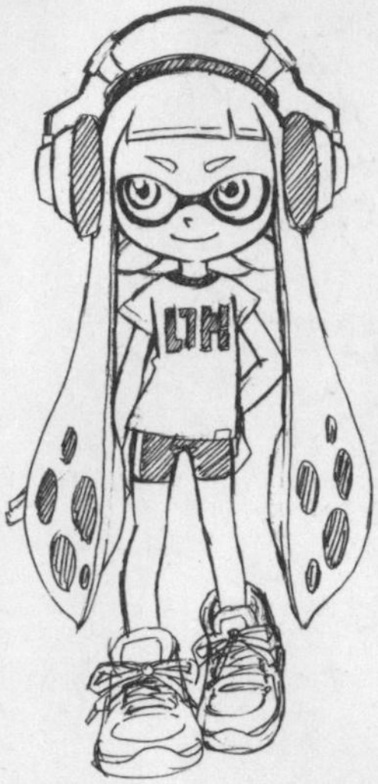

LTH

HEADPHONES

Weapon: Splat Charger
(but her Sub Weapon is Splash Wall for some reason)
Headgear: Studio Headphones
Clothing: White Tee
Shoes: Pink Trainers

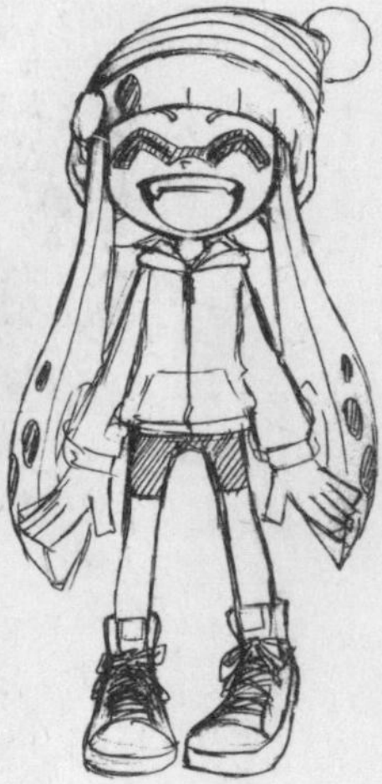

BOBBLE HAT

Weapon: Splat Roller
(but her Sub Weapon is Splat Bomb for some reason)
Headgear: Bobble Hat
Clothing: Green Zip Hoodie
Shoes: Cream Hi-Tops

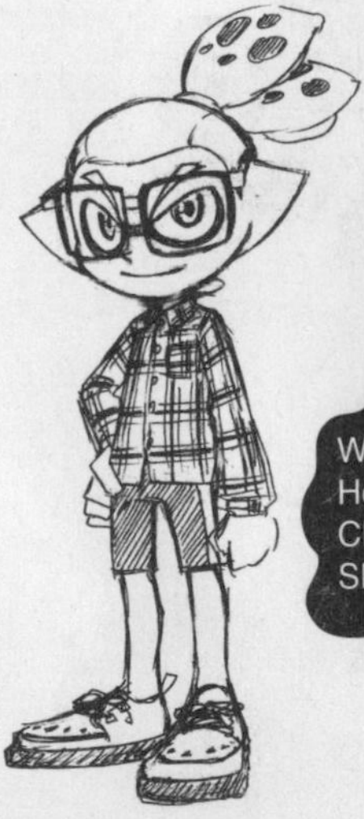

SPECS

Weapon: Inkbrush
Headgear: Retro Specs
Clothing: Vintage Check Shirt
Shoes: White Kicks

Splatoon
1

THANK YOU!

I paint ink on my work too!

Sankichi Hinodeya

Volume 1
VIZ Media Edition

Story and Art by
Sankichi Hinodeya

Translation **Tetsuichiro Miyaki**
English Adaptation **Jeremy Haun & Jason A. Hurley**
Lettering **John Hunt**
Design **Shawn Carrico**
Editor **Joel Enos**

TM & © 2017 Nintendo. All rights reserved.

SPLATOON Vol. 1 by Sankichi HINODEYA
© 2016 Sankichi HINODEYA
All rights reserved.
Original Japanese edition published by SHOGAKUKAN.
English translation rights in the United States of America,
Canada, the United Kingdom, Ireland, Australia and
New Zealand arranged with SHOGAKUKAN.

Original Design **100percent**

Printed in Canada

Published by VIZ Media, LLC
P.O. Box 77010
San Francisco, CA 94107

10 9 8 7 6 5 4 3
First printing, December 2017
Third printing, July 2018